CITY

(barcode) CW00833170

GARGO**YLES**

Paul D E Mitchell

There is no greater demon than a self-righteous soul with the wrong information.

In loving memory of Chris Thomas who went out of his way to help and encourage so many authors in Wales.

1

Wuggles Publishing

www.pdemitchell.com
for books by Chris Thomas, Sarah Wind
and many others

Thanks to Stella L Crews for her help and advice.

ISBN 978-1-904043-30-0
First Edition 2019

The Tower of Grieving

Milverburg was once the marvel of the West: a vast merchant citadel that rose up from the grey waters of the Milverbore like some immense broaching leviathan. Three causeways led to three viaducts across the estuary, each four miles long and bearing the railways that connected the countless workshops, factories, docks and stations to the mainland market places. Set into the outer walls were ten tall round towers from which merchants once kept watch upon their ships and those of their rivals.

On the roof of the northernmost tower, Harold Norman Porter was looking down from the battlement which gave him waves of vertigo as he was over nine hundred feet above the languid waves below. The views across the estuary were spectacular so he would spend hours brooding up here even in the ceaseless rain but today was unusual for this world: a late afternoon sun was blazing down for only the second time in six years.

This particular tower had twelve gargoyles equally spaced around the battlement like numerals on a clock face. They were all exquisitely carved but grotesque chimerae, some with wings, some with horns and all their faces were anguished and weeping. They leant over the battlements if they were about to cast themselves into the abyss to end their unbearable sorrow for each one represented a major disaster in the construction of Milverburg.

A woman emerged from the small turret in the centre of the roof that housed the entrance to the stairs. She strode across the flagstones to stand behind him but he did not turn around.

"I thought I would find you here, Light-Father," she said. "It's hard to tell where the gargoyles end and you begin." She peered down at one of the twelve weeping gargoyle heads set into the stonework below the battlement that discharged the roof rainwater through their mouths. "If you could walk around the base of this tower and look up, you'd see twenty-five miserable faces staring down at you instead of the usual twenty-four."

"Don't try to humour me, Fern. I'm not in the mood," he said bleakly. "You won't believe how many times I've wanted to throw myself off this damn tower."

"Of course I know. I'm a Wiccan," she said in a hurt tone. "That's why I've come to get you: we've let you brood up here long enough. I don't even know why you like this tower."

Irritated, he exhaled heavily before replying: "These gargoyles remind me of my honeymoon with Andrea in Paris. We went to the Notre Dame Cathedral which had statues and gargoyles just like these." He was silent for a while as he watched seagulls circling near the base of the tower. "But that was another time in another world before I lost my daughter and my marriage."

Fern closed her eyes and savoured the unaccustomed sunshine on her upturned face. "And so you ended up as a technician in some university," she recited wearily. "Drinking yourself to death. I've heard this all before, dear heart. Do you really miss that life?"

"Yes, I do. Well, no to be honest," he admitted reluctantly. "I spent all my time in that workshop well on my way to becoming an alcoholic until that hell-light or whatever it was knocked me out and I woke up in a railway depot surrounded by twelve urchins all armed to the teeth and calling me the Light-Father like I was some kind of messiah."

"The Scatterlings regard you as one," she insisted, looking at him with the concern plain upon her face. "They gave you a new purpose in life and you gave them *hope*."

He stood up and indicated his stained overalls, the baseball cap covering his thinning ginger hair, his stocky frame and steel toe-capped boots and the Japanese Empire katana strapped to his belt. "Hope? Just look at me!" he said bitterly. "I'm a technician. I fix machines; that's all I'm good for. I'm no samurai yet I had these pathetic delusions of grandeur and took you all to the Great Abbey and for what? I lost *five* of those kids! I love them as my own but I failed them! I don't *belong* here!"

She came close to him so that her face was just inches from his. "Be at peace," she said gently. "It's time to stop this maudlin self-pity. It's annoying and the children need you. You are *not* to blame for what happened there. All of us including your Scatterlings knew the risks yet we willingly walked the path laid out before us by the prophecies of Mother Moss."

"Some path!" he exclaimed angrily. "I failed those kids and every time I fall asleep, I'm back there in the Great Annex with you, Schimrian and that freaking *angel*!"

She closed her eyes and took a deep calming breath. "Yes, I know. You are not the only one plagued by night terrors," she said, placing a hand on her chest. "Fate summoned you here to be the Light-Father just as I was destined to be born a Wiccan."

He noted that she was dressed once more in the black lace-up linen shirt and trousers of the Wiccan Motherhood. She wore a white hemp belt with a black loin cloth bearing a Celtic triqueta in white and a rear loincloth depicting a triskele. He knew the clothes mocked the formal attire of the powerful, misogynistic Royal Conclave of Architects but it did not detract from her lithe figure one iota. Her face was beautiful with piercing jade-green eyes and framed by long black hair intricately braided and threaded through countless amber beads. How could he *not* love such a goddess?

She smiled having read his thoughts yet again. "As I love you, Light-Father," she laughed and kissed him briefly on the lips.

"That's not fair," he protested. "I'll never understand you or your craft yet you know *everything* about me. What *are* you, Fern? Witches are just fairy tales in my world: hook-nosed old crones flying about on broomsticks."

"The same prejudice prevailed in this world as well, dear heart. Do you know *why* we call ourselves Mothers?"

"Yes, I do listen to you," he assured her. "You told me that the Wiccans wanted to take that title away from the very religion oppressing them; to show the world that women could be something more than just nuns and chattels."

"Oh, I'm so happy you pay attention to a mere *woman!*" she teased and then she became serious: "Mother Moss had the power of prophecy and on my eighth birthday, she sat me down and told me that my one true path lay through the fires of Hell and into the arms of a saviour and she was right: it did."

"I'm no saviour, Fern, but dear God, *what* a birthday gift for a child! She must've scared the hell out of you."

"Oh, she did. I had nightmares for weeks but now I know well the price of prophecy. Seers are rare but they have the power to change Destiny itself as they perceive hundreds of possible futures and can steer the world down a path of their own choosing."

"Yes but for all her powers, we were only saved by David and a thirteen-year-old girl who *sacrificed* herself!"

"I know and I bless the short time that I knew her but…"

"Mother Moss was a *seer,*" he interrupted angrily. "She must've told Fierce to hide those grenades inside her stuffed toy and follow us into the Great Annex." He winced suddenly and pressed a hand to his abdomen; upon the wounds inflicted by Azrael, the insane seraph that Great-Abbot Schimrian, the head of the Order, had inadvertently brought into the world. The Wiccans were skilled in the healing arts but the pain still took his breath away at times. "She *knew* David would become a Tally-man and she *knew* Fierce would have to die to stop Azrael!"

Fern took his hands in hers. "You must rest, dear heart, otherwise you will never be free of him. You are newly healed but those wounds to both body and soul were *deep*."

He snatched his hands away. "Don't fuss over me! I'll be fine," he snapped. "Look, it's not just Azrael and Schimrian driving me crazy; it's Fierce. When those cables dragged her inside the Great Computer, I could see she was in agony but she didn't cry out; she just looked at me and she *smiled*! She *knew* she was going to die in there and she accepted it! How can I *ever* forgive myself or Moss for letting that happen?"

"She was a warrior," she said simply, tears rolling down her cheeks. "I failed her too, you know."

"I'm sorry, Fern," he relented, drawing her to him after wiping the sudden tears from his own eyes. "I'm being selfish, I know, but she could fight like that because she and her sisters were physically enhanced by parents who played God with the genes of their own children. That's not right."

"Had they not been enhanced then they would not have survived when the Order attacked their family."

"Mmm, maybe," he said doubtfully. "We'll never know for sure but they won't answer to their real names because of what the Order did to them and from watching their parents die from the Plague. They took their Scatterling names from Pious when he said that Shield protected her sisters, Mouse scurried about like a rat and Fierce defied him, slashing his face open. I suppose no normal eight year old could do that to a thug like him."

"Yet their parents vaccinated them just in time," she pointed out. "Even though they were already infected themselves."

"Saul told me about how their parents worked for Exodus Industries and when the Order bought the company, they set up a secret society and used the company's resources to give their offspring the same advantages in life as the Brothers had."

"As I told you, I infiltrated the Exodus labs in Crawcester to find them and warn them that the Order was designing a lethal virus at the Great Abbey but they would not believe me at first. Then one scientist in the Great Abbey lab finally told them that they were working on a virus that rewrote the host's DNA. They stole a sample and started working on a vaccine..."

"The Order found out they'd tried warning the press and the government so the bastards infected them with slow-acting versions of the virus just so they would pass it on to their families."

"Diana forgive me! If only I could've made them *listen!*"

She fell silent, her face grim, so he touched his forehead to hers in empathy. "You tell me off for beating myself up so why do you blame yourself for what those maniacs did?"

She shuddered and clung to him. "That's because I dream of the dead asking me over and over again why I could not save them!" she groaned. "We couldn't even cure the Ferals - we tried and tried but we were unskilled and too few in number... I..."

"None of that was your fault!" he insisted. "But I still can't forgive Mother Moss for sacrificing David, Fierce and the others just to save the rest of us. She..."

"I keep telling you that's the price of prophecy!" she fumed and pushed him away. "She *had* to tell Fierce she was destined to die. Fierce accepted that so why can't you?"

"Like I said; how could she *do* that to a child?" he retorted though clenched teeth. "How *could* she?"

All the love for him seemed to drain from her face and he knew that he was defenceless before her power. "Never forget that Mother Moss *foresaw* the vile torture and death she would have to endure to save her precious Scatterlings," she said icily. Such was the anger in her voice and the fell light in her eyes that he averted his face: he was no longer standing before a lover but a Wiccan who could destroy him in an *instant*. "Don't you *ever* disrespect her memory again!" she added, baring her teeth and pinching his face hard. "She sacrificed herself willingly as did Veneris, Rosemary and our precious Ferals: *one hundred and sixty of them!*"

He turned his back to her and folded his arms. "I'm sorry, Fern, I was angry at myself more than her," he began slowly. "You *know* how much I love you and you know I can't lie to you." Despite the dull ache of his wounds and the newer, sharper pain in his cheeks, he recalled how passionate their love making was despite their injuries: there was no way he could ever lie to her about *that*.

"I'm so glad you feel that way, dear heart."

His shoulders sagged. "*Please* stop rummaging through my mind like that," he said dejectedly. "My thoughts are *private*."

She stood in front of him with her hands on her hips, appraising him with her head tilted slightly to one side and an enigmatic smile upon her lips. She twirled suddenly and laughed: "So, when we lie abed together, all you can think about are my *breasts*? By Gaia's endless tears, how *shallow*!"

"I know. I'm a man," he conceded, raising his palms in a gesture of surrender. "Sometimes our brains are in our trousers."

She laughed again and threw her arms about his neck: "Such a strange saying but so apt in your case, dear heart." She rubbed noses with him. "But for all your faults, I love you. It pains me to see you rotting away in your tower or hiding from the Scatterlings in the docks but," she added, shielding her eyes from the sun as she gazed skywards. "See how Gaia favours you! You have magic beyond your empathy and our bed, dear heart."

Her scent was so distracting that he could barely think. Her touch was electricity sending sensuous thrills throughout his body: something he'd never known before - even with Andrea. She kissed him full on the lips, her tongue searching for his until all awareness faded but for the tsunami of lust surging through his veins.

She stopped suddenly and placed a finger upon his lips but he felt as though his knees were about to buckle. "Enough. We'll lie together soon enough, dear heart. I have news for you."

"Is it about Surl and the others?" he demanded anxiously, pulling back from her and placing his hands on her shoulders once more. "Well? Have you sensed them?"

"You have to trust our craft," she said, placing a hand on her chest. "Ivy sensed them close to Milverburg. In our hearts, we *knew* they'd survived…"

"I don't have any craft," he cut in impatiently. "All I have is the certainty that I left four children at the mercy of those lunatics. I hope to God Ivy is right and they've escaped because the last thing we need is more false hope."

She suddenly kissed him and placed her forehead briefly against his. "I trust her craft, dear heart, as I trust in you."

"Seriously? You trust me?"

"You are the Light-Father!" she said vehemently, startling him. "I keep telling you this! Azrael, Schimrian and Pious are dead so the Order will remain in chaos until a new Great-Abbot ascends the throne. We've had precious time to heal and *grieve*."

8

He pointed at the towering thunderclouds to the south with anvil-shaped heads already ninety thousand feet high and still soaring up into the stratosphere. "I don't know how much time we have, Fern This world is *dying*." He paused to wipe his face with a rag as the air was becoming incredibly humid. "Those storms are off the charts already after just *one* day of sunshine."

She shaded her eyes to study them. "I think they're moving towards us but what of it? It rained for *six years* before you came with not one day of sunlight like this." She sighed happily, closed her eyes, stretched her arms above her head and savoured the sun once more upon her upturned face. "Gaia is healing herself and even the waters below us will one day recede."

"I doubt that but at least those storms mean we don't have to worry about the Order for a while. Why are you frowning? I thought you be would be glad to see the rain again."

"No, dear heart," she said, folding her arms. "Pious is in my mind again. How could Azrael animate his corpse after Saul had pierced his heart? I fear that which I can't explain."

He laughed incredulously. "This from a *Wiccan*? In my world, people loved all these horror stories about the walking dead but I never thought I would see one for real. All I know is that the bastard stopped moving once Fierce set off her grenades inside the Great Computer and that's good enough for me."

A southerly breeze arose and stirred Fern's braided and beaded hair. She wrinkled her nose in disgust as it carried the necrotic stench of the Dead Marshes. "Maybe that devil-machine in the Annex created these abominations?" she suggested.

"Pious was nowhere near the machine when he was killed so it had to be Azrael. Given what you Wiccans can do, I have to admit that he must've been using some kind of necromancy."

"I see," she said doubtfully. "Then it is a craft we must fear. We've been lucky thus far but I fear that the Order *will* come for us soon. We must go and talk to Ivy and Nightshade."

"You're right. I haven't seen them for days."

"They're fully healed physically but like me, they grieve for Veneris and Rosemary and our poor Ferals…"

"At least they survived thanks to their Ferals. They destroyed every rotorcraft in that Angel compound but it amazes me that an albino like Nightshade could survive a beating like that."

"Why are you surprised?" she said raising an eyebrow. "Think of all the Mothers before us who endured both whip and flame. We survived centuries of persecution because we are of *Gaia*."

"I see that's all the answer I'm ever going to get so let's get back to Ivy: is she sure Surl and the others have escaped?"

"You and I were wounded, dear heart!" she reminded him sharply, placing a hand upon his chest. "Yet you were still able to lead us from the Great Cathedral and bring us here safely. We *had* to flee otherwise they would have killed us all."

"I know that in my head but not in my *heart*." He was distracted for a moment as lightning flickered ominously along the entire southern horizon. "They must have been the ones who killed the power in the Annex thinking back on it. If they've managed to escape from the Abbey I *have* to go and look for them. What about the other Scatterlings? Do they know about this?"

"No. We do not want to raise their hopes. You must work your magic, dear heart. You *must* talk to them. They are grieving for Fierce and they fear for the little ones."

"How can I? I can't even look them in the eye."

"You are their Light-Father!" she said fiercely, emphasising every syllable by poking him hard in the chest. "You've wallowed in your tower for weeks when you're the only father they have. They've never once blamed you for her death. They *love* you!"

"You're right: I should concentrate on the living not regret the dead. I promise I'll talk to them this evening."

"Finally," she beamed, raising her arms to the heavens once more. "The Light-Father sees the light. Hallelujah!"

"O joy! Sarcasm *and* telepathy!"

She suddenly frowned at him: "Forgive me for prying. I could sense Bas and Ibrahim were in your thoughts."

"That's because all the Scatterlings are genetically upgraded; they're stronger and faster than ordinary humans but their father went further than anyone at Exodus. He spliced the genes of *other species* into his own kids. He put cat genes into Bas and gorilla genes into Ibrahim. That man was a *monster*."

"He was that yet here they are," she said firmly. "They are part of our family; *your* family. Farzad paraded them naked as a testament to his own twisted genius so please go to them as soon as you can. They both need to talk to you."

"I will, I promise. I just had to get through *today*..."

10

She was surprised to see that his eyes were brimming with tears again. "Ah, what's so special about today, dear heart?"

"Ha! And you a mind reader."

"I *usually* try not to pry too much. You know that. What is it about today that vexes you?"

He took her hands in his. "As far as I can tell, today is the anniversary of the death of my own child, Rebecca, in another life, in another *world* yet here I am…"

"Then you must honour her memory by being a father to the Scatterlings and the Ferals but you cannot do that up here; one gargoyle amongst so many."

He winced. "I deserved that. What've you got there?" he asked as she presented him with a small silver-plated tin.

"It's for you. I searched all the shops in the lower levels this morning," she grinned. "I hope you like it."

He opened it and his eyes lit up. "Oh, thank God, cigars!" he exclaimed joyfully. "Real, genuine *cigars!*"

She curled her lip in disgust: "Foul things they are but you seem to need them more than your poor lungs do."

He extracted a cigar, peeled off the cellophane and sniffed at it. "I promise these will be the last I ever smoke. Mmm, as fresh as the day it was rolled," he sighed happily. He patted at the numerous pockets of his overalls in vain. "I think I left my lighter on one of the boats. Damn it, my head's all over the place!"

"You forget that I am Mother Fern of the First Degree," she intoned with a slight bow. The phrase reminded him of the coven upon the Hill Where It Never Rains. It was here he'd first met Fern and the other Wiccans with his soul somehow transferred into one of the Ferals that served them. "I am a Servant of Gaia, a Wielder of Earth yet I learnt a little of another element from Mother Rosemary," she touched the end of the cigar he had placed in his mouth. A coil of aromatic smoke curled skywards.

His eyes widened in awe. "What? You never told me you could do *pyrokinesis!*" he spluttered. He calmed down and inhaled a little smoke then slowly exhaled it upon the humid and pungent breeze. "I suppose I should not be surprised given that I saw Rosemary melt a hole through a brick wall. I just assumed you Mothers were stuck with the one 'element' and that was that."

"We have a little of them all but we are far stronger in the one. We're taught all the elements as part of our induction into the ways of Gaia but we are chosen by our defining element as Shield was when she manifested her power in Crawcester."

"You told me how you were taken from your parents as a little girl after you started talking to birds but you haven't told me much about your life as a Daughter. Why is that? Whenever I try to raise the subject you always find something else to talk about – the children, the Ferals, how the search for food is going. We make love, we sleep in the same bed but you're a mystery to me."

She pushed the hand with the cigar to one side and kissed him briefly on the lips then grinned impishly: "There's an old Finnish saying: if a woman cannot keep a man guessing then she cannot keep a man."

"Hogwash! You're the most beautiful woman I've ever met. I'm so in love with you it hurts but I know so little *about* you."

She looked down at the weathered flagstones beneath their feet. "I find it painful to talk about those days. As Daughters we grew up knowing full well the Mothers would kill us the second any evil thought took root in our hearts. It happened to my only friend, Clover. We shared a room and we lay together in the dark watches before the rituals of sunrise but she…"

"You've mentioned her name in your sleep a few times."

She looked ashen and chewed at her lower lip in silence for a while. "Pah! When I tread the dream-paths of Mag Mell, I am vulnerable to thee, dear heart."

"See? I know you think it's a pretty one-sided relationship when you use all those thees and thous," he said triumphantly.

"Formal speech is still common in Britannia," she huffed. "It's considered a mark of utmost respect."

"If you say so but you know everything there is to know about me: my family, my job, everything - yet *you* keep secrets."

She raised her face to savour the sun once more. "I loved her, Harold, almost as much as I love you," she confessed. "That's why these memories are so painful. Wiccans are shy of men so Daughters had but each other for solace."

"I know you're taken from your families," he sympathised, tapping some ash off his cigar "But why are you ashamed to admit you slept with a girl? It doesn't matter to me: I have *absolutely* no doubts about your current orientation."

"I am *not* ashamed!" she retorted angrily. "Ach! Why do men *always* assume that Wiccans are Sapphic? I will be more open in

12

time, I promise, but for now just be content that I love you with all my heart." She went to the nearest gargoyle and put her hand upon its head. "Do you know why they named this the Tower of Grieving? Do you know why these gargoyles weep?"

"Damn it, Fern, there you go changing the subject *again* but I remember you saying that each one represents a tragedy. I suppose every tower here has some bizarre story behind it."

"Before the world began to drown four centuries ago there was a thriving city beneath us but as the waters rose, the citizens were seized by the madness of vanity. They refused to accept their fate. They quarried the hills to the south and to the north and brought rock and stone to raise the causeways and viaducts to rebuild the city anew atop the ruins of the old."

"Impressive. I can't imagine how they ferried millions of tons of rock across an estuary like this with just barges."

"They laid down the first harbours and docks and for a while Milverburg prospered as a port while others foundered or had to be moved inland but still the waters kept rising."

"So they kept rebuilding the city and the viaducts but surely everything would collapse or sink into the mud?"

"This happened *twelve* times but as the saying goes: all the crows to Crawcester; all the mules to Milverburg. Levels buckled and walls fell but they kept on adding stone and rock until the sinking stopped and Milverburg rose up into the sky to become a fortress. These perimeter towers were built to watch over the estuary and each was named to honour a hero or battle during the Age of Invasions but this one was different," she smiled and patted the head of the gargoyle. "They placed these weeping gargoyles here to lament the original city now buried beneath us and all those who died raising each new Milverburg upon the old."

"I see. I'm sure I heard the sound of a drowned bell down there yesterday when the waves were breaking against the walls."

She smiled and sang a lilting folk song: "*Milverburg of old was paved with gold and the people dressed in silk but drowned were they in waters grey but only merrow mourn the soulless stones of Milverburg today.* There's more but you get the idea."

"Yes and you told me how the city grew so rich that all this insane architecture took place."

"Even a hundred years ago the world was a dangerous place but because Milverburg had survived blockades and bombardments,

13

wealthy merchants settled here and tried to outdo each other in creating a city of art and wonder."

"I suppose you could call some of it art but did *any* of them understand the meaning of taste or restraint?"

"I doubt it. We stayed here once on the way to spy on the Great Abbey. Mother Moss thought it would be an education to show Clover and I what true decadence was." She smiled at the memory. "Every level was filled with amazing statues, sculptures and gargoyles. Even the workers on the factory levels used to carve them in wood to mimic the merchants above. People in the Middle Cities used to say that there were more statues here than people so they dubbed it the City of Gargoyles. Mother Moss disapproved of them and she despaired of all the whores and tavern sots but we thought that Milverburg was *magical*."

"Magical? This place is a monument to all the servants and workers who lived in the darkness of the lower levels. I'm surprised there was no uprising or revolution here."

"The merchants were not stupid, dear heart! The workers' wages were thrice that of anywhere else in Britannia even Beorminghas and the markets were full of life and light. We went down to watch the ships being loaded and unloaded in the docks then we went to the railway stations to see the trains. You could smell every spice in Creation – it was the market place of the whole world."

He imagined the bustling crowds then he realised that Fern was probably projecting those images into his mind.

"I saw Assyrians, Inuit, Egyptians, Finns, Slavs, Chinese and even the Japanese Empire traders with their beautiful silk robes and wondrous swords but everywhere there were gargoyles and strange statues spouting water into fountains or sewage into foul drains and cess pools. We had such nightmares afterwards!"

"I'm not surprised," he said, stubbing his cigar out.

"An Assyrian asked Mother Moss if she would sell us to him so that he could take us to the Caliphates for the harems," she laughed. "We thought she was going to turn him into a pile of soot on the spot - she was *that* vexed with the idea."

"Sounds positively mediaeval," he noted dryly. "You want me to talk to Ivy and Nightshade so… what's the matter, Fern?

"There to the north-east, dear heart!" she cried, pointing and wide-eyed with fear. "Can't you see them? There are Angels in the air above Wealthorpe!"

He grabbed his binoculars from the flagstones and focussed them on the two black rotorcraft of the Order. The machines had been dubbed Angels decades ago by an unsuspecting world as they were exclusively used for medical aid by the Order. This was the same Order whose ruling Conclave had created and released the Virus of Revelation; a lethal plague that had left billions dead and mutated surviving children into Ferals by corrupting their DNA; activating redundant genes until they became animal-like and so deformed that they usually starved to death. The distant rotorcraft were Angels alright; heavily-armed Angels of Death.

"So much for the Order being in chaos!" he said despondently. "They must be from Bede. They could be looking for Surl and the others we need to … hey, what are you *doing*?"

"Hush, dear heart. I am trying to far-see with my craft," she explained, closing her eyes and pressing her fingertips to her temples. "I am in the thoughts of Father Ursaf of Bede… ugh! A disgusting mind full of schedules and circuitry! I am in the pilot's mind now: he is displeased to be despatched from Bede with such a violent storm front approaching. They're searching for people who've escaped the Great Abbey!"

His heart leapt with sudden hope: "Is it the little ones?"

"I'm not sure," she said, perspiring from the effort "They're looking for… for Abbot Michael! He survived the machine!"

"What? He was cut to ribbons. We saw all that *blood*."

"Nevertheless, he survived and they regard him as a traitor to the Order and want him dead." Her eyes snapped open. "Gaia protect us!" she gasped, sagging against the parapet. "I saw an image of Schimrian in Ursaf's thoughts: he's alive!"

"Bugger!" he groaned, his heart sinking. "That damned machine must've revived him somehow! Search their minds again. Are the little ones with him? I need to know!"

"I can't see them!" she said desperately. "They were not in Ursaf's thoughts but he does know that Abbot Michael had others with him that he'd freed from the Redemption Cells."

He gripped the hilt of his katana and a strange cold thrill ran through him at the thought of action. "If there's any chance of those kids being alive, we have to go out there and get them! I will *not* fail them again!"

~~~~~~

Scatterlings

Uppermost was a town built for the elite upon the roof of Milverburg. It boasted mansions, fountains, theatres, ornamental gardens, parades, galleries, banks, shops and government offices. Every building was adorned with art and sculptures but there was little theme or continuity to be found anywhere. The senses were overwhelmed by the jarring contrasts created by global merchants who cared little for context or aesthetics just as long as each could outdo the other with a statement of wealth and privilege.

Six years of constant rain and growing moss had not detracted much from the paintings and stonework but in the rare, bright sunlight, they made Fern and Harold feel particularly nauseous as they ran towards the Tower of the Sun at the centre of the township. They were sweating profusely when Harold called a halt and placed his hands upon his knees to catch his breath. "I keep forgetting how big this place is," he panted. "We're only halfway there. Can you contact Nightshade again to see if Kai is with her? He needs to be with us when we talk to the others."

Fern leant against the plinth of a tasteless pink statue of a cherub and wiped her brow with a shirtsleeve. She placed both hands to her temples and closed her eyes. "No. The wound Pious gave him is healing well but he refuses to leave the Ferals for he regards living with them as part of his penance."

"That has to stop," he said firmly. "He saved Fria and without his help we would have died at the Great Abbey."

"True but the others won't trust him for all his bravery because he still wears the field robes of a Brother and Shield and her sisters saw him lead children to their deaths in Crawcester."

"He was a postulant back then. He had no choice! Can you tell if the rest of them are in the Library yet?"

"They are. Nightshade has gathered them together and told them what Ivy has sensed and how we've seen Angels hunting along the eastern shores." She opened her eyes suddenly to stare at him. "They want to rush out along the viaduct to look for the little ones and poor Mouse is becoming hysterical."

"I should have spent more time with her too: she misses Fierce," he admitted guiltily. He glanced up at the sky as first distant peal of thunder sounded. Complex wisps of cirrus were streaming north and the sunlight began to fade. "I'm not surprised Michael turned

16

traitor after being shoved into that meat-grinder by Azrael but I can't believe Schimrian survived after having his skull crushed to a pulp! I've got my second wind now so let's get moving."

They resumed their run towards the Tower of the Sun that loomed over the imposing government buildings nearby. It was surrounded by a huge circular garden full of statues, ornate ponds and winding pathways. Around the perimeter of the garden were arcs of Bath stone mansions that reminded Harold of Bath Circus. These lesser merchants had no choice but to gaze up at the baroque majesty of the circular tower which bore twelve bands of stylised suns with ornate balconies separating each sun. The stonework had been painted a brilliant white while each carved sun was covered in gold leaf so that whatever the angle of the sun, one quadrant or another of Uppermost had been bedazzled.

The Scatterlings loved the tower as they'd all had luxuriously-decorated bedrooms and clean sheets for the first time in six years. The Ferals, Kai, Ivy and Nightshade used the servant quarters on the first three floors but Harold had fretted constantly about setting up a base in such a vulnerable building. If the Order ever reached Uppermost they'd all be trapped in the tower with nowhere to run to but the children had wanted to be as close to the sky as possible to enjoy the fresh sea air – except when the wind swept over the Dead Marshes that is.

As they crossed the drawbridge set down over a moat teeming with carp, three male Ferals scampered out to greet them with leers upon their ruined faces. "Lighfaahrer home, Lighfaahher ahhn Ferrrrnn arrrh luffers arh arh" said the leading male Feral. Harold could barely understand the gibberish spoken by most of the Ferals but he reddened at the suggestive nature of this one especially as he was nudging the other two in the ribs.

"Shhh, Godwin, such thoughts are not for one such as you," she chided good-naturedly, going down on one knee and ruffling his hair. "Our rest is over, dear heart. Tell Kai and the others to ready their weapons. We are going to fight the Order again."

A battle-lust shone in the eyes of the Feral who nodded eagerly. His clothes in tatters and his face almost dog-like, Harold could only imagine how handsome this Feral must have been before the virus had triggered his redundant DNA. He shuddered at the thought that amongst the ruins of this world, in crumbling, weed-choked towns and villages, the Order's holocaust ground on as the

17

viral mutations in their genes progressed and slowly purging them from the face of the Earth.

The Ferals retreated through the tower entrance with their instructions as Fern stood up and bared her teeth in frustration. "Let us not think of that any further lest we go insane. Come," she urged. "Only ten flights of steps to climb!"

"Have mercy, Fern," he groaned comically. "I'm still a badly wounded hero, you know!"

"The Order *has* no mercy! We must get everyone organised and save as many souls as we can. Come, Light-Father!"

"I really wish you would call me Harold," he grumbled as they began the ascent up the wide marble stairs that spiralled around the central column, opening out onto circular landings at every level. Not for the first time he imagined this central stairwell acting as a chimney if the tower ever caught fire and he had to shake his head to clear it drawing a glance over her shoulder from Fern.

"Then hurry up, *Harold*!" she urged.

"Oh, *now* you call me Harold," he wheezed. "When I'm on the verge of a cardiac arrest!"

"You need more stamina," she said sweetly as she waited for him. "Being bested by a woman is not good for the male ego."

"You will *not* get a rise out of me," he said, drawing in a deep breath. "I'm all for equality of the sexes!"

"So no whips and chains for me, then?"

He stopped dead when he realised how pointed that barb was. Wiccans like Fern had been persecuted for centuries. Never many in number, they had always opposed the Order and had paid a fearsome price. One of Fern's ancestors had been burnt at the stake for exposing the Minister for Alms Houses who was selecting poor and orphaned children for experimental procedures by the Fathers-Surgeon of the Order.

"No," he said simply as he caught up with her. "I would give my life for you, Fern, you know that."

She flung her arms around his neck and kissed him passionately until he really did think he was going to have a heart attack. She only disengaged at the sound of a discrete cough from the albino Mother leaning over a banister above them. "When you're done," Nightshade said pointedly. "We do have children to rescue."

They entered the main library which completely covered the tenth floor and was divided into four large connected rooms to

18

reflect the quadrants of Uppermost. At the long oak table in the North Room, Mother Ivy sat in an intricately-carved high-backed oak chair with her staff upon the table in front of her. "Welcome, Light-Father," she said, standing up and bowing to him.

"Please stop doing that, Ivy," he begged, taking a seat opposite her as Fern sat to his right. "It's embarrassing. How are your injuries? I'm afraid I've been a bit occupied lately..."

"That much is obvious," Ivy said bluntly and the children sat around the table nodded in agreement. "Brooding in your tower served no purpose but thank you for asking: my ribs have knitted well and the bruises are all but gone but, alas, nothing can bring my Ferals back," she added mournfully. "I can sense the little ones are indeed making their way here but I fear they may be being hunted by those Angels you saw."

To her right sat an eleven year old girl with braided yellow hair and a headband with mouse-ears upon it. She had two large knives strapped to her two belts and an ornate Iberian spear placed upon the table in front of her. She was dressed in leather-trimmed shorts, sandals and a crudely-stitched green leather jacket fastened with two buckles. She stood up, demanding to know why her Light-Father wasn't searching for her friends already.

"Be *quiet*, Mouse!" Nightshade commanded impatiently, taking the last vacant seat to Harold's left. "We cannot rush out there without thought otherwise all will be lost!"

"Yes, Mother Nightshade," she said timidly and sat back down. She looked sheepishly at Harold and smiled, gaining confidence in his presence. "I'm sorry, Light-Father, but I really want to go out and look for them! I miss my sister so much! Don't be angry with me, *please*, Light-Father!"

"I'm not angry, Mouse, but Nightshade is right. We don't know where they are yet but if they have escaped with Abbot Michael then they might be close to the eastern causeway."

"All paths lead the Order here to Milverburg," Nightshade said enigmatically. "Few is better, I think, and no Ferals." She pointed at the four oldest Scatterlings: "Saul, Ibrahim, Bas and Shield shall go with Fern and you, Light-Father: you need to lead them."

"Listen, all of you," Harold said urgently. "The Order is coming for us and I do not want us to get trapped in Uppermost where the Angels can get at us. We have to leave this tower so the rest of you get your weapons and packs and only take things that you need and get down to the docks. I've serviced three boats and we still have the Phoenix if we need her. Come on!" he barked, clapping his hands twice. "We haven't got all day!"

A squat youth with a livid scar disfiguring the right side of his face stood up, baring his teeth. "Why can't I go?" he demanded angrily. "I'm strong enough to fight beside the Light-Father!"

"You're not ready, Amos," Nightshade said curtly. "You're still too hot-headed. The Brothers will kill you unless you defeat the demon within you as Ibrahim has done."

"No!" Amos shouted. "I need to go! Surl is my *sister*!"

"Enough!" Ivy said in a voice with odd overtones to it. "I have discussed this with you before as has Fern and the Light-Father. Be seated, Amos - your time will come soon enough."

Amos perspired suddenly and tried resisting the compulsion to sit down to no avail. He gripped the sledgehammer on the table and his knuckles whitened. "She's alive but you will take her from me. That's why you would not let me return to the Great Abbey to search for her! Now I've learnt what it is to be her brother, you'll make her a Wiccan and she'll no longer be my sister!"

"Enough!" Harold roared, silencing the commotion around the table. "I see I need to spend a lot more time with you, Amos, but *now* is not the time. We *will* get her back!"

Amos folded his arms and turned his face away in disgust. "Ach! It seems I have no choice, Light-Father!"

"I'm sorry that you feel that way, Amos..."

"It's because we've hardly seen you since we came here, Light-Father," a tall, pale girl interrupted, staring down at her four long knives upon the table before her. Harold noted again how the Scatterlings always placed their weapons to hand especially at meal-times: six years of brutal survival had shown them that an unarmed child was a dead child in this lethal dystopia. "We all need your magic but you just work on the boats, mope in your tower or lie abed with Mother Fern," she added meaningfully.

"I know and I'm sorry, Fria," he conceded. "I blamed myself for losing the little ones but now we might have a chance to save them, it changes everything. As much as I wanted to, it would have been suicide to attack the Great Abbey again and rescue them."

"We always knew that the Order would come for us," Fern added. "We all hoped for months of peace here but that devil, Schimrian, is still alive and we are in great peril."

Saul, the leader of the Scatterlings, stood behind Amos and placed a hand on his shoulder. "We've been through the same travail as you but I've accepted that Shield is a Wiccan. Be at peace: their gifts will save us all. I'm convinced of it."

"You only say that, Eldest, because you're sleeping with her... *aiee!*" Amos yelped as Saul tightened his grip.

"I have no patience for your silly jealousies, Amos," Saul said dangerously. "You and I need to talk later as well."

Amos surged to his feet, his face red with fury as he rubbed at his shoulder. "It's not fair!" he protested. "Surl is my *sister!*"

Fern stood up and he subsided at the fell light in her eyes. A powerful wind suddenly whirled around the room carrying papers from nearby reading-desks. "Shield!" she commanded. "Do not let our anger and fear tear us apart! Control your power!"

"Yes, Mother Fern," she said humbly and lowered her head. The gale roaring about them suddenly ceased and the papers fluttered down to the floor.

"That's better," Fern said as Saul, Ibrahim and Bas headed for the door. "Join them and wait for us outside. I need to speak to Fria, Mouse and Amos." She waited until they had left the room and turned to the three Scatterlings who quailed before her anger. "Amos, I *cannot* allow you to turn against us when you have finally understood what it is to be a brother to Surl. If we have to flee Milverburg, she'll need your protection again."

"I'll protect her as well," Fria said bravely, clenching her fist to her chest. "Just as Bethwin protected me."

"Yes, Mother Fern, I'm sorry," Amos muttered with ill grace. "But you must get her back for me or I'll *never* forgive you."

"Much will change when you see her," Ivy assured him. "Hers is a truly dangerous power and carries with it grave risk if she remains untrained. If we do not guide her, Amos, the visions will drive her insane; they'll tear her apart. We will not do this simply to spite you but because it's the right thing to do for *her*. Saul is right: she and Shield could be the saving of us all."

"Yes, yes, I know this," he sighed, turning to Harold. "Father, what should I do? I don't want to lose her again!"

"You will not lose her, son. You have my word," Harold replied, glancing at Ivy. "Look, as soon as we get the little ones back you and I will go fishing, agreed?"

"Yes, Father but I beg you: *save her*."

"I will but now you must lead the others and the Ferals down to the main dock; the one next to the rail yard where the Phoenix is. I want you to keep our two escape options open. Gather food and water and wait for us there. We'll take a boat from the fishing dock but we might have to retreat on foot across the viaduct."

"But the Angels will see you," Fria protested suddenly. "They'll kill you with their chain-guns!"

Fern retrieved her jacket and raven-headed staff from the centre of the table. "You and Amos need to trust in our craft a little more," she said, getting to her feet "You recall how we fooled those Brothers in the Angels? I can do the same again."

"May God favour you, Mother Fern," Amos said impulsively. "I know I have much already to thank you for but…"

"Gaia favours us, Amos, not the God of the Order but you have a stout heart and Surl loves you. We *will* save her."

"Then by Saint Peter's teeth," he said impatiently. "What are you waiting for? Leave the evacuation to me, Father. We'll wait at the main dock and keep close to that large boat you repaired and refuelled last week. You have my word."

Fern and Harold nodded to each other and joined the four Scatterlings on the landing. "We need to get to the docks quickly," Harold said. "Do you have all your weapons?"

Shield gave him a peeved look: "Honestly, Light-Father," she sighed, displaying her stocked quiver of bolts, arm shield, sword and crossbow. "Do you *still* take us for babes?"

Bas adjusted her bow and quiver of arrows. Harold saw her ears twitch then she grinned, displaying her elongated canines.

Ibrahim smiled down at his younger sister and patted one of his axes. "Our inner demons are ready, Light-Father. May I suggest we use the shafts to get down to the fishing dock?"

Fern laughed as Harold made a face. "The Light-Father finds the shafts unnerving but they are indeed quicker."

"Fine, let's use the shafts," Harold agreed reluctantly.

After another loping run that left Harold gasping for breath again, they were at one of the elevator shaft entrances set around the perimeter of Uppermost. The elevators were essentially crude cages used for raising goods up from the docks and from the factories and shops on the other levels. Installed before electricity reached Milverburg, they could be operated in pairs by winches: one cage rose up as another descended. If the cages rising were empty, full cages descending could then rocket down at great speed with only the brake wheels running against the static hawsers set against the shaft walls to slow them down.

The Scatterlings had more faith in the brakes than Harold who was gritting his teeth as their cage plummeted down the pitch black shaft with Ibrahim reading off the level markings with a torch. It was only with two levels to go that he pulled the lever and sparks flew from one of the shrieking brake wheels. With his heart in his mouth, Harold felt the cage slow rapidly with the inertia all but pressing them to the cage floor. "We didn't need to fall *that* quick," he muttered. "I almost lost my breakfast."

Ibrahim shrugged in the torchlight as the cage locked into the dock platform and the cage-gate opened automatically. "Forgive me, Light-Father," he said throwing a large switch to his left. "Haste favours the bold as Mother Moss used to say."

The emergency lighting units about the dock area burst into life. Even after six years, the immense batteries had retained a charge which, Harold had to admit, was a minor miracle in itself. There were several diesel generators but he was wary about starting them up without servicing them first.

This dock had been exclusively reserved for the boats of the fishermen of Milverburg who trawled the Milverbore and the Gael Seas. Harold had spent some time exploring the lowest level and had serviced three of the sturdiest vessels in various docks and tested their engines as he knew their respite was only temporary. One of these was a small fishing boat with a powerful engine but he made the mistake of reading the Runic name again on the bow: *Ellendaed*. It translated as 'Deed of Valour' in his head but not before pain had ripped from one temple to another.

"Are you ill?" Shield enquired with some concern. "Your nose is bleeding a little, Light-Father."

"It's nothing," he said, pulling on a mooring rope to draw the boat flush to the dockside. "This is not my native tongue and new words are painful: whatever Moss did to hammer your language into my brain was not subtle. Get in," he commanded. "Fern? Are you ready to camouflage us?"

Fern sat cross-legged on the deck and laid her staff upon her thighs recalling her craft restoring it after it had been snapped in two by Azrael. "As soon as we open the dock-gates you must all keep quiet. If I lose concentration for a second, they'll see us."

Ibrahim ran to the end of the dock and threw his huge strength into turning the large wheel that drew the dock-gates apart. Water poured through the gap as the high tide was full and thus a little above the dockside levels. It would flood the whole dock area; the sea having risen again since they were built a century ago but Harold had no time to worry about that now.

He fired up the engines and the powerful boat surged forward with Ibrahim jumping aboard as it reached the gates. The smell of brine and the humid warmth hit them as they emerged and although the light was fading, they could see the Angels now circling like vultures near the eastern causeway. Fern closed her eyes and began a lilting chant in a long-dead tongue that made them feel light-headed while Harold steered the boat as close as he could to the viaduct, striving to keep as much of the ancient stonework between them and the sinister machines as possible.

The sun was almost hidden behind the clouds and powerful gusts of wind buffeted the boat as Harold slowed it down to approach the quay that jutted out from the muddy shoreline next to the causeway. There were one-storey buildings and cottages set some distance inland that Harold guessed had once housed the masons and labourers required to constantly maintain the gigantic causeways and viaducts.

As he moored the boat, he gazed nervously up at the Angels but they were now moving further to the east. He checked on Fern who still had her eyes closed as she recited her chant over and over again. He beckoned Saul to the bow and pointed at the cottages. "Your eyes are sharper than mine. Can you see anyone? There's no cover between us and that village so we'd be sitting ducks."

Saul looked at him quizzically then shaded his eyes to peer at the cottages and the woods beyond: "Why would we turn into lazy ducks? Fear not: I can see no Brothers in the village or amongst the trees. They would've seen the boat and raised the alarm by now. Bless Mother Fern: the Angels keep moving to the east! When they get beyond that tree line we can get to the cottages."

After what seemed like an age, the Angels dipped out of sight. Shield hauled the exhausted Fern to her feet then helped her ashore as Harold tied off a second mooring rope. "I'm too exhausted to far-see if the little ones are in the village," she told him.

"We'll search the buildings and if they're not there, we'll scout along the road and the rail track. Can you run?" he asked with some concern. "We have a hundred yards of open space between us and the cover of those cottages. Can you make it?"

"Yes, Light-Father," she gasped and after two deep breaths, she grasped her staff and set off at a fast pace.

"I wish you'd call me Harold!" he called after her. The others sprang forward to follow her leaving Harold bringing up the rear and struggling for breath. He patted the tin in his pocket. "Cigars are *so* not good for me," he muttered ruefully.

He caught up to them as they crouched down behind a garden wall. Saul placed a finger to his lips and motioned for him to keep low so he crawled up to the wall and peered over it. Between two cottages, he could see into the cobbled street beyond and his heart sank: two black half-tracks of the Order were parked there with groups of Tally-men and Brothers systematically searching the buildings and storehouses on the opposite side of street.

He sat down heavily with his back to the wall and looked at Fern. "We got lucky as they've started their searches on the north side so they haven't seen us or the boat yet," he said, drawing his sword. "We could circle around them but they would cut us off if we had to retreat back to the boat or the causeway. We've got no time anyway because as soon as they see the boat, they'll know we're here so what the hell do we do now?"

"We do what we always do," Saul shrugged. "We fight."

~~~~~

25

The Naked One

Abbot Michael was feeling a little faint from heat exhaustion as he stood at one of the east-facing windows of a farmhouse kitchen, meticulously wiping the dirt from the panes using a sleeve of his heavy Order field robes. The farmer had obviously been wealthy as the fitted kitchen behind him was spacious, well-furnished and the dressers were full of expensive Austro-Hungarian china but the once pristine fields were bramble-strewn and quickly reverting to woodland. Ivy was already smothering the exterior walls and in the thirty years time, he reflected, it would be as if this prosperous but isolated farmstead had never existed.

When they'd emerged from amongst the moss-covered trees of the Forest of Weal, they'd had no choice but to take the risk and hare across the overgrown fields and meadows to search for food and water in the only buildings for miles around. It was a desperate gamble but they'd been lucky: no Angels were in the air and they'd found some unspoilt tins of vegetable broth in one of the cupboards and a gas cooker on which to heat it up. It was barely enough to take the edge off their hunger but after a minute or so of hard work, the water from the old-fashioned pump over the main sink ran clear so at least they could drink their fill.

He drew his cowl about his head to keep his bandaged face in shadow as Surl, a girl of ten years of age, stood next to him. She came up his shoulder for she was tall and well-built for her age but she was completely bald with no eyebrows above her keen green eyes reminding him of a Tibetan monk he'd once met – only her powers exceeded that of any Panchen Lama he'd ever read about.

She wore khaki leggings tucked into her leather boots and a padded jacket fastened with two silver buttons over a plain green vest but all her clothes were filthy and reeking of mud and worse. She had a crucifix upon a golden chain about her neck but she was no novice monk: her favourite weapon, a machete with a thirty-inch razor-sharp blade, was in a sheath strapped to her back. She also had four long knives in sheaths attached to her belt or sown into her jacket. He'd seen her use them and had quickly realised that he'd never seen anyone as fast and as deadly as these Scatterlings.

"This sunshine is the Devil's work," he grumbled after checking that the fields and meadows to the east were free of pursuers. "This sunlight will make it easier for the Fathers and Brothers to pick up our trail. Well? What did your visions say? Can we rest here for a few hours? Will they find this place?"

"We'll be safe here until the storms come, Naked One," Surl replied, rubbing at her temples. She raised the crucifix and pressed it to her lips. "I swear this on my mother's death."

"I'm glad you haven't told the others why I'm called that. I'd rather they didn't know - for their sanity and mine."

Surl turned her face away as she suppressed a gag reflex: "It's up to you to tell the others."

He placed a gloved hand upon her head. "I pray to God that *you* aren't paying a similar price for your prescience."

"I don't believe in *your* God: the God of child-slayers," she said angrily, brushing his hand away. "Mother Moss saved us all at our Keep in Crawcester yet she paid this price you speak of for *her* prescience, didn't she? All we had left of her after Schimrian had tortured her was a severed head in a *tin*! This is all I have left of my birth mother so I kiss her memory *not* your precious Jesus!"

Michael bowed his head in shame: "You've every reason to hate me, child, though I had nothing to do with her death."

"My name is Surl *not* child and you had *everything* to do with the death of my family!" she retorted vehemently. "Without my gift, we wouldn't have made it this far, now would we?"

He glanced at the other three Scatterlings sat at the oaken kitchen table who were staring at him with undisguised loathing and hatred in their eyes, their weapons upon the table before them. He had to admit that the renegade scientists at Exodus Industries had done a remarkable job: any one of these genetically-enhanced children could kill a Tally-man in a *heartbeat* and for two weeks they'd wreaked absolute havoc at the Great Abbey before freeing him and five young men from the Redemption Cells.

"I'll grant you that, Surl," he conceded slowly. "We avoided the ambushes in Thaneton and Fosskeep thanks to your craft but your nosebleeds and migraines are getting worse. There's a large wood to the west and then we have to pass a village called Wealthorpe to get to the causeway. This is where they would set an ambush. I'm almost afraid to ask you to use your gift to find us safe passage: you could haemorrhage or suffer a stroke."

"Let me be the judge of that," she sighed wearily, suppressing a yawn. "I need to rest and so do the others. We've been running and hiding in woods and barns and ditches for seven days now and those men we rescued were already weak from being tortured by Pious and all those other devils at the Great Manse."

"Then I hope you're right about the storms: they'll help us slip past Wealthorpe and get across the viaduct. If the Light-Father and the Wiccans are there as you've foreseen, will they be able to aid us if the Brothers are guarding the causeway?"

"I've foreseen *something* happening at Wealthorpe to help us but it's too fuzzy: I don't know how my craft works but I think there are too many different futures for me to see clearly."

"Maybe a future you can't influence directly will always be difficult to foresee," he suggested.

"Possibly," she said after a moment's thought. "I have too few years to make sense of it. Anyway," she yawned, stretching her arms above her head. "I'm going into the dining room to sleep in one of the armchairs. The only thing I do know for sure is that we won't have to worry about the Angels above us."

"What?" he exclaimed, reaching out for her. "Wait! Come back! What you mean by that? We're vulnerable here!"

Surl didn't answer and left the kitchen but a boy of the same age got off his chair and came over to him and tried to peer up under the cowl but Michael averted his face.

"What do you want, Peter?" Michael asked, resisting the urge to hold his nose. Because of the constant rains and mud they'd endured on the road, he knew he was none too fragrant but the stench of the Great Abbey sewers still clung to the children.

Peter had a wide and open face smeared with oil and grime; his black hair matted and lice-infested. He was dressed in dark grey trousers, brown walking-boots, a long-sleeved green T-shirt and a grey jerkin with sheaths sown into it so that his five knives could be reached easily. Two of these could be screwed into the mount strapped to the stump of his right wrist which currently had a well-constructed metal claw attached to it.

"It's about those men: when I gave them their broth one of them asked me to tell you said he'd rather die here than be made into a stinking Tally-man while the others just want to kill you."

"I don't blame them," Michael laughed wryly, placing a hand on Peter's shoulder. Unlike the others, Peter could bear his touch without flinching. "You've looked after them well, my son. You have a gift. They're recovering but they must rest before we make a run for Milverburg when Surl's predicted storm breaks."

Peter placed his left hand on his gurgling stomach. "I hope that broth wasn't poisoned," he said anxiously. "I've had the squits three times already this past week."

"It's a miracle none of us have food poisoning," Michael sympathised, removing his hand. He handed Peter a jug. "Get them some water and make sure they drink as much as they can."

"Aye, for them *not* because you asked me to."

Michael made no response and turned to a girl with wild auburn hair who had about nine years by his reckoning and whose brown doe eyes belied a speed and ferocity that fascinated him. She wore a vest patterned with Celtic knot motifs, a filthy knitted jacket and a leather skirt over leggings and leather boots. She had two ancient war-axes in slings on her back and held another two in her hands almost perpetually. Unlike the others, she'd made an effort to wash the filth off her face and hands.

"What of you, Rabbit?" he asked as Peter filled the jug, the mechanism screeching thinly as he pumped. "How are you bearing up?" He knew he was just making conversation: she was exhausted, lice-ridden and brimming with a relentless hatred for the Order.

"Well enough, *God's butcher*," she said coldly. She picked up a whetstone and began honing one of her axes. "You asked me yesterday why most of us never use our birth-names. It's because we cannot bear the loss of our families. We've had to make a new family for ourselves. Mother Moss called me Rabbit because nothing could catch me yet all we did for six years is fight off dogs and Tally-men at our Keep until the Light-Father came to us in a blinding flash of light and worked his magic."

"All this reflects the divine madness that consumed us," he sighed heavily, sitting at the table. He lowered his head as he vividly recalled the ruling Conclave parading the seven-headed lamb that the Vatican laboratories had created after vying with the Order in genetic research. The Order had been founded upon the Book of Revelation comprising Twelve Tribes each with twelve thousand Abbots, Fathers and Brothers to complete the Blessed Number so this monstrosity was hailed as a sign from God. It created a tsunami of holy rapture that had swept aside all doubt in the Order as it unleashed its Virus of Revelation. Yet here he was six years later: a worm sitting at a table in an abandoned farmhouse seeking forgiveness from children he'd helped to orphan. Him! A willing agent of the Apocalypse!

29

"We actually thought we were carrying out God's works!" he said aloud, his voice dripping with self-loathing. "I *have* to save as many as I can before Satan drags my wretched soul to Hell."

"Hell would probably spit you back out," she sneered, going over to the window he'd cleaned to keep watch.

"Then why did you rescue me?"

"We heard that Schimrian's *thing*, Pious, was going to kill you and we were asked to save you and the others. I may have but a few years but Mother Moss taught me well the meaning of *irony*."

"Nevertheless, I'm grateful for the chance to save my immortal soul," he said, bowing deeply with hand on heart. "But I beg you: who asked you to save me?"

Rabbit curled her lip in disgust but kept silent and returned to her vigil as the youngest Scatterling looked at him and smiled sleepily. "Pup can't remember his real mother," he said, yawning hugely. "Bas is Pup's mother now... and Mother Moss was his grandmother before she was killed by Schimrian." He laid his head upon his arms and closed his eyes. "Pup tired now."

Michael regarded this seven-year old boy who always referred to himself in the third person as the most remarkable of the four. His dark brown hair was tied back into a ponytail and he wore a greasy leather jerkin over a T-shirt with Runic slogans, corduroy breeches and leather shoes. His main weapon, apart from two small knives in leather sheaths strapped to his belt, was an industrial-strength catapult that was almost impossible for an adult to draw back yet he'd seen this child kill a Brother with one of the ball-bearings he kept in the two leather pouches on his belt.

"Perhaps you should join Surl and sleep in one of the armchairs in the dining room," he suggested and Pup blearily complied, humming a lullaby.

A few seconds later Surl entered the kitchen and reseated herself at the table whilst glaring at him. "Did you know I had beautiful red hair once?" she said suddenly.

"I'm sorry, Surl, you had red hair?" he asked, perplexed. "I thought you were going to get some sleep."

"I would only keep Pup awake. I tried but all I could think about was how one of your Tally-men tried to smother me with a pillow. I had but four years then yet I was an Unworthy brat only worthy of murdering. Fria and Amos saved me. Fria stabbed him in the neck and Amos smashed his skull in with a sledgehammer until there was just this red... *mess*... full of sparks from the electrics of the Guides in his head." She shuddered and stared into the distance. "My hair fell out and I could not speak more than one word at a time until the Light-Father gave me back my voice."

"Did you start having visions after that trauma?"

"I think Mother Moss foresaw the craft in me but she couldn't find the Wiccan mark but I do have it. It was just hard to find."

"The five dark spots that Wiccans once claimed to represent the five holes of the Crucifixion?"

"Yes. She still tried to explain the craft to me and train me but I was too young to understand what she was saying. Besides, we were all too busy staying alive for her to do any more for me." She looked at him quizzically. "Now I *know* I'm a Wiccan, tell me why the Order hates us so much!"

He adjusted his cowl to make sure she could not see his bandaged face. "The Order has regarded them as blasphemous for centuries. I see this now as nothing more than jealousy and hatred of women who were blessed with such power."

"So if I'm caught they'll beat me and burn me at the stake?" Surl exploded, making Rabbit jump. "What God gave you *men* the right to kill women and girls just because we're *different*?"

"I won't lie to you," he said, raising his hands in a gesture of admission. "Even I, for all my scientific knowledge, regarded Wiccans as unholy abominations. I was indoctrinated..." he paused as he realised she could not possibly know what that meant. "It's when you are taken from your family as a child and told the same thing over and over again until you believe it but now I realise that *we* were the abominations not the Wiccans. I cannot undo such great wickedness but I will try to do some good before I die."

Surl indicated a spider spinning a web between some desiccated flowers in a vase in the centre of the table. "That spider has more chance of swinging my machete than you have of atoning for the death and suffering you've inflicted upon the world."

"Nevertheless, this *insect* will try to save you all if he can." He interlocked his fingers and took a deep breath: "I'm sorry to ask this of you but can you consult your visions... by the Holy Ghost!" he exclaimed fearfully. "I hear Angels! Did you foresee this?"

"Yes," she nodded, her eyes unfocussing. "Ah! I can see the Light-Father and Mother Fern! They're fighting Brothers and Tally-men in Wealthorpe but the Angels can't attack them as

31

they're above us." She gasped and placed her head on her arms. "No more! Ah! I'm tired of seeing so much *blood*!"

"They're circling above us, Surl," Rabbit confirmed, the fear making her voice crack. "They must know we're here!"

"I tried to make them think we were heading for Nuncernig or Epstall," Michael said despairingly, making a fist. "It didn't work! Those chain-guns can rip through brick walls."

Surl groaned and raised her head. "They won't open fire: I see this! At sixteen bells I *know* they'll leave then we must wait until the storm starts then we can get everyone into the woods to meet up with the Light-Father and the others."

"If they land and attack us, my handguns will make a difference," he reassured them, patting one of the holsters on his belt. "Fortunately for us, Schimrian decreed that Brothers and Tally-men cannot bear such weapons in Britannia."

Surl drew her machete and laid it on the table then checked her knives. "You'll use those toys soon enough but not just yet," she said dismissively and pointed at the ceiling. "Can you not hear? They're already moving away from us."

He cocked an ear. "You're right but they could be heading back to Wealthorpe," he suggested anxiously. "They could be going back to attack your Light-Father!"

"I think they'll be alright," Surl cried out, clutching at her head and screwing her eyes shut in agony. "Ow! All I see is *red.*"

"Stop scrying!" he insisted urgently. "Your nose is bleeding and you'll pass out at this rate. We'll just have to pray that God will bless us all and protect us."

"Like He protected the billions who died?" Rabbit snapped. "If you ever ask your God of Slaughter to bless me again, *deófolscín*, I will end you!"

Michael looked at the murderous intent in the eyes of such a young girl and flinched visibly. "God blesses whomsoever He wishes," he said quietly, wrapping his robes about himself again. He knew he stank and his skin itched horribly but he was nearly immortal thanks to the effects of the Revelation Virus upon his Order-nurtured genes and the infernal device Azrael had thrust him into to give him the bloodiest of epiphanies. He put a hand across his eyes and trembled violently at the memory. "You cannot kill me," he told her, his voice shaking. "My body regenerates from any wound. I can't die even if you stabbed me in my heart."

Surl tried to peer under his cowl to no avail. "All you can see in your mind are the knives and scalpels in that demon-machine that made you into the Naked One," she said with little sympathy. "The Devil was thus turned loose upon His own."

"You have no idea," he said bleakly.

~~~~~

Saul leapt over the garden wall with his katana drawn. Four Tally-men in long hooded black coats and armed with spears were guarding the half-tracks. They had their backs to him as they impassively watched the destructive searches of the cottages opposite. The nearest Tally-man never saw or heard the tall, slim youth approach from behind and looked down at the blade protruding from his chest for several seconds before his ruined brain registered that he was now dead. He let out a sound uncannily like a sigh of relief and crumpled to the cobbles.

By the time Harold reached Saul with his own katana at the ready, the other three Tally-men had been slain by crossbow bolt, arrow and axe by Shield, Bas and Ibrahim respectively. "Great plan, Saul, next time let's give a little more thought, shall we?"

Saul grinned without reply and flicked the blood off his sword as from the cottage doorways opposite, twelve Brothers with spears emerged wearing black field robes that ended at the knee, black scapulas of the same length, black trousers and boots. Finally, a large bearded man with the gold pectoral cross of the Fathers of the Order on his robes joined them along with fifteen Tally-men wearing their long, black, hooded coats. They too were clutching the long spears favoured by the Order. As there was no rain, their hoods were drawn back and the metallic Guides driven into their bald skulls glinted in the last glimmers of sunlight.

"Well, well, what do we have here, my sons?" the Father declared, drawing his sidearm. "This is not the Naked One and his Unworthy rabble but the very desecrators of our Great Cathedral! We..." He gagged on seeing Fern's attire and his face blanched with terror: "A Harlot of Satan!" he shrieked. "Brother Clegwyn! Get the begiuller from the half-track before she bewitches us!"

He aimed his gun at Fern but she brought her staff down hard upon the cobbled street and from beneath the raving Father, the ground erupted sending him twenty yards into the air and spinning like a rag doll. "I am Mother Fern of the First Degree!" she shouted up at him: "I am a Servant of Gaia and a Wielder of Earth! Thou wilt be one with the ghosts that scream for your soul! By the Triple Goddess, thou shalt defile this world no more!"

He slammed into the ground head-first and they clearly heard his neck and many other bones snap. He did not move again.

Harold hoped that his death would persuade the Brothers to abandon the Tally-men and flee but the sheer unreasoning hatred on their faces was plain to see: they would kill them for attacking the Great Abbey or die trying. Brother Clegwyn suddenly bolted for the open door at the rear of the nearest half-track but he never made it; collapsing to the ground whilst clawing in vain at the shaft of the crossbow bolt embedded in his throat.

A quick-witted Brother used the distraction and pressed a button on the control device strapped to the dead Father's arm. "Tally-men, use your spears! Attack!" he screamed into the microphone, the spittle flying from his lips. The Tally-men jerked to life as if seeing their attackers for the first time. "Brothers, use your dart guns! Do not fear the witch! We outnumber them four to one!"

Bas threw her bow and quiver to the ground and darted forward with incredible speed. Harold watched spell-bound as she leapt over a spear thrust at her and landed nimbly upon the Tally-man's shoulders. He tried to shake her off but her knife slashed through the wires connecting the metal Guides in his skull to the power and guidance unit attached to the base of his neck. She rolled clear as sparks flew from the device and the Guides; the Tally-man convulsing violently until bloody sputum erupted from his mouth and he toppled backwards lifeless.

She retrieved her bow and in one fluid motion, let fly an arrow into the heart of another Tally-Man. Harold had a moment to study this dark-skinned thirteen-year old girl and recalled how he'd tried to yank the cat ears from her head only to find they were real. She was as tall as he was only she was slim and her face had definite feline qualities as did her elongated teeth and fingernails.

In memory of her Egyptian mother, she wore a white polo-neck shirt with a band of Egyptian hieroglyphs about the shoulders. She had a leather belt with two sheaths for her knives, a short white skirt with Eyes of Ra all round the hem over white breeches and leather gladiator sandals on her feet. A Brother who'd worked for

Exodus pointed at her and screamed: "The Harlot's brought one of Farzad's vile chimeras with her! Kill it!"

Harold held his katana at the ready but he felt like a helpless bystander as Bas hissed, discarded her bow and quiver again then launched herself at the hapless Brother with her claws outstretched. He screamed in mortal terror before she sank her teeth repeatedly into his throat and ripped through his jugular vein.

Her older brother, Ibrahim, similarly dressed in shirt and leather trousers decorated with stylised hieroglyphs, blocked a Tally-man's spear thrust and grasped the shaft of the long spear with his left hand. He planted his feet firmly on the cobbles then heaved, pulling the Tally-man off balance. He swung the battle-axe in his right hand to catch his sprawling enemy full in the back of the neck almost cleaving the head from the body. "That's for Fierce!" he snarled, gripping his battle-axe in both hands and swinging at another Tally-man whose spear tip had missed his face by a hair's breadth. Despite the darts flying past him, he carved a bloody path through the ranks of expressionless Tally-men.

Harold saw that Shield was concentrating and using her craft to deflect the darts the Brothers were frantically firing at them. Some hit the Tally-men but their toxins hardly affected these lobotomised warriors of the Order. Harold knew each Brother also carried plasma-grenades and it would be but seconds before they recovered their wits enough to try and use them. He'd been hurled twenty yards by the plasma-grenade explosion in the Great Annex and did not want to repeat that experience again.

As if reading his mind, Bas grabbed her weapons and sprang onto the roof of a half-track and fired arrows relentlessly down at the Brothers, many of whom had cast aside their dart-guns in disgust and were fumbling for the grenades in their robe pockets.

He wanted to engage the Brothers but two more Tally-men charged at him and he was nicked by spear tips several times as he was slicing into the abdomen of the first one but he felt nothing. A roaring was growing louder in his ears but he couldn't decide if it was him or some wild animal making the infernal racket.

Saul and Ibrahim fought in utter silence now; utterly focussed on their foes. Harold thought everyone was moving in slow-motion compared to these two remarkable Children of Exodus. He noticed that Shield was free to use her cross-bow which she did with deadly accuracy felling three more Tally-men in as many seconds.

He swung his sword about wildly but it was of such exquisite workmanship that he felt it had a will of its own, slicing off a Tally-man's hand then thrusting through both coat and ribs as if through gossamer. A Brother sought him out and he was hard-pressed to avoid the thrusts and jabs of this more agile opponent.

"Unworthy filth!" the Brother snarled but then his eyes widened in fear. "Ware!" he cried. "The Wiccan is about to cast a hex!" He retreated to join the remaining six Brothers who were standing back to back in a defensive circle. Then the staff fell.

Harold felt a powerful seismic wave ripple beneath his feet. All seven Brothers lost their footing and their spears as the street beneath them erupted sending earth and cobble stones high into the air. "How the *hell* does she do that?" he muttered incredulously as he blocked a spear thrust. He stepped forward and drove his blade deep into the belly of his attacker then twisted it savagely. The Tally-man sank to his knees desperately trying to shovel his innards back into his torn abdomen. He looked up at Harold who saw sentience flicker in his eyes for one brief moment: "Finish me," he begged hoarsely, bowing his head. "*Please!*"

Fighting down a wave of nausea, Harold delivered the coup de grace; the head tumbling away from him. The Tally-men were all dead and Shield, Bas, Saul and Ibrahim were at work upon the helpless, prostrate Brothers. He watched in horror as knife, sword and axe rose and fell without hesitation; without mercy.

He started at a hand being laid upon his shoulder and turned to find Fern beside him, her face pale and grim. "They know they have no choice but to kill or be killed, dear heart, but I... Ah! Diana, save us! The Angels return too soon!" she cried out.

Rising above the trees at the eastern end of the little hamlet were the two black rotorcraft of the Order. Harold could see the barrels of their chain-guns begin to spin and he ground his teeth in helpless rage: "Oh, come on! You have *got* to be kidding me!

~~~~~

36

Angels of Death

"I understand your concern, my son," Father Ursaf said to Brother Spero, the pilot of Bede Angel Seven. "We know the fugitives were in the Forest of Weal but I'm convinced they did not get as far as Wealthorpe as Father Beorcraft believes. I don't think they're in the woods to the west either: they need food and water and the only likely place to find that is in that farm below."

"Are you sure, Father? You became confused and disoriented as Father Beorcraft and his Brothers entered Wealthorpe."

"I felt *something* affecting my thoughts, my son, but my mind is clear now. You said you felt it too, did you not?"

"Yes," the pilot nodded. "A migraine struck me every time I looked towards the Milverbore. Perhaps a Wiccan bewitched us into wasting our time searching these fields. Don't forget: Pious and all the Angel crews were sent southwards chasing illusions and phantasms while this Light-Father and his Wiccans rode a train eastwards to desecrate the Great Abbey."

"These approaching storms are a more likely explanation for our malaise. Abbot Pious was greatly overrated, my son. No Wiccan can bedazzle a sound scientific mind like mine but electrical energy in the air preceding a storm *can* affect a man's senses so that he may think he's under their malign influence."

Spero looked profoundly sceptical as he struggled to keep the rotorcraft steady then a savage downdraft caused both machines to drop fifty feet or so without warning. "One thing is certain, Father," he declared, beads of nervous sweat forming upon his brow. "Look at the height of those thunderheads! This is just the leading edge of that storm system: we won't be able to keep the Angels aloft once these storms reach us." He banked slightly and indicated the farm buildings. "Perhaps we should just strafe the farm and return to support Father Beorcraft. We can set down in the open spaces north of Wealthorpe and ride out the tempest there."

Ursaf shook his head slowly, deep in thought. "No, we cannot waste ammunition after losing all our Brothers-Technician at the Brigstowe armouries." He turned to the navigator: "Brother Gudflan, radio Bede Angel Three and instruct them to follow us down to get a closer look at those buildings. Tell them to keep their chain-guns trained on the farmhouse: there could be Unworthy souls waiting to ambush us."

Spero guided the rotorcraft down in a slow spiral, battling the strengthening cross-winds to allow the gunner in the nose-cone to keep his guns on target as did Bede Angel Three behind them. Suddenly, a brief radio transmission crackled through their headphones: "*We're under attack! Get back...*"

Ursaf glared at Spero who had given him a knowing look. "By Saint Peter's teeth, I am naught but Tythe's Blind Jester in this!" he conceded with ill grace. He jabbed the transceiver's send switch. "Bede Angel Three! Return to Wealthorpe! The Light-Father must be attacking Beorcraft and be careful: there must be Wiccans there to have sent us on such a damned fool's errand!"

As both rotorcraft ascended to head back to the hamlet, the gunner pushed himself back on his roller bed from the nose cone into the cabin between Spero and Gudflan. "Have a care," he grumbled. "That turbulence nearly cracked my skull open."

"Get back in there, Brother Piamadet," Ursaf snarled. "When we get to Wealthorpe, keep your guns trained on those cottages. If Beorcraft and his Brothers have fallen, the Wiccans and Ferals will be there along with their damned Light-Father."

Spero paled visibly: "He destroyed Schimrian's monster and the Great Computer with just his bare hands I'm told. Will we be able to take them out with just our two Angels?"

"By the Trinity, have some faith in me, Spero," Piamadet said sarcastically before returning to his station. He grasped the gun controls and Ursaf smiled with pleasure as he saw the barrels of the two chain-guns attached to the landing-struts begin to spin. These terrifying weapons could tear through brick and stone like tissue-paper but he was chastened to think that Wiccans could knock such powerful machines clean out of the sky as they had done in both Crawcester and Beorminghas.

"I would like to redeem these vile sports of Gomorrah as much as you, Father," Spero fretted as the Angel bucked violently in the increasingly strong gusts. "But another five minutes of these Satan-farts and we'll lose the tail rotor." He heaved at the levers as the Angels were hit with another downdraft. "Get ready, Piamadet," he shouted. "Wealthorpe is on the other side of those trees!"

Ursaf's eyes widened and his jaw dropped as the hamlet came into view and he saw in the fading light that the main street was littered with corpses. "Sweet Lord Jesus, they've been wiped out," he gasped in disbelief. "Every single one of them!"

"I can't see the enemy!" Piamadet yelled as the Angel hovered to the east of the hamlet, the panic evident in his voice. "What now, Father? I have nothing down there to shoot at! Where in St Luke's burning bones are these Wiccans?"

"They're not by the shore but there's a boat moored against the quay!" Ursaf bellowed back at him. "The Whores of Satan must have blinded us to its approach so they could launch a surprise attack on poor Beorcraft. It's been less than two minutes since they alerted us so the abominations *must* be hiding in those cottages - there's no cover between here and the woods."

He pressed the send switch on the transceiver: "Bede Angel Three: keep parallel to us. Destroy the cottages to the north of the street while we destroy the ones to the south. Use every bullet if you have to - there are Mothers down there!"

~~~~~

"Huh?" Harold exclaimed in disbelief as Ursaf's rotorcraft hovered before them with their chain-guns swivelling to and fro. "What are they waiting for? They have us cold!"

"They can't see us!" Fern gasped. "I'm in their minds: they're blind to us but only for a few seconds - my strength is all but spent! We must run beneath them, across the railway and into the woods." She turned to the others and shouted: "Run! I cannot hide us for long. They're going to destroy the cottages so if we don't move now, we'll die!" She clutched at his arm. "You must carry me, Light-Father," she panted, the sweat pouring down her face. "I cannot do this and run at the same time."

Harold sheathed his sword and swept her from her feet and staggered towards the woods after the others. As soon as they'd passed beneath the bellies of the machines, there was a flash of lightning almost overhead and the thunder melded with the roar of the chain-guns. Heavy-calibre bullets smashed every roof tile and beam into spinning fragments and tore the dry-stone walls apart as if two Norse gods were dragging vast hammers through the humble dwellings one after another until they lay in ruins.

Fern let out a shuddering cry as they reached the safety of the trees: "Ah, I am done! I must rest! I must rest!"

Shield put her hand on the Wiccan's shoulder after Harold had, somewhat reluctantly, set her on her feet. "You must tell me how you do that, Mother Fern. Teach me this spell that blinds!"

"Spell? We're not hags around some cauldron!" Fern wheezed, leaning on her staff and drawing in lungfuls of air. She watched as the two Angels completed the destruction of Wealthorpe, her face contorting in contempt and hatred. "Gah! Weapons fit for the children of the Devil!" she spat. "I mourn the honest masons and their families who lived here before the Great Plague. Not even their memory is safe from those sanctimonious pigs!"

"The Angels are struggling to stay aloft," Shield observed. All around them tree crowns swayed alarmingly as gusts impacted the woods. "Look! They almost collided!"

Harold grabbed Fern as she suddenly sagged against him. "The ground to the north is flat enough for them to set down," he fretted. "If they do that, they could be a problem when we need to get back to the boat." He looked up at the nearby firs, oaks and ashes as their boughs creaked ominously above their heads; the wind rising to a fitful roar that tugged at their clothes.

"We could just wait for them to land and attack them," Saul suggested hungrily as he cleaned his katana with a rag.

"No, Fern is exhausted and that's a lot of open space to cover. We can't wait for nightfall: we have to find the little ones!"

Saul nodded reluctantly and sheathed his blade. Suddenly he frowned and stepped forward to whip Harold's katana out of its saya. "Never, *ever* sheathe a bloodied sword, Light-Father!" he said in a shocked voice. "You'll have to oil this blade when we get back and flush the scabbard out and dry it. My father had many friends amongst the Japanese Empire traders who told him: '*honoh kiyen noh sama see-oh son-cheun seku dasai*' - you must respect the spirit of the sword." He wiped the blade clean and bowed deeply in the manner of the Japanese Empire as he returned the katana to Harold. "We fought well for 'kids', did we not?" he added.

"Yes, you did, but I'm amazed that you even noticed what I was doing with my sword during the fighting."

Ibrahim laughed as he wiped his battle-axes with a bloodied cloth. "Mother Moss trained us well. 'When in battle: eyes, ears and mind stay open' she used to say. We've practiced hard for six years and fought many battles even before you came." He flinched as with a deafening crack of thunder, a lightning bolt struck a tree overhanging the railway line and blew fragments of bark from the trunk. "Hoi, look, Light-Father! The Angels flee inland! *Cowards!* My inner demon *so* wanted them to land!"

Harold grinned with relief as the machines rose and headed northwards, harried by the violent gale. "I bet they thought they'd be vulnerable to attack," he reasoned aloud. "Good. That means we'll have nobody between us and the boat when we retreat."

"Now they're gone, Mother Fern, how will we find the little ones?" Bas demanded, inspecting her arrows and restocking her quiver. "Can you sense them?"

Harold was astounded to see that, despite the clattering presence of the Angels above them and the sinister whine of their chain-guns, Shield and Bas both had the presence of mind to pluck most of their bolts and arrows from the corpses as they ran beneath both rotorcraft. He realised again how little he knew of the true potential of these Children of Exodus but pondered the price they and their descendants might pay for their doctored genes.

Bas actually hissed with displeasure as the first large raindrops splattered down upon her head before Fern had revived enough to answer her: "I can't far-see them in my mind and they're too far away for me to 'far-talk' as you call it. I'm sure Surl's prescience will guide them to us but I did sense scores of Brothers to the east and north scouring the farms and woods." She massaged her eyes. "By the Triple Goddess, I'm so weary! We must find shelter and wait for the little ones as close to this road as we can."

"I'll scout ahead," Bas volunteered eagerly and she vanished into the dank and gathering murk beneath the trees.

Ibrahim smiled despite the rain now soaking through their clothes: something they were used to as it had rained continuously for six years since the Plague. "She's hoping to find more Brothers to kill. Her bloodlust has increased tenfold since our battle at the Great Abbey. I'm concerned for her, Light-Father, she may lose herself to the beast within and become worse than a Feral."

"I'm worried for her too," Harold assured him. "I've been so wrapped up in guilt and self-pity these past three weeks that I've barely spent any time with her or with you for that matter."

"We know you tortured yourself as Mother Fern does," Ibrahim said kindly, rubbing at the back of his neck. "You must remember that we all love you, Light-Father. You took us in and you got us out and you stood before Azrael and Schimrian. We fight to make you proud of us and to honour Fierce's memory." He secured both of his axes into the slings on his back and patted his muscular chest. "Besides, my inner demon rejoiced in that battle," he laughed then stopped abruptly as Fern glowered at him. "But he is now a very *small* demon," he assured her quickly, pinching his right thumb and forefinger together. "A mere imp!"

"Good, I have no desire to chastise thee again," Fern said icily. "Or remind you of our conversations on the matter of taking pleasure in killing. You children have suffered much - the Light-Father and I know this and we fear for your futures when we are free of the Order and Gaia smiles upon us once more."

"Better an uncertain future than *this* reality," Shield interjected. She started as lightning struck close by in the woods to the north of them. "We're not safe amongst the trees," she added nervously after the deafening peal of thunder had subsided. "I'm as wet as we were in the Keep. I really feel cold now."

"The Tower of the Sun has made you as soft as a kitten," Saul teased, embracing her. "Ow! What ails you?" he complained, rubbing at his bruised ribs. "That *hurt!*"

"I'm no helpless kitten needing protection," she said loftily, freeing herself from his arms. "I train every day at my craft and martial arts: I need no *man* to protect me."

"Don't look at me, Saul," Harold smiled, raising his hands. "She knows you love her but I wouldn't patronise her like that."

"Exactly, Light-Father," Shield huffed, folding her arms.

"You two *definitely* need to talk when this is over."

"We will, Light-Father," Saul promised, blushing crimson. "Mother Fern? Are you sure Schimrian's risen from the dead?"

"As far as I can tell from the mind of Father Ursaf," she assured him. She looked at this tall youth and appraised him again. He had a lean face with an intense gaze that met hers as an equal, a scar to the chin and long black hair that had been tied back and braided by Shield. What had impressed her most were his reflexes and the skill of his swordsmanship. She wished, not for the first time, that she could've witnessed his momentous battle against Abbot Pious, the deadliest member of the Order.

"Are you reading my mind?" he inquired suspiciously.

"A little," she smiled. "I can see you piercing Pious through the heart but I fear the dark magic that animated his corpse. I hope that he now suffers in the deepest depths of Hell."

"When Azrael died, he moved no more," Saul agreed. "But by my soul, I still fear that undead creature more than all the Tally-men and all the Abbots in the world combined."

"As do I," said Shield, taking his hands and ignoring Ibrahim's muttered jealousies. "But with Mother Fern and our Light-Father, we will defeat the Gross Thousands and free these isles."

"Dream of Paradise, if you must," Ibrahim said sourly, folding his powerful arms. "But this is *our* reality," he added, indicating the flickering heavens above. "At least my inner demon is happy: there are so many Fathers and Brothers yet to kill that he always has something to look forward to."

He whirled and drew his axe at a soft thud behind him only to find Bas grinning at him. "No axe in your hand? Tch! You're letting your guard down, brother," she teased.

"Did you find anything, Bas?" Harold demanded. He estimated that she'd jumped more than five yards to the ground with no apparent exertion. Her cold, calculating father would have been proud of his achievement in creating this hybrid child had he not himself been betrayed by the Order he'd served so well.

"Yes, Light-Father, a dozen chains from here is a wood-master's cottage set off the road and hidden from view. The roof is intact and dry enough inside. There are lots of cobwebs but it's free of bones. Follow me and keep away from the road – I'm sure I heard half-tracks but this thunder is making me deaf."

Ten minutes later they were safely seated on assorted chairs in the kitchen around a large rustic table. They listened in silence to the rain intensifying and hammering on the roof tiles while the last of the daylight faded. The kitchen was dominated by two ancient dressers decorated with intricate carvings of dryads, fauns and faces of bearded men with antlers. A rack was set against one wall and stacked with the tools of the wood-master's trade: axes, machetes, saws and serrated knives. The adjacent door led to an outhouse containing chainsaws and all manner of climbing equipment.

"I think I'll watch the road," Harold decided, taking out a small but powerful pocket-lamp from a pocket and switching it on.

"There are candles aplenty," Shield pointed out. "If we cover the windows we need not sit in the dark all night."

"At least there's no chance of Tally-men operating in such a downpour," Fern noted gratefully. "We'll light the candles but no chink of light must pass the drapes in case Brothers are nearby."

I made that mistake once in Crawcester," Shield admitted, getting up to draw the curtains. "But for Mother Moss we would've all been killed. I still have nightmares about that Father Alban and his whip. If I'd had a demon inside me then," she added, glancing at Ibrahim. "She would have howled with joy when he was torn apart by her vortex and the rain turned red."

They lit three candles and enjoyed their welcome light. Harold readied his sword and opened the door. It was pitch-black outside now the sun had set. "I'll check that the candle-light does not get through the doors and windows first." He turned and his heart almost failed as he beheld a large cowled figure, silhouetted by incessant lightning flashes, standing on the doorstep.

But for the lack of a scythe, Harold thought that he could have been looking at a manifestation of Death. Instead the man raised a gloved hand: "Ah, Light-Father, well met. I mean you no harm. I have four saboteurs here who would like to speak with you."

From behind him, a bald, bedraggled figure emerged and stepped timidly into the candle-light.

"Surl!" Harold exclaimed and stooped to embrace her. "I thought you were dead! I can't believe you're alive!" To his horror, tears coursed down his cheeks as she buried her face in his chest. "I'm so happy you're alright. I just… could not… find you! I am so, so sorry I left you behind!"

He looked up at Michael but he could not see his face as it was completely shrouded in the shadow of the cowl. "Thank you for saving them, Abbot Michael," he said simply.

"How could you possibly know my name?" Michael exclaimed then he noticed Fern. "Ah, the dark arts of the Wiccans, I see. The reading of minds is but a minor slight in God's eye when compared to the arcane panoply of their witchcraft."

Fern rose to her feet and brandished her staff. "Be civil, monster, lest I cast thee screaming from this world." She indicated the drawn weapons of the Scatterlings behind her. "Or perhaps I should let these children to pry open the gates of Hell for you."

"Forgive my unwise attempt at humour," he apologised, bowing deeply. "But this remarkable child is helping me undo a lifetime of indoctrination and prejudice." He went outside to usher in the others and soon the kitchen was so crowded that more chairs had to be found and more candles lit. Fern had to use her 'voice' to prevent Saul, Bas and Ibrahim from attacking Michael, dressed as he was in the field robes of the Order.

Michael closed the door and watched silently as Pup, Rabbit, Surl and Peter were swamped in endless hugs and kisses from their elders as the five victims of the Order sat in a corner, staring at the candles as if seeing their comforting light for the first time in their lives. Harold waited until the hubbub subsided. "I'd better go and keep watch," he said as they became too overcome with joy to speak. "While I'm out, can one of you see if there's any gas in that cooker? The rest of you: search the cupboards and the rooms for food and anything else we can use."

"We will, Light-Father," Bas promised as she hugged Pup after swinging him round several times until he was dizzy.

He pecked Fern on the cheek. "I really hate the rain," he grumbled in martyred tones making her laugh.

After Harold had left, Fern approached Michael with a frown upon her face. "Shall I read your mind to find out *why* you saved these little ones and those poor men?" she said candidly, conscious of Ibrahim still glancing at the cleric with murderous intent.

"The answer is simple: because they saved *me*, Wiccan," he whispered into her ear. "Condemned to a living hell by Azrael, I was about to be killed as an abomination by another abomination but they freed me from my cell and found me these robes. They are remarkable. I am nothing but a maggot in their eyes but they've been my epiphany; my final awakening."

"I want to know *why* the Order has turned on you and why you now decry and betray the Order you've willingly served all your adult life and blindly followed unto the ruin of all humanity. Tell me, monster, why should I believe you?"

"Because the Order reviles me as the Naked One."

"What do you mean by that? Are you naked because you've finally cast off your mantle of arrogance and delusion?"

"Oh, it's far more *literal* than you could ever imagine, Wiccan," he said quietly. He unfastened his sodden robes, pulled back the cowl and removed his gloves and the bandages that hid his face. He let them all fall to the floor. "Behold."

Saul had to leap forward to catch her as she fainted.

~~~~~

45

By Candlelight

"Saint Peter's *teeth*," Saul choked as his eyes widened and bile rose in his throat. He laid Fern gently upon the floor and turned his gaze away. "Ugh! We must tell the Light-Father of this!"

Michael said nothing but drew on his clothing and gloves, reset the bandages about his face and raised his cowl. "Do as you wish," he said dismissively as the others continued to stare at him apart from Bas who was being wretchedly sick in one of the sinks. "But the Wiccan and the rest of you needed to see me as Azrael made me. *Now* do you understand why I wish to help you?"

"I can see why the Order wants to kill you," Saul replied, his voice shaking. "Gods, how can you bear to live like that? I would kill myself rather than be… be *that*!"

"I deserve no less. When the Conclave showed us the Vatican's seven-headed lamb, I harboured doubts about it truly being a Sign of Revelation but after spending my whole life bathed in doctrine, my faith in their belief was absolute."

"You had *doubts*?" Saul exclaimed in disbelief. "You could've warned people! You could've raised the alarm!"

"I was overwhelmed by a holy rapture that affected everyone at the Great Abbey so that all I could focus on was New Jerusalem. Before that, Exodus scientists at the Great Abbey had told me of the Virus of Revelation and how dissidents in the company had tried to warn politicians of the danger but nobody listened. Besides, I was so afraid of Schimrian that I wouldn't even *try* to tell anyone. This," he said, indicating his body. "Was supposed to be a form pleasing to Azrael but it was God who punished me for my sins. I dare not add to such an infernal tally with suicide."

"Unh!" Fern groaned, sitting up and rubbing her forehead. "I do indeed deem thee punished," she said formally, glaring up at him. "I have no craft to undo this but forgive me: so many murdered souls haunt my dreams that I will *never* pity you!"

"I seek no pity nor deserve it yet I see that you punish yourself for our sins," Michael noted with some surprise. He held out a gloved hand to help her to her feet. She shocked the children by accepting that hand. "What an extraordinary thing to do. Why take on such a burden when I see in you a pure soul?"

"Pure for a Harlot of Satan, you mean?" she said archly, placing a hand upon her heart. "Inside me reside countless generations of

Mothers your Order put to death for revealing the cruel truth behind its virtuous façade." She frowned as she studied him: "Oh? Who is this Father Bucheort I see in your mind? Oh? He was *crucified*? Is there no end to the Order's cruelty?"

Michael did not reply for Bucheort had been a brutal disciple of Pious who had been rumoured to have snapped the neck of at least one postulant. His death in Crawcester, allegedly crucified by the Wiccans, was not mourned by many at the Great Abbey. He bent down to retrieve her staff from the flagstones and examined the ornate and exquisite carving of the raven at the head. Its diamond eyes shone eerily blue in the candlelight and the black mahogany wood of the staff felt somehow alive in his hands. He hastily presented it to her. "Curious," he murmured, flexing his fingers as if they pained him. "I thought these arcane rods were affectations; mere badges of rank amongst the Wiccans."

"You claim to have studied our craft so you should know they are more than 'mere badges'," she smiled enigmatically, displaying the matching raven amulet set on the leather thong around her neck. A massive peal of thunder rattled all the windows. "We can't leave here while this storm lasts so you can tell us what's happening to the Order. Was Azrael's body destroyed and...?"

"I *knew* they were magic," Ibrahim interrupted, approaching the staff to study it. He turned and wiggled his fingers at Shield who bridled at the gesture. "Be wary, Eldest!" he warned in ghostly tones. "She'll use her staff to put a spell on you!"

Saul wrapped his arms about Shield's waist and held her close. "She already has," he laughed. "I'm bewitched!"

"As you have me, dear heart," Shield replied fondly but Rabbit forced her way between them and pouted up at Shield making her smile. "I've not forgotten you, little Rabbit. Oh, dear heart," she said tenderly, sweeping her up in her arms. "I thought I'd lost you along with my poor sister!"

"Pah! I see you find comfort enough with *him*" Rabbit huffed, glaring over Sheild's shoulder at the bemused Saul. "You'd better not treat her badly, Eldest, or I'll ki-."

"Stop that!" Fern snapped, raising a hand. "There'll be no more threats to kill, even in jest, when we've just found each other! Let us not think of death and look to life instead. Shield. Peter, Bas, obey the Light-Father: search every cupboard for food. Saul, check that gas cylinder and you, Ibrahim, the cooker. *Now*, please!"

Rabbit and Pup approached Fern and tugged at her white hemp belt as the others set to their tasks. "We're not that hungry, Mother Fern," Rabbit said with Pup nodding in agreement. "We found some broth in the farmhouse earlier," she explained, pointing at the five men in the corner as they talked quietly amongst themselves. "It wasn't much so we want you to make sure they eat first. Peter's been looking after them but they're still weak. I… " She stopped, wiping at copious tears with a filthy sleeve. "I'm sorry, Mother Fern. I have so few years for this… I…"

"Pup needs a hug too!"

Fern knelt and comforted them as intense thunderclaps rattled the crockery upon the shelves. They closed their eyes in rapture then Pup burst into tears as well. "W-we were so afraid, Mother Fern!" he sobbed. "But suh-Surl saved us over and over again in the dark places beneath the Great Abbey. We…"

"Shh, dear hearts," Fern said gently. "Don't tell your tale just yet - the Light-Father needs to listen and work his magic upon all four of you. Dry those eyes then take a candle and go and check the bedrooms to see if those poor men can use the beds."

"I'm not crying," Rabbit sniffed, blowing her nose into her hand and wiping it on her trousers. "They had some rest at the farmhouse earlier so they may not want to sleep again. We don't even know their names – they've not spoken to us much."

"They won't want to talk to anyone else after weeks of cruel torture but they'll heal in time. It's getting cold - see how they shiver! Find them blankets if they won't use the beds. Go, dear hearts, please do as I ask of you." As Rabbit and Pup hesitantly obeyed, she beckoned Surl to come to her and put a hand on her shoulder. Michael leant against the door to watch them intently.

"What of Abbot Michael? Can you see his path?"

"Yes, Mother Fern," Surl said gravely, dabbing at her nosebleed with a cloth. "The visions hurt but I can see he is a monster still though salvation does lie before him."

"Then I will strive to live up to your augury, young *seer*," Michael vowed, bowing deeply.

"I hope so, Naked One," Surl said pointedly then turned back to Fern: "I'm so *tired*. I feel so *thin* inside."

"I understand, Daughter," Fern said, embracing her. "Unless we train you, this power *will* consume you."

"As my research indicates," Michael added smugly.

48

Fern raised a hand to silence him. "You'd dissect her living brain like a Tally-man's, wouldn't you?"

"Despite my sins and Azrael's curse, I'm a man of science still," he replied blandly. "I'm curious as to how her gift works; how her brain perceives visions of the future but I'd never harm her. I'd hardly need to dissect myself, now would I?"

"Indeed not. But keep your counsel while I attend to the little ones. I forgot to check them for injuries."

"We've none of consequence, Mother Fern," Surl murmured happily, enfolded in the arms and scent of the beautiful Wiccan. "Save for memories we'll never forget and a constant fear of death." She trembled and buried her face in Fern's bosom.

"Be at peace, little one," Fern crooned, feeling a new and powerful maternal instinct stir within her heart. "The universe has been so cruel to you Scatterlings but the Light-Father and I will do our best to change that. If he can bring back the sunshine like he did today, he can do *anything.* Amos is waiting for you in Milverburg, don't forget. He wanted to come but we denied him: he's far too rash in battle and puts others in mortal peril."

"I know but I want to see my b-brother!"

"All in good time but first things first: if the four of you are uninjured then go and help see to the needs of those men."

"Yes, Mother," came the muffled reply. Fern was deeply moved at the omission of her name but it was almost five minutes before Surl let go of her and by then the five men had been seated at the table as pans of broth and rice simmered on the cooker.

Fern was conscious that Michael was intently studying the Scatterlings. "Their parents' gifts have served them well, Mother Fern," he observed on meeting her gaze. "Surl bears no visible mark of the craft so the Exodus scientists must've succeeded in replicating the craft in her through genetic manipulation."

"I doubt it," Fern replied cautiously. "Our craft is not something you 'men of science' could possibly understand."

"Not yet," Michael conceded. "I've studied your history and your 'craft' for decades and much lies beyond current rationality, I'll admit, but in the end, everything is just physics."

"I dread that day when a man such as you reduces me to a mere *formula*," Fern retorted.

"Amen to that," Michael said ironically. "Hark to that thunder! Each bolt sounds a Dolorous Stroke upon the thighs of Cernunnos.

I see no need for the Light-Father to stand sentinel." He indicated Surl: "She could scry whether or not he should remain out there in this deluge. Well, young oracle, what say you?"

Surl came up to Fern and again solicited comfort: "You say you worry about the visions making me ill yet you keep asking me to use my power all the time. Why?"

"Forgive me: I need to speak to the Light-Father before we flee westwards again. We might not get another chance to talk."

"I see," Fern said bitterly. "You cannot share such information with a mere *woman*, is that it?"

"No, I am now far beyond the chauvinism of the Order, as you saw, but you are indeed a natural mother to these children as he is a father and you should *both* hear what I have to say."

"It's safe to call the Light-Father," Surl said, wincing in pain. "We must leave at eight bells to get to the boat. That's the best time but it will be hard: we'll have to fight again."

"I'll go and get him," Michael offered, reaching for the latch.

"There's no need," Fern replied and placed her fingertips to her temples. Within seconds, Harold was inside the kitchen with the rainwater cascading off him.

"Now *that's* what I call rain," he grinned ruefully. "The road's a river and lightning is smashing down tree limbs all over the place; sparks everywhere. I felt a shock from a few of them. Ah, I see those men are getting some hot food. Good." He turned to Michael and touched his forehead in emphasis: "Fern communicated to me what Azrael did to you," he said. He grasped the hilt of his katana meaningfully. "I think we can trust you but if you *ever* betray these children, I *will* terminate you."

"If you can," Michael shrugged. "I'm immortal: unless you sever my head from my body, I will regenerate. Azrael arranged it thus to provide eternal sport for him in his hellish Jerusalem."

"So what did you want to talk to us about?"

"Let's go somewhere private," Michael insisted. He led them into the front room and set two candlesticks on a dining table. He carefully checked the drapes and applied a match to the candle wicks. He sat down carefully in one of the musty armchairs. "May I say how glad I am to finally meet you, Light-Father?"

Fern and Harold sat next to each other on the sofa opposite him. "Skip the pleasantries!" Harold prompted impatiently. "What about Schimrian? How the hell is that bastard still alive?"

"That 'immortality-machine', as they now call it, continued to function despite the explosion. Thanks to you and that child, he was resurrected and not mutilated as I was."

"He has to be brain-damaged," Harold said, shaking his head slowly in disbelief. "We heard his skull being crushed."

"Not so. He's recovered most if not all of his faculties though his skull remains somewhat misshapen and he did fall into a temporary dementia from the trauma. It's as though his precious Azrael had never turned on him so he curses your young Scatterling for killing his 'beautiful son' yet she saved the rest of us from Hell being made manifest by that Satan."

"And you?" Harold said. "Why did they turn on you?"

"I was blamed for the loss of the Great Computer as they saw me cursed by God. As I later heard from the postulants, Tally-men who were connected to the Great Computer through their barracks computers went berserk all across the globe."

"What? All of them?" Harold demanded eagerly.

"No, not all," Michael said after a pause. "Some Tally-men were in rest mode and were not connected to their barracks computers. The Order in Britannia is depleted and in disarray because of this massacre and the fact that you attacked at the perfect moment when many Fathers and Brothers were still on routine Inquisitions in the Middle and Northern Cities. I presume this Mother Moss you speak of foresaw Azrael's ascension?"

"She never told us; only Fierce knew," Harold said with a heavy heart. "She kept that secret from us until she pulled those fuses."

"Fierce is the young Scatterling who destroyed Azrael?"

"Yes. Kai told us there were only forty or so Brothers there so I *knew* we had a chance, you see," Harold grinned, making a fist. "Only there must've been a hundred at least but it didn't matter in the end because we were guided there not to destroy the Great Abbey but to fulfil a prophecy of Mother Moss."

"So I understand but Kai didn't mislead you," Michael pointed out. "Some eighty Inquisitors returned that very morning and he couldn't have known how many were in the laboratories or the garages and smithies. Anyway, to finish my tale, I was thrown into a Redemption Cell. Camus, my oldest friend, came to visit but he vomited at the very sight of me so I never saw him again."

"So there is only one Abbot left at the Great Abbey?" Fern asked shrewdly. "What of the rest of the Order, Michael?"

"The Twelve Tribes have been decimated and the surviving Fathers and Abbots scattered across the globe want to return to the Great Abbey but Schimrian refuses them as he doesn't want to face a challenge to his authority. However," he added, raising one finger then two in emphasis: "There is not one Abbot but *two* at the Great Abbey. Pious is very much *alive* – if you can call that living death life. I'm well versed in the arts of electrics and circuitry but what sustains him, I cannot say. The postulants who brought me food as punishment told me of the terror they have of him: his heart doesn't beat, his flesh is cold and he draws no breath except to speak."

"So how are you declared the abomination and not him?"

"Simple, Light-Father, Pious was the only creature in this world that Schimrian trusted implicitly so he declared his resurrection to be a miracle from God who wishes him to continue Inquisition until the world is cleansed of the Unworthy *and* the Ferals."

Fern gasped in shock: "What? Have you not done enough to those poor children yet they're now to be hunted down and *slain*?"

"Yes, though they're now much closer to beast than man, Azrael deemed that they could become fertile and bear young; populating the world with strange chimerae and hybrids."

"Nature will find a way," Harold agreed. "Radiation, mutation; anything could happen in such a huge pool of damaged genes. There must be hundreds of thousands of them out there."

"Possibly millions," Michael conceded. "The odds could yield mating pairs but most if not all of the offspring will be unviable. Cancer, hunger and deformity will eventually kill them off."

"And at each innocent death another ghost shall stand at your shoulder and at mine," Fern said bitterly, her eyes glistening with tears. "I name the whole world *Heofland*: a world of ghosts and death created by nothing more than misogyny and exegesis."

"Call it what you will," Michael shrugged. "But thanks to you and Azrael, only five Abbots, forty Fathers, six hundred Brothers and less than a thousand Tally-men remain in Britannia."

"What about the Angels?" Harold demanded anxiously.

"Father Ursaf had six at Bede and nine others were flown there from Norton and Wyehold making fifteen in all and two more may be salvaged at the Great Abbey."

"God, that's more than enough," Harold groaned, lifting his cap to run a hand through his hair. "Does the Order have any other aircraft in Britannia?"

"I heard that Ursaf struggles to maintain all the machines in working order as the spare parts are all but gone. The three propellercraft and the one long-range jetcraft at Bede bear no armaments and luckily for you, they were too unskilled to salvage any military aircraft even before half of them were slain."

"Now there's a small mercy," Harold said bleakly. "What about the rest of the Order?"

"Across the globe, less than twelve thousand survived Azrael's betrayal but be warned: with their New Jerusalem denied, they're vengeful and still numerous enough to hunt you down. In time, they'll eventually disobey Schimrian's orders and make their way to these Hallowed Isles to challenge him. They won't all come at once however as these storms keep getting more violent and there are few ships that can withstand such maelstroms."

"I see. We can make a stand in Milverburg then," Harold decided, still unwilling to trust Michael. "I think we can defend the place even if all six hundred attack us at the same time. We could fight a guerrilla war in there for *months*."

"Ah, good, you're thinking like a general," Michael approved. "Surl's visions decreed that you were at Milverburg but this would have been our destination in any case. You intrigue me, Light-Father: you dress like a car mechanic and that strange cap bears Romanic letters in a language I can't read. Azrael considered you to be of another world as was he in essence; forged from that alien device at the heart of the Great Computer."

Harold glanced at Fern who nodded approval and held his hand. "I come from another plane, Michael. It's the same Earth but in a different dimension where a different history has played out and my Great Britain, as it is called there, has not drowned though it may do soon as the climate's heating up."

"Ah, I'm glad to learn that my belief in parallel worlds was well founded! I'd guessed as much for Azrael stole from you small but complex items of circuitry unknown to our science which he used to create and power his emergent form."

"We call them microchips," Harold explained, extracting one from a pocket in his overalls. "See? These are tiny computers with connections small enough to link to nerve endings. What I don't understand is how quickly he adapted and replicated them. God knows what would have happened to us if he'd disconnected those umbilical cords."

"I imagine what happened to me would have seemed like paradise to the rest of his victims," Michael agreed sombrely, interlocking his fingers. "As I said, it may be weeks or months before survivors arrive in Britannia but the resulting power struggle could delay or disrupt any siege of Milverburg."

"Schimrian and Pious still have six hundred and forty men here," Harold reminded him. "You said fifteen Angels were left flying but could more Angels return to Britannia?"

"In time but most must return by ship as aviation fuel is scarce and the survivors are wary of setting sail in these storms."

"That's good to know but, basically, even if we kill every member of the Order in Britannia and destroy all fifteen Angels thousands more will come after us no matter what we do?"

"Yes, in time, but don't despair completely. As I said, they have radio links but the atmosphere is too disturbed to make long-range communication reliable. Many survivors can't be contacted and the abbeys and outposts in Scotia and Eirann have fallen silent. The equatorial storm systems are so intense that I suspect those in the Southern Hemisphere are stranded there."

"So a lot less than twelve thousand?" Harold prompted.

"There will be enough. You may be able to resist six hundred in the labyrinths of Milverburg for some time but not when thousands lay siege to the city and all its levels."

"We'll defend ourselves!" Fern declared hotly grasping her staff. "We must ensure that the deaths of Rosemary, Veneris and our Ferals were not in vain." She turned to Michael as a bleak thought struck her: "What happened to their bodies?"

"Ah, I regret Pious forced the postulants to desecrate and dismember their corpses then burn them in the furnaces of the smithies but of your brave young warrior-maiden, not one scrap of flesh remained. The Great Computer was vaporised and the alien device with it, taking down all the slave computers and erasing all the data. The main generators were destroyed by Surl and the others so the Great Abbey is still lit by candlelight. There you have it: this is all that I could glean from my Redemption Cell before your brave Scatterings freed me."

"How were they able to look at you?" Fern asked. "I'm curious as the very sight of your face made me faint."

"Surl brought me these robes and bandages and was able to bear my disfigurement as she was no doubt prepared by her visions. She wisely did not let the other three see my condition or tell them of it as we fled with the five prisoners they insisted on saving."

"The rain is easing a little," Fern noted then she flinched as more large hail clattered down upon the slates. "Ach! Another false hope! Yes, Surl, what is it? We still have much to discuss with Michael. We need to know what Schimrian is planning."

Surl was stood in the doorway and was joined by Pup, Rabbit and then Peter. "No, you're done with him for now," she announced gravely. "We've fed the men and the others are looking after them so now we four have need of our Light-Father and Mother." With that, all four of them wriggled around Harold and Fern on the sofa and snuggled up to them, with Surl eventually seated on his lap and resting against his chest contentedly with her eyes closed and his arms wrapped around her.

Michael hauled himself to his feet and bowed: "I leave you to weave your magic as I suspect these brave children have yet more harrowing tales to tell. We must talk at length, Light-Father, for I see a kindred spirit in you."

"I doubt that," Harold frowned. "I can never absolve you of your sins, Michael, but we *will* talk later. These children are the reason I'm here and I love them as my own so if you could leave us alone for a while, I would be grateful."

"Then weave your magic well, Light-Father," Michael said and bowed again before leaving the room.

Despite being soaked to the bone and with Surl half-asleep on his chest, Harold said briskly: "Right, who wants to go first?"

~~~~~

Duct Rats

"Small stones create avalanches; small deeds victories" - Thomas Tythe

A death's-head moth fluttered frantically in front of Surl's face. She turned her head to follow it and beheld in time the Tally-man thrusting a knife at her. Years of relentless training by Mother Moss served her well as she leapt back and drew her machete. Amos and Saul had spent days honing the edge and she held it out in front of her as the two Tally-men with hideous leers upon their normally impassive faces just stood and stared at her as Peter, Fria and Pup formed up behind her, brandishing their weapons.

"Scatterlings," one hissed malevolently. "More sweet innocent *toys* for me to play with." Surl sensed that someone or some *thing* was speaking through this soulless creature. She couldn't bear to look into their eyes for she sensed a powerful consciousness of absolute evil that wanted to consume her body and soul.

The other turned to the prisoners they'd just released from the Redemption Cells in this corridor. They were naked but for soiled loin-cloths and weakened by weeks of relentless torture for the Order needed them to be broken and compliant but most of all *conscious* when they lobotomised them, driving the Guide wires into their remaining brain tissue. "I've had so much *pleasure* watching my acolytes play with these pathetic beings but now they've served their purpose as I serve mine."

The four children watched in horror as he selected two of the prisoners and plunged his knife into their hearts. He licked the knife blade sensuously as they slumped lifeless to the floor. "Ah, I sense a craft user!" he gloated, grinning at Surl. "Such a rare delicacy but you must thank your precious Light-Father for your swift death. He approaches and I must be there to welcome him!"

As the two Tally-men began to advance, Surl kept Pup, Peter and Fria behind her as they retreated along the corridor. She was at a loss what to do for she'd had no vision of this but Pup didn't hesitate: he fired his catapult and a heavy ball-bearing struck the Guide on the right temple of the nearest Tally-man. It emitted several bright sparks, causing him to twitch and arch his back. The second Tally-man received another ball-bearing upon the Guide set into his forehead and as they both began to spasm, the children launched themselves forward as one.

Almost without thought, Surl ducked under a poorly-aimed knife thrust and swung her machete at the first Tally-man, slicing through the backs of his knees. He collapsed to the floor, flailing vainly about with his knife. "He's down! He's down!" she exalted and struck again and again at the knife-arm as he tried to jab up at her from the floor. She saw that his face was emotionless with no trace of the demonic presence that had turned her innards to water so she was free to hack at him, a white-hot rage coursing through her veins as she remembered the pillow smothering her...

Peter had ducked under a jab from the second Tally-man but got too close and a powerful arm was clamped around his neck. He stabbed the Tally-man in the thighs repeatedly with the knife in his left hand but it was useless: the Tally-man had no pain receptors and raised his blade to strike but Rabbit attacked him from behind, leaving one of her axes embedded in his back. He flung Peter away and vainly attempted to reach the axe handle as Pup kept firing ball-bearings at his head.

"Rabbit!" Surl cried out as she circled her grounded foe, looking for another opening. "Cut through the wires!"

Rabbit leapt high into the air to rake her axe though the wires at the back of the skull. The results were spectacular: the huge Tally-man went into a fit and crashed to the ground. He writhed and gurgled then died as bloody foam sprayed from his mouth spattering Rabbit who shrieked in dismay.

Surl did the same to the first Tally-man with her machete and he too convulsed in a pool of his own blood before dying.

"Help us," one of the prisoners gasped, clinging to the wall as he watched Rabbit wrench her axe free from the Tally-man's back. "We cannot fight after all this torture. You have but few years but we beg you: use those weapons well and put us out of our misery otherwise they'll make us monsters like *them*."

Surl knew that these young men had been teenagers when the Plague struck yet they possessed a rare natural immunity. Mother Moss had told them at the Keep how female survivors were killed immediately yet male survivors were captured to serve the Order as mindless drones. "Don't ask that of us," she groaned in anguish. "We'll come back for you, I promise!"

The man sagged to the floor in despair: "So be it, child, but promise me this: kill as many of them as you can. It may help us to endure the torture a little longer when we are captured again."

"Go through there," Surl urged, pointing at the door leading to the armoury. "We saw rations and water flasks in there. Take the robes and weapons, dress yourselves as Brothers and make your escape in the confusion."

"Aye, we shall try," the man agreed, forcing himself back to his feet. "We're as weak as babes but we shall die as free men. Get up, all of you!" he commanded, his voice growing stronger. "We *will* avenge our families! Thank you," he added as he herded the others down the corridor. "My name is Ken Glascae of Scotia, born of the fabled Aberlour Clan. What's yours, child?"

"Surl!" she said proudly, drawing herself up to her full height. "I'm no child but a Scatterling of Crawcester. I see you all in my future for I am blessed with the gift of foresight!"

"Farewell then, Surl of Crawcester! We have no choice but to fulfil your prophecy!" he replied with a slight bow and with that, they staggered into the armoury, closing the door behind them.

"I'm fine, thank you for asking," Peter grunted, retrieving his knife and getting to his feet. "Ouch. That hurt. Ow."

"Oh, you'll live," Surl said sarcastically. She winced as bright, vivid images flooded into her mind and pain lanced from temple to temple almost driving her to her knees. She looked around in panic and saw another death's-head moth fluttering at the door at the far end of the corridor. As she reached it and held out her hand to touch it, it dissolved into a puff of dust and her heart ached. "Oh, Mother Moss," she moaned. "I miss you so much."

She started at the sound of something smashing above her head. "Pup missed that camera earlier," he explained.

"Well done, Pup," she nodded, rubbing at her forehead as the pain subsided. "You must destroy every camera you see after we go through that door. Can you do that?"

"Yes, Surl," Pup grinned, adjusting the two large bags of ball-bearings on his belt. "Pup likes breaking things!"

"Get ready," she warned them as she turned the handle. "I've had no visions of what's in there. We… what's that noise?"

"Sounds like explosions and gunshots outside," Peter said, tightening one of the leather straps on the small shield attached to his crippled forearm. "I can hear people screaming too."

"We have to get into the power room or the Light-Father will die. They are facing something terrible in the Great Annex and…" she shuddered and went blank until Peter shook her hard by the shoulders. "I think it's what was in those Tally-men... a *devil*," she gasped. "We have to stop the begiullers in the walls hurting Mother Fern and we have to find a way to stop the Tally-men getting their orders from the Great Computer."

"How do you know this?" Peter demanded.

"I see it, I see it!" Surl hissed, tapping her right temple. "It hurts to use my craft but Mother Moss is guiding me."

"Um, yes, Mother Moss," Peter muttered, unconvinced. He recalled her wizened head kept in the tin at the Keep and shivered as he heard once more her cries of agony as Schimrian and his Brothers brutally tortured her. "I hope she really is watching over us," he said, shaking himself free of the thrall. "I'll go first."

He pushed open the door carefully and peeked into the room which was filled with twenty computer terminals set upon four rows of desks. "It's deserted," he sighed with relief. "The Brothers must've gone outside to join the fighting."

"Go now!" Surl whispered urgently. "Let's get to that far door and into the power room before they find us."

As they crossed the room, Pup took out two wall-mounted cameras with his catapult. They had almost reached the power room door when Surl shushed them to be quiet and pulled them behind the last row of desks and told them to hide.

A split second later, the door crashed open and two flustered Brothers entered. One of them actually sat on the desk Pup was hiding under. "Brother Edward," he panted, the fear making his voice tremble. "What in the name of God's Holy Lamb possesses the Tally-men? They're running everyone through with their spears all across the Great Abbey!"

"Wiccan devilry possesses them, Theo," the other replied in a calm, bass voice. "I have no idea how they've done this but the accursed Mothers are responsible for this sacrilege. The Holy Father alone knows what they've destroyed with their explosives but it looks like they've targeted the fuel stores first."

"We've grown soft and complacent these last six years thinking that no Unworthy survivor could ever pose a threat to us but fear not: Schimrian and Pious *will* defend the Great Cathedral! The Wiccans are few in number: they cannot win."

"Yes, yes, Theo, but what about the *rest* of the Great Abbey? We're being overrun by their Ferals and now the Tally-men have turned on us! See those blank monitor screens over there? It defies all logic but these same few Wiccans have taken out most of our security cameras. Look, even the Redemption Cell cameras have failed. This is a well-planned attack."

"Even if the Unworthy break free, they will not get far once we redeem these Harlots of Satan and their beast-children."

"True, Theo, but I cannot hide here while our Brothers and Sisters are being slaughtered. We must join the Inquisition!"

"Abbot Camus will flay us alive if we leave our posts!"

Edward ran a hand through his coarse black hair in exasperation. "Hear me: they would have targeted the generators by now if that was their plan so why are you prevaricating? Remember: a coward dies a thousand deaths; a hero only one!"

"Gah! Now you're quoting Thomas Tythe at me again!" Theo grumbled, curling his lip in disgust. "I'll join you in this but don't blame me if Pious personally redeems the pair of us."

There were racks of spears and dart guns by every exit door throughout the Great Abbey and after arming themselves, the two Brothers left leaving the four children to breathe a huge collective sigh of relief as they cautiously emerged from under the desks.

"Tally-men killing Brothers!" Peter exclaimed gleefully. "Why are they doing this? Are they remembering the torture?"

"No," Surl said, shaking her head. "The Great Computer has control of them. It's how Azrael commands them."

"What? Who is this Azrael? I thought Schimrian was the evil one," Rabbit said, checking her axes and knives. "Why is this Azrael killing all the Fathers and Brothers?"

"Schimrian wanted an angel for a son but he's raised a demon that enjoys killing for the sake of it. It was in those Tally-men just now! We have to shut down the generators or this Azrael will kill the Light-Father and Mother Fern but Fierce...."

"But Fierce?" Peter echoed. "But Fierce *what*?"

"Oh, nothing," Surl said quickly and opened the door.

The power room was dominated by two massive diesel-powered generators with a bank of equipment to their left and large fuel tanks to their right. The air stank of diesel oil and ozone and the concrete floor thrummed beneath their feet as the generators span, powering the whole complex. "Peter! See those engines?" Surl insisted, pointing at the twenty-foot high machines. "Mother Fern is in my head telling me they make all the lights and the computers work in the Great Abbey. We *have* to destroy them!"

"How can we stop these, Surl?" Rabbit asked, gazing around the huge room in fear and awe. "They're gigantic: we're only small children and those Brothers will be back soon!"

Peter had climbed on some crates to peer out of the windows set high in the eastern wall. "Mother Veneris and Rosemary are down there in the street," he reported excitedly. "Their Ferals are fighting all the Brothers and Fathers! Ah! Mother Rosemary is down and Veneris... wait! The Tally-men have just stabbed a Father *and* all the Brothers in the back down there and - oh no! Mother Veneris has a spear in her too! Ah! Kack! She's *dying!*"

"Mother Fern says there's nothing we can do!" Surl shouted up at him. "We *have* to save the Light-Father and the others and shutting down these machines is the only way!"

"Yes, Mother Surl," Peter said acidly as he clambered down. "The Tally-men have run the Father and Brothers through but..." he spluttered, wide-eyed with fear. "They are not... not..."

"Yes, they are not dying. I see this in my visions. Azrael is using a dark magic to keep them alive. Forget them! We *must* save the Light-Father and Mother Fern!"

"Then let's try this," Peter suggested, hefting a heavy wrench. He opened an inspection hatch on top of one of the generators and dropped it into the gearing housing of the diesel unit and jumped clear just in time as the gears jammed instantly with a deafening noise and metal fragments shot upwards through the open hatch while others slammed into the casings.

"One down, one to go!" he crowed and repeated the process with the second generator yielding the same result. The strip-lights went out and blue emergency lamps flickered into life as the stricken machines began to tear themselves apart with one armature shaft completely shattering its bearings.

"Mother Fern says we must destroy these devices along the wall as well!" Surl cried out, clutching at her forehead. She gritted her teeth, grabbed a sledgehammer from a tool-rack and smashed the screens and control panels for the generators so that the engines could not be shut down. There was a bank of power supply feeds and screens for the radio masts and satellite dishes so she laid into these with all her strength until they were unrecognisable.

Panting from the exertion, she threw aside the sledgehammer and looked around the power room. Peter and Pup were breaking phones and screens on the two desks by the main doors but Rabbit was nowhere to be seen. Her heart leapt with fear: "Rabbit? Where are you?" she yelled though her cupped hands.

Rabbit emerged from behind one of the stricken generators and beckoned for them to join her. "We can't go through the doors so I've opened up this ventilation duct I found," she explained. "It's wide enough for us crawl through so follow me – ugh! Kack! It's full of cobwebs!" she cursed as she crawled in.

Surl remembered this from a vision and blessed Rabbit's good sense and instincts: they could not possibly escape any other way. Whatever door they tried, she foresaw their capture and death.

She almost hurled Pup in after Rabbit and Peter then she followed them in, pulling the grill back into place. Mercifully, it stayed in position and through it she could glimpse Brother Theo racing to the shattered control panels and frantically trying to shut down the huge engines as they screamed and belched smoke with their gearing loads removed and their mountings failing.

"What do we do now?" Peter demanded of Surl. "Can Mother Fern tell us where we need to go to be safe?"

"I can't hear her in my mind any more but I know this duct joins a vertical shaft a little further on with rungs that will take us to the roof. We have to climb up there before the flames reach the fuel tanks otherwise the heat and fumes will kill us."

Suddenly the sound of a massive blast shook the duct. "What was that?" Pup shrieked. "Pup nearly wet himself."

Surl groaned as she concentrated. "A bad thing and a good thing just happened. I think the Light-Father and Mother Fern and the others will be able to escape now that Azrael's dead!"

In the gloom, the others accepted this without a word as they crawled along the duct, feeling their way by touch as the feeble blue light filtering through the grill faded. Here it joined many others at the base of the large vertical shaft that she had foreseen.

Peter fished out a glow-stick and shook it violently to initiate the chemical reaction. He took a headband out of his pocket and with some difficulty because of his claw; he threaded the glow stick into the loops sewn into the head band. "I'll take the lead," he offered. "Just follow my light and don't let go of the rungs!"

The following minutes were etched into their souls forever. A cacophony of shouts, screams, booms and clangs echoed past them as they climbed. They began to feel hot and already the fumes from the stricken diesel engines were making them nauseous. "Hurry,"

Surl urged as she followed the others. "This shaft will become a chimney for the fire once it takes hold!"

"We have a problem, Surl," Peter called down. "There's a fan set into the shaft: it's going to be difficult to climb through. Why is it here and not on the roof like in the train sheds?"

"I don't know but we can make it: my visions say so!" Surl replied. She was sweating heavily and knew that she was lying but she was also wise beyond her years: better a false hope than none at all as Mother Moss had told her. "Just climb through it, Peter. If the electrics come back, the fan blades will slice us to bits!"

Peter cursed and thrust himself between the blades but he lost one of his knives as the hilt snagged and it was dragged out of its sheath. It narrowly missed Pup as it banged and clattered down into the darkness beneath them. "Hah! I'm through," he gasped. "Here, Pup, give me your hand! There's a small ledge around the shaft above the fan and some more rungs."

"Pup is scared," Pup whimpered, too frightened to let go of his handholds. "The air's bad. Pup can't breathe properly!"

Rabbit immediately grabbed the rung beneath Pup's midriff, hauled herself level with him and braced her feet. "There, Pup, now you cannot fall as I can catch you now. Now, reach up, that's a good Pup, that's a *brave* Pup!"

Trembling, Pup extended a hand. Peter heaved him up onto the ledge but he cried out in pain as he did so as he was hanging from a rung by his claw and the weight almost tore the leather sheath from his arm. His stump still had not healed and a trickle of blood oozed through the stitching. He made sure Pup had a good handhold and footing before he adjusted the straps, hissing with pain as he did so. "I can't help you," he admitted reluctantly. "I'm bleeding and my stump can't take any more weight."

"Pfft! I am Rabbit!" Rabbit declared. "I could hop to the top and never stop!" Nevertheless, it took her three attempts to clamber up through the blades and join Pup on the rungs. Wisps of acrid white smoke began to rise past them.

"Hurry, Surl!" Peter fretted. "There's a red glow down there!"

"Then move out of the way!" Surl snapped as she wriggled past the blades, her sweaty hands scrabbling for a grip as the light from the glow-stick sent vast eerie shadows dancing about them. "Start climbing again, all of you! We have but seconds to get out of here! Come on, Pup! Quick as you can!"

63

With Peter crying with pain at every rung, the last stage of their nightmare journey began as the air grew foul and hot about them. Rumbles and booms echoed up from below until Pup cried out: "Pup sees daylight up there!" and his pace increased.

The others caught up with him and were eternally thankful for that pale light. "Pup! Jump out!" Rabbit cried out, her voice hoarse with fear. "My lungs are burning! I want to get out of here!"

"There's a cap on top of the duct," Pup wailed. "It's too narrow for Pup to get through!"

"It must come off," Peter said. "Otherwise, why have these ladder rungs in here to maintain the fan? Push up as hard as you can, Pup. Rabbit, you hold on to him in case he slips."

"The edge of the cap is bending, Peter, the metal is very thin! Pup thinks he can squeeze through."

"Be careful, there's a drop onto the roof," Surl warned after a violent cough. "Try and go feet first through the gap."

"Pup's almost through... *eep!*"

"Pup? Are you alright?" Rabbit squeaked in panic.

"Unh!" Peter grunted as her foot slipped and he received her boot sole full in his face. "Kack! Rabbit!" he screamed. "I almost fell! I can't put any weight on my claw!"

"Sorry, sorry, sorry," Rabbit panted. "I'm sweating so much, the rungs are slippery. Pup? Are you there?"

"Pup fell - it's about six feet to the ground but Pup isn't hurt. You'll have to make the gap bigger before you climb out but there are rungs on the outside as well."

Rabbit heaved frantically and the rain cap twisted to one side so all three of them were soon lying on their backs on the sloping lead roof of the generator block gulping in lungfuls of fresh air. There was a dull roar and tongues of flame erupted from under the rain cap then the duct disgorged clouds of toxic black smoke to join the pall from the fires now raging across the Great Abbey.

A gigantic gout of flame erupted from the Angel compound to their south as a rotorcraft exploded inside a blazing hanger. Debris flew high into the air including a rotor-blade that tumbled out of the sky to strike the dormitory of the Brothers-Technician.

"Why are you smiling, Surl?" Peter asked. "We're trapped up here and this building could explode any second!"

"No, it *won't*," she sighed, wiping the sweat from her forehead with her sleeve. She wrinkled up her nose for the air now reeked of burning athidol and plastic. "That rotor-blade just saved Ivy and Nightshade. Veneris and Rosemary are gone but the others are still fighting in the Great Cathedral. Let's get away from these ducts and chimneys – hack! – this smoke is making me feel sick."

She led the way up and over the roof of the Great Annex that adjoined the generator block and out across the flat roof of the surgery units on the southern flank of the Great Annex. She shuffled on her bottom to the edge and the others joined her as more titanic detonations raked the Angel compound shaking the masonry beneath them.

To their left was a tall, ugly, grey accommodation block - one of two in the Great Abbey that housed the Tally-men. Before them was the ornate Gothic-style building which was the luxurious residence of the elite Brothers and Fathers who serviced the Great Computer and the Conclave's favoured Brothers-Surgeon and Fathers-Surgeon. Beyond were the walls and the plain white-washed buildings of the Sisters' Enclave. Smoke billowed from broken windows in every building.

"There are fires *everywhere!*" Peter cackled with delight. "Hoi! Take the judgement of God upon thy pates, thou sinners!"

"Pup wishes Mother Moss was here to see this," Pup sighed sadly, dangling his legs over the edge. "More fireworks!" he exclaimed, pointing at a great ball of flame billowing skywards as the last of the Angel fuel stores exploded. More followed, this time behind them, as the last of the fuel reserves for the Order vehicles in the north-east of the Great Abbey erupted, sending shrapnel, tiles and masonry spiralling high into the air.

The sun was sinking behind the black clouds forming to the south and west but in the distance beyond them, anvil-clouds rose snow-white and menacing into the stratosphere. "Down there!" Pup squeaked, pointing. They could see the Apse of the Great Cathedral and emerging into the broad avenue of the Sisters' Processional were figures running and regrouping by the Library. They saw the last of Veneris' and Rosemary's Ferals join them but then a large group of Brothers emerged from the Apse and charged. "Look! The Light-Father's hurt and so is Mother Fern!"

There was no mistaking their precious Light-Father and his red baseball cap, waving his sword and screaming defiance at the Brothers while clutching at his stomach. "Sweet Mary, save him," Rabbit prayed anxiously. "Ah, the Ferals are going berserk!"

"There are more Ferals coming up from the station!" Peter said excitedly. There was no mistaking the long white hair of the albino Mother as she was half-carried by two of her Ferals. "That's Mother Nightshade and she's injured too!"

"So is Mother Ivy," Surl added. "This will be remembered as the Battle of the Great Abbey yet we can't help them."

"Can't you guide us down?" Peter demanded hopefully. "You know: with your visions?"

Surl wiped her nose with the back of her hand and showed the fresh blood to him. "No, I can't. Mother Fern told me that if I try to 'see' any more I could have a fit and *die*."

"Oh? So we're stuck here?" he gasped in horror.

"For a while," she admitted as a death's-head moth fluttered in front of her face only to vanish in a puff of dust. "Trust me."

"Look!" Rabbit shouted. "They're charging the Brothers again and driving them back. They're winning!"

Surl drew up her knees and rested her chin on them. "No, they're not," she said, grimacing with pain. "More Brothers are coming and they have begiullers! They have to retreat to the Phoenix now or they'll all be massacred."

"Bas! Bas!" Pup wailed. "Please come back for Pup!"

There were flashes as pipe-bombs, hurled by Ivy, exploded amongst the Brothers allowing Fern and the others to flee in good order towards the station gates. Pup burst into tears as they were lost to view behind the drab walls of the Sisters' Enclave.

Surl put her arm about his shoulders as he sobbed. "Shhh, dear heart, we will be safe enough. There are ducts and sewer tunnels everywhere beneath the Great Abbey where we can hide. Be brave because Fate and Mother Moss have this great destiny awaiting all of us. It will be *such* an adventure that we can write our own saga one day and we'll call it The Tales of Pup the Mighty and his Catapult of Justice!"

"Hallelujah, you stopped him crying," Peter muttered, huddled up in misery. "Even if we ever get off this accursed roof, we'll be knee deep in kack till we're slaughtered like piglets. Some adventure! So what's this 'great destiny' of ours then?"

Surl turned to him and grinned: "Sabotage."

~~~~~

Schimrian

"You wanted to see me, Eminence," Abbot Camus said wearily as he entered the Great-Abbot's extensive Gothic chambers on the top floor of the Great Manse. Columns supported the ribbed vault roof nine yards above their heads and the shuttered windows and the door were set into pointed arches. There had been a ceiling in here and an attic above but Schimrian had them removed to expose the carved angels set at the base of the diagonal ribs who gazed down upon him as he sat at his imposing mahogany desk.

He was dressed in his immaculate formal vestments but Camus noted that he was also wearing a complex, gold-embroidered dalmatic with the emblem of the Order dominating the chest: the cross in lieu of the rod of Asclepius and coiled about by the two Hippocratic snakes of healing. He knew that the Great-Abbot had taken to wearing the dalmatic constantly since his temporary bout of dementia but for some reason Camus found that it made Schimrian seem even more menacing and capricious. '*How is that possible?*' said a small voice in his head. '*He created this dystopia.*' Another voice chimed in, mocking: '*Try not to soil yourself!*'

There were candles burning in various recesses and on the desk but the far corners of the chambers were lost in deep and dancing shadows. The storm raged above the Great Abbey and Camus felt his heart sink as he thought of all the havoc the pounding rain was wreaking on the fire-damaged buildings. The Great-Abbot was still reading some papers and hadn't acknowledged his presence. "I have much to do, as you know, Eminence," he prompted, wringing his hands. "With so few able souls to assist me."

Schimrian sighed theatrically, placing his papers into a folder then he poured some brandy into two large glasses. "Please be seated, my son," he said quietly, indicating the chairs in front of his enormous mahogany desk. "We have much to discuss."

Camus swallowed nervously as he sat down. The chairs in front of the desk were deliberately lower than Schimrian's so that the interviewees felt like naughty schoolchildren called before a stern headmaster. He knew the psychology of it but it was still effective only more so in his case. It had been difficult with Schimrian ranting and raging constantly for two weeks after being dragged half-alive from Azrael's machine in the Great Annex. His friend, Abbot Michael, had not been so lucky and the mere thought of

67

what had emerged from that device made the bile rise dangerously in his throat. He blinked and realised that Schimrian was staring at him with a hand raised above the desk.

"Oh! Forgive my disrespect, Eminence!" he flustered and rose to kiss the Great-Abbot's proffered ring of office. He sat back down heavily. "I-I must apologise for wearing overalls and being oil-stained and unkempt in your presence, Eminence, but I can't work on machinery in my vestments or even my field-robes..."

"Peace, my son," Schimrian insisted, raising a hand to silence him. "Your work-attire speaks eloquently of your selfless efforts to restore our Order. I could hardly expect you to strip engines with a mitre upon your head and a crozier in your hand." He slid a glass of brandy across the desk towards Camus. "Please, enjoy this token of my esteem. We have a thousand bottles from the revered vintners of Provence-Ardechia and such exquisite brandy is best savoured in virtuous and blessed company is it not?" He swirled the liquor in his glass, holding it up to the candle-light. "Such colour, such aroma," he sighed before downing it in a single gulp. "Ah, such divine fire to the belly, such holy warmth in one's veins."

Camus cautiously sipped at his brandy before replacing the glass on the desk. Schimrian had terrified him to the core before the attack but after two weeks of vitriol and garbled pronouncements in the near empty Great Cathedral, this sudden calmness was unnerving as he had *never* received praise or such familiar compassion from the Great-Abbot in all his years of service.

He glanced over at Schimrian's computer-desk and was shocked to see that all three consoles and their screens had been systematically smashed to pieces. He quickly turned his attention back to Schimrian who had steepled his delicate, long fingers and had a smile on his face that made his blood run cold.

"To business, my son: we are three weeks on since the death of my precious Azrael and yet not one Abbey Angel is functional. I would welcome some good news, my son, for this is our darkest hour: our Redemption Cells are almost empty, all our scientists are dead and Revelation slips ever further from us as we speak. Is our New Jerusalem but a fool's dream, hmm?"

"N-no, Eminence," Camus stuttered. "I-it is not."

"Ah, good," Schimrian nodded, the smile broadening. "You are my most trusted savant of machinery and circuitry so forgive me if I test your faith and patience at times. You are a role model to our postulants and novices as well as the more... *naïve* Brothers and thus you are held in high regard amongst them."

Camus recognised the danger he was in immediately. "Y-you have no need to test my faith or my loyalty, Eminence, but how can I repair buildings, computers, radios, Angels, communications, generators with only twenty Fathers and Brothers skilled in such arts? While you were, um, indisposed, parts went missing, equipment failed for no good reason and untended buildings constantly caught fire: the Great Abbey is *dying*, Eminence. I have been without sleep for *days*!"

"I am now fully recovered from my malaise," Schimrian said then paused to refill his glass. "And I know what stalks your dreams: phantoms, ghosts; the will o' the wisps of a guilty soul. The Brothers inform me of your nightmares but still thy fears: I am conscious of the impossible burden placed upon you."

"Then call in more survivors from Britannia and Europe to staff the Great Abbey and help me... I *cannot* do more: the damage done by the Ferals and Wiccans to the hangars is too extensive..."

"Yet, as we have explored in depth, you let two Mothers escape when you had them both at your mercy."

"We had but *one* begiuller wielded by Brother Althayne," Camus protested. "If my Brothers had firearms, we would not have lost all but two of our Angels. Althayne was cruelly struck down by a rotor blade and the Mothers I had at my mercy were freed: they wielded their arcane arts and then their Ferals tore my technicians apart. That albino Harlot got into my mind and forced me to shoot yet more of my Brothers and had she not lost count of the bullets, she would have had me shoot myself!"

"Yes, yes, my son, their foul craft is indeed powerful; vexing to the mind; tortuous to the soul." Schimrian paused to sip yet more brandy that was bringing colour to the high, pale cheeks of the most powerful man on the planet. "I myself was bewitched in Crawcester as I redeemed an ancient Hag so I lay no blame at your feet, my son. I merely broach the subject as we have just received word that those same three Wiccans we let slip may have just slaughtered Father Beorcraft and all his Brothers."

"How?" Camus gasped, wide-eyed. "Father Ursaf was aiding them, was he not? I understood he'd taken two Angels from Bede to support Beorcraft in the search for the.... um, Naked One and those Unworthy prisoners he set free."

"Bede serves us well, my son, but Father Ursaf reports that the hamlet of Wealthorpe is strewn with the corpses of our Brethren and Tally-men. He suggests a sortie came ashore in a boat and ambushed them as they were engaging the Unworthy."

"Ah, so Father Ursaf and his Angels were *not* at Wealthorpe when Beorcraft was attacked?"

"He was not. He has now fled north to land and wait out this storm but he claims he was bewitched into thinking the refugees were hiding in an isolated farmstead to the east of Wealthorpe. He was certain he was right and Beorcraft was wrong so, once again, the sin of arrogance has thwarted our most holy ambitions. Ursaf shall feel my wrath, my son, of that you can be certain."

"Was the Light-Father there, Eminence?"

"He is confident that he killed the Unworthy who were hiding in the cottages but due to his cowardice he would not set down close to the hamlet to verify matters before the storm was upon him. We must therefore assume the Light-Father and his witches were indeed at Wealthorpe and both Beorcraft and Ursaf have failed us in every respect. What stratagems can your agile mind devise to rid me of this troublesome creature, hmm?"

"A boat indicates that the Unworthy must reside in Milverburg, Eminence, or in one of the towns on the southern banks of the Milverbore. If I were them, I would choose Milverburg: the place has ten levels; each one a town; each one a maze."

Schimrian curled his lips in disgust: "Pah! Milverburg was ever a *Gomorrah* of merchant excess and debauchery but I concur, my son, this vile city must indeed be their refuge. We therefore need all our remaining Angels to land upon Uppermost at the same time as three forces of our Brothers-Martial advance along the viaducts."

"I agree, Eminence, but our boats must take to the Milverbore as well to sink any vessel that flees Inquisition as the Angels could be grounded by poor weather or poor visibility."

"Excellent thinking, my son! I know you're exhausted but I want you to co-ordinate the ships and Angels to form a blockade of Milverburg. However, we must first redeem the Naked One before he reaches this Light-Father - do you not agree?"

"Aye, Eminence. I agree," Camus nodded, licking his dry lips. "He knows the Order well and was unparalleled in circuitry and computers. His knowledge of our systems runs deep. He could do us far more harm than the treachery of Brother Kai. He…"

Camus paused as he became aware of movement in the shadows then a familiar figure stepped into the candlelight. The face was corpse-white but the livid scar upon it was blood-red as were the eyes. Like Camus, he wore black overalls set with the small silver emblem of the Order which only the Abbots could bear on their vestments and working clothes. He had a sword strapped to his belt and a heavy calibre machine-gun slung over his shoulder.

There was a sharp wheezing intake of air into lungs no longer needed for the earthly requirements of breathing but for speech delivered in a voice as cold and as merciless as the grave: "*I* seek the honour of redeeming the Naked One, Eminence."

"Ah, Pious, you provide me with solace," Schimrian smiled indulgently. "You are my staff and my shield in these trying times. It's a pity you cannot savour this excellent brandy but the Lord fashioned you thus to carry on His mighty works."

"If I m-may be excused, Eminence," Camus stuttered, getting to his feet. "The two Angels that landed on the roof of the Brothers' dormitory during the desecration of the Great Cathedral are beyond repair after the roof collapsed but we've been able to salvage two of the Angels in the compound. I w-will resume working on them and inform you when I've completed the repairs."

"Not yet, my son; stay seated," Schimrian insisted and Camus flopped back down. "We still have much to discuss."

"What of the Naked One?" Pious whispered hungrily. "I wish to set forth and redeem him *immediately*."

"All in good time, my old friend, all in good time." Schimrian smiled again at his old protégé. "Please, lay aside your weapons and lend us your wisdom."

Asthmatic hissing issued from the Abbot's dry lungs as he bent over the desk to kiss the seal on the Great-Abbot's ring. Camus could not bear to look at Pious's face but gazed instead at his white hands where the veins were black for no heartbeat sounded within those creaking ribs. How could he move? How was he possessed of the strength of ten men? Everything about the man was unholy yet here he sat with the eager, predatory smile of the Pious of old and with the full unquestioning support of the Great-Abbot.

"Camus is more than capable of this task, Eminence," Pious approved. "However, I crave your indulgence. After I hunt down the Naked One, I wish to lead the ground assault on this Babylon; this poisonous canker in the midst of our most Holy Britannia. We shall raze this affront to Heaven in our wrath and let the Milverbore reclaim the smoking ruins. Will you join us, Eminence, in our most holy assault on this last redoubt of the Unworthy?"

Schimrian's smile vanished instantly and he ran a hand through his thinning hair, subconsciously feeling for the protrusions left after the machine had reformed his shattered skull and restarted his heart. "You *know* I cannot leave the Great Abbey untended, my friend, and none other is worthy enough to sit on my throne. None! Camus would have me flood the Abbey with Abbots and Fathers when I must first interview them to determine who is worthy of my trust and who is *not*."

"As you wish, Eminence, but you ask too much of poor Camus here," Pious smiled, placing a hand on the Abbot's shoulder making him shudder for it felt as hard and as cold as marble even through the thick fabric of his overalls. "He was beset by so many problems that we suspected Unworthy spies were amongst us but we searched in vain. It is a pity that the others *altered* like me did not stir again after Azrael perished but such is the Will of God. I am thrice blessed to be allowed to continue His great work."

"Yes, so many dead," Schimrian grimaced, steepling his fingers again. "With so few left to bury them, the corpses were putrefying. I am eternally grateful that you took charge, old friend, and saw to the burials and cremations with such efficiency."

"The postulants and novices just needed motivation, Eminence, so when a postulant defied me at the Library shortly after the attack, I buried him alive to set an example to the others."

Camus shook his head slowly. "You l-left the boy in that coffin for three hours before you exhumed him! He is of no use to anyone and soils his bed constantly. With so many Sisters killed, there are too few to tend the greenhouses and see to our laundry. In fact, this tempest above us is destroying the few remaining greenhouses we have left. Food rots on the vine and we have to work in these stained and unclean garments."

"Nevertheless," Schimrian said icily, his eyes narrowing. "This one cruel example did mean the cremations and burials were all completed by this morning. As for the dead Sisters, I mourn their loss but there remain three dozen healthy Eves: more than enough to restore our Twelve Tribes in the centuries to come. Now that all our dead Fathers, Brothers and Sisters are finally at rest, rejoice for God has restored my clarity of thought and my purpose."

"Hallelujah," Pious rasped. "I so wearied of holes being dug and corpses being burnt. Camus, however, has a point: we must allow more Brothers and Fathers in here as soon as possible before your throne sits amidst nothing but a rainswept ruin."

"Not yet!" Schimrian shouted, slamming his hand down upon the desk. "This will happen on *my* terms. Some Brothers and Fathers will be loyal to Abbots whose own loyalties lie with their Tribes while still others answer only to the Conclave. In this darkest hour, I *must* be certain of their veracity!"

"What say you, Camus?" Pious wheezed.

Camus knew they were toying with him and despaired but out loud he said: "It has to happen quickly. Maybe the Brothers-Technician at Norton can help us as I know they're loyal to you, Eminence. We need more Brothers well-versed in electrics and mechanics to repair our satellite communications, computers and generators. We are salvaging parts from nearby towns and villages as well as the Southern Cities but at this rate it will be *months* before I can restore electrics across all the buildings here let alone salvage spare parts from the wrecked Angels. We also need more aviation fuel or they will be grounded anyway."

"In truth, my son, it is all *most* frustrating," Schimrian said, indicating the smashed computer equipment. "All our devices are useless and we are almost blind and deaf to what is happening across the globe." He paused to delicately open a Bible at a marked page. "It is at times like these that the dialogues of Job aptly remind us of our need for humility: *God does not trust his heavenly servants; he finds fault even with his angels. Do you think He will trust a creature of clay, a thing of dust that can be crushed like a moth? We may be alive in the morning, but die unnoticed before evening comes. All that we have is taken away from us; we die, still lacking wisdom.*"

"Forgive my ignorance in these matters, Eminence," Camus ventured, wiping the nervous sweat from his brow with a rag. "But what relevance has this quote to our crisis?"

"It contains a profound warning about how all things are transient even with the blessings of our forefathers, my son," Schimrian said with a thin smile, his eyes alive with manic fervour. "Like my loyal Bucheort, tormented and crucified in Crawcester by those vile harpies, we are but frail and fallible creatures in the eyes of Our Lord God and his Hosts."

Camus immediately thought of Azrael as the ultimate golem; a satanic creature of clay according to Michael who had described the events in the Great Annex to several novices who then spread the details to those they trusted in the Great Abbey. A small but suicidal voice in mind urged him to put this theory to the Great-Abbot but he could see that the irony would be completely lost on Schimrian and Pious. He recalled a phrase from an unknown Slavic author: *when caught between two hungry wolves, do not put on a fleece and bleat.* "This I see, Eminence," he said carefully. "But I beseech you: enlighten me as to its significance."

"The Lord guided me to these Holy words because for weeks, death's-head moths had tormented me day and night until I recovered my wits through the wisdom and patience of Job. The epiphany is clear, my son: we must restore ourselves in the eyes of God; we must Inquire of Milverburg; we must redeem these Harlots of Satan; we must *crush* this emissary of Lucifer; this so-called Light-Father!" he seethed, banging his fist on his desk in emphasis: "You will both lead the Last True Inquisition and make of this task a new scripture to be revered for millennia yet to come!"

Pious grinned, drawing his sword from its scabbard as peals of thunder shook dust from the masonry far above their heads. "I promise you, Eminence, your Inquisition shall be *glorious.*"

~~~~~

Nightshade

Complex bolts of lightning arced and forked ceaselessly from cloud to cloud as Nightshade sheltered beneath the immense Gothic archway of the eastern railway entrance into Milverburg that was aptly sculpted as the mouth of Thor, the Norse god of thunder. The wind roared from the south-west so the veils of rain did not reach her but violent gusts and eddies whipped her long milk-white mane this way and that until, sighing with irritation, she laid down her staff and tied her hair back into a pony tail.

She did not flinch as the tip of a spear touched her spine and a voice cried out: "You let your guard down, Mother Nightshade! I could've been a Tally-Man and run you through!"

"I doubt it, Mouse, because your spear is not what it seems," Nightshade smiled, keeping her back to the young girl.

There was a shriek and a clattering of the spear upon the flagstones. "My spear turned into a *snake*," Mouse cried out in horror. "It tried to bite me!"

Nightshade stooped to pick up her staff then handed the spear back to Mouse, marvelling at its exquisite workmanship. Inlaid with silver, it was superbly balanced and had once belonged to an Iberian prince some three hundred years ago. "Silly Mouse, I *knew* you were behind me and as for the illusion: well, I *am* a Wiccan! So, are all the others as restless as you?"

Mouse handled the spear nervously before standing it upright to look up at the beautiful but enigmatic albino Wiccan. "Yes, Mother Ivy just threatened to turn Amos into a warty toad *again*," she said dejectedly, moving closer to Nightshade to solicit an embrace and watch the immense display. "He's such a bull-pat at times but he's unbearable now he's worried about his sister."

"He *was* mourning for her but now he knows she's alive, it's only natural that he wants to tear the world apart to find her."

"But he's been *awful*; swooning like some helpless maiden in a saga." Mouse put the back of her hand to her forehead and struck a forlorn pose: "If only I'd been a real b-brother to S-Surl she would not have needed a w-w-wig!"

"Tch! Such mockery is cruel, Mouse; shame on you."

"But it *is* funny when we have no joy in our lives."

"I understand, dear heart," Nightshade smiled, placing her hand on Mouse's head. "We Mothers had no real childhood to speak of either." She paused as a blinding flare of light was instantly followed by a thunderclap that left their ears ringing. "Glorious Diana, preserve us!" she gasped. "That was *close*! I think it struck one of the towers on Uppermost."

"The Light-Father told me how hailstones make the lightning as they rub against each other in storm clouds. He said lightning is so hot it makes the air explode to create the thunder. It's strange to think that Thor's hammers are made from *ice*!"

"So the Light-Father did find time to teach you something. He is a most unusual man. I'd love to see his world with my own eyes. To think they sent men to the *Moon*!"

"Me too but he hasn't talked to me about Fierce since we got here," Mouse said sadly, a tear trickling down her cheek. "I just wanted to talk to him so much about losing her but he was always so sad about her death and leaving the others behind."

Nightshade put her arm about Mouse's shoulders and drew the girl close to her. "Dear heart, guilt is a dreadful burden. The Light-Father blames himself for Fierce and the others who died so you must forgive him. He needs to heal too."

"But we need his magic," Mouse pouted.

"I know, dear heart, but remember; he was also wounded by an evil the like of which this world has never seen: something even darker and more terrible than the Order." She gazed at the heavens: some of the bolts were so gargantuan that they seemed to crawl from one horizon to the other. "Maybe this evil has manipulated the Order all along," she murmured thoughtfully.

"I know the Light-Father was stabbed by Azrael but you, Ivy and Fern were badly hurt too yet you never seemed to be as worried about the little ones as he was."

"We *were* worried, Mouse, but the Light-Father does not understand Surl's gifts as we do. We always... *believed* that they would somehow survive in that dreadful place."

"So Surl *will* become a Mother one day?"

"Yes, she may become as powerful as Mother Moss so we must get her back at all costs. Because she is a seer, perhaps the only one left in all of Gaia, she may prove to be the only hope we have of surviving this nightmare."

"Surl has no craft mark so how can she be a Wiccan?"

"The mark could be *anywhere*," Nightshade replied, poking Mouse playfully and making her giggle. "It could be here or here or

76

here - we just haven't seen it *yet*. We know her gift is *not* due to the genetic manipulation of the scientists at Exodus although you and the other Scatterlings bear much of their legacy."

"I know," Mouse said miserably, making rapid thrusts and parries with her spear against an imaginary foe. "I'm stronger and faster than most children my age but I'm so tired of being hunted by the Order - they even hunt me in my sleep."

"Oh? Are you still having that dream you told me about?"

"Yes the one where the three of us are riding in the Barnacle on the River Craw and racing through the broken Copper Bridge with masonry crashing into the water all around us but when Shield and I turn around, Fierce is no longer with us. Suddenly, we arrive at this calm lake where the sky is blue and the sun is warm on our faces and our parents are sitting in a rowing boat."

"Is your sister always with them in the dream?"

"Yes and she's waving at us. There's an old man steering the boat: Mister Helfburn who owned the house in Crawcester where we stayed after the floods. We found him dead in his chair; he was watching the river and drinking whisky as he died."

"Then I envy him in some ways," Nightshade said, hugging Mouse tightly as the clouds above them were illuminated by vast flares of blue-white light. "Shield told me of your adventures so it is not surprising that you dream of them so. Your dream is simply telling you that she sails the shores of Avalon with your parents. Poor Mouse, you've seen so many things that no child should ever see but here we are: two small gargoyles standing in Thor's mouth and watching Gaia in all her fury."

"I'm so tired of being frightened, Mother Nightshade."

"As am I, dear heart, yet we will protect you and cleanse Gaia of the Order. I swear this on the blood of my fallen sisters."

"I hope so," Mouse smiled gratefully through her tears. She let her spear fall to the ground once more, wrapped her arms around the Wiccan's slender waist and buried her face into her chest. "I miss my parents so much! Do you remember yours? You haven't told us anything about where you're from."

"There's little to tell, dear heart," Nightshade said in self-deprecating tones. "I am what I am: Mother Nightshade of the Fourth Degree; a Servant of Leo and a Wielder of Fire."

"Hmph! That says everything and *nothing*," Mouse huffed. "So are you saying you were hatched out of a Wiccan egg?"

77

Nightshade laughed then waited for a titanic rumble of thunder to die down. "Ha! An odd choice of words, Mouse, but I'll tell you of our coven first. Mother Rosemary was of the Sun: she could wield the Light of Creation so her 'element' – if you want to call it that - was that of Helios, the Sun God. She could breathe life back into those souls stranded at the Gates of Death and guide them back into this world. The Eirannau used cross the Gael Seas to visit her as they revered her as *Dian Cnecht* reborn in female form."

"So was she more powerful than you?"

"I was not quite her equal but, amongst the Mothers, I was still respected," Nightshade smiled modestly. She opened her free hand and above the palm an intense glowing sphere formed and Mouse could feel the heat upon her face. "I, too, can melt brickwork and set the greatest of fires but I also have craft enough to confuse the minds of our enemies as you just found out with your spear."

"Ugh! The snake was so *real*," Mouse shuddered. "I could feel its scales in my hands and I heard it *hissing*."

"That's because it was a fooling of *all* your senses. We call it a *geis*. Fern is as strong as me in that facet of the craft and one day, Shield and Surl may possess such gifts and insights."

"But I thought Wiccans could only wield one element?"

"Not so but we are strongest in the one that calls out to us and awakens us. Fire called out to me but we all have other gifts such as telepathy and telekinesis to some extent what people used to call 'far-speaking' and 'far-moving.' All of us can cast illusions of one sort or another but, as I said, the ability in casting the '*geis that blinds*' varies greatly from one Mother to the next."

"What about Mother Veneris?"

Pain crossed the delicate features of the Wiccan and the fiery sphere faded away. "Oh, I so grieve for her, dear heart! She was a Wielder of Water and a friend and a mentor to me. She could've raised a wave high enough to drown this citadel twice over but those infernal begiullers laid her and Rosemary low at the Great Abbey before they could wield their full power. None before them would have survived had their craft been unleashed."

"Mother Rosemary frightened me," Mouse admitted. "Her irises would change colour when she was angry and all the shadows about her seemed *wrong* somehow."

Nightshade looked down at Mouse with some surprise: "Well, you *are* perceptive and no mistake."

"But what *were* those shadows?" Mouse persisted.

"It's hard to explain but Rosemary could stand at the Portals of Hell *and* the Gates of Heaven as a Bearer of Souls and what you saw was a manifestation of those souls. The people of Eirann called her the *Wibrana* and brought gifts of carved ravens and one of them carved the staff that Fern now bears."

"A Bearer of Souls? So she could heal people *and* see ghosts like Mother Fern does all the time?"

"Hmm, not so: Fern's ghosts are phantasms created by her guilt whereas Rosemary could actually converse with earthbound souls. Before the Great Plague, many powerful people sought her aid in wresting secrets from the dead. She would always encourage those souls to abandon earthly ties and cross into the Light but now there are *billions* of vengeful shades roaming Gaia bearing a rage great enough to tear reality apart. Everyone in the Order would be naught but ash if that hatred ever became corporeal."

"Huh? Corporeal? What does that mean?"

"Ah, how can I explain this, Mouse? You're all so mature for the years you have that I keep forgetting you're still children! You know when the hairs on the back of neck stand on end and you feel a chill when there's nothing there?"

"Yes, sometimes," Mouse said doubtfully. "Mother Moss told me that was just a ghost walking through me."

"Exactly! One ghost has a little physical presence which a few of us can see but imagine four billion angry spirits all focused in one place: they could bring down a mountain range!"

"Ah, I see," Mouse nodded then she looked up at Nightshade with a worried look on her face. "Now that Shield is a Mother, will she go mad if all these ghosts start speaking to her?"

"Fear not, like Rosemary, she will not lose her wits nor will we take her from you."

"Will she be taking the dead into the Light?"

"No, we feel she has not craft enough to be a Bearer of Souls," Nightshade replied carefully. "But she *was* strong enough to keep you from entering the Gates of Death with Fern's help."

"I remember but I got so suspicious of Shield once: she spent so much time with Mother Moss in that office building then she would come back to the Keep, white as paper and trembling."

"Mother Moss determined your sister's element of awakening to be Air which she honed at that Keep of yours in Crawcester. To be

79

trained like that is painful and can drain the hardiest of souls. Your sister will become very powerful but she must learn to control that power or it will consume her and we'll have to..."

"You mean if she ever becomes *evil* from using her power," Mouse interrupted angrily. "You'll kill her like all those other poor Daughters you've murdered!"

"Please understand, dear heart," Nightshade sighed heavily. "This is not something that we Mothers are proud of but we have no choice in the matter. History had shown us again and again that evil Wiccans left unchecked become dark and terrible creatures. They were the origin of so many dark fables about witches and created all those centuries of prejudice against us but you don't need to worry about Shield: her heart is *pure*."

"I know. That's why I love her so much. She kept Fierce and me alive in Crawcester but at the Keep, like Fierce, she kept her secret from us until she destroyed those two Angels out in Beorminghas," Mouse said proudly. "Long before we got to the Keep, we almost died in the flood on the Craw but she made our rope bounce out of the water and onto a mooring post. We didn't know at the time but *that* was when she first used her power but she has no time for me because she's so *besotted* with Saul."

"It's natural to be jealous of her falling for Saul. She is indeed your sister yet she is also a beautiful young woman whose heart is awakening to love," Nightshade laughed kindly. "Hah, in such a world their love gives me such hope and joy!" She cupped Mouse's cheeks in her hands. "You see, Mouse, Daughters were forbidden from taking lovers but that is just foolishness with mankind all but destroyed. When this madness is over you'll mature as your sister is now doing; you'll seek out a man; you'll fall helplessly in love with him and then you'll have lots of little mouselings!"

"I don't want mouselings! I want my sisters back!"

"Please, dear heart, don't cry again. You hate Mother Moss for making Shield keep a secret from you and for setting Fierce upon her grim journey but never forget that Fierce accepted that fate willingly knowing that she would have to sacrifice herself to save her sisters – such was her love for you. I bless her for even I with all my craft, could never have shouldered such a burden for so long knowing full well the time and manner of my death."

Mouse waited for another earth-shaking roar of thunder to subside. "What of you? You never answered my question. Who are you, really, Mother Nightshade? What's your real name? How did you become a Mother? When did you awaken?"

"Ah, Mouse, you do know I'm an albino?"

"Yes, I can see that," Mouse grumbled. "I'm not stupid."

"I did not say that but many people believed that albinos were a portent of evil and the midwife actually fainted when I was born. However, my parents were both well-educated and they accepted my condition but then they found the mark of the craft upon my left shoulder. Everyone knew of the mark of the Wiccans so they hid it as best they could but, alas, they made many naïve enquiries about Wiccans and so the Order knocked the door one night and forced their way into the house."

"How did you escape?" Mouse gasped.

"Diana protected me. My parents had to watch as a Father inspected me for the mark knowing that the make-up could rub off at any moment. He left after sympathising with them for having such a 'damaged' child and he actually wished them well!"

"By Saint Saul, your parents were brave."

"Yes, they were but my very earliest memories are ones of fear as they struggled to keep my secret safe and my shoulders covered at all times. I was thus very lonely and bored as a child until my craft stirred one day when I had but six years and was about to start school. I was yet to feel the call of my defining element but straight away things became… *difficult*."

~~~~~

"Bordan, she's doing it again!"

"She's doing *what* again, Kendra?" Bordan demanded irritably, putting down his newspaper. "God's teeth! It's difficult to have a conversation with you when you're bellowing down the stairs from the landing while I'm eating my breakfast in the kitchen!"

"Well, come upstairs then!"

Bordan muttered several pithy comments about bachelorhood before levering himself to his feet with a heartfelt sigh of resignation. He trudged upstairs and along the landing to find his wife hovering at the doorway of their daughter's bedroom. He looked over her shoulder to see their six-year old daughter sitting cross-legged on the floor and waving her hands to and fro.

"Ah," he groaned, putting a hand to his forehead. "Telekinesis! I thought it was just a myth put about by the Order to discredit the

Wiccans. I've not seen one scientifically documented example of far-moving and the Wiccans always deny it exists."

"Yet there it is," Kendra said, stifling a sob. "She's far-moving! Same as yesterday only I thought I was hallucinating when that ball floated across the room."

Five stuffed toys were marching in unison around their little albino daughter who was singing a nursery rhyme: "*March, march, march, little soldiers, march to the music of the band...*"

"That's no myth, Bordan, or do you deny the evidence of your own eyes?" Kendra whispered. "The craft is manifesting in her. We can't send her to school even after all the preparations we made with the principal to deal with her albinism. What would a teacher do if they saw her doing *that*?"

"Look, Da, my toys are alive! It's *magic!*"

"Yes, Ellete, it *is* magic," he said carefully. "Can you ask them all to lie down so you can get dressed and have breakfast with us? I have to go to work soon."

"Okay, Da," Ellete smiled and waved her hand once more. The toys flopped to the floor and she started pulling off her nightdress and stopped suddenly. "Oh! I don't feel so good," she whimpered, clutching at her head and swaying.

Kendra swept her up in her arms as Bordan inspected the toys. "You're right: there is no way we can send her to school after *this*," he groaned. "But if we keep her home, our neighbours will start asking even more questions than they are now. The prejudice is bad enough but if they ever found out she was a Wiccan they would burn this house to the ground and us with it! That happened to a family up in Hind only last month."

Kendra cradled her daughter who was already beginning to revive and whimper at the tone of their voices. "I'm sure Eowynne Unwin has already reported us to the secret services - her brother is a Master of the Royal Conclave of Architects and you know how close they are to the Order and the shareholders at Exodus!"

Bordan sighed and ran a hand though his hair in exasperation. "She's not the only one, I'm sure of it."

Kendra kissed her daughter on the forehead. "It's why we have constables visiting us all the time: the neighbours keep telling them that we're keeping her prisoner."

"Yes, I know," he laughed wryly. "It's our good fortune that the constables believe us rather than those tattle-tells when they see that she's an albino. They're good men but poor Ellete will never understand why they're so afraid of those blood-red irises of hers. I don't want her to lose her innocence but we can't hide a craft this powerful and we can't keep her home from school."

Ellete began to wriggle in Kendra's arms. "We have friends working for Exodus. Maybe they can suppress the genes causing this without their managers finding out. We have to try, Bordan, otherwise they will take her from us!"

"How can Exodus help?" he shrugged. "They still do a lot of work for the Order and they won't be able to explain how a small child's brain can generate enough power to make dolls and toys come to life. It must require a lot of energy so it's no wonder she nearly fainted. Look, she has a nosebleed as well."

"I'm really hungry, Ma," Ellete mumbled, snuggling against her mother as if nothing had happened.

"I bet you are, dear heart," Kendra murmured soothingly, dabbing at Ellete's nose. She showed Bordan the small spots of blood on the tissue, the unvoiced concern plain upon her face.

"I want to go to school and make some friends!"

"I know you do, angel, but the other children don't have magic like you do. If you made toys dance around, they might be too frightened to play with you."

"I'd never be mean," Ellete said, patting her mother's face. "I'll keep it a secret. Are bad people coming to take me away?"

"We won't let anyone take you, Ellete," Bordan reassured her. "We'll keep you secret; we'll keep you *safe*."

"I love you lots too," Ellete said simply then she screwed up her eyes: "Um, I think I had a weird dream last night."

"What do you mean by that, dear heart?" Kendra asked.

"There was a tall woman in funny clothes, holding this big stick and she came up me and called me her daughter and I said I'm my mummy's daughter not yours and she said 'for now' and then she went away and I woke up."

"See, Bordan?" Kendra said bitterly. "The Wiccans are far-seeing into her dreams! Telepathy, damn you! You just *had* to talk to them about her craft mark again."

"As *you* did when she was born," he retorted angrily. "Only they know what the craft entails when no scientist on this Earth can explain what they do. We may have no choice but to give Ellete to the Wiccans – they're the only ones who can protect her."

83

"Never! Because some parents *do* get to see their girls again," Kendra said through gritted teeth. "The ones they send home *dead*. We can no more trust them than we can trust the Order and the government. Remember when the newscasters were calling for the Wiccans to be tried for murder even though the autopsies proved that they all died of natural causes?"

"I know, I know," Bordan conceded, going to the window to study the busy main street at the front of the house. "But I don't know what else we can do! If we keep her home the authorities will ask why she's not at school but if the Wiccans take her, for some reason the police just stop asking questions."

"Oh, the Wiccans see to *that*. Even I have to admit their abilities are real but they can't have her."

"Ah, Kack! I think we have a bigger problem."

"What do you mean? How can it be any bigger than *this*?" she demanded incredulously, indicating the toys on the floor.

"Trust me: it's *worse*. A police car is in the street and two vans with the markings of the Order. There are about fifteen or so constables and Brothers all talking to each other and pointing up at the house." He ran into one of the rear bedrooms for a moment then rejoined his frightened wife. "They haven't posted anyone at the rear of the house yet. Thank the Virgin Mary we had the foresight to see this day coming!"

"Do we really have to run away *now*?"

"Yes, we do: we have no choice. I'll barricade the front door while you grab those two suitcases we keep packed. Make sure you pick up our wallets, papers and passports from the bedside cabinet and wait with Ellete by the back door. Hurry, dear heart," he urged, taking her by the shoulders and pressing his forehead against hers. "Please. We have so little time left to us!"

"Are we playing hide and seek?" Ellete asked innocently.

"Yes, dear heart," Bordan said, kissing his beloved daughter on the head. "Only we must make sure they *never* find us."

~~~~~

Small Shadows

"What do you mean by sabotage?" Peter demanded as he revelled in the carnage taking place all across the Great Abbey. "How can four 'kids', as the Light-Father calls us, take on hundreds of Brothers and Fathers?"

Surl smiled as Pup ran in little circles behind them shouting "Pup the Mighty!" with excitement at each blast and gout of flame. "Not hundreds now, Peter, and most of the Tally-men are dead. We have to finish what the Light-Father started!"

"Pah! You really do sound like the Eldest," he grimaced. "All I want to know is will this gift of yours protect us? Hoi! Look over there," he urged, pointing at the southern horizon. "The sun is going down and more big storms are coming this way. We can't stay up here all night in the lightning and the rain."

"He's right," Rabbit agreed. "Seeing the sun again today was wonderful but I can smell the lightning on the breeze. What shall we do now, Surl? Where can we hide?"

Surl pursed her lips and pointed downwards. "There are endless tunnels and sewers under the Great Abbey. Because there are so few Brothers left alive down there, I think we can stop them repairing their Angels and their machines until we find a way to escape to Milverburg and find the others."

"Milverburg?" Peter exclaimed. "Is that where your visions say the Light-Father will be waiting for us? That city in the estuary with statues and all those dried up corpses on the platforms?"

Surl hissed in pain and pressed a hand to her forehead. "Yes, yes. I see them waiting for us in a beautiful golden tower but all about them is *dark*. Ah, it hurts when I try to see too much! We *will* get to Milverburg but not right away."

Rabbit peered over the edge of the roof again. "Hoi! We could climb down the outside of this building using the pipe-work but Peter can't climb as his stump's injured. We'll have to find another way down." She turned to look at Surl as a thought struck her: "Can you see if Schimrian is still alive or did the Light-Father kill him? Huh? Why are you shaking your head?"

"Something worse than Schimrian was down there waiting for him," Surl choked and shuddered. "Schimrian created a monster called Azrael; a fallen angel full of madness and evil. Azrael made the Tally-men kill all those Brothers and Sisters because it amused him. He stabbed the Light-Father and killed many thousands of them all across the world before he was killed but I think Schimrian is still alive down there in that strange machine."

"Why can't we just escape now?" Rabbit insisted fearfully. "Why do we have to stay here when Mother Fern and the Light-Father failed to destroy this place?"

"They did not fail! The Angel of Hell is gone," Surl retorted, the tears coursing suddenly down her cheeks. "But Fierce died in that explosion down there... I saw it... she had plasma grenades inside her Honey Bear and blew herself up to save us all... and Mother Moss knew! She *knew* that Fierce was the only one who could kill Azrael otherwise he would have destroyed *everything*!"

"No, you're *wrong*!" Pup wailed, wrapping his arms around her. "Mother Moss loved Fierce! Surl cannot be right! Use your magic to bring Fierce back! Please!"

Surl's shoulders sagged as she wiped at her eyes again. "I would if I could, dear heart, but I'm not a Wiccan like Mother Fern. I have so few years and I'm scared too but my visions say we must stop them repairing their rotorcraft and the generators. I-I-I am not sure," she groaned, rubbing her forehead. "But if we flee now, the Order will kill us all in Milverburg by landing those Angels in the city and blocking the docks and the railways. Ah! Ah! I cannot see any more – *it hurts, it hurts*!"

Rabbit embraced Surl and comforted her as the four frightened Scatterlings huddled together. Acrid smoke drifted past them and scattered drops of heavy rain began to fall from the darkening skies above. A train whistle blew defiantly in the distance as the Phoenix, the locomotive that had brought them here, reversed westwards on the railway line that ran through the Great Abbey separating the Angel Compound from the rest of the site.

"No! They can't leave us here!" Rabbit sobbed.

"They can and they *must*," Surl said grimly, pointing down at the surviving Brothers and Sisters racing to and fro across the sweeping expanse of the Sisters' Processional. "The Battle of the Great Abbey is over."

"What about the rest of the Ferals?"

"Most of them perished," Surl said, wiping at her tears again. "Sweet Mary, Rabbit, they fought so bravely but so few of them survived! Thirty or forty I think. Oh, and Mother Veneris and Mother Rosemary are dead as well."

Rabbit put her hands on her hips. "We'll have to mourn them later," she urged decisively. "If any of those Brothers look up here, they'll see us. Hah! If Surl's visions can't find us a way down then leave it to Rabbit to find us a warren!"

She pointed to the roof of the Great Cathedral and the tall bell-tower at its south-eastern corner. "Look, there's a door and there must be stairs in there we can use to get down to the ground. There can't be any Brothers inside when there's been fighting and so many fires are burning everywhere."

Surl nodded wearily. "Yes, but we need to be careful because the ledges are exposed. We could be seen if anybody looks up at the roof. Well then, Rabbit, lead the way."

The ledge was indeed narrow and slippery with mould and mildew with a sheer drop to their left. They resorted to crawling as Peter wondered why the architects of this huge structure had given so little thought to the safety of the workers who maintained the roof. A rising wind tugged at them and Pup whimpered in terror for the full ten minutes it took them to reach the door which was mercifully unlocked. Shuddering with fatigue, they entered the musty and oppressive silence of the belfry.

Pup shrieked at skittering noises above them in the rafters and shadows fluttered past their faces in the dark. "Ugh, bats," he shuddered, waving his arms above his head to ward off the whirring wings. "Ugh! Pup can hear them talking to each other in those nasty little squeaks of theirs."

"It's how they see," Rabbit explained. "I read it in a book back at the Keep. They make those sounds to detect objects in the dark. Their huge ears hear the echoes so they never crash into anything. It must be hell for them when this bell rings!" she smiled, reaching out a hand to touch the rim of the thirty-ton brass goliath.

"Ignore them, Pup, they're a nuisance but they can't hurt you," Peter said, crossing to the ladder and peering down into the gloom of the stairwells below. "This leads onto the stairs. Follow me, but be careful," he warned, clambering onto the ladder. "The rungs are very narrow. There's not much light down here and this glow-stick is almost done."

With their hearts in their mouths, they gingerly descended the hollow tower using the flights of steps set against the walls. There were no safety railings and feeble daylight streaming through the small arched windows merely made the sense of vertigo worse until

Pup had to stop to pee as he was so frightened. He then lay upon the cold stone steps, his face pressed against the wall and his eyes screwed shut. He was trembling and whimpering for a mother he had never seen and a family he had never known.

Rabbit instinctively knelt beside him and kissed him on his sweat-soaked forehead. "She would think Pup is a brave Pup," she crooned, copying his way of speaking in the third person. "She would want Pup to be strong because inside his little body beats a warrior's heart. She would want Pup to get up and *fight*."

Pup stared for a long while into Rabbit's large, dark brown eyes and relaxed. He put a hand up and ran his fingers through her unkempt auburn mane. "Would she really tell Pup that? Pup has had dreams about her - she has no face but she sings Pup a lullaby," he murmured: "*Let the angels fill your dreams with cakes and queens and magic beans...*"

"Enough, Pup," Rabbit coaxed gently and hauled him to his feet. "We're near the bottom now. Just keep a hand on the wall and don't look down. Just keep moving and keep your eyes on me. That's it. Good Pup. We'll soon be on the ground."

"Yes, where all those angry Fathers and Brothers are running around," Peter grumbled. "I just hope the fires keep them busy."

Surl sat down suddenly so that he almost tripped over her. "Saint Paul, Surl!" he exploded. "I almost fell!"

"Shhh! Hide the glow-stick and lie flat on the stairs!"

Such was the tone of urgency in her voice that they obeyed instantly. A second later, the tower door immediately beneath them opened and two Brothers, clutching spears, entered and gazed up into the darkness of the tower above them. "Makes me nauseous to look up at that bell," one grumbled. "There's no accursed Unworthy in here! They all fled on that damned train they hid in the woods to the west of the station."

"Nevertheless, Father Leored insists we search everywhere for stragglers," the other shrugged, shining a strong torch upwards to illuminate the beams of the belfry far above them. "With the Annex destroyed and Schimrian dead, we're vulnerable to another attack. All our radios are dead, don't forget."

"Tchah! I'm glad that lunatic is dead. I pray we can elect a new Great-Abbot a little more visionary and a little less *insane*."

Watch your tongue, Brother Cyrus, they may resurrect him yet: he was in that satanic machine and that survived the blast."

"Verily I say unto you, unless a kernel of wheat falls to the ground and dies, it remains only a single seed. But if it dies, it produces many seeds."

"Enough quotes! Come; let us move on to search the other towers before darkness falls. Remember, all the electrics have failed so we'll have to make do with candles and torches."

"Then throw out the worthless slave into the outer darkness; in that place there will be weeping and gnashing of teeth."

"By Saint Peter's beard, Cyrus, will you *please* stop quoting the Scriptures at me? We could run into the Unworthy at any moment – it's an ill time for attempts at levity."

"As you wish, Brother Luke," Cyrus laughed. "But the cowardly shall have their part in the lake which doth burn with fire and brimstone, which is the second death."

"No human being can tame the tongue. It is a restless evil; full of deadly poison," Luke retorted in disgust and slammed the door behind them leaving the children able to draw breath. What little daylight eking through the small windows was fading as Peter ran swiftly down the remaining stairs, knife in hand to open the door a crack. The other three gathered behind him anxiously.

"There's nobody around but there's a lot of thick smoke out there. It'll hide us but where do we go, Surl? If we can't find a way into those tunnels we're finished!"

"Stop being a worry-wart," Rabbit chided "There's a sewer access over there next to the wall of the Great Annex."

"How would you know *that*?" Peter asked sharply.

"Huh! Mother Moss always taught us all to use our eyes and see *everything*," Rabbit said loftily. "When we were on the roof I looked for manhole covers and there it was. The sewers won't run under big heavy buildings like the Cathedral but I think Surl is right: there must be lots of places to hide down there."

"Hallelujah, Mother Mary, we get to swim in kack or we get killed," he groaned. "So it's the kack for us. Come on; let's run while this wretched smoke stays on the ground!"

They hared across the hundred yards of open space with the acrid fumes burning their lungs then, using an abandoned spear, they prised the cover up and descended down the rungs into the putrid darkness of the sewer system. Rabbit struggled to pull the heavy cast-iron cover into place but the darkness became total as Peter's glow-stick suddenly faded.

He exhaled noisily with frustration as he took his two remaining glow-sticks from his jacket and shook them into life. He was about to throw the spent glow-stick into the sewage flow when Surl grabbed his arm.

"No!" she hissed. "It'll be found!"

"So you can foresee what happens to kack?" he asked with an incredulous grin. "Ha! That is quite the gift!"

"Mother Moss taught us well," she retorted crossly. "She said we should never leave clues for your enemies to find. Amos said our Da was always telling him things about thinking like a soldier. I wish I could remember him..."

"This is *not* the time to think of our lost parents, Surl," Rabbit interjected firmly. "Peter's knife is still in the duct down by the generator room, remember?"

Surl glared at her for a moment then massaged the bridge of her nose. "True, Rabbit," she conceded. "But it will take weeks to clear away the wreckage in the power room and check the vents."

"Huh! I didn't mean to drop the knife! Some saga this is going to be," Peter muttered, holding his nose. "Oh, let's get going before I vomit from the stench."

The crumbling brickwork of the sewers was barely higher than their heads as they walked along the ledges set into the rounded walls. In the pale light of their glow-sticks they made their way past lines of chittering rats which paid them little heed. Surl was leading the way until she eventually she found a rotting door set into one wall where the sewer opened out into a cubic inspection chamber leading to six smaller tributary sewers.

She carefully pulled the door open which creaked ominously upon its rusty hinges. "We're here," she declared and led them into an ancient cellar which had wooden benches around a large oak table and cobwebbed shelves set into three walls.

The fourth wall was covered with racks of hundreds of bottles of wine. "Some of these are over sixty years old," Peter announced after reading the labels. "This must have been a wine cellar that the Brothers have forgotten about. Mmm, Surl, can you smell cooking? I can," he said, sniffing at the air hungrily. "Wonderful! Better than a nose full of that kack out there."

"We're below the kitchens where the Sisters prepare the food for all the men in the Great Abbey," Surl explained and sat down gratefully upon one of the benches. "These will be our beds and this will be our Keep for the next two weeks or so. Ah," she winced and wiped at her nose again, the blood bright red upon her sleeve. "I can't see any more! It really hurts!" she groaned, closing her eyes. "All I can see is the colour red, red, red, *red*!"

"I'll check that opening over there and see if there's a way up into the kitchens," Peter said decisively. "Did your visions earlier warn you if there any Brothers are up there?"

"No but I don't need second sight to know that the Sisters do all the cooking so no Brothers will be in that kitchen!"

"Good. Sisters are less likely to kill us if they catch us. Pup, you stay to look after Surl and I'll see if we can find some candles and something to eat. I need some fresh bandages and ointments for this damned stump as well. Can you use your power, Surl?"

Surl put her arms on the table and rested her head on them. "No, I just said I can't see anything but red when I try," she grimaced, closing her eyes. "Sorry but you're on your own."

"As always," he grumbled, clutching at his stump. "By the teats of the Holy Mother, this *hurts*. I'm sure it's infected."

"Hurry then," Rabbit urged, peering into the dark. She took hold of one of the glow-sticks and in its feeble light she could see stairs going upward. "I think we might be able to get up into the kitchen. Mmm, I can smell the cooking now!"

"Be as quiet as possible," Surl whispered urgently. "Sisters are not that clever but they have keen ears."

"We have less than half an hour before those glow-sticks burn out," Rabbit noted. "I'll take this one and Pup, you keep that one and look after Surl for us."

Pup readied his lethal catapult. "Pup will kill any Brother who comes in here," he declared bravely but the shaking in his voice betrayed the raw fear of a child orphaned by Armageddon.

Peter nodded his approval and scurried after Rabbit as she climbed the musty stairs that seemed to go up forever before reaching another long-forgotten store room with large wooden shelves against all four walls. There were cartons, jars and pots galore upon those shelves all shrouded in cobwebs and dust.

Between two shelving units they found a door boarded up from the inside. There was a faint chink of light that drew them to a small crack in the door. "Strange," Peter murmured. "Whoever placed these boards here must have come up from the sewers but why would they do that?"

Rabbit peered through the crack. "Who cares, Peter? There's a hallway lit by candles on the other side but I can't see much: the crack is too small and the light is too dim. I don't think there's anyone around though."

Peter tugged at one of the pieces of wood and it came away easily in his hand with virtually no sound. "Hoi! The saints are with us, Rabbit: the boards are full of dry rot," he grinned. A few seconds later, he had freed the door. "Aw, there's no handle or door knob," he groaned in despair. "We can't open it."

"Wait," exclaimed Rabbit, rooting around on the floor. "Here's the spindle, but there's no way to turn it in the door lock."

"Let's see," Peter said, extending his hand to take it. "Ah, all we need is this nail to go through this hole in the spindle like so and we insert it like this. Now, give me the glow-stick." He placed it securely in a pocket inside his jacket. "There's light enough out there and we do not want to leave it behind as a clue."

"I would *not* have dropped it!" Rabbit sniffed.

They started a little as the door swung easily inward to reveal a narrow table set against the door frame with lit candles set upon candle-sticks at each end. A faint haze of smoke hung in the air but there was no sign of any Sister as occasional booms and rumbles from the exploding fuel drums shook faint puffs of dust from the arched ceilings above them. To their immediate left, the wide hallway ended at an ornate arched portal into the kitchen.

They crawled under the table and entered the kitchen warily, their weapons at the ready. In the waning daylight from the dozen leaded windows set high in the walls and the ruddy glow from the ranges and oven fires, they saw on the tables closest to them something they'd never thought they would see in this world again: mounds of freshly baked bread and pats of butter.

There were also boxes of candles and matches so that they could not believe their luck: "Don't take too many," Peter cautioned, shoving loaves and butter pats onto a tablecloth. "They might get suspicious and come looking for us."

"We need to check the other tables and pantries for some cheese or smoked meat first," Rabbit decided. "We can't live on bread." She went around another kitchen table then screeched in horror. Peter was by her side in a flash with a knife at the ready.

"Oh, oh, I see," he whispered in horror, struggling not to heave and puke. There on the floor were three Sisters with their throats slashed; their bodies bearing countless puncture wounds and their habits drenched crimson with their blood.

"Saints save us, look at their faces!" Rabbit whimpered, clinging to Peter. "The poor souls have been *butchered*."

Peter shook himself free of her. "No, Rabbit! Do *not* pity them for they serve the Order! We must take this food and get back to the others now or we'll end up like them."

He added cheese and dried meat onto the tablecloth along with fourteen candles and a box of matches then drew all four corners together as well as he could, hissing with pain as his claw was now virtually useless. He joined Rabbit who was standing transfixed with her mouth open in abject fear. She was quaking like her namesake but, after years of relentless training, she had both her razor-sharp axes at the ready.

"Oh, what now?" he demanded irritably then a cold thrill ran through him as, in a blur of motion, he dropped his burden and whipped out his longest knife.

Spear in hand and silhouetted by the candles burning in the hallway was the unmistakable shape of a Tally-man.

~~~~

Stone Ghosts

Muted rumbles of thunder could be heard even in the lowest level of Milverburg. In the dim emergency lighting that the Light-Father had restored to the docks and railway stations, Amos could not take his eyes off the Phoenix; the magnificent Cambrensis Class Locomotive that had taken them from their Keep in Crawcester to the Great Abbey and from there to Milverburg. Even though it had stood untended in a railway shed in Crawcester for six years, the brass fittings still gleamed as new in the dim blue light apart from bullet marks on the cabin roof from sniper-fire as they'd barrelled though Beorminghas, the City of Towers. The interiors of the blood-stained carriages were another matter: the two hundred Ferals they'd taken to the Great Abbey had not travelled well.

The forty Ferals who'd survived the Great Abbey played and swarmed atop the carriages and the engine cab of the Phoenix but he could see they were on edge: suddenly standing stock-still for moments at a time, peering into the vast and endless shadows about them like meerkat sentries on a Kalahari mound.

He had given up arguing with Mother Ivy about why he was not allowed to help the Light-Father rescue his sister after she'd glared at him and put a finger to her lips. He couldn't utter a single sound until he was a hundred yards away at the colonnaded entrance of the Western Merchant Dock where the merchant ship that the Light-Father had serviced was waiting to take them away.

He could hear the countless other vessels fretting gently at the quaysides as the dock-gates to the Great Harbour were open even though water lapped over the wharves during high spring tides. It worried him: the open gates meant they could escape but the Order could also slip into the lower levels while they were asleep in the Tower of the Sun. The Ferals kept constant watch on the estuary and the viaducts but he feared this was not enough.

He also knew it would take too long to fire up the faithful Phoenix in an emergency even if anyone could stomach riding in the carriages so the gaudy merchant boat was their only chance of escape but he would miss riding on the train: the wonder of that epic journey would never fade despite the visceral horrors he'd witnessed at the Great Abbey.

He stiffened as *that* vile memory resurfaced: the one where the Tally-man was pressing a pillow down on the face of his little sister. Grasping the shaft of his sledgehammer tightly he vividly relived bludgeoning the Tally-man to a bloody pulp and splattering his little sister with blood as he did so. He remembered the look on Fria's pale determined face as she stabbed and stabbed the Tally-man. He shuddered: what was it the Light-Father had called it? *Post-traumatic stress* - that was it: a lifetime of cold sweats and night terrors to look forward to. O Hallelujah.

"I saved her, God! What else could I have done?" he growled, shaking his fists at the shadow-shrouded masonry above him. "I still have too few years to understand why you let this happen to us, to *everyone*," he raged. "But by Saint Peter's bones, I vow that I will get stronger to protect my sister and prove to the Light-Father that I'm not some helpless, quivering *maiden*."

"Do you want to see how helpless *this* quivering maiden is?" said an ice-cold voice behind him.

He turned to see Fria glaring at him with both the long knives in her hands pointed at him. "You're no helpless maiden," he said carefully, taking a step away from her knife-tips. "You carry three sharp blades strapped to your back, three to your thighs and you tread as silently as Bas does." The corner of his mouth lifted in a rare half-smile. "And you can fight."

Her green eyes narrowed dangerously. "Don't coddle me with weasel-words, Amos. I know you were reliving how we killed that Tally-man again but I keep telling you: it's *pointless*. I will not dwell on that or how badly you treated us before Mother Moss saved us because if I did, I would stab *you*."

He let his shoulders slump and turned away from her to stare at the docks that were fleetingly floodlit by lightning flashes through the dock-gates, sending complex flaring shadows amongst the boats and cranes. "I knew not of your anaemia and I was without heart and hope until the Light-Father's magic began to heal me. You often dream of that hospital where your friend, Bethwin, became a Feral and you walked upon rats and corpses to find food..." he choked down a sob of self-pity. "Mother Mary, we're only children yet here we stand in the bowels of a monstrous city, hunted by monsters and haunted by the memories of monsters!"

Fria remained silent as he dabbed at his treacherous tears and studied the vast vaulted spaces of the West Central Core but the gloom could not hide the massive columns supporting the colossal weight of the nine levels above. Three railway lines crossed the viaducts with each passing through a station before entering the Core and, around the titanic central column decorated with carvings of ash trees and dryads, they were inter-connected to allow through-trains to shuttle between Port Kent, Beorminghas and Brigstowe. When the Phoenix had steamed through here in such utter darkness, she was convinced that they were in some endless tunnel of Hell but, miraculously, the points were set so as to send them onto the Port Kent line and the Great Abbey.

She shuddered as she recalled how the few surviving lamps on the Phoenix had faintly illuminated grinning, desiccated corpses upon the seating of the station platforms. She could not imagine why they'd crawled there in their last moments but she was grateful that the Ferals had cast them all into the Milverbore. The Light-Father had since shown her how freight trains were diverted onto the dock sidings to swap cargoes with brightly-painted merchant ships so now she would give her eye-teeth to have seen the hustle and bustle of this world trade centre at its peak.

Amos pointed at the oppressive bulk of the central column, seeking a diversion from their dark thoughts: "That one is called Askr Yggdrasil," he told her. "The Ash Tree of Life."

Fria sheathed her long, ultra-sharp knives slowly for even in the dim light she could see his ragged facial scar, inflicted six years ago by a brutal and sadistic Father, and it still made her blood run cold. "*Yggdrasil shivers, the mighty ash; the old tree groans and the giant slips free*," she murmured. "*From the lake beneath, the Fates unchained: Urd, Verdandi, Skuld; the maidens three.*"

"I've never heard those rhymes before."

"If you'd spent more time with Mother Moss instead of sulking you would have learnt much at her feet. Songs of Viking, Saxon, Celt and Cymrig she sang to us and such sagas! Oh, I miss her..."

"She would not wish you to shed tears, Fria," he said kindly, wiping at his own eyes with the back of his hand. "She despaired of me. She kept telling me to wait for this magical Light-Father and so for five long years I waited not really believing he was real..."

Fria saw him place a hand to the scar as he often did when he was reliving all the dark times they'd lived through. As a result of the horrors they had witnessed, he'd almost lost himself in an alter-ego and had refused to answer to his true name until, in a blinding flash, the Light-Father had stepped into their world and given them hope and made him Amos once more.

96

She'd followed Harold down to the docks a week ago to watch him work on a fishing boat. He explained to her as he worked that he needed to ensure every dock had a boat that they could use to escape and this was only the third. Finally, she remembered how he'd wiped his hands with an oily rag after coaxing the powerful engines back to life and waited patiently while she bombarded him with chatter and endless questions about his magic.

"There's no magic, Fria, just the empathy I've learnt from my wife and being with you Scatterlings."

"Yes, but why did Amos call himself Scar?"

He ran his hand through his thinning hair and replaced his cap while trying to figure out how to explain something this abstract to a traumatized and heavily-armed child. "Do you know how the human conscious and sub-conscious works?"

She wrinkled up her nose in concentration, transforming her from warrior to keen elementary student and for one precious moment he savoured that. "Um, Mother Moss told me the brain has a conscious part that looks after your mind so that you can think and make the body do things like fight and eat. Yes?"

"Not bad," he told her. "So what does the other part do?"

"All the stuff you don't want to think about like breathing, keeping your heart beating, digesting food and balancing?"

"Excellent!" he exclaimed, making her beam with pleasure. "But the subconscious is more complicated than that. It can create alternative personalities to try and protect the conscious mind when that person has been overwhelmed by trauma and horror."

"Like a kettle boiling over, the subconscious lets the memories flow away in separate channels down its side."

She recalled the look of absolute astonishment on his face before he laughed out loud. "I keep forgetting Exodus enhanced the whole package: brains as well as brawn! Anyway, like your kettle, the conscious mind loses its identity when this happens."

"Amos used to say that he deserved his injury for failing to save his family then Surl went mute so she wouldn't have to call him Scar. Even Peter started calling himself Claw for a while."

"I know. Amos has regained his true self but he still has a lot of healing to do as do you, Fria of the Long Knives."

She understood what he was getting at and drew her long blades to study them and knew that her soul-name; her Scatterling-name was now bound to her weapons as they were to her.

As they slowly ascended the Western Circumference Stairway by torchlight, he described the many scientific wonders of this strange, alternate reality of Great Britain and why he no longer had any regrets about being dragged into her world to find a new purpose in life. He even told her that he now loved her as much as the infant daughter he'd lost so tragically! She'd yearned to hear so much more but he'd repeatedly withdrawn to the Tower of Grieving or worked in the docks so she could not question the silent hug he'd given her nor the tears in his eyes... oh, *Father*!

She stood next to Amos who held his nose: "Phaw! What have you been doing, Fria? You smell like a field of flowers!"

"Huh! Nightshade and Fern decided that I should smell of something other than kack, dirt and rotting leather. You should try it some time, *peasant*!"

"Perfumery?" he teased. "Gaia's most fearsome warrior: Fria Rafson of the Long Knives reeking of lavender and of roses? I fear the readers of our great saga would not believe this! They would flip over the page in disgust and fan their faces!"

"Ach! You're still a bull-pat, Amos Crawin, and you smell like one," Fria huffed. "I have but thirteen years yet I'm a girl for all my martial skills and fast approaching birthing age."

Amos caught the tone in her voice and for the second time in six years he did something intentionally kind for her and in a gentler tone, he said: "Mother Nightshade whispered this to me but I had noticed this on my own, Fria. Please do not tell the others I am saying this otherwise they will think I've gone addled in the head but when you embraced me and called me *brother* after all I had done to you and Surl, my heart was forever lost: you are my *dúnelfena*; you will always be more than a sister to me."

Fria's elven features went crimson with shock then she flung her arms around his neck. Her scent completely overwhelmed his senses so he could no nothing but embrace her fiercely.

"Forgive me," he whispered.

Her eyes were closed, her face upturned and he felt faint stirrings of arousal; it was new and exciting and the blood began to pound in his veins. He was about to kiss her when he saw forty Ferals grinning expectantly atop the Phoenix and its carriages. With all the leering and nudging, he needed no translation.

He ignored them and only slowly disengaged from her arms at the sight of Kai smiling and Ivy waving at them in approval. "Let us wait by the boat," he urged, his face reddening. "Too many prying eyes are watching."

"Let them watch!" Fria declared. "I care not what they think of us." Nevertheless, she followed him into the gloom of the dockside. The spring high tide was receding and the lowest of the wharves were above water, glistening in the feeble emergency lighting. Here, the thunder was louder and they could see gentle waves lapping in from the Great Harbour that protected the gates and entrances to all the southern and western docks.

They stood by the merchant boat that slowly chivvied at its moorings. Railway sidings ran alongside the north western edge of the dock and they could see the hulking shapes of the dockside cranes that had once transferred the cargoes of the merchant ships directly to and from the railway wagons. The lighting in the dock was slightly less than in the Core and emboldened, they embraced each other tightly before Fria took the initiative and kissed him full on the lips. The pounding of his blood became a tsunami and he passionately returned his first real kiss.

Their mutual bliss lasted but ten seconds as there was a scraping noise on the vessel and they pulled apart, weapons instantly at the ready as they crouched in defensive stances. "Beware, thieves and foes, for we are armed! Reveal yourselves!" Fria cried out. "We are the Scatterlings of Crawcester and we fear *nothing*! We've slain countless Brothers and Tally-men!"

"We fear the light!" said a young female voice from behind the door of the wheelhouse. "For light brings the Order and Death upon us. You'll bring the Brothers here! We'll not reveal ourselves but we'll kill you if you stay any longer in our city."

"Milverburg is *ours*," another voice added, again a young female with an odd accent: "We are *déathscufan*. We know you both well, Fria Rafson and Amos Crawin: we do not fear you; we will kill you because you will bring the butchers here."

"You call yourself death-walkers?" Fria said contemptuously. "Pah! Shadow-mice are what you are." She regretted it instantly as an arrow shot past her right ear, the fletching nicking the edge and drawing blood. Without hesitation or thought, they both dropped to their bellies to present smaller targets. "We are not your enemies!" she shouted angrily. "We follow the Light-Father and we have Wiccans with us! We attacked the Great Abbey and killed many Tally-men and Fathers and Brothers!"

"But you did not kill them *all*," the first voice said angrily. "The Angels still fly and will come for you. They'll come for *us*. We chased them out of Milverburg and we could have lived here in peace for ever and ever but now, because of you, they will come again and destroy Milverburg with their flying machines and the Brothers and their Tally-men will hunt us!"

"How many of you are there?" Amos demanded as Fria dabbed at the nick to her ear and ground her teeth in frustration.

"We are *déathscufan*. We are many."

"No you're not. Our Ferals knew you were watching us as their senses are keen. They named you stone-ghosts and they told us of your whisperings in the air shafts."

"Liar! We are the ghosts that bring death. Your beast-children have sharp eyes and ears but they are as dull as clay."

"You are but two girls," Amos retorted. "They said they only heard two female voices but we didn't believe them at first."

Fria frowned. "If you want nothing to do with us, what are you doing on our boat?"

"The Beomodor is *our* boat!" the second voice cried out. "My father and her father owned it and we sailed the seven seas with our families and our cargo. We won't let you take her!"

Amos and Fria turned to see Ivy and a few curious Ferals approaching them. "Stay back!" Amos warned. "They fired an arrow at us. They are Scatterlings like us!"

"Ah, yes, the Ferals know of them," Ivy replied, striding forward. "They wanted to hunt them down but we denied them that dangerous pleasure. Come forth, children, for we mean you no harm! You have my word as a Mother."

"Wiccans are *evil*. Our friend from the Arnearsen clan was taken away by Wiccans like you and she came home in a coffin; her face as white as snow!"

"I have an arrow aimed at your heart, witch," the first voice said dangerously. "Go away! We are *déathscufan*."

Ivy threw her arms wide as she stood above Fria and Amos. "Then kill me, child. I care not what you call yourselves but you are *not* murderers. If you had meant to kill me you would have fired upon me from the shadows when you've been spying upon us these last three weeks. You could easily have killed Fria had you wanted to. Come forth into the light where we may gaze upon such fearsome creatures. We mean you no harm."

There was an expectant hush where even the nudging and jostling of the boats and the lapping of the water seemed to cease. Then came the whip of two arrows from the shadows on the boat and Ivy let her Crescent Moon staff fall to snatch both of them out of the air; one in each hand. The arrow tips were poised mere centimetres from her silver pendant of three moons; waxing, full and waning. Fria and Amos watched open-mouthed as she began to strain, her knuckles whitening and perspiration beading her brow, as if the arrows were somehow possessed and seeking to bury themselves deep within her chest.

After what seemed an eternity, she relaxed and let the arrows fall before retrieving her staff from the flagstones. "It's safe to stand, children," she said thoughtfully. "They're gone from the vessel. How? I know not but I can sense them no longer."

Fria got to her feet put a hand to her injured ear and she could see the traces of blood even in the dim light. "We'll have to kill them if they *ever* do that again," she seethed, her eyes glinting dangerously as she drew her knives. "They could've killed us."

"But they did not, dear heart," Ivy smiled, placing a hand to Fria's ear. There was a short stab of pain and Amos drew close to study the injury.

"The bleeding has stopped!" he exclaimed in awe then he turned to Ivy who was sill peering into the shadows on the boat. "Those arrows were alive with magic, were they not?"

"Good. You're beginning to develop an open mind," she replied absently. "Yes, the craft is at work in those two! They're untrained so I can't tell whether they'll be useful or a threat to us yet they've survived in this dangerous place for six years without parent or guidance. It would be better if I dealt with them." She turned to stare candidly at them both. "You must *not* seek them out for I fear you'll be no match for their craft or their archery."

"We'll see about *that*!" Fria snarled, leaping aboard the boat to search the wheel-house and cabins. Ivy waited patiently as Amos fidgeted anxiously, ashamed that he could not bring himself to follow Fria. A few minutes later, she rejoined them brandishing a parchment with a crude drawing of two girls holding hands: one with short black hair and one with short fair hair. They both had bows and were surrounded by corpses full of arrows.

Ivy took the drawing and studied the Runic letters scrawled beneath. "At least we now know their names," she smiled. "I must tell my sisters of this discovery. It seems we may not be the last Wiccans left alive in Gaia after all."

"But they tried to kill you!" Amos protested. "Why should we not hunt them down and kill them for that? We cannot let enemies wander about unchallenged in Milverburg!"

A fell light shone in Ivy's eyes as she gazed down upon the scarred youth. "The whole world has been trying to kill them just as the Order has tried to kill you and your sister. They are *not* your enemies; do not be too quick to judge. Did *you* not try to kill Shield when you first encountered her in Crawcester?"

Amos pursed his lips and guiltily lowered his eyes for Ivy was both terrifying and beautiful with the pearls adorning her long brown braids gleaming in the feeble lighting. "The Light Father has healed some of my pain and I suppose he could work his magic on them," he conceded grudgingly. "Like us, they have but few years and have no doubt seen far too much for ones so young."

Ivy bent forward to kiss him upon the brow as lightning once more illuminated the entrance to the docks. "Gaia bless you, Scatterling, you have come so far in such a short time but I fear that you will yet test the patience of the Light-Father."

A deep booming rumble of thunder silenced them for a moment as it seemed to shake the very flagstones beneath their feet. Ivy cocked her head as if listening to distant voices. She pocketed the drawing and placed an arm about Fria's shoulders. "Come, children; let us return to the others. This will be a night full of sadness and storms and in such darkness tales unfold into shields against those fell creatures at the edges of our dreams."

Amos looked over his shoulder at the Beomodor as if expecting a hail of arrows at any moment. "And now we've got two stone ghosts to add to those tales," he said nervously.

~~~~~

102

From Pillar to Post

Nightshade fell silent as a great swathe of hail clattered upon the flagstones. Mouse looked up at the enigmatic Wiccan, who was lost in thought, her red irises unfocussed as long-buried memories resurfaced and tears mingled with the rain upon her face. Mouse wrapped her arms around her waist and hugged her, driven by such a deep, natural empathy that Nightshade eventually smiled.

"Bordan and Kendra sound like wonderful parents," Mouse said. "I can't recall my parents' faces as I had so few years but I do remember being loved. I still remember the sun in our garden, music and marquees full of roast chicken and *cake*..."

Nightshade embraced her, set her mouse-ears straight and placed a hand upon her cheek. "Dear heart, I too remember mine from the perspective of a child: I was small and they were *giants* bending down to whisk me up into the sky and swing me round and round and round while I laughed like a jester and then they would put me down and I would be so dizzy!"

"Me too," Mouse smiled wistfully. "So what happened next? Did the Order and those constables catch you?"

"Shh!" Nightshade commanded, putting a finger to Mouse's lips. "I'm far-speaking! Ah, Ivy has just met our two stone ghosts and ah hah! Amos has declared his love for Fria." Another broad smile graced her perfect features. "Praise the Triple Goddess! Cupid's arrows still fly true in this ruined world of ours."

"Pfft!" Mouse huffed. "You would have to be as dull as ditch water not to see them blush whenever they're close to each other. What *does* she see in a lizard like him? All he used to think about was his scar and killing Tally-men. He was *so* cruel to her and Surl when we lived in that shop in Crawcester."

"Surl sees past his scar and forgives him for how he behaved – this is the Light-Father's magic at work, Mouse. This Harold Porter is truly a most remarkable man."

"*Please* tell me the rest of your story," Mouse begged. "You can't end it with you trapped in the house!"

"Well, as I said, my parents had always expected the worst and so they were well prepared that day..."

~~~~

103

"Kendra! You *have* to let go of the wall and drop down into the lane. I can hear them knocking at the front door!"

"I can't, Bordan! It's too far down. I'll break my ankle!" she whimpered, clinging desperately to the capstones.

Bordan silently cursed his decision to brick up the lane access door some months ago after some youths had crept into their garden to throw bricks through Ellete's bedroom window. He climbed up onto the garden water-butt and straddled the eight-foot high stone wall then he firmly prised her fingers free and lowered her gently down, wrenching his back in the process. It was a mere three feet below her flailing heels but to his terrified and disoriented wife, it was an abyss.

The two suitcases were perched on wooden crates next to the water butt so he grabbed them and dropped them down to his wife almost knocking her to the tarmac. He jumped down off the water butt to sweep Ellete up in one strong arm and, hissing with pain from his protesting back muscles, he scrambled back up the wall and passed her down into Kendra's waiting embrace.

Ellete's eyes were saucer-wide with fear but she uttered nothing more than a muffled 'eek!' into her mother's bosom.

Bordan rolled over the capstones on his stomach and dropped down into the lane, jarring his back again. "Ach! Listen!" he hissed through clenched teeth. "They're smashing through the barricade. We have *got* to get to my car in Silversmith Road. Down this side alley, quickly now, before they send men round to cut us off. The Fates favour us today: they expected us to wait in the house like lambs for the slaughter!"

He grabbed the suitcases and with Kendra carrying Ellete, they emerged from the gloom of the side-alley, which was cluttered and overgrown, into the bright sunlight of Silversmith Street. Bordan allowed himself a split-second of self-congratulation for always parking his car here and walking around to their front door: it was ten minutes every day that was now very well spent indeed.

The street itself was empty of folk as most of its inhabitants were at work or in school and only the traditional gargoyles and carvings that ornamented the houses frowned down upon them. Kendra put Ellete into the back seat and strapped her in as Bordan loaded the suitcases into the trunk. She was about to climb into the passenger seat when she stopped to gaze around her beloved neighbourhood, burning it into her memory.

"Hark at the birds singing," she said, fighting back tears. "Everything is so peaceful here but now I'll never see my friends again. Oh, Bordan, what are we going to do?"

"What we've always planned to do," he said a little sharply. "We're going to survive and protect our daughter. Now, for the love of all the holy saints, get into the car!"

"Patience," she retorted angrily. "Do not play the *déofolscín* with me, husband! We've lost *everything.*"

"But not our lives, Kendra," he said, strapping himself in. "Where beats a human heart, there beat the wings of hope."

"Quoting song lyrics doesn't help," she snapped, slamming the car door. "We can't go to our families as we'll put them in danger from the Order and the police. You know what the Government *really* thinks about the craft!"

"History shames them and stays their hand these days," Bordan grunted sarcastically as he gunned the engine into life. "They tolerate the Wiccans even though the Order whispers acid into the ears of politicians who know full well that burning women alive at the stake is no longer acceptable in our 'enlightened' age." He turned to look at their daughter who was cowering at the sharp edges to their voices. "I'm sorry if this is frightening you, Ellete, but we're going on an adventure."

"But you keep shouting at each other!" she grizzled.

"I know we are, dear heart, but we're scared too. If we weren't a little bit scared then it wouldn't be an adventure now would it? Listen, I have something for you I bought yesterday. It's in that bag next to you. You can open it while I drive the car."

As the car pulled away from the kerb, Ellete pulled out a stuffed toy. "It's a Honey Bear!" she squeaked happily, squeezing it. "Thanks, Da! I *love* Honey Bears!"

"Well, you wanted one last Christmastide but I couldn't find one in the shops. You'll need something like him to cuddle as we have a long trip ahead of us." He turned to Kendra, who was cradling her face in her hands and weeping silently from shock and fear, and placed a hand on her shoulder: "Look, you have to find the strength to endure for Ellete's sake. We have no choice: we cannot give her to the Wiccans and magically return to our jobs and our friends as if nothing had happened."

"I'll miss Brigstowe," she said miserably. "All our family and friends live here. Our parents and grandparents lived here. Where can we go? The police or the Order or the Architects will find us: they're powerful and their eyes and ears are *everywhere*."

A faint smile touched Bordan's lips. "Oh, you wound me so, dear heart. I work for the Government, remember? I know *exactly* how the police and the intelligence services operate and what legal constraints are placed upon the Order."

"What do you mean?" Kendra asked suspiciously.

"Well, for one: do you think the registration plates on this car match my real name and address?"

"How can it be otherwise? It's the law!"

"No, it's registered to a fictional teacher in Brigstowe. Stephen Henwin forged the registration documents for me."

Kendra exhaled noisily. "And no doubt your artist friend, Dunstan, has painted us new identity papers? What about our social registration and tax documentation?"

"Check the glove compartment."

Kendra did so and found two sets of papers plus a false birth certificate for Ellete. Her jaw dropped. "Blessed Mary, I never suspected you were *this* prepared!" she gasped. "You could've picked a better name for me than Cassandra Geowine!"

"We even have our own bank account but there is only enough in there for two months at best and yes, I didn't transfer any money from our account; I set it up with cash. They've only begun to computerise the bank systems so it'll be hard to trace us."

"You told me you were demoted last year!" she said angrily. "So *that's* where all the money has been going while we were going short! You could've told me."

"I wanted to, Kendra, believe me, but I couldn't risk you letting it slip to your friends over coffees and card games," he sighed resignedly. "I hope you can forgive me." He glanced over his shoulder at Ellete who was playing contentedly with her Honey Bear. "We'll have to dye her hair but I don't know what we can do about her eyes and that snow-white skin of hers."

"Dark glasses," Kendra suggested. "And make-up. She has only six years but she's so clever that I'm sure she'll be fine. We can say her eyes were injured by an accident or an illness and that she cannot bear bright lights. We must be careful: superstitions and rumours about albinos are rife in the villages."

He nodded. "I know but the make-up should work. Ah, look, we're in the countryside already. I feel much better putting the city behind us," he smiled with relief. He checked the rear mirror again but the road behind them was eerily empty of traffic.

"Will we take one of the Arthburg ferries?"

He sucked at tooth, deep in thought. "No," he said eventually. "The police and the Order watch all the estuary ports and the coast police there are extremely vigilant – even those papers will not fool them for long. We'll take the road to Cairhold then get onto the Bede Road, swing north through Rackgate, head west through Beorminghas and on to Crawcester. They'll not expect us to hide in plain sight in one of the Middle Cities."

"It's a pity we can't hide in Anseld or Edelingaeg or even in Fellholm. They're so isolated we'd be safe there."

"When our money runs out, we can't eat dirt no matter how safe we are." Bordan said patiently. "Besides, strange and desperate folk dwell on those islands and who knows what they would do to Ellete. My colleagues reckon that centuries of in-breeding have left them eternally wary of 'in-comers' and 'mainlanders' as they call us. We might try Epstall or some of the other quieter coastal villages if Crawcester doesn't work out."

"Da, you and Ma need to be careful," Ellete said suddenly, her eyes closed. "Something bad is waiting for us. I can *feel* it."

"Kack!" Bordan exclaimed. "A road block: police *and* a half-track from the Order. They're stopping everybody."

"The Order?" Kendra exclaimed in horror. "Surely, they can't have had the time to organise roadblocks to stop us?"

"Impossible but I've never heard of the Order and police forces collaborating like this before." He pulled the car in behind a line of thirty or so vehicles and stopped, his knuckles whitening on the steering wheel. "We still have time, Kendra. Pile her hair up under a hat and put on that make-up. Don't hesitate, just do it! Ellete?" he said over his shoulder. "Ma is going to give you a tan and we're going to pretend that you're a little girl called Freda Geowine. Ma will be Cassandra Geowine and I'll be Geoffrey Geowine. Do you understand? It's important."

"Yes, Da," Ellete nodded excitedly. "Are we going to be like actors in a play?"

"Clever girl, that's right," Kendra approved, climbing into the back seat. She quickly stuffed the little girl's snow-white hair under a bobble-hat and applied hints of make-up to bring a touch of colour to her cheeks. "Now, when the police talk to us, pretend to be asleep. Do *not* open your eyes or they will see your red irises. Keep them shut whatever happens. Promise?"

"Yes, Ma," she smiled and immediately pretended to be asleep even to the point of faking a little snoring.

"She's adorable!" Bordan laughed despite the seriousness of their situation. He re-started the engine and rolled the car forward twenty yards. "There are dozens of police checking drivers so the line is moving quickly. Get ready: here they come."

A black-uniformed officer approached the car as Kendra quickly hid her make-up bag. "Papers, please," he said curtly, holding out a large gloved hand.

Bordan complied and as the bored officer checked the forged documents he tried to strike up a conversation: "It's too warm to be out in this sun, officer. Are you looking for terrorists?"

"As you'll no doubt have heard from the newscasts, sir," the officer replied patiently. "There have been six unsolved robberies and murders in Arthburg and one in Milverburg. Some of the murders were gruesome to say the least; pretty ritualistic in fact so we think a Heofland gang is responsible."

"I'm sorry to hear this," Bordan said, perplexed. "Why would the Order be interested in a few cut-throats from Heofland?"

The officer relaxed and handed the papers back. "Heofland is a dangerous place and God alone knows what goes on in those Black Valleys so the Brothers claim they have an urgent need to study their genes for mutations and resistance to diseases."

"I see," Bordan said, trying to calm his jangled nerves. "We're going to Beorminghas to see family and friends so I hope you catch them. Do you know if that city is free of these villains?"

"Only the local scoundrels and the Aldermen to worry about there, sir," the officer smiled. "Worry not for we in the Southern Cities Police Force will catch these brigands before the day is out. This Father from the Order wishes to speak with you," he shrugged. "As you know, the Government has granted them medical priority over all things *genetic* in Britannia."

He paused to look into the back seat and grinned approvingly. "At least your little one is a blessing: nothing worse than a whining brat on a long car journey!"

He went back towards the cordon but a Father, dressed in the shortened field robes and grey hooded scapular of the Order, strode forward with clipboard in hand and stopped him. After a brief conversation, the Father came up to the car and bent down to gaze past Bordan at the sleeping Ellete. "What a pretty child," he murmured with evident disinterest. "I'm sorry to burden you and your loved ones, Mister Geowine, but we are surveying the current racial and medical characteristics of the Southern Cities. I wonder if I could take some family details of you and your wife."

"Certainly, Father," Bordan said, gazing up into the impassive face of the cleric and noting the mirthless eyes, thin lips, the long, sharp nose and receding hairline. "My family is grateful for the medical services the Order bestows upon us and we are more than happy to repay that blessing but you have me at a disadvantage: do you have a name, Father?"

The Father stroked his short black goatee beard and peered over his prince-nez glasses into Bordan's eyes for several eternity-stretching seconds. "Please forgive my lack of manners, Mister Geowine," he said formally with a brief bow. "You may call me Schimrian, Father Schimrian, and may it please you to know that I am forever at your service."

Beginnings

Heavy hailstones threatened to smash the tiles for a few seconds then thunderclaps salvoes made conversation impossible. Finally, it subsided and the storm paused as if it were a living thing drawing breath for a fresh assault upon the senses. Surl had fallen asleep upon Harold's chest with a contented smile upon her face and did not stir at all during the cacophony. He was conscious of their damp clothes and felt claustrophobic and somewhat pinned down as she was a dead weight in her slumber.

Fern placed a hand upon her head and concentrated. "Diana has blessed her with a deep and dreamless sleep," she said. "She's utterly spent, the poor child. She's hardly slept for three weeks but she feels safe and loved in your arms, dear heart, as do I," she added suggestively making him blush. Peter was looking at him quizzically so he coughed to hide his embarrassment.

"So you and Rabbit were trapped in the kitchen by the Tally-man," he prompted. "Well? Did you have to fight him?"

~~~~~

"Why is he not attacking us?" Rabbit demanded in an urgent whisper as the Tally-man stood motionless in front of them, blocking their way into the hallway. His hood was pulled back and they could see the dull glint of the metallic Guides driven into his bald skull. He raised a hand to touch the one embedded into his right temple as if listening to a radio message then took a sudden long and rasping breath that startled them.

Peter looked over his shoulder at the great oak door on the far side of the kitchen. It was their only means of escape but he feared it would lead them out into the Great Abbey grounds and certain death. His heart was fluttering with fear but the Tally-man was making no move to attack them or even point his spear at them.

"Peter!" Rabbit whispered. "He can't see us!"

The Tally-man's head swivelled from side to side as he scanned the kitchen and then to their immense surprise he purposefully strode between them as if they were completely invisible and carefully laid his spear on the nearest table, resting a hand on it for a moment as if trying to recall some pleasant memory.

"Hoi, monster!" she cried. "What are you doing?"

110

The Tally-man turned to face her and a chill ran down her spine as those soulless eyes regarded her for a full ten seconds as if she was some insect unworthy of the energy to swat. He brushed past her to retrieve a large wooden tray and began stacking bread, butter and cheeses onto it. Too fascinated to bolt down the hallway, the children watched him as he calmly went about the kitchen. He paused to stare impassively down at the mutilated corpses of the Sisters for a moment then he simply stepped over them again and again as he got on with his task.

"Ah, now I understand," Peter said brightly, kneeling to pick up their scattered provisions and bundling them back into the tablecloth. "He's back under the control of the Brothers but he's not been programmed to search for us or to deal with the Sisters; he's just been instructed to collect food for them!"

Intrigued, Rabbit stood in front of the Tally-man who simply stepped around her to collect another loaf of bread. She even waved her hand in front of his face only to have it gently brushed aside as if it was an annoying fly. "Shall I slice through his wires?" she suggested, readying her axes and circling behind him.

"No!" Peter said quickly. "Think about it: they sent him here to get food so if he fails to return and they find his wires cut, they will know that someone has been in this building and start looking for us. Leave him be: let's get this food back to our new Keep."

"Wait," Rabbit said as the Tally-man lumbered out of the kitchen, bearing his overloaded tray. "We need that." She went to a shelf and took down a medical kit.

"Ah, well spotted, Rabbit." Peter sighed with relief but he also cursed himself for not thinking of it first. "Even the slightest pressure on my stump is making me feel sick but we need water as well. I can manage this; you fill those two large jugs under the tap. Can you reach?"

"Just about," Rabbit puffed as the jugs were almost a third of her size yet she managed to fill them at the sink. "Phaw! They're heavy but I think I can carry them. If any Sisters have survived this madness, I pray they don't notice they're missing."

"Mother Moss said that Sisters were bred by the Order to be as brainless as the Tally-men so I think we should be safe."

Rabbit struggled heroically with the jugs of water and they were soon back in the cellar after Peter had checked that the door into the hallway was secure and braced with several stout pieces of wood.

He was surprised to see in the pale light of the glow-sticks that Surl and Pup had found a musty old broom and had swept the place free of debris, cobwebs and rodent droppings. He pinched his nose: the cellar still stank of kack and sewage because of the gaps in the rotten access door. They'd also found bales of linen in the store-room that had been wrapped in plastic and had fashioned four crude beds on the wide wooden benches.

"We met a Tally-man, Surl," Rabbit began breathlessly. "But he never even looked at us!" She paused and looked crestfallen: "Ah, but then you already know through your visions."

Surl smiled wryly, tapping her temple. "No, I can't see anything right now. You'll have to tell me what happened. I'm so glad that we have all this food and water: I was so worried!"

Rabbit launched into a breathless account of how she found the bodies of the Sisters and their encounter with the Tally-man.

"At least we know we need not be afraid of Tally-men unless they're instructed to come after us or they go berserk again," Surl said thoughtfully, looking at Peter who nodded. "Pup, be patient!" she chided as the youngster rummaged through the bundle, dropping a wheel of cheese onto the flagstones. "Well, Peter? Did you remember to get some crockery?"

He almost rose to the bait but laughed instead: "I'm sorry, your highness," he said with a mocking bow. "But we do appear to be short of cutlery too but in the storeroom there were boxes that may contain plates and other things we might find useful. Look; you missed those candle-holders on the shelf over there! Let's risk lighting some of the candles - these glow-sticks are almost done and I'm tired of the dark. Ugh! Listen to the rats in the stonework: I hope they keep out of the cellar when we're sleeping."

"We need to find some more glow-sticks or electric torches," Surl suggested as she watched Pup tearing bread and cheese apart with his teeth. "I think he's hungry," she laughed then her own stomach made a loud noise. "Let's at least try and slice and butter the bread and cheese," she said, mimicking Mother Moss. "We must behave in a civilised way even if there is no civilisation left... I... " she trailed away, suppressing a sudden treacherous sob.

"I miss her too," Peter sympathised, placing his hand on her shoulder. "I think you're right: she *is* watching over us somehow."

Surl shook herself free of her misery to light three candles and savour their warm and comforting light. "First things first," she said briskly as shadows danced around the cellar walls and Pup nearly choked until Rabbit enthusiastically slapped him on the back. "Let's have a look at that stump of yours."

~~~~~

Kai started as a hand was placed on his left shoulder. "Ah! Mother Ivy! I didn't see you there. How are Amos and Fria?"

"Fria had her ear nicked by our stone ghosts and her pride was sore wounded but she'll live and she and Amos have a lot to think about. We need to find these two girls before they attack us in earnest as they show signs of the craft. I'm not accustomed to having arrows fired at me like that."

"So they could be Daughters? I suppose this must be so as they've survived for six years in this stupid mausoleum. We hear them whispering through the air-shafts in the stables. I think they were doing it to drive the Ferals wild. It takes me a long time to settle them down after they do that as they thought that they were real ghosts in the beginning."

"What exactly do you mean by 'stables'?"

"Our quarters at the base of the Tower of the Sun."

Ivy frowned at him. "Our Ferals are *not* animals, Kai," she said dangerously. "They are naught but human children subjected to cruel disfigurements. They suffered much as we strove to reverse their mutations at the Hill Where It Never Rains."

"Ah, it was their idea," he said defensively, desperately seeking to change the subject. "What of these stone ghosts? Do we hunt them down when the others return?"

"No," she said, displaying the drawing. "I want them to learn to trust us and join us for they are victims of the Order just as we are. They're not the reason I came over to talk to you. I need to find a way to stop you brooding like this as I fear for your sanity. I know you want to take care of our Ferals but they are valiant and independent souls: they love you, they say, but they're not animals to be shepherded. They know full well you do it out of a sense of guilt and not because of any love for them."

"Ah, I see," he said, crestfallen. "I thought I was being useful but I have failed in that small atonement as well."

"You did well at the Great Abbey, dear heart, and you turned your face away from a great evil yet you still wear the field-robes of the Order. I must ask the Light-Father to weave his magic upon you because you do not endear yourself to the Scatterlings by wearing the very symbol of the madness that destroyed their families and made of Gaia a world of bones."

"A change of clothes will not make them trust me, Mother Ivy, but fear not: I don't blame them for hating me as much as I hate myself. I beg you to leave me be: I've had this talk before with Mother Nightshade and Mother Fern and I will not change my mind on this. The Order was my whole life, body and soul, just as being a Daughter was yours. Thus I wear these field robes as a reminder of my unspeakable sins while I do penance and pray to Almighty God every day for His mercy."

"And so you cling to the image of some vast male deity sitting on a throne amongst the clouds and judging you!" she said archly. "I'm not burdened with such foolish notions, dear heart. That's why I beg of you not to punish yourself for events you could not control. You were just a child; an innocent in all this."

"I'm no innocent but how could you ever understand me? You Wiccans have no concept of sin or divine punishment, you have no sense of good and evil," he said angrily, returning his gaze to the Ferals still chasing each other about the Phoenix and its soiled carriages. "You may wish to revel in such decadence but I am of the Cloth: I need to absolve my sins whilst I am chaste and find a way to reclaim my place at God's right hand."

She tightened her grip on his shoulder and turned him to face her. He saw a dangerous light in her eyes and gulped nervously. Shadows flowed across the floor to the feet of the Wiccan as her anger flared: "Thousands of Mothers were put to lash and flame by your holy Order for the crime of being *different*; for the sin of being powerful women so never, ever again tell *me* what is good and what is evil, Kai! I will never forgive Schimrian for his torture of Mother Moss: applying pliers, barbed wire and all manner of tools to her naked, frail body before beheading her. These are the foul creatures who taught you the concept of sin; of what is good and what is evil. How in all the ruins of Gaia could my anger at such monstrous acts ever be construed as *decadence*?"

"I-I'm sorry," he flustered, reddening. "I'm still blind to such things: I have but eighteen years and much to learn."

He breathed a sign of relief as her fury and the shadows about her faded. "That's better," she nodded. "An opened mind is but the first step on the road to wisdom but you do indeed have much to learn about a great many things."

As before, he found himself unable to turn his head away. Her proximity, the beauty of her face and her subtle but heady scent suddenly aroused him. He shuddered and quickly tried to shut the thoughts down but not before she had raised an eyebrow:

"Oh, so you *do* possess earthly desires for all your faux piety," she said with a faint smile and sensuously drew a long forefinger down his cheek and under his chin. "Perhaps you would like me to teach you the ways of the flesh as well, hmm?"

His cheeks flushed crimson: "Now you mock me because you can reach into my mind! Do I not punish myself enough?" he seethed through clenched teeth. "Hear me well: I led innocent children like lambs to the slaughter during the Year of the Rats till none were left but the Scatterlings and two stone ghosts."

"As I tell thee, dear heart: you had no *choice*."

"I have no count of them, Mother Ivy," he confessed, screwing his eyes shut to fend off the tears. "But in my dreams and even in my waking thoughts I see every face, every drop of blood; I hear every scream, every plea for mercy, every twisted grin on the faces of the Fathers and Brothers as they butchered them in the name of God: may He save my soul."

He felt her hand upon his face again and her voice was soothing: "I know your tale well, dear heart. You were taken from your family in Crawcester as a postulant: part of the Order's centuries-old arrangement with the Conclave of Architects that your family was party to. You had no choice in the pact as you were the eldest male in that line and in return the Order manipulated the bloodlines of Architect families for hundreds of years so that they could harvest clerics such as you from their ranks."

"Yes, my family was well feted by the Order. My father was ranked as Stonemason amongst the Architects and my uncles were Aldermen of Crawcester. Then the Virus of Revelation triggered my DNA as the Order ordained thus I am now both immortal and damned," he groaned, hanging his head in despair. He placed a hand to his side. "The wound Pious gave me was deep but not even a scar remains. I will have centuries in which to contemplate and repent my sins. I am however spared the sin of suicide," he added bitterly, shedding a tear. "Apparently I cannot kill myself unless I completely sever my head from my body."

115

"You may heal swiftly but there is no guarantee that you are immortal, dear heart. It may interest you to know that Wiccans also know how to extend life. I have fifty years for example."

His eyes widened in total disbelief and he looked her up and down: the lithe figure; the skin toned by Persian heritage and again he had to avert his eyes as he felt waves of arousal coursing through his limbs. "You mock me again," he accused. "You have but one year tallied to one score. You are beautiful…"

Again she forced him to look at her. "Why thank you for such sweet courtesies, young knight," she laughed delightedly. "I seek not to mock you but to distract you. Mother Fern and the Light-Father torture themselves and so do you. For Diana's sake: you had no choice in the actions you carried out. When you did not obey, you were beaten without mercy and steeped in the brutal misogyny of the Order until your free will was crushed."

"I *did* have a choice: I could've run away or refused to act as a Judas-goat to those children but I did not because Britannia was emptied of souls and foul with the stench of rotting corpses. I was too afraid to act and I now think that my grandfather foresaw what was coming: he tried to stop my father signing the papers but they took me nevertheless. Even my family name, Helfburn, was denied me." He smiled suddenly. "But was it not the strangest of coincidences that Fierce and her sisters sought refuge at his house? It's a comfort to me to know that he died in his favourite chair, drinking his favourite spirit and watching the River Craw that he loved. He used to take me fishing along the river banks."

"Good," Ivy smiled again, making the blood pound through his veins as the crescent Moon atop her staff was almost touching his cheek. "You must seek out and treasure all the light you find in your memories. You saved Fria did you not?"

"Yes," he conceded. "I tried to save many others but with little or no success. I swapped her medical notes with those of another girl in her ward who was near death."

"It's to your credit that you did so despite the risk," Ivy nodded. "This is one good deed at least to salve your guilt."

"Not so," he grimaced, shaking his head. "Because I was forced to watch Father Pious slit that girl's throat believing her to be a Child of Exodus. He thought it would be *educational*. She was alone and helpless; in pain and terror; begging me for help but I couldn't move. I did nothing but stand and watch as her bright red

116

blood flowed and the light faded from her eyes and, may the Devil take me, I can't even remember her *name*."

"Fria told me her name was Cora. She was stricken with the Plague but still robbed of dignity in death by that *devil*," Ivy explained quietly, drawing a little closer and making his heart race even more. His senses reeled as she now had about her the million faint aromas of the deep flora of her craft.

"Cora," he repeated, painfully aware that his voice had risen in pitch. "I will honour her name and her memory."

Profoundly unnerved by the beautiful Wiccan, he stepped back but found himself pressed up against cabin of the Phoenix with no escape. He looked past her and noticed the Ferals were no longer near the Phoenix but were chasing each other amongst the forest of columns or chattering excitedly to Fria and Amos.

"W-what else d-do you want of me?" he stammered.

Ivy smiled and pressed relentlessly forward again. "Kai, I am a Servant of the Moon, a Bearer of Quintessence and a Wielder of Darkness and I pledge to thee, youngling, in the name of the Mother of All, I will protect thee and save thee if I can."

"I assure you, I c-can save myself," he blustered as her lips were now but inches from his. He tried to move away from her but could not. "Have y-you bewitched me?" he demanded.

"Mmm, only in the corporeal sense," she murmured softly, her lips brushing against his. "I must remind thee that where a human heart beats as fierce as this, there is always *hope* – even for me."

"But I must redeem myself for my sins," he groaned. "I cannot yield unto temptation. Get thee hence, *please.*"

A spasm passed across her face and she pulled back a little. "Redemption? Gah! The Order has reduced that word to a blood-soaked synonym for *genocide*, Kai. You must find new words to utter in their place as you seek out your new path."

"Why are you standing s-so close to me and why are the Ferals not laughing at me? What are you doing?"

Ivy pressed her body against his and kissed him full on the lips. He responded instantly, passionately, their tongues searching. His passion was so aflame that he thought he would faint but he noted that she, too, was breathing heavily, her eyes closed with pleasure. She leant her staff against the Phoenix and cupped his face in her hands. "A simple geis; a spell that blinds the eyes, dear heart: it looks to them as though we are just talking here awhile."

She repeated the questing kiss again and his heart hammered in his chest as he circled his arms about her waist and held her tight. After several minutes, she pulled away to kiss him on the forehead. "See? There are things in life worth holding on to."

"You.... *Jezebel*," he panted heavily. "You toy with me because of my youth; tempting me away from my faith."

"It's nothing to do with faith, dear heart. I simply wish to purge the guilt devouring you. But," she added mischievously, leaning forward to nibble at his ear. "When all is done, we *shall* lie together for six days and nights or more, young Kai."

She stopped and cocked her head to one side as he coughed and reddened to the tips of his ears. "Ah, Mother Fern and the Light-Father are safe! They fought and killed a Father and many Brothers at Wealthorpe and now they hide deep in the woods…"

"Oh, thank God for your 'far-speaking'," Kai sighed, relieved that she had released him. "I'll have less on my conscience now. What's wrong? You don't look well at all. What horror is Mother Fern revealing unto you?"

She shuddered and picked up her staff to raise it and release the Ferals, Fria and Amos from her geis. "A disturbing image of someone you know well: Abbot Michael. He lives but Azrael disfigured him for his amusement and the Order seeks to kill him as they feel he is marked by God for his sins."

"Abbot Michael?" he gasped. "Why? There was no man more devoted to the Order - and the kitchens - but he *was* kind to me and taught me electrics and physics whenever he could."

"Be that as it may," she said, placing a hand on his shoulder. "He was blighted by Schimrian's demon and will have need of you as he too seeks to atone for his monstrous crimes."

"I see. Then I will do what I can to assist him at your request," he pledged, placing his hand upon his chest.

"Thank you, Kai. Now shall we rejoin the others?"

He blushed crimson once more and turned from her, squirming in acute embarrassment. "Um, if it pleases you, Mother Ivy, I will remain here in the shadows awhile to… um, reflect on all that you have revealed to me."

"Why, bless you, young knight!" she laughed brightly, placing a hand to her cheek as a coy young virgin might do when receiving her first declaration of love. "You flatter me with such 'reflections'. I will leave you be… for now."

Meetings Destined

"So it was Schimrian who stopped your car at the roadblock," Mouse exclaimed, wide-eyed. "Un-*geh*! Are you sure?"

"Absolutely sure," Nightshade nodded. She waited as another deafening peal of thunder made the ground shake beneath the soles of their feet and the hail returned, some large pieces smashing onto the stonework before them sending ice fragments skittering across the flagstones. In the gloom and flickering lightning beneath the belly of the storm, Mouse watched fascinated as plumes of water erupted from the surface of the murky estuary below.

After three minutes of the thrashing roar and ice impacts that damaged the statues and ornate masonry above the Mouth of Thor, the hail core moved slowly northwards. "Look at that green glow in the clouds, Mother Nightshade! I've only seen that colour once before in Crawcester. Is it an evil omen?"

"I'm no meteorologist, dear heart, that's a scientist who studies the weather, but I'm told the glow is caused by large hailstones falling and rising in big storms on strong updraughts. Praise Diana, it's moved away: my ears are ringing."

Mouse gazed up at her impatiently: "Schimrian?" she prompted. "How could you know it was *that* Schimrian?"

"I had but few years yet I knew from the sound of his voice that I was in the presence of absolute evil. I felt the same malevolence when we entered the Great Abbey. I knew then that if he ever beheld my blood-red eyes, I would've been killed as a witch the instant he found the mark of the craft upon me."

"You didn't see his face though, did you?"

"Of course not! I was supposed to be asleep, remember?"

"Oh. Yes. Forgive me. I *am* listening."

~~~~~

It was getting stuffy in the car as they fought down the rising panic in their chests, waiting silently as Schimrian read through their forged papers and made meticulous notes. "Have you always lived in Brigstowe?" he asked pleasantly as he returned their papers. "Can you tell me a little of your family's history? We can always go through each Great Census of course but we want to know if there are genes out there that can help us succeed in our holy task to rid the world of all known diseases."

119

"What do you mean?" Bordan asked, puzzled.

Schimrian stroked at his goatee then smiled patiently: "The Census can only tell us so much about family histories. Think: did you have a grandfather who never had a cold or a great-great-grandmother who lived to receive one hundred and ten years from Our Lord for example? Was there a cousin who was abnormally strong or fast or excelled at academic subjects? Do you understand the reasoning behind our holy endeavour?"

"Yes, I think so," Bordan said carefully. "You wish to identify and isolate the best of the genes of humanity for our children and their children. I have read your literature."

"Ah, that is so good to hear," Schimrian murmured, ticking a box on his clipboard sheet. A thin knowing smile formed upon his face but his eyes remained cold: "The Wiccans and certain media demagogues spread falsehoods about us so it is a pleasure to deal with educated folk for a change. So tell me: is there anything outstanding in your family bloodlines?"

"Well, I'm just a humble teacher at Brigstowe South Academy where I've lived all my life and my darling wife, Cassandra, is but a humble housewife…"

"My dear Mister Geowine," Schimrian admonished. "There is *no* such thing as a humble housewife. The Sisters of our Order are revered as all women should be. There is nothing humble about gestating life such as your young Freda there. The day is warm so do not let her overheat as she slumbers."

"We'll be careful," Kendra assured him. "As for remarkable family members, I'm afraid we must disappoint you, Father Schimrian. All my side of the family were average across the tables: average height; average strength; average life spans and we got ill often – my grandfather died of sclerosis."

"Ah, how unfortunate," Schimrian said distantly leaving them unsure as to whether he was referring to their genes or her fictional grandfather. "And what of you, Geoffrey?"

"A long line of schoolteachers, I'm afraid, and my maternal grandfather was a tailor with no special skills as I can recall. May I ask what you do with all this information?"

"Ah, you may: it's no secret. When we find a bloodline of interest we map the double-helices of that family and isolate the genes that confer long life, resistance to illness, intelligence, rapid healing and so on. We have a new computer at the Great Abbey that collates the information that we have mapped of the human genome. We hope one day to create medicines that are tailor-made for individuals to cure specific cancer and brain ailments and so on. Is this not a worthy goal for our Order?"

"It is, it is," Bordan replied hastily, aware of the evangelistic edge to Schimrian's voice. "I teach the sciences to baccalaureate level but I can't conceive of a computer powerful enough to compute something as complex as human DNA."

Schimrian consulted his clipboard and scribbled a few notes upon it. "There was little progress as computing is in its infancy, I concede this, but we've made several astounding advances in that regard at the Great Abbey and we are close to building a machine capable of such a feat. I tell thee: these decriers of Intelligent Design need but to look at the sophistication of our genes to see the Hand of God at work. "

"Something was found in Heofland, was it not?" Bordan asked shrewdly, wiping the perspiration from his forehead with a large handkerchief. Schimrian's unblinking gaze was deeply unnerving but curiosity steadied his nerves: "A newspaper reported that one of your Fathers found an ancient computer in a cave."

"Sensationalist rubbish, Mister Geowine," Schimrian scoffed. "You shouldn't take such nonsense as gospel truth. However, what we did find *was* unusual: a Cymrig youth near Caer Brenia possessed of phenomenal skills in electrics and mathematics. In this blighted village we found this pauper boy surrounded with books and papers all covered in calculations."

"That is unusual for Heofland. The villages there are completely isolated from the rest of Britannia; even more so than the clans on Anseld, Edelingaeg and Fellholm."

A look of profound disgust crossed Schimrian's face as the Order often condemned the inbreeding on those islands. "Quite so yet even amongst the jungles of the southern hemisphere, genetic surprises surface almost daily. It's a shame their immune systems can't cope with the diseases of our civilised world," he sighed theatrically. "We have so much to do and to learn even from the degenerate brigands of Heofland. Hopefully, we can prevent the police from being, um, too *enthusiastic* when they are found."

"This new computer that you are building," Bordan prompted, a nagging doubt gnawing at his heart. "Will it be available on the market in the near future?"

121

"Not for some time. We recruited this remarkable young man and completed his education with the help of Exodus tutors. However, he's made such staggering advances in computing theory that we'll need decades to master his innovations. Fear not, we shall make such knowledge widely available in due time but only when we are satisfied that such technology will not be used to design and build weapons of mass destruction."

"I understand and commend such caution," Bordan agreed carefully. "These are dangerous times with the Japanese Empire threatening war again. I'm sorry we can't help you much with your survey but forgive us: we urgently need to get to Beorminghas."

"Of course, I'm sorry to delay the three of you," Schimrian said with a slight bow. He straightened up and moved away from the car window then paused to gaze into the back seat with a frown upon his face. He opened the rear car door, causing Kendra to gasp involuntarily, and placed a hand on Ellete's forehead but she did not react and grumbled sleepily. "Forgive my impertinence but I yielded to my medical concern for your daughter: I had thought her unnaturally flushed in this heat but her forehead is cool."

Bordan glared at him as he withdrew from the back seat and quietly shut the door. "If you are done with us, Father, we need to press on with our journey before the full heat of the day catches us. They do predict another heat-wave, you know."

"Indeed they do. It was a pleasure to meet you. God speed you and watch over you."

"And thee," Bordan responded formally and gunned the engine into life. "Good luck with your survey."

As Schimrian stood and watched the car weave its way through the roadblock and recede into the distance, he was joined by one of the more curious Brothers. "Were there genes of interest in that family, Father?" he asked. "You spent a long time with them and we have a long line yet to interview."

"Indeed, my son," Schimrian replied, rubbing his thumb and fingers together. "But can you tell me first why a child who has but six years is wearing make-up, hmmm?"

They whirled at the sound of tyres screeching behind them. A van erupted from the waiting line of vehicles and slammed into two police officers hurling them high into the air. The passenger let loose volleys of obscenities and gunshots but the Brother did not hesitate for one second: he picked up a metal barrier and hurled it through the windscreen. The van swerved, missing Schimrian by mere inches, and ploughed into a police car. The impact flipped it onto its side and it slid down the road in a shower of sparks.

The occupants scrambled out brandishing weapons but were met with a withering fusillade of fire from the incensed police officers seeking revenge for their fallen colleagues.

Schimrian brushed at some dust on his field robes and retrieved his clipboard. "I bless your good reflexes and resolute heart, my son," he said to the Brother who nodded, making no reply for he appeared to be relishing the spectacle of the Cymrig brigands being shot repeatedly at close range.

"Ah, our Heofland friends have met with an untimely demise. How unfortunate," Schimrian sighed as the shooting abated. "We can always salvage some samples, I suppose. I'm not familiar with you or your colleagues from the Burslen Abbey but I have use of someone like you. I'll ask Abbot Cystig to transfer you to the Great Abbey. I feel we are astray of late and so I intend to *personally* see that we fulfil our holy destiny as ordained in the Book of Revelation. Do you have a name, my son?"

The young Brother grinned wolfishly. "Pious, father, they call me Pious. How may I be of service to you?"

~~~~~

Michael sat with his back to Shield and the others in the kitchen as he devoured the broth marvelling at how the preservatives and canning process had served the food so well. "A small miracle," he murmured to himself: "One that I ill deserve." He was aware of Shield's presence standing next to him and the scent of damp clothing, fresh blood and soap fragrance from her recent bathing at Milverburg. "Yes, child?" he enquired patiently. "What do you want? - apart from my prolonged and painful demise that is."

Shield took the empty bowl from him, placed it in the sink then she pulled up a stool and sat next to him. "I will not deny that I resist a powerful urge to kill you where you sit but the Light-Father would consider me to be the monster not you. I've killed many Brothers and Tally-men today and even this deluge cannot wash their tainted blood from my clothes but such is the world that you and Schimrian created. Please don't turn from me: I wish to look you in the eye as I speak."

Michael complied and found himself gazing into the eyes of a beautiful and powerful young warrior who was the polar opposite of the timid rabbits caged in the Sisters' Enclaves. "What would have me say, my child?" he asked, tilting his head slightly to one side. "The crimes of my Order are so vast that I have no words to convey the horror of it yet you have now seen me Naked as the living embodiment of that unspeakable arrogance."

"That I have and yet I do not pity you."

"As I said to your Wiccan: I desire not your forgiveness nor do I deserve your pity."

"You will receive neither from me. You are what you now are because of what you did to bring about this bloody Ragnarok; this... this *nightmare* without end. You..." Great sobs wracked her body but she held up her hand to forestall Saul from coming over to comfort her. He reluctantly rejoined Bas and Ibrahim who were applying bandages and salves to the wounds of the five victims who were still unable to voice their gratitude.

Shield composed herself and glared at Michael: "You helped Schimrian create a physical body for the Devil that my sister gave her life to destroy. Without her, Hell and all its demons would have been made manifest all because of *you.*"

"I honour her name but, as I said before, both I and Camus were cowards. We kept the machines working and the Angels airborne but before that we worked on the Great Computer for twenty years ever since Schimrian found that machine in a cave in the Black Valleys and brought it to us at the Great Abbey. I asked him how he found it and he claims the 'voice of God' revealed it unto him while our Brothers scoured the wastes of Heofland on a mission to find Cymrig samples of DNA."

"Because they wanted nobody to survive their precious virus," Shield scowled. "Mother Moss told me of your 'surveys'."

"That may have been so for the Abbots and the Conclave but most ordinary Brothers genuinely wanted to serve mankind but those fools in the Vatican experimented with animal genes until they created a seven-headed lamb that survived."

"How could such a creature survive? Your Virus is destroying the Ferals but none of them have more than one head!"

Michael shrugged: "I know not but on my journey here, I was thinking that God or the Devil intended that creature to be viable. Then, guided by an angel or tempted by the Devil, someone in the

Vatican betrayed them and smuggled it out of the laboratories. They sold the monstrosity to a carnival owner who obviously did not understand the significance of the creature he proudly paraded. Naturally, it attracted world-wide attention until it was seized by the Order and taken to the Great Abbey for analysis."

"Why was such a creature so important to the Order?"

"Because the Twenty-Four of the Conclave beheld the creature and its seven heads, each with one horn and one eye upon it and concluded that the lamb was the One True Lamb as foretold in the Book of Revelation; a creature heralding the opening of the Seven Seals upon the world to bring about the Day of Judgement. With war and famine already rampant, they decreed that the first three Seals had already been opened and thus we opened the Fourth. Now every night the Fifth Seal opens unto me."

"What do you mean by that?"

"I forget that you haven't read the Bible. Every night the souls awaiting Judgement surround my bed: a countless horde beyond the reason of guilt or conscience or logic. I hear them cry out: '*O Lord, how long before thou wilt judge and avenge our blood.*' Camus sees them too but not Schimrian or Pious - oh no, not *them.*"

"Mother Fern sees them too."

Michael made a gesture of negation. "No. As you heard me tell her earlier, her apparitions are figments of her misguided guilt whereas the shades I see are *real.* The manner of their death binds them to this world; adding to our sin and our punishment." He placed a hand across his eyes. "Every night is a torture until we pass out from exhaustion: the mind can only take so much before it shuts down and oblivion claims us for a few sweet hours."

"I see," Shield said coldly. "Mother Moss often told me that spirits were real but they held no fear for us for we survived the Year of the Rats and the endless rains of Crawcester. We saw such sights that even the vilest of shades would seem as angels to us but we've never seen a ghost."

Michael looked up at her. "I think *you* have for such is the Wiccan gift and do not deny this: I see it in your face."

Shield blushed and averted her eyes. "In Crawcester, during the first of the great floods, I and my sisters sheltered in a house on the banks of the River Craw and I admit I beheld the spirits of my parents and the old man who used to live there, Mister Helfburn. I thought I was hallucinating to see such visions but Mother Moss assured me otherwise. I now know that he was none other than Kai's grandfather by happenstance."

"Hmm. Happenstance indeed. Such coincidences are rare so I suspect a Higher Design is at work. I had no belief in earthbound souls until the Great Plague and since then Camus and I have endured nightly swarms of vengeful spirits." He fell silent for a moment. "Enough of me; tell me of Brother Kai. He has shown far greater courage than I in this. Do you not think he is a remarkable young man? I fostered his interest in science as he has a keen mind and was unbowed by the oppressive routines of the Order. I was… fond of him almost as a father would be. He was too young to be party to our monstrous schemes of genocide so I would know if you Scatterlings can forgive him for his sins."

Shield pursed her lips and stared into his eyes again. "He saved Fria but he did so at the expense of another girl in the hospital and I saw him lead two children to their brutal death so the answer is no despite the bravery he showed at the Great Abbey."

"His bravery is far greater than you can ever imagine given the brutal subjugations of our postulants and novices. He had to rebel against every fibre of his being and every tenet of his faith to help you. Their young minds are filled with the mistrust and hatred of women especially Wiccans; the Whores of Babylon as they are so described in the teachings of the Order."

"I'm no whore but I do bear the mark of the craft and I have received the staff of a Wiccan," Shield said proudly, watching him for a response. He gave none. "Why are you not recoiling in horror and making the sign of the cross at me?"

"Given my appearance, do you honestly think I would react to anything? However, despite all that Azrael did to me, I thank God that I still retain the scientific curiosity that often warred with the rigid theology they drummed into me. I tried to retain an open mind even during the experiments with that accursed machine that Schimrian brought back to the Great Abbey."

"If that machine was so accursed, why did Schimrian bring it back from Heofland? Why did the Order use it?"

"Schimrian was mesmerised by it. Abbot Cystig was in charge of electrics but he indulged and mentored Schimrian in all things. He was too easily flattered and bedazzled to see the true nature of the man or the dangers in that infernal machine. I would only go near it under sufferance as it had an aura that made my skin crawl."

"And you suspected nothing?" Shield said with an eyebrow raised. "Are you lying to me?"

"I had my doubts but it was an engineering marvel: a multi-faceted sphere with a band of portals at the equator but its power was almost spent after being damaged and trapped in the cave. We surmised that it had once travelled between worlds like your Light-Father who proved my theory about parallel realities."

"The Light-Father has told us of his world and how there may be millions of worlds all side by side…."

"Indeed. Why would the Creator stop at just one Creation? The device resisted our attempts to study it. It emitted flashes of light that rendered Brothers unconscious and it would rise into the air, warping the benches and flooring beneath it before crashing back down to earth. Waves of fear emanated from it and Brothers would curl up on the floor in foetal positions and soil themselves."

"So this thing was beyond your ken yet you persevered and brought the End of Days upon us," Shield said, aghast. "But I begin to see that it was not just the Order at work."

"Ah, now you begin to grasp the full sin of our arrogance," he said, spreading his hands. "I'm convinced the Devil steered that device into our reality with the Order providing the fertile soil for his demon seed. We finally managed to open the casings and found a container of dead brain tissue attached to its central processors. Schimrian found a still living brain cortex and placed it into the container. The device immediately became active: before we could react, it sealed itself up and floated into the Hexagon where we saw cables move on their own connecting the sphere to the computers in the Hexagon and the rest of the Great Annex."

"How can cables move by themselves?" Shield demanded, frowning. "It's impossible, surely?"

Michael chortled: "Ha! This from a *Wiccan*? I know of no physical mechanism that can impart kinetic energy over a distance even though we knew Wiccans can 'far-move' objects. We were transfixed by this telekinesis as terminals started powering up and began communicating with our programmers. To save face, we pretended to Abbot Cystig and the Conclave that we intended this to happen to keep both our positions and our privileges. Then at some point Azrael was born."

"From what Kai told us, the Light-Father concluded that he began as something called an artificial intelligence."

"He is indeed an insightful man but I believe the sphere already contained Azrael's will. The machine that contained him did not present itself as a threat then, some eight years ago, he revealed himself to a few of us and completely seduced Schimrian and Amherus. He helped us to design the Guides, the begiullers and showed us how to design the Virus to confer immortality."

"I can't believe they didn't question any of this! What in Mary's name did you think the Guides were for?"

"Ah, the Guides were originally designed to restore mobility to paralysed patients as we could use them to bypass breaks in spinal cords. We had some initial success but then a few scientists at Exodus voiced their concerns about the Guides being used as coercive devices but the Conclave had them dismissed."

"Why didn't the rest of the Order take them seriously?"

"Because countless medical innovations flowed from the Great Computer as they began to call it so we all convinced ourselves it was benign. The rest you know from your experiences at the Great Abbey and only when that door closed upon me did I at last recognise the full extent of my cowardice and my sins."

"And *now* you seek redemption?"

"In the proper *Christian* sense of the word, aye."

One of the former prisoners looked across the table towards them. "Listen well, Abbot," he said in a voice croaking from a lack of use and much suffering. "I forgive you."

Michael's eyes widened and his jaw dropped. "You can't do that, my son. You cannot forgive a man who would have stood by and watched you torn apart to become a Tally-man."

"Nevertheless, I forgive you. I reject all the hatred in my heart as it poisons me: body, heart and soul. As these wonderful children, these Scatterlings have shown us: we must become better than you or we become less than beasts."

"I rejoice that you've regained your voice, my son," Michael said, the awe evident in his tone. "But such forgiveness is beyond the power of mortal man. What birth-name do you have?"

"You should know it well enough," the young man said. "I survived for six years in Oldhayne, losing everyone I loved to Plague, dog and rat only to be captured and tortured in the Great Manse. I'm Marc Onderhelm; your younger *brother*."

~~~~~

Brother Ignatius

"Thank you, Surl," Peter said, admiring the neatly wrapped bandage on his stump. "The antiseptic is working already: it's less painful now. The Light-Father is right: if I get a major infection in this I could lose my whole arm or even my life."

"It was raw and there was some bleeding but I've disinfected the bandages as well. Mother Moss taught us well the healing arts," she reminded him, closing the medical kit. She scratched at her back. "We need insecticide lotion next: we still have lice from the Keep and I don't want any more flea bites. Six years in the rain in Crawcester and we were nothing but insect fodder!"

"We got rid of the fleas," Rabbit agreed around a mouthful of bread and cheese. "But, yes, the lice are definitely back."

"Pup is scared of the rats in the walls."

"I know, dear heart," Surl sighed, ruffling the young boy's hair. "There's not a lot we can do about them at the moment."

"The food will attract the rats unless we can find somewhere to keep it safe." Peter pointed out. "I saw some jars with lids in the store-room we can use." He reached across the table for his claw but Surl placed her hand upon it and shook her head. "What are you doing?" he grumbled. "I need it to carry the jars!"

"Your stump must be allowed to heal and that claw mount is far too small," she insisted. "Leave the jars to me. We have a lot to do tomorrow. It must be close to Nine Bells of the evening up there and we all need to sleep."

"The explosions have stopped," he noted, cocking an ear. "We did a lot of damage to the Order today but I wish the Light-Father had taken us with him."

"As do I," she nodded. "But we'll make him proud of us."

"Can you see him in your visions?"

"No, I'm too tired now, I think: the visions have gone away – maybe forever. I just don't know."

"Hmm, I still think you're meant to be a Mother," he said stoutly and then he smiled: "Maybe we can find you a staff and you can throw lightning bolts at the Tally-men!"

"Ha. I don't feel any power in me apart from the visions," she shrugged, smearing butter on a slice of bread and adding cheese to it. "Unless you call a rumbling tummy a power," she laughed as the visceral noise subsided. Peter's stomach followed suit and they both started to giggle with Pup breaking wind until the sound of traumatised children enjoying a brief moment of joy echoed and re-echoed down the dark sewage tunnels sending rats skittering into crevices and masking the sound of approaching footsteps.

"Ah, this is *so* good," Peter grinned contentedly, wiping butter from his chin. "Almost as good as the food the Mothers made for us in Crawcester. What was it that Mother Moss used to say? An empty belly is the best judge of food?"

"Yes, something like that," Surl smiled.

Pup burped loudly then yawned hugely. He clambered onto one of the makeshift beds set against the wall and drew the linen sheets about him. "Pup misses Bas already," he whined. "She always used to sing Pup a lullaby. Can you sing Pup one?"

"Perhaps you can sing one to yourself," Peter suggested kindly.

Pup's brow wrinkled with the effort and his voice wavered with emotion as he sang: "*A cat once walked, on the skyline of the roofs, as silent as a thief, silhouetted by the Moon, a shadow-thief; a clever thief, who stole a silver spoon…*"

They froze as a deep, rich baritone voice responded beyond the rotting door leading to the sewers: "*…from the Mistress of the House, and a stranger to the truth, he stole all six gold teeth, from her husband's mouth, then the rattle from the baby, who then stole the cat's lament, and set up a mewling cry, that stole the hearts of passers-by, who chased the clever cat, and tied about its neck a bell, ending eight of his nine lives…*"

There was a rap upon the door as they extinguished the candles and readied their weapons. They could see torchlight through the gaps in the rotting wood. "I mean you no harm, little ones, I am Brother Ignatius of the Tower. Will you allow me safe passage? I know that you're armed. However, there is something in that cellar that I need then I will leave you in peace. Don't pretend you're not in there: I can hear you breathing and whispering."

"How can we trust you?" Surl said shakily; there'd been no death's-head moth or premonition to alert her to the approach of this danger so maybe he wasn't a threat – she just didn't *know*!

"I could have crept away and alerted the Great-Abbot as to your location but I haven't done so. Your friends could've killed me earlier today but they spared my life so I wish to repay such undeserved mercy. May I enter?"

"Yes," Surl said warily. "But be mindful or you die."

The door creaked open and they were all but blinded by his torchlight. "Ah, excuse me, little ones," he apologised. He switched on a small battery-lantern from his rucksack, set it upon the table and turned the torch off. "That's better," he smiled engagingly, helping himself to bread and cheese as they all pointed their weapons at him. He sat down and began to eat. "I see you've acquainted yourselves with the kitchens. I take it you brave young souls got left behind when the Light-Father retreated?"

"That's obvious," Peter said fiercely. "Why are you here? Why are you not calling for help? We could easily kill you."

"I dare say you could, my son," Ignatius said blandly. "Mmm, fresh bread and cheese: wonderful. It's such a wonder that the Sisters grow so much wheat in their greenhouses that I need wine to appreciate it, methinks." He stood up slowly and went to one of the wine racks and selected a bottle. He opened it at the table then extracted a goblet from the rucksack and filled it. The children watched wide-eyed and silent as he drained it in a single gulp and wiped his mouth with the back of his hand. "Ah, that's the prescription filled," he beamed. "Now I suspect you want to know the *second* reason I'm not betraying you to the Order, yes?"

"Yes!" Surl scowled, studying the lean, grey-haired cleric with a mixture of suspicion and loathing. "We would."

"Because I don't care a jot if the Order gets wiped off the face of the Earth," he said frankly, refilling the goblet. "Believe me: I had nothing to do with the Virus of Revelation or the Tally-men and I want nothing to do with *this*," he added, pointing to the small Hebrew tattoo on his forehead denoting his Tribe. "I argued with Father Schimrian when he showed us the Vatican's monstrosity; the seven-headed lamb. He grew vexed with me when I said that it wasn't a Sign of God so he exiled me to my tower. As prisons go, it's bearable. I have a warm fire, books and wine aplenty and the postulants and novices pay me clandestine visits. I still try to educate them in poetry and literature - such is my life."

"So you've lived in luxury while we've lived with rats and dogs and being hunted by the Order for six years!" Surl spat. "We are but children yet we've had to kill to survive. You could've warned everybody what this Conclave of yours was planning!"

"I only knew that they regarded the mutant lamb as a Sign," Ignatius confessed, cupping the goblet and bowing his head. "I was excommunicated; banned from attending services and masses in the

Great Cathedral but I was still able to wander around the Great Abbey after dark. Only two Exodus scientists in the laboratories would talk to me. They told me that they knew the Conclave was planning something apocalyptic and that I should look to my books while they looked to their children. I presume they meant you: the Children of Exodus whom they've blessed with above average strength, intelligence and vitality." He raised his goblet in a toast. "Please put down those weapons as I mean you no harm. In fact, if you'll let me, I propose to help you."

Pup went up to the cleric and studied his face closely. "Pup believes you. You smell really nice," he smiled, hugging him. Tears formed in the old cleric's eyes as he gently returned the hug.

"Bless you, youngling," he croaked, his voice crackling with deep and complex emotions. "I never thought I'd hear the sweet innocent sound of a child's voice again!"

"Your bloody-handed Order saw to that," Peter snapped. "We lost our families. Some of us watched them *die*."

"As did I, as did I," Ignatius sighed. "I had brothers and sisters and they all had children that I was fond of. How I used to love spoiling them at Christmastide and Easter! When the Plague struck, I broke exile and rushed to Danelief to help them but many of my relatives died in my arms, cursing me to Hell. I saw the Inquisitions begin and learnt of torture in the Great Manse and in Redemption Cells across the world then I saw my first Tally-man. My heart and soul now dead as stone within me, I returned to my prison to drown my impotence in copious amounts of alcohol."

He looked at the faces of the children, noting the terror and suffering they'd endured; children who'd had to fight and kill to survive in the world his Order created. He sighed and stared into his wine, pursing his lips. "Now I hear the dead lament in the dark watches of the night outside the windows of my tower. I hear them cry when the wind howls and weep when the rain falls. The only thing that dulls their voices lies in this cellar."

"Was it you who boarded up the door?" Peter asked, finally placing his knife back in its sheath.

"Yes. I took to exploring the sewers and catacombs under the Great Abbey in my exile. I laid a table against the doorway in the hallway upstairs then boarded up the door. The Sisters soon forgot that they ever had a store-room and a well-stocked wine cellar here as there are so many other cellars. They're not bred for intelligence, bless them, and I know now they were designed to be naught but incubators for the Conclave's twisted New Jerusalem."

"So if you aren't going to betray us to Schimrian," Rabbit said nervously. "Why would you risk helping us?"

"As I said, I owe my life to your friends' mercy and see in you the nieces and nephews I watched die. I would thus honour their souls and their memories." He placed a hand upon his heart. "It's no less than that and no more than that. I have no loyalty to Schimrian or his Conclave. I prayed for their deaths every day but the world remained blighted by their presence."

He helped himself to more bread and cheese. "Forgive me: I am unlikely to be fed while this chaos lasts. If you come with me now I'll guide you to my tower then you can escape westwards under cover of darkness along the railway tracks."

"No," Surl said, folding her arms. "We *need* to remain here! We intend to sabotage the Order before we leave."

"Good Lord, such resolve in one so young!" he exclaimed, setting Pup onto his feet. "You really are Children of Exodus! To have such few years and hold such great ambition; yet you are still younglings and many Brothers and Tally-men remain alive up there. There's a malaise in this Great Abbey beyond your meagre skills, little ones, thus I beg you: you must flee!"

"We will *not*," she said resolutely. "We are the Scatterlings of Crawcester and we follow the Light-Father."

"Yet he abandoned you here."

"He had no choice! He was wounded in the Great Annex. He only had enough strength to save the others."

"Ah, forgive me for doubting him: his assault upon the Great Abbey was a masterpiece of strategy and no doubt young Kai served him well. And you, youngling: you seem so sure of yourself for one so young when so many have perished today."

"Not enough," she replied coldly.

"I'm told many of your Ferals died," he pointed out. "And two of your Mothers were killed after they destroyed the fuel dumps and many weapons and begiullers. The Light-Father's victory was a Pyrrhic one at best. It was madness to assault a place this large with so few followers but he did well to escape, I'll grant him that."

"The madness was yours," she retorted. "What happened today was set in motion by Mother Moss. She was a powerful seer who foresaw that the Order would use a strange machine to raise a demon and that our friend, Fierce, would destroy it by sacrificing her life to set off plasma grenades inside the Great Computer. Do you know anything of this demon?"

"What demon? When they untied me, they told me that they'd found the remains of an angel with wings amongst the debris of the Great Computer. I didn't believe a word of it but they were in raptures, blaming the Light-Father for its death and that of the Great Abbot. They even claimed that the Wiccans used their dark arts to force the Tally-men to kill Fathers and Brothers and then raise many of them from the grave!"

"That's not true! Schimrian's demon, Azrael, controlled the Tally-men and those dead Brothers! He may have looked like an angel but that *thing* was going to open the Gates of Hell."

"I only have your word for that," he said doubtfully.

"The Sisters in the kitchens are dead too," Peter told him. "The Tally-men must've killed them: they were stabbed by spears hundreds of times; they were *mutilated.*"

They saw the remorse in the old man's face as he lamented their deaths. "Ah, I didn't know," he groaned. "They were innocent; the purest and sweetest women in all of Creation. I hope Schimrian is truly dead if he did indeed summon a demon as you claim."

"What happened to him?" Peter insisted.

"They told me they can see his dead body inside that machine but it's still active despite there being no electrics." He drained the goblet and levered himself upright to begin loading his rucksack with bottles of wine. "I fear necromancy may be at work in the Great Annex. This is definitely no place for you children."

"We *have* to stay," Surl said resolutely.

"Then I pray you change your minds soon," he sighed.

"I still find it hard to trust you," Peter said candidly.

Ignatius paused to indicate Pup: "This child has clearer insight into my soul than you have. I have no desire to betray you or go forth into an empty world so I'll hide from the shades and the shadows with my precious books, safe in the arms of Bacchus."

He hoisted the clinking rucksack onto his back with some difficulty and stepped out onto the sewer ledge. Surl picked up the lantern to return it to him but he held up his hand: "No, keep it, youngling. I've found that candles are not much use in sewers as there are pockets of gas and sudden draughts that snuff them out. It'll last three days then I'll give you another."

"Thank you," Surl said, painfully aware that without her visions, she had nothing but her gut instinct with which to gauge this amiable alcoholic. "How do we find you?"

"Ah, bless you for honouring me with your trust," Ignatius smiled, bowing slightly. "It means a lot to an old man like me. Follow the main sewer south but keep to the left until you reach an overflow tunnel raised four feet above the sewer level on the right. The main sewer carries on under the Angel Compound while this tunnel serves as a storm overflow and opens out into the River Elver. You can also escape that way as there are no grilles. As you crawl down the tunnel, you'll come across an inspection shaft that emerges in a small enclosed courtyard at the rear of my tower. It's usually left unlocked but knock six times on the door and I'll come down to meet you if I'm not in my cups or asleep!"

"Goodbye, Brother Ignatius," Surl said returning the bow.

"How are you so sure you'll be safe here?" he asked shrewdly. "Are you relying on the predictions of this Mother Moss or are you a Daughter yourself? Tell me - not that it will change things - but do you bear the mark of the craft?"

She was about to proudly declare she was a seer but a death's-head moth fluttered in front of her face only to vanish in a puff of dust. Startled for a moment, she blustered out a lie: "N-no I have no mark - it's just that the Light-Father trained us well."

"Ah, pity. I had hoped to meet a Wiccan in the flesh to compare her to the propaganda of the Order I've endured all my waking days since they took me in as a postulant. Now, before I go, I would like to know what names you all have."

"I'm Surl, this is Rabbit, that is Peter and Pup you know."

"Pup likes you!" Pup added brightly.

"And I like thee, Pup," Ignatius laughed, the years seeming to fall from his lined face in the dim light of the lantern. "Fare thee well then, children. I'll bring you food and water when I can. Six knocks, remember, six knocks!"

He waved goodbye and pushed the door to. They listened in thoughtful silence to the sound of his retreating footsteps and the fading clink of wine bottles until they could hear nothing but the susurration of the waters gushing down the sewer on their way to the derelict sewage plants of the Kentish Meres.

~~~~~

Audiences

Schimrian gazed at the two trembling Brothers standing before his desk. "Forgive the lateness of the hour," he smiled thinly. "But I noted both of you were absent from Compline where I thought the Gloria in Excelsis Deo was *especially* poignant."

The Brothers bowed their heads but remained silent apart from a jointly whispered: "*In manus tuas, Domine.*"

Schimrian drummed his fingers on his desk for a few moments. "Be that as it may, I know you labour hard at restoring our Great Abbey and such lapses are forgivable but you also missed Vespers. We have to maintain our devotions, my sons, or we may as well be Ferals. But, because of these creatures and their Master, only five Abbots, forty Fathers, six hundred and forty-six Brothers and less than one thousand Tally-men remain in all Britannia."

"Yes, we know this, Y-your E-eminence," the shorter of the two Brothers, Theo, stuttered, his work-robes becoming increasingly patched with nervous sweat. "Our l-losses have been great thanks to his accursed Wiccans corrupting our Great Computer."

"Indeed. Yet three weeks and one day have passed since these Harlots of Satan desecrated our Great Cathedral and brought down our Christ in Majesty! After all this time, however, we remain in a mediaeval stupor, reading our Scriptures by candle-light. The Great Cathedral, by divine contrast, was indeed magnificently lit by candles but, alas, our stores of large candles are sore depleted. Therefore, before we worship in the dark, what of your repairs in the generator rooms? Have you made *any* progress at all on repairing the very machines that you failed to guard, hmmm?"

"We have already begged your forgiveness, Eminence," the second Brother, Edward, explained desperately while clasping his hands together. "We were overcome with concern for our fellow Brothers and joined the battle to chase these desecrators out of our Great Abbey. As for the repairs: Abbot Camus has tried his utmost these past three weeks, Eminence, but we Brothers and Fathers-Technician tally but twenty and both generator engines were *thoroughly* destroyed. Only we and four others here have the engineering skills to restore electric generation..."

He paused as Schimrian's eyes had narrowed dangerously at the praise being directed at Camus. Schimrian finally sighed, gesturing impatiently for him to continue.

"Um, we have just finished dismantling them and clearing the foundations of debris. The fire-damage has been addressed but, as you know, the control panels and communication relays were all smashed and needed repair most urgently. There is some good news: Father Aten has found and retrieved three portable generators from Beorminghas. We can restore electrics to the Great Manse and the Great Cathedral but not to the rest of the Great Abbey. We were servicing them so we've missed our devotions."

"Ah, yes. Bless Father Aten! I am glad he survived our travails as he was ever one of our more efficient Inquisitors. Now you have these generating machines, when will we have our electrics?"

"Tomorrow," Theo said quickly. "Before Compline."

"I am delighted to hear this, my son. Some of the Order may regard candle-light as divine ambience but I regard the shadows they cast as portals of Hell. I would see all at all times thus my patience is taxed. I concede I was... unwell from the explosion in the Great Annex but I had expected more progress."

Theo glanced at Edward, who nodded nervously for him to continue. Only two weeks prior to this day, Schimrian had been screaming in tongues at them before being restrained and led away by Pious but they found this new compus mentis incarnation of the Great-Abbot infinitely more unnerving. "The portable generators run on scyfol and as it's a light fuel, there's little left in Britannia. We lost most of our reserves here during the attack and the many fires since then have destroyed the smaller stores such as the one in the Library. We calculate we can only run the portable generators for a month at most unless we get fresh supplies."

"Ah, yes, those *fires*," Schimrian nodded thoughtfully. A spasm of venomous rage crossed his face that made the Brothers struggle to restrain their bowels from loosening. "We lacked the foresight to keep such generating machines at the Great Abbey and there were *far* too many incidents to be happenstance while I was... indisposed. I was mortified to learn that all of you, including Abbot Pious, thought they were mere acts of God! You can imagine how disappointed I was on regaining my senses but we are where we are. With Abbot Michael confined, Pious could not identify who may have been responsible but he does now have a suspect: someone we have overlooked for far too long."

"Ah, we..." Theo spluttered. "...are glad there has been some progress. We did indeed think that the fires were accidental as there were so many burning candles left untended. We see now that saboteurs were afoot but the sabotage was so subtle as if they knew exactly where to strike yet hide their tampering…"

"Exactly," Schimrian agreed, raising a forefinger in emphasis. "The Light-Father is evil but even sore wounded as he was; he did not leave any of his minions behind. I see his dark mind now: full of malign intelligence and strategy! That's why Pious concluded that one of us, a traitor to the Order, was responsible…"

"Ah, I pray that he does not think it was us," Theo said, the fear evident in his voice as he suppressed an almost suicidal urge to point out that leaving saboteurs behind was a common historical strategy of retreating armies. "We toiled night and day to repair the damage to the radios and relays and we…"

"Be at peace, my son," Schimrian said sharply, holding up a hand to forestall the blustering. "If I had found any fault in you other than a desire to help your fellow Brethren, you would both have been left, naked and bound, on the shores of Erdethric as sport for the Ferals that now infest that island. I'm told that they've recently developed a taste for human flesh…"

"Yes, b-bless you, Eminence," Theo stammered and fell silent, despite the overwhelming sense of relief, the nervous sweat kept trickling down his back. He could see why Schimrian found the deep and writhing shadows in his chambers threatening especially from the corner of the eye as both Brothers expected Pious to step forth into the candlelight at any moment and slay them.

"Well, proceed, my sons," Schimrian prompted impatiently. "What of the main generators and our fuel situation? I hear that Bede has enough athidol to supply our needs. Yes?"

Edward nodded quickly. "Enough for two years while Father Ursaf has arranged for tankers to be made ready and the roads checked. As for the main generator engines, we have yet to find a suitable heavy transporter that is still operable and a safe route to get them here but we *will* find a way, Eminence."

"I am sure that you will, my son. Now to the main reason I've called you here. I worry for Abbot Camus as I have over-burdened this worthy soul. He, Abbot Pious and I are set to gather all the remaining Order in Britannia at the Great Abbey, at Bede, Burslen and at our Abbey at Wyehold. We have determined that this Light-Father has taken refuge in Milverburg and we shall shortly Inquire of him and all his ungodly entourage."

Theo brightened up at the news: "This is most encouraging, Eminence. So will we now recall the Angels and aircraft searching Britannia and focus on this accursed city?"

Schimrian nodded then glanced over his shoulder at the candle-shadows in the recesses. The two Brothers saw the revolver upon the table and the wreckage of three smashed terminals on the computer desk. They looked at each other in trepidation. "As you determined for me, we have but twelve thousands left across the world. Now that our communications are improving, I've ordered them to continue their Inquisitions and to eradicate Ferals but they whine and bleat that they're no longer equal to the task. No more so than that *coward*, Abbot Amherus." He paused to stare at Theo meaningfully: "He was your mentor once, was he not?"

Edward's eyes widened in concern for his friend but Theo recognised the danger he was in immediately: "He was, Eminence, but I soon determined under his tutelage that his pearls of wisdom were rarely supported by facts nor were his interpretations of the Scriptures sound. I did pay my respects as befitting his rank but no more than that, Eminence, I assure you."

There was an agonising pause as the Great-Abbot's eyes bored into the inwardly-quaking Brother but then the moment passed and Schimrian indicated that they seat themselves before his desk in the chairs they had been ordered to stand beside. He poured them all some brandy from an exquisite glass decanter into cut-glass tumblers and bade them drink their fill. "I am promoting the two of you to the rank and privileges of Father-Technician," he explained benevolently. "I am fully satisfied as to your loyalty."

Both Brothers relaxed visibly and enjoyed the warmth of the fiery spirit now radiating outwards from their innards. "This is excellent, Eminence," Theo approved, staring at the decanter. "I have not tasted such as this for decades. Thank you."

The smile faded from Schimrian's face and his eyes hardened. "It was well-earned, my son, but there is subterfuge still afoot and I have need of your services. I want you to watch Abbot Camus and all your colleagues closely for me. I doubt not their veracity but these are trying times and we cannot brook doubters or challenges to my authority during the holy task laid out before me for I am the only one capable of building our New Jerusalem!"

"What would you wish of us when those now abroad from these shores return?" Edward ventured.

"I've made it clear to them they are *not* to return with so many Inquisitions unfinished yet I fear that many will ignore my wishes. The surviving Conclave Abbots and their acolytes have voiced a particularly strong desire to return to these hallowed isles and were unconvinced of my arguments though they continue to pay me lip-service. Many hundreds of their Tally-men have already been slain out of their deep mistrust as to their reliability."

Theo looked aghast: "Can they not understand that it was a malfunction in the Great Computer created by the Wiccans which could not affect those Tally-men who were resting?"

"They're not as technically enlightened as you, my son. They point out that all but two of our Brothers-Surgeon were taken from us and few remain who are skilled at the electrics of the Guides. They question the need for Tally-men and thus I conclude they may soon abandon their righteous tasks."

"What shall we do if they return?" Edward reiterated.

Schimrian's brow furrowed as he steepled his fingers. "I shall cross that foul Styx should it flow before my feet. They will come to learn that I disdain the faint of heart and those who would so lightly discard the binding tenets of our faith."

"When and if they return, Eminence, you may count on us," Edward pledged, hand on heart.

"And I, Eminence," Theo added.

"Good, good," Schimrian beamed and the Brothers felt like two huge millstones were being lifted from their necks. Schimrian waved a hand in dismissal and presented the Ring of the Order for them to kiss. "Do not take long in moving your belongings into your new residences," he warned them as they reached the door. "I expect you to fulfil your pledges to restore our electrics. Now go forth, my sons, and remember this during your toil: what the Lord bestows, the Lord can so easily take away."

It was only when they reached the sanctum of the generator room that they fully relaxed. Rain and hail smashed into the high windows and here amongst the ancient masonry of the Great Manse they could feel the thunder reverberating deep within their bones. They lit as many candles as they could find until the large room was ablaze and swept clean of shadow though each flame guttered in the draughts created by the immense storm raging above the Great Abbey. Wind whistled and moaned through gaps in the window frames and through the air vents.

There was a small table and two chairs by one of the portable generators. Theo extracted a bottle of whisky and two small silver cups from his locker and set them upon the table. "I've no idea why I put this bottle in here but I'm glad I did now. It's been a tumultuous time, Edward. Let there..."

Edward raised a hand. "Let me stop you there. If you quote Thomas Tythe at me, I will punch you in the face. I've no stomach for his medieval scribbling at the moment."

"Scribbling? The greatest playwright Britannia has ever known? Philistine!" Theo snorted as he poured the whisky and sat down. There was still bread and cheese on the table so he made them both a sandwich in silence until Edward had ceased his nervous pacing and seated himself.

"Fine, Tythe then," he conceded. "I am Lord Althayne in 'The Seven Cardinal Sins' before Cardinal Bancheron trying to weave excuses for Bishop Manswick at the end of Act Four when being forced to help entrap his old friend. Satisfied?"

Theo smiled and fetched a battered book from his locker and found the page. "Ah here it is: *how thou hast blinded thyself with loyalty, my dear Althayne, when thine own weakness; thine own cowardice, thine own debaucheries hast delivered you into my hands. For thou art mine, naïve soul, and I shall save thee from a devil who presents to thee a mask of friendship; a deceit to thine eyes; a fair voice to thy fey vanities.* Ah, if Tythe could see us now as we sit in the Hall of the King wondering whether Bancheron and Manswick are both the Devil playing flawed men who trick and coerce poor Althayne into betraying his friends."

"So do you take Camus to be devil or a fool?"

Theo drained his cup and sighed. "No, he's a lost soul like Brother Ignatius, the wisest fool of all. Six years in his little tower by the railway free from Matins and Vespers and any thought of regret as he addles his wits in wine and books."

"At least, like Althayne's tragic Fool, he tried to warn us about the Conclave," Edward said, raising his cup in a toast and draining it. "It's too late for us to play the Fool, my friend: *the curtain has fallen and the Scythes of Time sweep the theatre clean of watchful souls but for those that linger, bound to this weeping earth, unaware their corporeal forms have cruelly ceased.*"

"Bancheron," Theo nodded sagely, adding more whisky to the cups. "He had the Fool blinded for that impertinence in front of his master yet here we sit in the Hall of the King wondering whether we be Fool, Althayne or a spectre in the gallery."

"Pfft, I'm solid enough," Edward said, resting his chin on a hand. "Like Ignatius, we buried our consciences in work and prayer and cared naught of the outside world unlike Camus..."

"Unlike Camus," Theo agreed. "He's told me often enough of his sleepless horror; of the nightly shades that tormented both he and Abbot Michael before he became the Naked One..."

Edward shuddered. "It made Camus vomit. What think you of that angel they say was spawned in the Great Annex?"

"There were wings and strange flesh but none alive witnessed it but for Michael who told of it when he and Schimrian were pulled from that infernal device some now call the 'immortality machine.' I'd love to study it as the circuitry is far, far beyond my current comprehension of electrics but Camus forbids it."

Edward gazed about the vast room and its sea of candles. "As would I but I can no longer deny we were party to Armageddon despite the holy rapture we felt at the time and the theological justification dripping from Conclave tongues. We..."

"We experience doubt and guilt? Fear that we will stand before God and be sent to Hell Eternal? Yes, at last we are. I feel a change in the air and not just because of this accursed storm but we must play Althayne for now and not the Fool otherwise we will be naught but food and sport for the Erdethric Ferals."

Edward drank some more and wiped his mouth with the back of his hand. "Six years of sweet oblivion in prayer and electrics!" he laughed. "And only now we hear the faint cries of those slain by our Order. *What bitter irony, Lord Althayne,* said the Fool, *for all that my orbs have been wrenched from my poor skull, I still see thee clearly: a pragmatist; a fine synonym for a coward; one who would still save his friend for all his cruelty and folly but whose soul drowns in fear and his resolve in copious wine; a shallow pantin hoisted this way and that by cardinal sins and strings...*"

"So we betray all and bury our consciences for another day of sweet life upon this storm-tossed ship of death?"

"We do, Edward. The world is dead and we killed it. This is an existence where we accept the wisdom of Ignatius and seek oblivion not salvation for, like the Bishop at the end of Tythe's tragedy; we cast aside our mantles of justification and bare our chests for the twin swords of redemption and damnation."

142

"Enough classical literature, Theo," Edward begged him. "My heart beats, there is whisky and food enough on this table to stave off such thoughts for now and for now it is *enough*."

Theo raised his cup again. "Here's to enough," he slurred happily. "Here's to the wisest fool in the Order: Ignatius!"

Edward clinked his cup against Theo's. "Ignatius!" he grinned.

~~~~~

Even in the oppressive and lightning-rent darkness stifling the Great Abbey and the fields and orchards round about, wafts of smoke could be seen being torn from the chimney of the tower. The lantern-lit topmost room was a study with curving plastered walls all painted white, great mahogany bookcases stuffed with all manner of publications, tables bearing rare porcelains and treasures looted by ardent postulants and novices for the only Brother in the Great Abbey to ever show them any kindness or respect.

A coal fire burnt brightly in the ornate tiled hearth that hissed occasionally when the largest of the hailstones gained entrance to the flue beneath the battered metal chimney hood. A large bottle of Alsace vintage and a half-filled glass sat upon an Indian coffee table which was inlaid with extraordinary marquetry using exotic woods. An old wind-up gramophone was playing the Third Sonata by the renowned Austrian composer, Valdus.

An incense candle smouldered on another table and a plate of bread and cheese lay on the floor by Brother Ignatius who sat at his desk in an ancient wooden chair carved with Celtic motifs of Cernunnos and running stags interlaced with brightly painted knot-work. He was reading a translation of Cicero and making notes in the margins. He gazed up at the needlework banner above the fireplace that repeated one of his favourite sayings attributed to Cicero: *a room without books is like a body without a soul.*

There were three floors to the station tower each with high ceilings and each accessed via an exterior stair case attached to the western side of the tower. The ground floor was the kitchen, toilets and office and could also be accessed from the small enclosed courtyard. Ignatius could not be sure, due to the tumult of the storm, but he thought he heard someone enter the ground floor and begin ransacking the place. His heart pounding, he crept to the door

143

and locked it wishing that there was another escape route as the faint and muffled sounds of destruction continued.

The Third Sonata drew to a crescendo and fell silent but for the click of the gramophone needle on the innermost groove. Ignatius strained his ears but all was quiet. "It must have been the wind or some novice venting his despair," he reasoned aloud to himself but nevertheless he retrieved a heavy fire-iron from the hearth.

Suddenly beneath his feet, he heard his bed being hurled across the bedroom and his wardrobes tossed against the walls to be reduced to splinters. It lasted four minutes but seemed like an eternity to Ignatius who began trembling. "Ah," he breathed aloud. "Dear Lord, protect me from the Devil within and without!"

He heard the door wood creak ominously until the lock failed from the superhuman pressure applied to it and flew across the room. Pious emerged from the darkness of the stairwell and drew back the cowl to reveal a predatory grin that froze the very marrow in his bones. With all his might, he brought down the fire-iron which bent on impact, tearing a large flap of flesh from the Abbot's scalp and revealing the white bone beneath.

Pious rocked slightly from the blow then reached up to press the flap of flesh back into place while glaring at the trembling cleric. He held it there for thirty seconds then took his hand away.

Ignatius shuddered violently and the fire-iron clattered to the floor for he could see neither blood nor a sign of any wound. He thought he would faint as dead lungs wheezed in air not for oxygen but for the act of conversation:

"Ask me how I did that?" Pious said in a voice as dry as the Vatican catacombs. Ignatius could not utter a sound such was his abject terror. "Ah, I'm afraid I have no explanation, Brother Ignatius. Let us just say that I am blessed by Our Lord God and let us not question His beneficence like some pagan or perhaps the Unworthy creature that carved your chair, shall we?"

Pious advanced upon the quaking Brother who retreated and made the sign of the Cross. "Forgive my poor welcome, Eminence, but I thought I was b-being attacked by the Light-Father. What do you want of me?"

"Ah, Brother Ignatius, I am on but a minor errand for the Great-Abbot: he wishes me to Inquire of you."

~~~~~~

144

Strange Rains

"Is that a vortex up there?" Mouse said nervously, pointing at a snaking funnel illuminated by lightning. "We saw one six years ago from the museum in Crawcester where we were hiding from the Order. Huge hailstones smashed all the skylights and statues to pieces! They were much bigger than the ones earlier and they whistled as they fell: they were the size of *boulders*!"

"By Helios, you've had some adventures," Nightshade smiled. "That's not a vortex but a waterspout and look: it's dissipating already. Milverburg cannot be hurt by any vortex so we're safe here. The worst of the lightning is moving north too but this rain is like watching a waterfall cascade. Listen to it pound upon the flagstones! I can't recall rain as heavy as this."

"Six years ago was bad," Mouse insisted. "That was when the first great flood swept away the Copper Bridge in Crawcester. We've had many storms since then but not one this heavy for a long time. Even the storm three weeks ago was nothing like this."

Amidst the deluge, something heavy thumped down onto the flagstones in front of them and that something flapped and slithered but the dim light beneath the clouds had faded so they could not see what was making the sound. Nightshade whispered an arcane chant in a long-lost tongue and the lion's head atop her staff began to emit white light. Then she laughed as more objects landed on the flagstones before them and on the viaduct until there was hundreds of them writhing about, scales glistening in the pale light. "Fish!" she cried out as another series of lightning flashes dispelled all doubt. "Strange rain in a strange world: we'll eat fresh fish tonight. Praise Diana and the Triple Goddess for their bounty!"

"I hope it's a good omen, Mother Nightshade."

"Food when a belly is empty is *always* a good omen, dear heart! That waterspout was sent by Gaia to aid us, I'm sure of it. It sucked these creatures high into the air and dropped them into our laps. We'd better find some baskets to collect as many as we can before the seabirds take to the skies and steal this feast from us."

They hastened back into the bowels of Milverburg and within minutes twenty excited Ferals were romping through the relentless downpour with boxes and woven baskets, filling them to the brim with fish whilst chattering and teasing each other. Mouse began to appreciate how good their night-vision was as she could barely make out their fleeting, darting shapes except during the more lurid lightning-flashes that left their images seared upon her retina like a photograph. Two minutes later, they retreated bearing their prizes to show Kai and the others, leaving Mouse and the enigmatic Wiccan alone in the Mouth of Thor once more, listening to the dull roar of the rain, illuminated by the faint glow of her staff.

They felt a warm wind on their faces and withdrew further into the tunnel as veils of rain angled towards them. Nightshade sniffed the air. "Even this deluge cannot wash out the ashes of Africa," she mused aloud. "But the wind is shifting to the east and the storm is losing energy. I fear it will dissipate before dawn. That's only six hours away and we must get some rest. If the weather sets fair tomorrow, who knows what devilry will come our way?"

Mouse dropped her spear and buried her face in the bosom of the Wiccan catching her by surprise. "What ever is the matter, dear heart?" she said, holding Mouse close to her with her free hand. "I had hoped you'd tell me more of your tale about the Crawcester museum and how you met up with Amos, Fria and Surl."

"A cruel memory, Mother Nightshade," Mouse sniffed, the tears coursing down her face. "Four years ago we were searching for food in the centre of town and we were attacked by a huge pack of dogs. Leo and Jana could not run as fast as us as they were still unwell from eating bad food. The dog pack ate them alive and as we ran away, we could hear them screaming and begging us to save them. Saul and David never forgave themselves and we all cried for *days* until Mother Moss told us that they were destined to make that sacrifice as it allowed us to survive when they could not."

Mouse buried her face in the albino's bosom again and shuddered and howled. "Peace, little one," Nightshade said. "The Light-Father is right: whenever a memory like this afflicts you, you must speak of it and let others lend you their strength by listening. Cry, dear heart: I'll always be here for you. We'll face the dark memories and the nightmares together. We'll prevail together."

"I'll never forget Leo and Jana," Mouse sobbed. "And now I've lost my sister as well as my parents. It's not *fair*!"

"I know, Mouse, I know. I lost my family as well but I will never forget them: they will always be in my thoughts."

Mouse wiped her eyes as the rain slackened only for the heavens to be rent by fusillades of lightning flashes, some of which struck the rails on the viaduct sending currents sparking past them along the tracks. The discharges worked their way into the Core making one of the Ferals by the Phoenix leap into the air as he was playing on the tracks, still wet from harvesting the fish.

The display distracted Mouse and, after the rattling thunder had faded northwards, she looked up at the Wiccan. "The Light-Father is right: I have to confront each memory as it surfaces. If you don't talk about it, he said, it's like bottling poison inside you."

"This is true. He's really perceptive for a man."

"I love him, Mother Nightshade. He's like a father to me and you're now like a mother to me. Thank you."

Nightshade was taken aback: "Ah, you do me a real honour, dear heart. I don't know what to say."

"How about telling me what happened after Schimrian almost caught you and your parents at the roadblock."

Nightshade pursed her lips and then sighed. "I suppose I, too, must honour the Light-Father's dictum though the tale does not end well - like so many in this dark grimoire of a world."

~~~~~

"Phaw!" Ellete snorted in disgust. She had her head out of the rear car window like a hound savouring the breeze but the day was already swelteringly hot. "What is that *stink*?"

"Mind your head doesn't blow off, Ellete!" Kendra joked, glancing over her shoulder.

"Don't be silly, Ma! What's making that awful smell?"

"We're on the Dead Marshes Road, Ellete," Bordan explained. "See that big fortress and those bridges across the Estuary? That's Milverburg. You can just about see it through the haze."

"Un-*geh*! I can see it! It's *huge*! I thought it was an island, Da!" Ellete chirped. "Oh, this is like going on holiday! Honey Bear says he's excited. Honey Bear wants ice cream!"

"Ha! I bet he does," Bordan laughed. "That smell is the Dead Marshes and it's always worse in hot weather. They say people get lost in there and it sucks down birds and animals too. The corpses and the rotting vegetation create that foul odour."

"Yrch! I hate it," Ellete grimaced. "Mouldy cabbage and rotten eggs smell nicer than that… or a kack after a bad tummy."

"That's enough about toilets, dear heart," Kendra admonished. "I don't want you getting travel sick again."

147

"Speaking of toilets, we can go when we pull in to get some scyfol at the highway station this side of Rackgate," Bordan said decisively, tapping at the fuel gauge. "This car uses a lot of fuel and we could use some food, coffee and ice cream. It'll be another thirty minutes or so. Can you wait that long?"

Ellete flopped back into her seat, folded her arms around her Honey Bear and pouted: "Hmph! I suppose so!"

She turned to stare out of the rear window. "I'm glad that awful man back there isn't following us. I could hear this horrible voice whispering to him in his head. His hand was as cold as *ice*. He made me so *scared*."

"He scared us too but you were a great actress, dear heart," Kendra said kindly. "You made us both so proud of you!"

"But why was I born like *this*, Ma?"

"Hmm, I'll leave that one to you, Kendra," Bordan grinned.

"Thank you *so* much, dear heart," Kendra said sarcastically, digging an elbow into his side. She turned in her seat to stare at her daughter. "It's called genetics, dear…"

"Oh, *that's* a good start," Bordan interrupted only to receive another sharp jab to the ribs.

"Ellete, when a man and a woman come together they each give a little part of themselves, mix it together and start a baby growing in the woman's womb and then, nine months later, she gives birth to a little boy or a little girl."

"Yes, but *why* am I so different? If part of me is you and part of me is Da mixed together then I should have brown hair and brown eyes! Am I *really* your daughter?"

"Shhh, stay those tears, dear heart," Kendra soothed, taking her daughter's hand. "It's complicated and you need many more years to understand it all but every so often, something goes wrong in the mixing that makes babies. Da and I both have a part of us that's defective and if those parts come together, the baby can't make the pigment that gives colour to skin and hair so they stay white and the irises can turn a blood-red colour like yours."

"Oh! So I'm *defective*!" Ellete sobbed, yanking her hand away and burying her face in her Honey Bear.

"That went well, *ow*!" Bordan yelped. "Hoi! That is going to leave a bruise! Perhaps we should have waited a few years."

"I think we should just let her cry it out," Kendra said, staring despondently at passing clumps of bulrush, reed mace and cattail that marked the living boundary of the Dead Marshes. "She has to know she's our daughter and we love her!"

"She has but six years, Kendra," Bordan said placatingly. "How much did you understand of the world having tallied but six years? You probably can't remember anything."

"Oh, I do, Bordan. In primary school, they taught us of such things at her tally but she hasn't been to school yet." She turned to her daughter again. "Listen, Ellete: you are *not* defective; you're an albino and our rare and precious and beautiful daughter. How could anything so beautiful possibly be defective?"

"But I can make magic and you can't," Ellete whinged. "So I *must* be made wrong. Is that why those men want to hurt me?"

Bordan wisely kept his council as he knew Kendra would probably break a rib next time. Something caught his eye in his rear view mirrors. "Kendra, there are two black rotorcraft flying low along the road behind us," he said with some concern. "Surely the police can't be after us already?"

Ellete immediately took an interest, wiped her eyes and knelt on her seat to gaze out of the rear windscreen. The Angels roared overhead causing vehicles travelling in both directions to swerve so that it was a minor miracle that no collisions occurred.

"Ach," Bordan snorted in disgust. "Those were Order rotorcraft not the police. I know they must be ferrying patients to hospitals for emergency treatment but their pilots always fly low to show their contempt for us lesser mortals; the Unworthy as they call us."

"Oh, I thought we were going to be taken," Kendra fretted. "Bordan, I'm so frightened!"

"Be at peace, dear heart. I'll put the car radio on."

Kendra rested her head against the car window and despite her despair she was lulled into a doze by the tepid mass-produced melodies of several Government-approved folk bands. What felt like a moment later, she was being gently shaken awake by Bordan. "We're coming into Rackgate," he explained. "Look: there's the highway station. You'll feel better after some tea and something to eat and I believe Ellete still wants her ice-cream."

"And one for Honey Bear!"

"And one for Honey Bear," he laughed. He pulled into the car park that was already shimmering in the intense late-morning sunshine. "We mustn't use bankcards or cheques if we can avoid it," he said, counting the bills in his wallet.

"But these 'Asphalt Sovereign' places are so expensive!"

Bordan gazed at his wife and grinned. She had said it in such a petulant and matter-of-fact way that he briefly had the illusion that they were simply an ordinary family on vacation.

"What's so amusing, Bordan?" she frowned.

"Nothing. I just realised how beautiful you are."

"Pfft! Flattery is the discourse of fools and demons."

"Aye, there's some truth to that," he sighed. He opened the rear door and helped Ellete and her Honey Bear out of the back seat.

"It's so *hot!*" Ellete complained. "This hat is making my brain melt like cheese on toast and my clothes are hot too!"

"You have to wear trousers and the long-sleeved top, dear heart," Kendra explained. "And the hat and those glasses. You'll have to play the actress until we get to Crawcester, understood?"

"Yes, Ma," Ellete grumbled rebelliously and stomped off ahead of them, leading the way to the cafeteria part of the station.

They entered a large hall full of plastic furniture and tacky wall paintings depicting Celtic, Norse and Saxon legends. There were serving hatches at the far end behind a counter made to resemble a battlement. Waiters in black shirts and trousers wore aprons each bearing the motif of a crown surrounded by stars and runes as they flitted to and fro amongst the hubbub, wiping tables and clearing away used plates and cutlery. To Kendra and Bordan, it was the epitome of poor taste and crass consumerism but to Ellete, cosseted and cocooned all her life, it was a magical palace.

"Let's get this over with," Kendra said, grabbing Ellete's hand. "People are staring at us already."

Bordan shrugged his shoulders as they joined the back of the queue. "No, that's just normal paranoia, dear heart. We're just a normal family on a normal vacation so relax."

There was a family in front of them with a young blond boy in a plain shirt and shorts holding his mother's hand. He was staring at Ellete but he could only see his reflection in her mirrored lenses. "Ma, Ma, there's a strange blind girl behind us," he said several times, tugging at her hand. "She's *weird.*"

"Shh, Cedric, it is not polite to point at people or call them names," she said curtly, wagging a finger at her son. She turned to Kendra. "I'm so sorry but he's usually so well-behaved."

"That's okay," Kendra said, greatly relieved. "It happens all the time. My daughter isn't blind or weird but she suffered a viral infection as a baby that damaged her retinas so she can't bear bright light - it causes her so much pain."

"Oh, I see," the woman said, guiding Cedric away from Ellete. "But does she need to be bundled up like that? Cedric! Stop staring at the poor girl. Be grateful that you have your health and you can run about without sunglasses." She knelt down and put a hand on Ellete's shoulder. "I apologise for my son's rudeness. You've been through some hard times, dear heart. Please accept my blessings for your good fortune and your good health."

Kendra nudged her daughter. "Manners, Freda, what do you say to the nice woman?"

"Thank you," Ellete simpered and bobbed a curtsy.

The woman stood up and was in raptures. "Oh, how *precious*," she gushed. "How I wish I had a daughter to go with my three boys but we had to stop at the three boys unfortunately."

Her husband laughed good-naturedly at Bordan. "The spirits were willing but the bank balance was weak! Families these days often have more children than they can feed then they expect our government and our taxes to pay for them but not us!"

"Very commendable," Bordan nodded, deciding that he felt he should dislike the man immensely but the man's round face and engaging demeanour had caught him off-guard. "We, alas, have but one child yet we count our blessings."

"Ah, yes, I expect the medical bills for the poor child were crippling, no doubt," the man sympathised. "But good for you: too many parents surrender custody of their disabled children to the orphanages run by the Government and the Order..."

"It's scandalous: we hear such rumours about their treatment even in Accyngate," his wife interrupted in a quiet voice, looking around nervously to ensure that they could not be overheard. "The local orphanage was shut down last year as some of the children went *missing*. Some in Accyngate say that the Government and Exodus were using them in *experiments*!"

"Ah, I wouldn't know," Bordan dissembled. "We've heard nothing of this in Brigstowe and we have three orphanages there. Accyngate, you say? I thought you were from the northern reaches of the Middle Cities from the accent," Bordan smiled. "I'm afraid that we've never visited your home town."

"Oh, we have a new Cathedral," the man huffed proudly. "We're no longer just a market town on the northern borders of the Middle

Cities. Accyngate became officially chartered as a Middle City in its own right last Whitsuntide!"

"Congratulations," Kendra said brightly, enjoying the banality of the conversation. "We're taking a vacation in Crawcester but we might take a trip north to Accyngate."

"Then you'd be most welcome," the man nodded, proffering Bordan a business card with both hands. "Please look us up if you do make the journey. If we're free, we would be delighted to show you the more interesting sights. I am sure we can disprove the myth that Middle City folk are inhospitable and wary of strangers. We have a lot of tourists these days. We…"

"It's our turn to order, Aaron," his wife interrupted, indicating the counter. "The boys want the meat pâtés and potato chips."

"Thank you," Bordan said, bowing slightly and accepting Aaron's card with both hands in the manner of the traders of the Japanese Empire. "I hope you enjoy your vacation too."

"We hope so," Aaron shrugged as his wife grudgingly ordered for the family as it was obvious Aaron wanted to carry on talking to Bordan. "We're planning to go through Fosskeep and head down to the Tamemere Piers where all the amusement parks are. We *were* going to Arthburg for the festivals and shows but they were cancelled following those incidents with those Cymrig brigands. It's a national shame that King John the Merciless showed too much mercy to those Cymrig swine!"

Bordan's eyes widened at the casual, racist callousness of the statement. "It *was* called the Great Massacre for a reason," he pointed out delicately. "Even after centuries of recovery, there are but twelve thousand Cymrig alive today."

Aaron tutted: "Yes, I know and every one an inbred genetic nightmare according to the Order. Why else would they attack and murder innocent citizens?"

"Why else, indeed," Bordan replied blandly. "After all this time, they still seem to harbour an irrational hatred towards Britannic citizens for the Massacre. You'd have thought they would've let it go by now. After all, history is history."

"Well said," Aaron grinned, completely oblivious to the irony. "They are more vexatious than the Fellholmers and Longspit clans could ever be. Anyway, our food is ready. It has been a pleasure to meet you. I do hope that we will meet again in Accyngate but please forgive me: I know not your names."

"Geoffrey Geowine, at your service," Bordan said formally, shaking Aaron's hand. "This is my wife, Cassandra and my daughter El... I mean Freda."

Aaron looked puzzled for a moment then smiled broadly. "Well met then, Geoffrey and Cassandra. My wife's first name is classical too: Hera; obviously an omen that we'll meet again. May God watch over thee and thy vacation."

Kendra and Bordan returned the bow. "And thee and thine," they responded formally. Bordan watched Aaron pick up the second tray of food and then the family wandered off in search of a table with Cedric racing pell-mell around his stoic brothers.

"Hera indeed!" Kendra scoffed. "Their little Cedric is a nest of vipers to be sure but if I'm to be Cassandra then those two are definitely Clytemnestra and her lover, Aegisthus."

Bordan ordered their sandwiches and ice creams but the counter assistant apologised that the coffees and chocolate milk would be awhile: the machines had broken down so they were making the drinks with kettles. He gave them glasses of water for free. "We'll bring your drinks to that corner table over there in about ten minutes," he said, pointing. "We'll discount the tea and coffee because of the inconvenience," he added, bowing.

They carried their trays to the table and seated themselves after waving at Aaron and Hera who were two tables away from them and struggling to control Cedric who was leaping around with the toy aeroplane given away free with the children's meals. Ellete took a token bite out of her sandwich before launching into the ice-cream. Bordan could not resist a dig at Kendra: "So who am I?" he teased. "Am I your Apollo or your Agamemnon?"

"Huh! Neither," she said in a tragic voice. "More like Ajax the Lesser snatching me away from my helpless family."

Bordan laughed: "You are indeed the queen of tragedies but for some reason I can't explain I fell hopelessly in love and married you despite all the fey glamours about you."

Cedric ran past their table making aircraft engine noises and was evidently irritating all the families around them. "I almost feel sorry for his parents," Kendra whispered. "They call it hyper-activity like it's some kind of disease but it's all down to failures in parental discipline. Ah, here come the drinks!"

"Thank Almighty Zeus," Bordan said, continuing the mythological theme. "I desperately need some coffee!"

The harassed and overworked waiter had several other orders balanced on his tray so he didn't see Cedric dart between two tables to trip him up as he approached their table. Bordan felt the world was moving in slow motion as the man tumbled forward and all the cups and their contents were propelled towards Ellete. He saw the look of horror on Hera's face as she rose from her table then something miraculous happened: for one moment, the cups and most of the hot liquid had simply stopped dead in mid-air but not all of it: some reached Ellete and she yelped in pain.

The cups and the suspended liquid fell to the table in a cascade but Kendra reacted instantly and hurled their water at Ellete where the hot tea and coffee had splashed her. She tore off Ellete's glasses and hat to hastily wipe her face and neck, making sure there were no scalds but removing the make-up in the process.

Hera approached the table with a look of mortification on her face. She had literally hurled the bawling Cedric into his father's arms then helped the waiter back onto his feet while apologising profusely to him, bowing Japanese-fashion until he was placated and left to fetch a mop, pan and brush to clear the debris.

"By Saint Basil's bones, forgive me: I am so sorry," she began, wringing her hands as Kendra dabbed Ellete with paper towels from her bag. "Your sandwiches are ruined as well. I'm so sorry; we cannot get Cedric to sit still! Um… is Freda unharmed? I hope she's not scalded. Bu… bu…" she gurgled to a halt and stared open-mouthed as Kendra had moved out of the way so she could see the little girl clearly. Glaring at her was a child with pure white hair, snow-white skin and blood-red irises that made the hairs on the back of her neck stand up on end. "Oh! She's an *albino*!" she gasped and almost fainted. "An *albino*! God preserve us!"

"Now you know why we lie and why we cover her up," Bordan said angrily, indicating Hera. "We do it because we are sick of seeing reactions and prejudice like *that*. We live in modern times, Hera, but people hang on to their mindless superstitions."

Hera had her hands to her mouth but she rallied quickly and her face became serious. "I can only humbly apologise again. We are not medieval in Accyngate, I can assure you but," she paused and broke into a smile. "She *is* striking and she caught me by surprise." She bent down to speak to Ellete: "I think you're beautiful, Freda. Sometimes, being different is good. You're going to have so many boyfriends when you grow up!"

Ellete, pouted and stared out of the window. Hera stood up again and put her hands on her hips. "I don't blame her for not speaking to me but let me make it up to you. I insist on replacing your ruined food and drinks. Will you at least let me do that much by way of making amends for Cedric?"

"That's very generous of you," Bordan told her as three waiters arrived and started mopping up the puddles and clearing away the broken cups and plates from both floor and table. "But we need to get some scyfol and resume our journey."

"No, you just move to the next table while they clean up and I'll be right back with fresh sandwiches and more ice-cream for Freda. Would you like some of their special double chocolate ice-cream, Freda? They say it's worth going to war over it!"

After a nudge from Kendra, Ellete nodded: "Yes, please."

Hera scurried off leaving them to move to the next table with more paper towels handed to them by the waiters to dab at their clothes. Kendra noted with spiteful satisfaction that Cedric was still crying his eyes out but she doubted that he was seriously hurt. He was also the object of angry glares and comments from many other diners who clearly shared her opinion of him.

"A lot of people were staring at Ellete. Thank the stars we're not in Cheal or Oldhayne," Bordan muttered. "This is not good: we only need one person to call the police and we're troll-meat but if we flee, I'd expect Hera to call them herself."

"Then we stay and accept the Accyngate peace offering," Kendra sighed, resigned. "You can take the top off as well, Ellete, now that everyone's seen you. We're on holiday after all and you get the expensive ice-cream that we can't afford."

"Ah, that's better," Ellete grinned after removing the wet over-shirt. She had a Honey Bear t-shirt underneath that was coffee-stained but presentable. She stiffened and put a hand to shade her eyes from the bright light streaming in through the nearby windows. "That woman is talking to the people at the counter and pointing at us and those waiters were talking about me too."

Hera arrived with fresh sandwiches and coffees and the biggest bowl of chocolate ice-cream Ellete had ever seen. She was blushing furiously. "We've been asked to leave," she explained. "They can never grasp what makes him like this so I understand how you feel about the prejudice you experience." She bowed again and fought back tears: "May God bless thee and thy journey."

"And thee and thine," Bordan responded suspiciously. "The counter staff seemed to be asking a lot of questions about our daughter. What were they saying? Are they afraid of her?"

Hera saw that Aaron and the boys were at the exit and waiting impatiently for her. "They were just ignorant dullards: I had to explain to them what causes albinism and that she wasn't about to curse them. Hopefully they'll leave you alone. Farewell."

Bordan watched them leave and saw that the curiosity of other families seemed to be satisfied. "That could've been worse," he said. "But thanks to her, we've got time to enjoy our food."

He was wrong.

~~~~~

Abbess

Surl awoke in the pitch black dark and no matter how she tossed and turned on her makeshift bed she could not find sleep again. She'd had no dream or vision so she felt truly blind for the first time in years but she felt no fear only a curiosity about her powers and a fleeting hope that she was becoming 'normal'. The cellar was quiet apart from the waters gushing past the access door, rats skittering in the stonework and the gentle snoring of the others with Pup mumbling the word 'cake' every so often.

Despite her age, she had been honed by years of remorseless training by Mother Moss so she found her machete by touch and only then did she turn on the lantern and set it to emit a dim glow. She felt a sudden and overwhelming need to do her toilet and realised that she had given this little thought before bed so she sheathed her weapon and padded upstairs to the store-room where, to her relief, there was a bucket which she used gratefully.

She tore strips from some linen sheets to wipe herself clean and recalled peeing on Amos's shoes six years ago as they hid from the Order in an inspection chamber in the garden while their parents and their brother and sister were tortured in the family home. She wept silently, recalling how she somehow knew they were dead and picking flowers to place beside their blood-soaked bodies.

They'd lived in their grandparents' garage for a while after the elderly couple had refused to let them into the house for fear of the Plague. She remembered how Ruff-Ruff, the Feral, joined them and how she could *feel* her grandparents dying before the arrival of Mother Moss. She ground her teeth with a new resolve: the Order would pay for their crimes; every last stinking one of them!

Mindful of Peter's warning about rats, she found a large lidded jar and carried that, strips of linen, the bucket and the lantern downstairs with great difficulty. She opened the sewer access door and tipped the bucket contents into the water racing past with the runoff from the torrential rain still falling above ground.

She was glad she could swill the bucket out as the water was almost level with the sewer walkway and she wondered how it was so high yet the cellar did not flood then she remembered the overflow tunnel Ignatius had told her about. The water appeared to be clean so she breathed a sigh of relief and washed her hands before returning to the cellar to store the food in the jar.

She sat on her bedding and listened to all the sounds about her: the water, the others breathing and the faint sound of the Great Bell tolling six times to call the Order to Matins. She closed her eyes and crossed her legs - as Mother Moss had taught her to do - and let her mind drift upon the sounds. She opened her eyes suddenly as she could clearly hear a lamentation echoing down the stairs; a sound that set her heart leaping with fear.

She took the lantern and with her machete drawn, she warily ascended the stairs again and tiptoed up to the door leading into the corridor. She was glad Peter had propped the door shut as there was a lot of activity on the other side of it. A caterwauling was issuing from at least three female throats and she presumed that they were mourning the dead Sisters in the kitchen. There were other voices; frantic and disjointed:

"So many Sisters are dead!"

"Oh! There's blood *everywhere*!"

"How can we prepare food with their bodies lying there?"

"Why did the Tally-men kill so many of us?"

"Will the Abbess do something about this? We can't leave them in the kitchen lying on the floor like that!"

"Many greenhouse panes have been broken by the hail and many of the crops are ruined. What shall we do?"

"If the sunlamps don't work, the plants won't grow!"

"There were fires and explosions all night!"

"What's happened to the electrics?"

"They got into Magdalene House and not one Sister survived!"

"In Saint Mary's, they were murdered in their beds!"

"And Saint Catherine's. All dead! All dead!"

"So only the Abbess Manse and our House were spared?"

"Yes."

"Oh, so many dead! So many dead! So many dead!"

"What will become of us?"

"I don't know. Oh, Abbess! Bless you! You survived!"

The tumult in the corridor subsided and another female voice spoke with an authority and intelligence demonstrably lacking in the others: "Sisters, I have visited all the Houses in the Enclave and I'm afraid only those of you in Saint Agnes House and in my Manse were spared this calamity. The Fathers tell me that the Wiccans and their cohorts attacked the Great Cathedral yesterday and bewitched the Tally-Men into attacking us."

"We saw them by the Eastern Processional after we'd delivered food to the Fathers' Lodge. The beast-children came at us but they were only interested in fighting the Brothers."

"Oh, oh, how could the Fathers let the Harlots do this?"

"What about Matins, Noon Prayer and Vespers?"

The Abbess spoke curtly in a raised voice: "Stop babbling! We will *not* observe them this day and we will gather at my Manse for Compline as there are now but three dozen of us left alive."

Exclamations of horror and weeping resumed then a lamentation by several sisters began but the Abbess silenced them: "Enough! We are Sisters of the Order and we have much to do! Sisters Anna and Freya: you lay sheets upon our departed sisters in the kitchen. The rains have eased so, Sisters Audrey and Darlene, take bread, sausage and cheese to the postulants and novices…"

Surl listened intently and began to gain a picture of the losses sustained by the Order and how few Brothers, Sisters and Fathers remained alive in the Great Abbey. She peered through the door crack on hearing heavy footfalls in the corridor but the table banged suddenly against the door startling her and making her gasp. Tally-men were lumbering past into the kitchen with stretchers to begin the removal of the dead Sisters. Many of the Sisters clamoured in fear at the sight of the Tally-men with a few becoming hysterical until the Abbess silenced them; slapping several across the face when they were beyond the reach of words.

The Abbess continued issuing instructions until all the Sisters were given tasks but one thing that struck Surl was the rapid change of mood of the Sisters from caterwauling and moaning in despair to singing psalms in clear bright voices as they set about their duties. It was like a switch had been thrown to erase their memory of the dead. She could hear the blood being mopped from the floor in the kitchen and food despatched across the Great Abbey as it stirred into a shattered and ghastly parody of its former life.

The corridor fell silent for several minutes and Surl was about to return to the cellar when she realised the candles in the corridor had been extinguished yet dawn had only just begun. She immediately switched off the lantern but it was too late:

"I know you're there, child," the Abbess said. She was sitting on the corridor table and talking quietly through the split in the door wood so that the Sisters in the kitchen could not hear her speaking: "I heard you gasp and beheld your lamplight."

Surl cursed herself but held her tongue and waited in an agony of suspense for several minutes of absolute silence.

"So be it, child," the Abbess sighed heavily. "I would've loved to hear the sweet voice of a child again to fill the emptiness in both my womb and my heart. I saw the four of you emerge from the bell tower through the pall of smoke so I presumed you were left behind after your so-called Light-Father retreated. Let me now bear my soul to thee: I had no part in the genocide wrought upon the world but I did sense a foul shadow growing in the Great Abbey some ten years before the Plague was released. After the Plague, it got stronger until I couldn't bear to be near the Great Annex - such was the satanic malice I felt emanating through its walls."

The Abbess fell silent for a minute. "I could put no words to this evil but in my heart I knew that it was somehow corrupting the Conclave and shrouding the Brothers' hearts. Thus when the monstrous Seven-Headed Lamb was found, they sent forth the Virus without question. Like yours no doubt, my family fell to the Plague and my faith was tested and found wanting. Brothers were filled with an insatiable hatred and sent to hunt down survivors across the globe; slaughtering infants and innocents; branding them all Unworthy to justify each atrocity."

She laughed bitterly: "I am brought low: confessing my sins to a mute Child of Exodus through a crack in a door: a poor excuse for a confessional. Forgive me for I have sinned, dear heart, and for six years I've been trapped here out of despair and a sense of duty to my precious, helpless Sisters; my little flock."

The door creaked as the Abbess gently leant her back against it. "You may not believe me, dear heart, but I *despise* the fact that my Sisters were genetically *bred* for generations to be brood mares in this so-called New Jerusalem. I was told, even *after* the Plague, that the Order had provided sanctuary for all these simple-minded women who would otherwise be preyed upon in a cruel world. Fool that I was, I believed them but I soon realised how *misogynistic* the machinations of the Conclave truly were!"

There was another pause yet Surl could not move as she was mesmerised. "Then the Tally-men were created to assist in the Inquisitions – so called as to legitimise the butchery. How my poor Sisters quailed at the screams from beneath the Great Manse and the thin, young men in chains being led into the Redemption Cells. Redemption: oh, how that holy word has been twisted! I heard how

160

their brains were being sliced open and those Guides driven into their skulls to create slaves without conscience. I care not if the Wiccans turned them upon us or not: it was no more than the Order deserved for stealing their bodies and their *souls…*"

The Abbess faltered and stifled several choking sobs: "With the world gone, I remained and countenanced one unspeakable horror after another. I closeted myself in my Manse and prayed until I could pray no more. I became like Brother Ignatius in his tower: he to his books and I to my precious Sisters; keeping them chaste and safe from the grasping lust of Brother, novice and postulant."

There came another pause as the Abbess collected herself. "Ah, still listening I see," she chuckled. "I can almost hear your heart beating but fear not: I will not harm thee but heed my words: flee the darkness that ensnares us and be wary of Wiccans. Fear their powers and remember that they are not of God and may lead thee astray onto even darker paths. I think we'll meet again before all is done but I must leave you now and tend to my poor brood mares. Farewell, Child of Exodus. Pray for me and wish Brother Ignatius *kali uyeia* when you see him next."

Her slow footsteps faded leaving Surl bewildered and panting heavily as she switched on the lantern. She slapped herself hard in the face several times. "Stupid, stupid, stupid Surl!" she muttered angrily then, her heart heavy with self-contempt, she returned to the cellar to find Peter awake and lighting candles.

"Good morrow, fair maid," he smiled, bowing gallantly.

"There's *nothing* good about this day nor am I a fair maid!"

He looked crestfallen at her tone: "Hoi! What's wrong? I was only trying to cheer you up."

After she had told him everything she'd overheard, he thought for a moment then shrugged: "If this Abbess was going to raise the alarm, Surl, she would've done it straight away not waited until there was nobody in the corridor and then poured her heart out to you. She hates the Order for killing her family and she feels she has nowhere to go so she stays to look after the Sisters."

"Yes and now we know how few Brothers and Sisters remain alive but I made a stupid mistake with that lantern: if my brother was here, you can imagine how he would scold me!"

"The Sisters are as brainless as sheep so you could not know that they had a wolf as a shepherdess but this is good news: we can stay here in the cellar until we escape! Besides," he grinned. "You know

Amos is a bull-pat with no compassion or sense of humour so stop being a worry-wart: maybe she'll help us like Ignatius and then maybe she won't. How did she know he was in the cellar?"

"Oh, she must know about the wine racks down here and how he likes his drink," Surl said thoughtfully. "Having two people who know about us is not good but we have no choice: we have to trust them because if they were going to betray us they would have done so by now and we would all be dead."

"Then stop belittling yourself," he said stoutly. "We still live thanks to you and your visions and we can do a lot of damage before we escape. With your power we can do *anything*!"

Surl bowed her head: "My visions have stopped for now. I can't foresee what we must do next or how to avoid capture. The sun is almost up and we must try to sabotage something after breakfast with or without my visions." She pointed at Rabbit and Pup who were slowly starting to wake up. "Let's get some breakfast ready for the little ones first."

She opened up the food jar as Peter set plates for them. She buttered hunks of bread for them all and cut the cheese and dried meats into slices with one of her knives.

Peter put a piece of linen over his forearm and stood by Rabbit and Pup as they wiped the sleep out of their eyes. "Good morrow, sir and madam," he said, imitating a supercilious waiter in a Crawcester restaurant that Saul had described to them. "Your table awaits and we have quite the breakfast menu: bread and cheese, bread and dried meat, cheese and dried meat or bread and bread with some excellent water to wash it down."

"Pup's confused," Pup said blearily. "Did you hit your head?"

"He's pretending he's a waiter and we're the rich diners," Rabbit yawned. "I would rather the blow to the head, to be honest."

"Tch! Such ungrateful guests! Chef *will* be upset!"

Surl laughed, grateful for the distraction. "Play along, you two, otherwise he'll sulk and complain about his stump for *hours*."

With martyred expressions, they allowed themselves to be shown to the table by Peter who readied the chairs for them and tucked in strips of linen to serve as their bibs. He so enjoyed the role that Pup and Rabbit eventually entered into the spirit of the charade ordering venison and champagne for their evening meals. Suddenly, there was a scraping outside the sewer access door followed by six rapid knocks but before the first knock sounded, all four children were

162

already away from the table in fighting stances and holding their weapons at the ready.

After two minutes of bated breath, Surl gingerly opened the cellar door but Ignatius was long gone. In the dim light of the lantern she beheld on the walkway a thermos flask, a jug of fresh milk and two rolled up parchments tied with string. She opened the thermos cap slowly and sniffed at the contents. "Hot tea!" she exclaimed, her eyes widening. "Quickly, Rabbit, light two more candles and bring those cups to the table."

As Rabbit complied, Peter unrolled the two parchments. He examined them with the lantern and smiled: "Ha! We don't need your visions now, Surl: this one is a plan of the Great Abbey and the other is a map of the sewer system beneath it. Look: Ignatius has written exactly where and when we need to strike!"

Surl gazed at the parchments and saw that Ignatius had marked out the access routes to fuel stores, garages, the generator room, the former Exodus laboratories where begiullers were made, the Angel hangars, the Great Manse and the Great Annex. "Bless Ignatius: we have a chance," she sighed with relief. "We might be able to stop them from searching for the Light-Father and the others."

Pup paused from slurping at his hot tea. "Does that mean we're not going to die?" he asked brightly. "Are we really going to finish the Saga of Pup the Mighty and his Catapult of Justice?"

Despite her heavy heart, Surl nodded and forced a smile: "Yes, we will live to tell the Saga of Pup the Mighty but finish your food first: we can't bring down the Order on an empty stomach!"

~~~~~~

"I think I need more food," Peter declared as his stomach growled loudly. "I can barely hear the rain and thunder!"

Surl yawned, stretched and snuggled into Harold's chest again pinning him to the sofa. "Uff! She's solid for such a young girl," he muttered ruefully. Her machete was still in its sheath and he had to take it off her as the hilt kept digging into his shoulder. He noticed with mild surprise that his katana was also making its presence felt and he realised how quickly it had became automatic for him to keep a weapon to hand. In the candle-light, he could see how all four children were the same. Rabbit leant against Fern with a contented smile on her face - and an axe in each hand.

Peter had paused in his tale to sit in one of the arm chairs and finish the second bowl of broth that Shield had brought him. As he drank the broth, Harold saw how he was hampered by the knife attached to his stump and the naked blade on the armrest.

Pup was gently snoring on the other side of Fern with a drawn knife still in his hand. Harold clearly saw Fern's growing maternal feelings for both children as she held them close to her: a small pool of solace in their nightmarish, dystopian childhoods.

"I hear your thoughts, dear heart," she said candidly. "I too wish I could grant these poor children a peaceful life."

He was about to reprimand her for using telepathy but his ire dissolved in the deep adoration he had for this beautiful witch - even though he knew he would never fathom her powers. His world had no such creatures except in fairy tales and myths but then it struck him: the university had been awash with rumours about inexplicable events happening around that bizarre patient of Doctor Smith's. He'd seen the vending machine embed itself in a wall then he'd witnessed the hell-lights and the shadows and then he'd been translocated into this world. He had no rational explanation for these events yet here was: the Light-Father!

He listened to the rain hammering onto the roof and the bass reverberations of the thunder shaking both innards and the dust from the ceilings and shelves and decided that there was nowhere in the universe he would rather be. He saw damp patches forming in the ceiling corners and resisted a sudden irrational urge to go upstairs and fix the hail-shattered tiles.

"This home will soon succumb to the elements," Fern sighed. "As will millions of others," she paused at the sound of shouting and a brief scuffle in the kitchen. She turned to Peter who was staring at her, his eyes shining brightly in the candle light: "Ignore them, Peter: it's only a family reunion. Please, tell us what happened next in the Saga of Pup the Mighty."

Peter patted his stump and Harold's eyes widened. "Yes, Light-Father," he grinned. "Brother Ignatius made this wonderful new leather sheath for me. It fits *perfectly.*"

"Then tell us more about him," Harold urged. "This storm will last for hours so we have all the time in the world."

~~~~~

164

Wolf and Worse

"Brother Spero," Father Ursaf said loftily. "I deem the worst of the storm has now passed. I need you to go out and see if there is any significant damage to our rotorcraft."

Spero's inventive expletives were completely drowned out by a savage peal of thunder. "I'm sorry, my son," Ursaf said with exaggerated patience, cupping a hand round one ear: "Could you say that again? I completely missed your wisdom on the matter."

"I will *not* check the accursed rotors and the Angels by torchlight in rain like this," Spero snarled, reining in his expletives with difficulty: he was beginning to acquire new layers to his loathing of the portly Father especially as Ursaf had just eaten most of their rations without sharing them. "The lightning is striking limbs from the trees over there and a bolt could easily ground through an Angel. So curse me to hell and back if you will, Father, but I *refuse* to do your absurd bidding."

"As would I," Gudflan added, shivering. "And curse this place too: we can't find anywhere dry to sleep!"

Savage crosswinds buffeted the ruined farmhouse, tearing at the broken tiles above their heads. Ceilings had long collapsed so torrents cascaded unhindered into ground floor rooms with only the kitchen left dry apart from puddles on the flagstones. Father Ursaf and both Angel crews had been soaked to the skin and bruised by hail as they raced across the fields in search of shelter. Hailstones now lay deep upon the ground and inside the farmhouse so that their breath steamed in the ice-chilled air.

One room contained the skeletal remains of the family who had perished at the height of the Great Plague with their clothing all but rotted from their bones. In the ghoulish humour now rampant at Bede, their skulls had been placed upon the kitchen table and lit candles set atop them. Ursaf bit his tongue at this sacrilege as six years of regret and isolation had created this macabre mindset amongst the Brothers-Technician at Bede as a way of dealing with the sheer weight of guilt now bearing down upon their souls.

The Bede Angel Three pilot, Brother Marcus, grimaced as he gazed through a broken window pane at the lightning flashes. "The hail and ice could compromise the electrics," he fretted anxiously. "And if the rotor-blades are badly dented then the Angels might not be airworthy at all."

"We had no choice but to set down in *these* fields and ride out the tempest in *this* building!" Ursaf snapped irritably. "Perhaps you would have preferred a night in the Angels or taking shelter with the Wiccans in the ruins of Wealthorpe, hmm? There's no guarantee that we redeemed them all – they've already bewitched us once this day, remember?"

Marcus glared at him: "We *were* bewitched, Father, but the Great-Abbot will brook no excuses for failing Father Beorcraft," he pointed out. "Unless we get airborne at first light and resume our search for the Naked One and his Unworthy followers, he will send his monster, Pious, to Inquire of us. He…"

"Remember how he threatened to gut you at Bede, Father?" Piamadet interjected. "According to our contacts at the Great Abbey, the Wiccans killed him and glamoured him into some kind of walking corpse. He buried a postulant alive for disobeying him so the Holy Ghost alone knows what he'll do to us."

The Bede Angel Three gunner, Brother Hneftal, ran a hand through his long lank hair and coughed nervously. "They say he is a worse sight to behold than poor Abbot Michael. His flesh is cold, his veins are black, he draws no breath and he lifts Brothers clean off their feet with just one hand."

Father Ursaf nodded. "So they say, my son, but Pious was a monster well before the Wiccans bewitched him. He made my blood run cold every time he passed through Bede but there are other darker rumours: my sources say the Harlots conjured up a demon that destroyed the Great Computer and that's what sent our Tally-men berserk. This is all hearsay: we need to go to the Great Abbey and determine the truth of it for ourselves."

The Bede Angel Three navigator and radio operator, Brother Durwyn, a tall and round-shouldered man, laughed ironically: "No, Father, Schimrian was paranoid before the attack but they say he was a raving lunatic for two weeks; spitting at shadows and speaking in tongues. Even though we've suffered great losses, he would have Pious run us through if we ever dared set foot in the Great Abbey. Some of his Brothers-Inquisitor also survived the battle and they are to be feared as well."

"Those are dark ones indeed," Hneftal agreed quickly. "I didn't meet any of them at Bede but they say there was not one spark of Christian mercy in their souls. Pious had these psychopaths accompany him on all his Inquisitions: in truth they are the Locusts

166

to his Abaddon. They had to be reined in otherwise there would not have been a single Unworthy soul left alive for the Redemption Cells. Unfettered by conscience, they glory in fell deeds."

"Ah, now there's a mixed blessing for you," Piamadet muttered sarcastically. "Tally-men: I never suspected the Conclave and their confidants were capable of such barbarity until they started bringing them to Bede in the half-tracks five years ago. They are tortured for weeks in the Redemption Cells below Schimrian in the Great Manse before the lobotomies - their screams are his lullaby. They must remember being tortured: perhaps that is why they sought revenge upon us. What say you, Father?"

Ursaf massaged his face and sighed wearily: "A darkness was upon us: we hardened our hearts to their suffering and thought not of the knives of our Fathers-Surgeon. Thus we paid a heavy price, my son, with half our brethren slain at Bede. The remaining Tally-Men were not connected to the barracks computer but we have no guarantee that they're free from bewitchment."

"All these years, I would often gaze into their eyes hoping to find a spark of humanity," Hneftal confessed. "But no: they are soulless golems that would kill their Worthy masters in an *instant*."

"Then we should destroy them all," Piamadet said earnestly, clenching a fist. "Every single damned one of them! We had nothing to do with their Redemption so why should we endure this threat? Yes, they can clean toilets and corridors well enough but remember how we had one pick up a red hot rivet last Eastertide and he just stood there as it burnt through his flesh. Then, three weeks ago, this same Tally-man gutted Gregorius and Aspenald before me - I barely escaped with my life!"

"Ah, that's because you were always so fleet of foot," Hneftal laughed nervously.

Piamadet scowled darkly and pointed his spear at his tormentor: "How would *you* like to be gutted, snake-tongue?"

"Be at peace, Brother," Hneftal said, making a conciliatory gesture. "I meant no disrespect by my jest for I hid like a child in the cold store while our Brothers were slaughtered in the refectory. I only came out when the massacre was over."

"One was about to kill me too," Durwyn shuddered, wide-eyed at the memory: "I was cornered with his spear pointed at my innards then the Guides in his skull sparked and he toppled backwards like a felled tree. He was dead before he hit the ground."

167

"They all fell as one and every single dead Tally-man had that damned smile upon his face," Piamadet added angrily. "I see them in my dreams every night; smirking at me as if they're sharing some divine joke at my expense."

"Let us not gnaw at these bones, my sons," Ursaf said decisively. "It has been hard for all of us at Bede: we had no part in designing and unleashing the Plague but we are of the Order and that's all we have left. We have no other home or purpose. We must..."

"The damned need no purpose, Father!" Marcus said bitterly. "Bless Camus and Michael: they kept the worst of the zealots away from our airfield yet here we are," he added, waving a hand at the kitchen and the row of grinning skulls on the table. "For six years we all shrank from discussing the Tally-men, the Plague and our part in Armageddon but in this place, having buried sixty of our friends at Bede, such self-delusion is an insult to God!"

Ursaf exhaled heavily and massaged the bridge of his nose. "Listen, my son: we did *not* shrink from discussing the Plague these last six years; it's just that we knew that such discussions were a distraction when we had duties to attend to. We survived..."

"*Why* did we survive?" Piamadet interjected, tears coursing down his face. "We all went into this collective fugue as the Plague was released; we put all thought and conscience aside and clung to this false illusion of a New Jerusalem like the drowning rats we are. The Conclave and the Order slaughtered billions for *nothing*. We, blessed lambs that we are, sacrificed our families for *nothing*. What say you, Father Ursaf? Away from our warm beds and full bellies at Bede, behold: the Lord has guided us here to reveal unto us the *true* fruits of our labours."

He walked to the table and cocked an ear at one of the skulls: "What's that? You would like us to fix your roof? Well, that's going to be a bit difficult, Mister Farmer: as I was only telling your lovely wife and children earlier, all the tradesmen around here became naught but rat-droppings and dog-turds six years ago. What's that you say? You bless the Order? Quite right too, you disgusting Unworthy *peasant*!"

"Enough blasphemy, Brother!" Ursaf said curtly. "What would you have me do, hmmm? Schimrian has recovered his wits so his plans for a New Jerusalem will no doubt resume regardless of our losses. For now, that has to be enough for us because we still have Wiccans and Ferals out there to deal with."

Ursaf knew full well that contemplating their part in the Order's genocide had resulted in six Brothers and a Father committing suicide since the desecration of the Great Abbey. Even though the Virus had made them almost immortal, it was disturbing yet somehow comforting to know that he could die if he drank enough poison. Ten others had sought succour in the screaming halls of insanity and were incarcerated in secure cells leaving him with only fifty able-bodied Brothers to keep Bede operational.

He'd been hard-pressed for six years to keep them all focussed on their tasks especially during the Year of the Rats when the smell of rotting corpses drifted across the airfield but in the last three weeks it had become impossible. It was as though a veil had been ripped away from their souls and they could finally accept the enormity of the sins committed in their name. Prayer and sermon became nothing but a hollow lip-service to a vengeful God.

"Don't forget their Ferals," Gudflan pointed out, breaking the uncomfortable silence. "The Wiccans managed to train hundreds of them to attack the Great Abbey. I'm told they were adept at biting out throats and if they struck at Bede, we would be defenceless! We could all end up like that brute, Father Bucheort!"

"It's a blessing that we're allowed to carry plasma-grenades," Piamadet growled, wiping at his eyes with his sleeve. "But we need firearms and more begiullers, Father! We cannot defend Bede with these damned *toys*."

Ursaf patted his holster. "Even these would be of little use if they attacked us at night, my son," he pointed out. "The Wiccans got into the mind of Camus and made him shoot his own men and Ferals can see in the dark. I suspect Schimrian will be planning an Inquisition after our losses at Wealthorpe and it has to be against Milverburg: its endless labyrinths would make the perfect lair for this so-called Light-Father and his witches."

"I hope they don't expect us to attack Milverburg!" Durwyn burst out, his knuckles whitening as he grasped his spear. "I'm a Brother-Technician not a Brother-Martial! I would be useless in a real battle as most of us would be. Why should we care about them anyway: the Brothers-Martial sneer at us and call us 'oily rotor-monkeys' behind our backs."

The conversation became heated as they rounded upon the many and varied shortcomings of the Brothers-Martial so Ursaf, grateful for the distraction, went to the door to watch the Angels as they were illuminated by incessant lightning. "I expect Schimrian will ask us to attack any boats escaping from Milverburg, Father," Marcus said as he joined him. "Or command us to land in Uppermost. There are parks there where we can easily set the Brothers-Martial down. I do not relish this but we should be safe enough in the air, would you not agree?"

"Unless the Wiccans bind our senses again like they did to the Angel crews in Beorminghas," Ursaf replied despondently. "I was proud of my mind and my discipline yet I was so easily sidetracked at Wealthorpe. We were at least spared the fate of the Angels in Beorminghas: they flew straight into *buildings!*"

"But *Milverburg!*" Marcus persisted. "The Queen of Babylons will be crawling with Ferals and ghosts. I went there once with Abbot Balthus so I know how our Brothers-Martial will have to search all ten levels for Wiccans and fight Ferals at every turn amongst those vile and decadent murals and *statues...*"

"Tch! Statues are not corruptors of the soul, my son," Ursaf snorted. "And vengeful ghosts are but flickers in the corner of the eye magnified by a fevered imagination..."

Marcus passed a hand across his eyes. "Pah! Now you quote Chenikov at me," he sighed. "Thank God for the books we have at Bede and their blessed diversion otherwise I would be in a secure cell myself! I tell you this, Father: I would sell my worthless soul here and now in a *heartbeat* for a glass of rum."

Ursaf studied him with a worried frown. The Brothers at Bede had all but exhausted their supplies of alcohol, sleeping tablets and potions they had meticulously looted from the ruined shops and pharmacies of the Southern Cities. For three weeks they had drifted abed in soul-searing dreams and now no amount of alcohol could numb them to the fact that half of them had been slaughtered and their families sacrificed because of a mutated Vatican *animal.*

Marcus raised his hand and called for the others to be silent. "I cannot be sure in all this lightning but there's something moving out there by the Angels!" he cried.

"It's probably just a pack of dogs," Ursaf said, straining to see through the veils of rain. "I can't see anything. Let us not panic and extinguish the candles until we are sure."

"Could they be Ferals, Marcus?" Spero demanded nervously as the others joined them. He had drawn a plasma-grenade and was attempting to set the fuse timer with such fear-fumbled fingers that

Gudflan had no choice but to take it from him lest he accidentally detonated it amongst them.

"It's hard to tell," Marcus replied anxiously. "They must be Ferals for dogs could not swarm so over the Angels."

"I *knew* the Conclave were fools to let these damned mutants survive!" Hneftal shouted above a peal of thunder.

"The Conclave believed that the Virus would kill them off," Ursaf retorted. "Another divine jest played upon us if you will."

"Well? Will they attack us, do you think?" Spero asked, his voice trembling in near panic. "They'll rip our throats out!"

"Keep your nerve, Brother!" Ursaf ordered, struggling to master the fear threatening to overwhelm his senses. "Keep your weapons to hand and ready the grenades. It's just primitive curiosity about the Angels. Ferals are usually afraid of the Order and I doubt any Wiccans are out there in this tempest to guide them."

A peal of thunder faded away and there came a howling from unseen throats that froze the marrow in their bones. "Saints have mercy! They have wolves with them!" Gudflan groaned. "By the bones of the Martyrs, Father, have you heard of such a thing?"

Ursaf frowned. "I've heard rumours from several Inquisitors that this is so in the North but why are you surprised? Ferals are nothing but beasts themselves after all this time."

Marcus took a large torch from the table and returned to the door. "Father, I think you need to come and look at this." Ursaf joined him on the porch as the Brother switched on the torch and swept the powerful beam in an arc before them.

The hail had started to melt into the sodden ground but against the white blanket they could clearly see hundreds of dark shapes massed about the farmhouse and, in the torchlight, hundred of pairs of eyes glittered with hunger and unspeakable intent.

Ursaf felt his bowels turn to water as he slowly drew his firearm. Each lightning flash left a vivid image on his retinas and he could clearly see their bared fangs as a deep mass growling merged with the rumbling of the thunder. He and Marcus stepped back into the kitchen and quickly bolted the door shut.

He checked the safety was off on his gun and addressed the wide-eyed Brothers with a quote from the Book of First Peter that popped unbidden into his mind: "*Be alert and of sober mind, my sons!*" he cried out. "*Our true enemy prowls about us like a roaring lion looking for someone to devour! Resist and stand firm in our*

171

true faith because we know that our Brothers throughout the world undergo the same travails! We can't guard all the ground floor windows or the roof so we must make a stand in this kitchen!"

Stirred from their daze, Hneftal and Piamadet placed the skulls and candles upon kitchen units and jammed the table and chairs into the hallway to form a barricade as there was no door separating the kitchen from the rest of the farmhouse. Piamadet primed the fuses on their four plasma grenades and placed them on a stool as the others set their spears and loaded their dart guns.

"Gudflan, Durwyn and I will guard the kitchen windows, Father," Spero said, his face deathly pale in the flickering candlelight. "How many of them are out there, Father? Is there any point in me trying to use this damned begiuller?"

"Keep it to hand, my son," Ursaf replied, trying to calm his own hammering heart. "I doubt any Wiccans are out there but we can use it if they besiege us as it does affect Ferals. We know the sound waves confuse dogs so it'll work on wolves as well."

"How many?" Spero insisted, the fear clear in his voice.

"A horde beyond count," Marcus answered grimly. "Ferals and wolves enough to surround this farmhouse thrice over."

Spero's shoulders sagged: "Ah, this is not how I envisaged my end but a fitting irony nonetheless for I can bear my guilt no longer. Will you take my confession, Father? No? I suppose only our Lord God Himself could do that; such is the magnitude of our sins." He went down upon his knees and prayed: "Receive our Unworthy souls, O Lord, and forgive us our transgressions. Grant us this day a swift and merciful death, amen."

Ursaf said nothing as the others sank to their knees briefly and chorused: "Amen." A cold shiver ran down his spine as he saw in their faces that they fully expected to die in this place, bereft of hope and salvation in the face of divine retribution.

Spero got to his feet and placed his dart gun and spear on the work surface by one of the two double-casement windows and set the fuses on his two grenades as did Gudflan and Durwyn at the other window. Then they waited; each wrapped in silent terror and beset by swirling black thoughts and unbearable guilt about their lost families. They gazed at the skulls with the guttering candles still atop them and the skulls gazed back.

There was a lull in the storm and they realised that the howling without had faded into an expectant silence. Then came a tentative

172

scratching of claws on the farmhouse door that made their neck hairs stand on end. Marcus and Ursaf looked at each other and flung themselves against the door just in time as something powerful and heavy slammed into it, rattling the door frame and sending the topmost saddle keep flying across the room.

"God's breath!" Marcus hissed through gritted teeth. "What in all Seven Levels of Hell was that? A battering ram? This door won't hold with just two bolts left! A few more charges like that and the hinges will go as well!"

"Not if we brace it," Ursaf said, feeling a pain in his chest as he struggled to draw breath. "We can but hope it lasts the night. What can you see through the windows?"

"Not much!" Durwyn said shrilly. "Just pairs of eyes staring in at us." He jabbed the tip of his spear through a broken window pane at a face creating a yammering that seemed to come from all around them. "Hoi! That's for the Great Abbey!" he crowed and thrust again at another face only this time the tip was caught by several pairs of strong hands. "Gah! This is why we need firearms!" he cursed as it was torn from his hands. He went to grab his dart gun from the work surface but the spear was thrust back through the broken pane and pierced his throat beneath the larynx. Gudflan couldn't help him as he was frantically stabbing at powerful hands reaching in to try and open the window latches.

As Durwyn collapsed slowly to the floor clutching at his mortal wound, the door was impacted again and again but it held with Marcus and Ursaf throwing their weight against it. "Unh!" Marcus grunted. "We'll not be able to hold this door for long. One of you use the begiuller! It might buy us some time!"

Hneftal turned to Ursaf: "The windows in the other rooms are being smashed in," he shouted. "They'll be at our throats next!" He was perspiring heavily and shaking but he paused to gaze up at the ceiling. "Hark! They're in the room above us! Well, will you hear our confessions now, Father?"

Ursaf glared at him as another huge impact rattled both the door frame and his teeth and he could hear the floor boards being ripped up above their heads. "Now is not the time, my son!" he bellowed. He gasped as he saw the shadows moving in the corridor behind Hneftal and the acceptance of death in the Brother's eyes.

"*Now* is the only time we have left, Father."

~~~~~

173

Journey's End

"Lovely," Ellete beamed, pushing away her empty bowl. She then burped as loudly as she could: "Urp! Better out than in!"

"Ellete, how…" Bordan began then he winced. "Gods! I swear your damned elbows are made of steel, Ken… Cassandra," he grumbled, rubbing at yet another bruise. "Freda Geowine, we raised you better than this. Where are your table manners?"

Ellete was about to reply but she shivered violently and wrapped her arms about herself. "Brrr, I feel so cold," she complained.

Kendra checked the other diners and apart from the odd sidelong glance they were ignoring their albino daughter though the waiters and waitresses were still staring at her. She smiled as she could almost hug that obnoxious brat, Cedric, for his antics earlier. "You just froze your head eating that ice cream so quickly."

"No, Ma, it's something I can't explain. We *need* to go," Ellete insisted. "Something's not right. See? They keep talking about us at the counter and there's a man in a suit there too."

Bordan took another bite out of his sandwich and relished another mouthful of coffee before turning to look. "Hmph, whoever thought Asphalt Sovereign coffee could be this good? I think they're just curious about having a beautiful albino in here. Don't worry: we'll be safe enough for now."

"I don't know, *Geoffrey*," Kendra smiled, pretending not to look herself. "Two more men in suits just arrived. They've gone over to talk to the manager and now they're pointing directly at us. This is more than just Rackgate bumpkins warding off the evil eye. One of them is using one of those mobile phone units."

Bordan finished his coffee in a single gulp and hastily wrapped up their remaining sandwiches in serviettes. "Mobile units are used exclusively by the military and the secret services under the Ruhr-Köln Anti-Terrorism Agreement," he said nervously. "Why are they here? Surely, they can't be interested in Ellete?"

"Her craft," Kendra suggested, keeping her voice down. "The Defence Minister admitted last week that he'd asked Wiccans to work in his clandestine defence units so it's only natural to assume the secret services would be interested in girls like Ellete."

"You might be right. I heard the Mothers turned him down so he plans to legally force them to co-operate but I can't see his Bill getting through Parliament…"

"Please, Da, we need to *go*!" Ellete said urgently. "There's a voice in my head telling me to tell you there are Order half-tracks coming and a rotorcraft as well."

"What? A Wiccan's in your head?" Bordan demanded. "Kendra, we have to assume it's true so put these in your bag - we might not get a chance to eat later! Come on, let's go!"

Kendra stuffed the wrapped sandwiches into her bag and placed the lid on her coffee cup. She bundled up Ellete's top, hat and glasses then they walked quickly to the main exit but, as they'd feared, the two men had beaten them to the punch and awaited them in the lobby. They made it plain that they were armed.

The larger of the two showed them his identification badge: "I am Agent Alfreyus of His Britannic Majesty's Secret Services and this is Agent Jonarsson," he said politely. "We were contacted by the Brigstowe police and alerted to the Order's interest in your daughter: she is striking isn't she? The manager contacted our Rackgate office as young girls of her... *complexion* are extremely rare. We also know one of the staff contacted a Father in the Order in Stepperton so they're on their way here."

"We guessed as much," Bordan scowled. "You have to let us go. We can't let them take her: she'll be nothing but an experiment for the rest of her life if they don't kill her first."

"True, the Order and their Exodus contractors do have certain medical liberties in Britannia, Bordan... yes, Bordan, we do know your names: we're not stupid, you know. We also have leverage over many people working in Government offices including those like your Mister Henwin, whom we reeled in years ago for his somewhat third-rate forgeries."

Bordan's heart sank: "Ah, so he gave you our registration plate details some time ago?"

"Indeed, sir," Jonarsson grinned. "We appreciate it's not much of a choice but we'd like to train your daughter and employ the two of you. The Wiccans and the Order are your only other options. Be mindful that police officers tend to sympathise with the Order because of the free medical services they provide."

"So you're not going to arrest us?" Kendra prompted anxiously. "Do you mean we're free to go?"

Alfreyus rocked his hand from side to side with a pained expression on his face: "Mmm, not exactly: we have considerable discretion in this regard under various Security Acts. We, like you, are apprehensive of the Order and their influence in the world. Rumours of child abductions and experiments are making our masters nervous as do the politicians linked to the Conclave of Architects which, in turn, controls the Upper House. The Wiccans have been warning Ministers for decades about some Armageddon they say the Order is secretly planning but, naturally, nobody in their right mind would ever trust a Wiccan."

"Politics," Jonarsson sighed theatrically. "You see, sir, certain scientists in Exodus have also taken to warning the Cabinet about the Order's long-term ambitions concerning genetic manipulation and breeding programs so," he added, indicating Ellete. "We've been instructed to investigate both the Order and the Mothers. We believe that your daughter is a craft-wielder as she's albino and you've been keeping her from school…"

"And your somewhat indiscrete enquiries about the craft were reported to us *and* the police," Alfreyus added. "If you come with us you will both be well paid, live in comfortable Government accommodation and you'll be able to keep in close day-to-day contact with Ellete as she trains with us. What say you?"

"Well, I say…. hello, gentlemen!"

"I'm sorry, madam, this is Government business. It does not concern you," Alfreyus said firmly, turning to regard the woman who was smiling up at him. She was dressed in a floral summer frock and her red lipstick was striking against her pale skin and long black, braided hair. "Please go on through to the cafeteria, madam; we're just leaving. Please have a good day."

"Is it truly a good day? It's certainly rather warm and sunny," she beamed as Kendra and Bordan stared at her. She placed her hand on Ellete's cheek whose eyes were as wide as saucers. "Ah, Gaia bless you, little Daughter: you recognize me, don't you? Poor thing: you have such a hard journey ahead of you."

"I'm sorry, madam," Alfreyus huffed, displaying his badge officiously. "But I must insist that you go back inside the building or we'll have you arrested as this is none of your business."

"Oh, but it *is* my business," she said, her voice taking on a keen edge. She turned to Bordan: "This is the part where you *run!*"

Alfreyus tried to speak but he clutched at his throat. "Seems the cat's got your tongue, young man," she smiled and turned to Jonarsson who gasped and hastily dropped his firearm as if it was biting his hand. "I can only hold them for a little while, Bordan," the woman said over her shoulder. "Now *go* – and don't go into any more highway stations. Hurry! The Brothers are almost here and I can't deal with all of them at once!"

Bordan fought down his shock and amazement and turned to lead Kendra and Ellete through the main doors and out into the sun-baked car park. The two agents staggered after them but then abruptly sat down on the tarmac with their backs against the wall of the building, their eyes unfocussed and their mouths slack. The woman gave them a wave as they pulled onto the highway.

Ellete was excited as she clutched her Honey Bear. "That was a Wiccan!" she crowed. "She was using magic!"

Kendra sighed with relief as they sped away. "That's the only explanation, Bordan. Those men were like marionettes. How can anyone control another person's body like that?"

"Magic, magic, magic!" Ellete burbled happily.

"She *had* to be a Wiccan," Bordan frowned, his knuckles whitening as he grasped the steering wheel. "I don't know what to make of it. I've never seen anything like it."

"And what did she mean when she said *that* to Ellete?" Kendra fretted as she turned to look at her daughter who was hugging her stuffed toy with a contented smile on her face. "I'm so worried for her, dear heart. Are we on this hard journey she spoke of now or is there a worse fate awaiting her?"

Two black Order half-tracks roared by on the other side of the road their lights ablaze and sirens howling. Bordan glanced over his shoulder to see Ellete hiding in the foot-well. "I honestly don't know, Kendra, I honestly don't know. We're low on fuel but we should be able to make it to a garage I know in Stepperton and there's a small back road near it that heads north towards Apulder. We can bypass Beorminghas completely and we could cut west to Accyngate and drop south into Crawcester if we need to."

"What's the point? We're fugitives with forged, useless identity papers," Kendra sighed, leaning her head against the window in despair: "We're completely on our own!"

"You have me and Honey Bear!" Ellete chirped.

"That we do, Ellete," Bordan said with forced cheerfulness. "With you and Honey Bear we have nothing to worry about!"

An hour later, after refuelling at a sleepy backwater garage, they were on the narrow country road north of Stepperton heading for the ancient market town of Apulder set deep in the rural areas miles away from the sprawling Middle Cities. Bordan pulled into a lay-by near the hamlet of Bexley and killed the engine. "I need to take a break," he explained so they climbed over a style into a meadow that sloped away from them and sat down on a blanket to finish their sandwiches. They enjoyed the view as Kendra shared the last of her cold coffee with Bordan and Ellete made daisy-chains by an ancient stone monument called a *cruagrac* set in the meadow to their south and covered with weathered Celtic carvings.

The sun was beating down and it felt as though they were a million leagues from Brigstowe and all their troubles. The silence was near perfect as birds sang, bees buzzed about them and a breeze lifted dandelion seeds high into the air. Bordan laid down on the blanket with his hands behind his head to stare up the complex wisps of cirrus. "I wish we could stay here forever," he sighed but his bliss was short-lived as they could hear a vehicle approaching rapidly from the south.

"I don't believe it!" Kendra wailed. "Can't we have just a moment's peace to ourselves?"

"Curse me for being an idiot," Bordan growled, gathering up the blanket. "Kack, they're stopping! Quickly, we'll hide behind the hedge up there in case it's Alfreyus or the police."

"Ellete doesn't seem worried," Kendra pointed out. "Maybe they're just tourists stopping to see the monument."

"With our luck, I doubt it. Ellete! Come here now!"

Ellete shook her head. "A voice is telling me to stay here and hide behind this rock thing. I'll be safe here."

"Ah! The Wiccan's in her head again!" Kendra moaned.

Bordan peed through the hedge to see three armed police officers inspecting the car. "Keep calm and follow my lead. They'll be looking for an albino child not a couple of locals."

An officer climbed the style and spotted them straight away. "Is this your car, sir?" he demanded, removing the strap on his holster. "Only there's a call out on the registration plates."

Bordan threw his hands up. "No, officer, we're from Mancetta, the next village over. It's my day off and we're walking the field paths to Ansley. We're planning an anniversary meal in the tavern at the crossroads: the Fox and Hares."

The officer relaxed and smiled: "I see. Did you see anyone leave this vehicle? Was there anyone on the path? We're looking for a couple with a small child who's an albino."

"An albino?" Bordan asked as the other two officers joined them. "By the Bones of Saint Lucius, that's a rare thing to be looking for! No, we certainly haven't seen an albino!"

"Why are you carrying a blanket?" a second officer asked.

Kendra looked coy: "Um, it's our anniversary and we... um, you understand... out here in the fields... we..."

The officer reddened and the other laughed at him and nudged him in the ribs. "That's very, um, romantic. Just keep an eye out for the fugitives. They've abandoned their car but they can't have gotten far and they may be dangerous."

"Worse than Cymrig brigands," the other officer added.

"They'll be making for the railway station in Mancetta," the third officer suggested. "They know their vehicle registration has been identified. I'll guard the car while you two head on down the road." He turned to Bordan. "I suggest you don't keep your wife waiting for that anniversary meal, sir. I'm married and the last time I forgot an anniversary, she didn't speak to me for three weeks. Mind you, the first two weeks was a blessing," he laughed. "Sorry, madam, that was just my little jest! Well, off you go and enjoy your meal. Blessings be upon thy anniversary."

Bordan bowed and took Kendra's hand and they headed south, along the hedge with his heart hammering in his chest. Kendra was squeezing his hand painfully tight as they walked slowly and calmly away from the officers one of whom was sitting on the style and watching them. She was shaking and fighting down great choking sobs of fear and loss. In a few short hours it had come to this: they had nothing left but a handful of banknotes, a blanket and the clothes they were wearing whilst walking in a meadow in warm sunshine beneath an impossibly blue sky.

They passed the monument and she risked looking back at Ellete who was sitting cross-legged out of sight of the officers with a little crown of daisies on her head and clutching her Honey Bear with a strange smile upon her face. Behind her it looked as though the circle of Celtic figures carved upon the stone were worshipping her as a goddess adding to the surreal quality of their situation. Then a shot rang out: she thought her heart would stop such was the fright she felt. She sagged to her knees and Bordan had to roughly haul her to her feet to face the three officers who were striding towards them with their firearms drawn.

"Wise move," the first officer said as they raised their hands.

"You must think we Middle Cities officers are country yokels," the second officer snarled. "Your descriptions just came through. Get down on the ground, the pair of you. We need to do a body search for weapons and any drugs you might have."

The third officer threw Bordan to the ground roughly and as the other two pointed their weapons at Kendra, he pulled Bordan's arms behind his back and handcuffed him. Kendra stepped forward to assist her husband but she was backhanded across the face by the second officer and knocked to the ground where she suffered the same indignity with blood trickling from a split lip.

The second officer knelt down, grabbed a handful of hair and yanked Bordan's head back. "Gods above, you bastard, you two were laughing at us back at the style, weren't you? It's lucky the secret services want you in one piece or we'd be beating the life out of you right now. Now, where have you hidden your little freak of a daughter? Where is she?"

"B-by the stone, officer, but please don't hurt her: she's only a child and an innocent in all this."

"Ah, there she is," the second officer smiled and stood up. "No wonder we couldn't see you: all white against a white stone in the sunlight. Gods save us, look at those devil-eyes of hers."

"Quite the freak," the third officer laughed. "Well, little demon-brat? Shall we give you to the secret services or to the Order? Better not: their surgeons would probably put you in a jar!"

Bordan and Kendra despaired but then they frowned in puzzlement as Ellete's smile did not waver an inch as she stared at the three officers, two of whom were aiming their weapons at her. She held out her right hand with her palm facing them and tilted her head to the left a little. "Fire," she said.

Instinctively, Kendra and Bordan averted their faces and a split-second later they felt an intense pulse of heat. There were no sounds but birdsong, the breeze amongst the nearby trees, distant police sirens and a rotorcraft circling far to the south.

"What in the name of all that is sacred just happened?" Bordan gasped, rolling onto his side. Ellete was still seated by the stone as she grinned and gave him a little wave. A fine ash was drifting down around them or floating away on the gentle breeze and there was a stench of scorched human flesh and cloth. He saw three red glowing pools of metal nearby and knew that these were once the firearms of the three officers. "What did you do, Ellete?"

180

Ellete shrugged and said nothing but hugged her Honey Bear tightly. She leant against the stone with her eyes closed and then slumped sideways to the ground completely unconscious. "Ellete!" Kendra cried out hysterically. "Ellete! Dear heart? Are you alright? Speak to me! Can you hear me? Ellete!"

As they lay there helpless, the horror of what had just happened began to dawn upon them. Kendra licked her torn lip and spat out some blood. "She killed them, Bordan!" she shrieked. "She turned them into a cloud of *ash* in an instant! Oh, my God," she moaned. "Oh, my God, save my little girl! This can't be happening! Oh, my God, spare my little girl! God, she *can't* be a Wiccan!"

"Unh!" Bordan grunted as he struggled up into a sitting position to stare at Ellete. "She looks as though she's sleeping it off," he said with some relief. "But there's no doubt about her power. Her element must be fire and it called out to her." He hung his head and wept bitterly: "Oh, Ellete, what in God's name are we going to do? How can we save you now?"

From the corner of his eye, he could see a figure climbing the style on the other side of the meadow and coming up the slope towards them. As she approached, he recognised the woman from the Rackgate cafeteria: "Hera?" he exclaimed in disbelief.

"Hello, Geoffrey or should I say Bordan?" she smiled. "We're parked on the other side of the woods over there on the Bethlehem Road. Stay where you are. I'll get the handcuff keys from the police car. I know where to look: *she* told me."

Within a minute, Hera was back to unlock the handcuffs and give Kendra a handkerchief to mop the blood from her lips and chin. "I don't understand?" Kendra said groggily, holding her head as the blow had been quite heavy. "Why are you here? I thought you were all heading to the Tamemere amusement parks. Bordan? Can you check Ellete? See if she's alright."

"Oh, she's just exhausted, the poor thing," Hera said, her face sombre: "You see, we owe the Mothers a favour. I lied earlier: we *do* have a daughter whom they took from our hands as her craft manifested. We were stopped at the fuel pumps at Rackgate when one of the Mothers approached us and told us to come here. She was wearing this pretty summer dress and she had long black hair all tied in braids. Did you meet her?"

Bordan had picked up Ellete and sat down next to Kendra to cradle her sleeping body in his arms. "Yes, we did. Ellete seems fine but she's sleeping deeply. Is this what happened to your daughter when her powers went out of control?"

Hera sat down next to them. "I'm sorry about all the mud on me," she apologised. "I'm not really dressed for walking across the fields like this but we haven't got long to wait. Yes, it happened to her and the Mothers told us that her element, water, had called to her because the next thing we knew water exploded into the house from under the ground and all the water mains in our parish in Accyngate burst. Her power was incredible and we couldn't handle it just as you can't handle Ellete's craft now."

"You must have known she was marked?" Bordan asked.

"Oh, we'd seen it and prayed and prayed we were mistaken. After she'd been taken from us, the Order made our lives a misery with their enquiries and always taking blood samples. They play the angel in the hospitals but there's something not right in the way they treat people: they think they're so superior to us."

"So did you see her again?" Kendra demanded, stroking Ellete's silky white hair as she snored gently.

"Bless her, she looks so peaceful," Hera sighed. "Yes we saw her a few times after they renamed her Clover but she was so distant. It was as if she barely remembered us at all. Poor Aaron and the older boys were heartbroken and Cedric's behaviour became difficult but he can be an angel and a very good actor."

"What do you mean by actor?" Bordan exclaimed. "He was a little monster in that cafeteria!"

"I must confess that his tripping the waiter up was no accident," Hera admitted guiltily. "The Mother wanted to see if Ellete's craft was starting to manifest before she took action. Once she saw those cups hovering in the air above the table, she knew your daughter was about to be called by her element but certain events had to play out according to her visions."

"What do you mean? Play out?" Kendra demanded angrily.

"The Mother who stopped us is a *seer*," Hera explained, gazing at the carvings in the nearby monument. "You had to be in a field away from a town or a village and you had to see her power unleashed. She knew these three officers were destined to die today but if Ellete had awoken in an urban environment, she would have killed dozens if not hundreds of people!"

She looked candidly at them as another vehicle pulled into the lay-by and a door slammed. "You know this is where you part with your daughter, don't you?" she said sadly. "You two will come with us and we'll take you to Accyngate. Aaron is well-connected and we can hide you there. Take what you need from your car but you'll have to leave it here. What happened here will become a mystery in the sensationalist press. The Mother told us that the exposure will make the police and secret services leave you alone and all sorts of conspiracy theories will circulate so that even the Order and Exodus will stop searching for you."

Bordan cried openly so that tears fell upon Ellete's face making her stir a little. "Please! We can't give our little girl up and never see her again." He turned as a woman stood next to him. "You!" he said angrily, looking up at her. "You planned this!"

Gone was the floral dress and smile and in their place was a grim middle-aged woman in the traditional costume of the Wiccans based on the mockery of the traditional garb of the misogynistic Conclave of Architects. She held a black staff with a silver swan as its ornament and the wings outstretched so that the design resembled an Egyptian ankh. "I am Mother Moss," she said. "I have come to take Ellete and keep her safe. You can try and stop me taking her but I advise you not to. You've seen her full power and you know in your hearts that great tragedy will befall others should your love for her outweigh your wisdom."

Kendra's shoulders sagged and her heart ached. "Is this her hard journey then?" she said as Ellete stirred and raised a hand to touch her mother's cheek. "We have to let her go?"

"She will do great things with her powers in the darkness I foresee when the heavens tremble and Gaia falls. Fear not: you both will flourish and bear two more wonderful daughters and be with them at the End of All Things. Go with Hera and her family: let them shelter you and give you a new home."

She handed Hera her staff and bent down to lift Ellete effortlessly from Bordan's unresisting arms. "Follow me, Hera. You can get their belongings from the car for them. I think they need a moment to themselves."

As the women walked towards the style, Bordan and Kendra saw Ellete wave at them then she rested her head upon the Mother's shoulder and closed her eyes. Bordan crawled across to Kendra to hold her in his arms and together they grieved for their daughter and wept soundlessly at the injustice of the universe.

~~~~~

Lamentations

*"Give sorrow words; the grief that does not speak
knits up the o'er wrought heart and bids it break." - Shakespeare*

Nightshade put a hand across her eyes and sank to her knees with her head bowed. There was a pause in the thunder as the storm moved slowly northwards, the gusts of wind faded and the rain eased to a fine drizzle. Silence fell but for the lapping of the waves against the vast viaducts and stoneworks of Milverburg.

Mouse, her heart afire with empathy, wrapped her arms once more around the distraught Wiccan. "So you killed those three police officers but how could you know?" she said in Nightshade's ear. "You had but six years. You were no different from us Scatterlings: we've killed to survive. We had no choice and neither did you. I'd love to sit in a cafeteria eating chocolate ice-cream with you but that will never happen in this world."

"As would I, dear heart, but when I said 'fire', it was so much more that just a *word*," Nightshade groaned and laid her staff upon the flagstones. She placed her hands over Mouse's hands. "My element called me and I embraced it because those stupid *men* were hurting Ma and Da. I killed them, Mouse!"

"Shield tried to tell me what she felt when she took down those Angels in Beorminghas but she couldn't find the words."

"It's hard to explain but your whole soul reaches out into the infinite: it touches the edge of the cosmos and collapses back down upon the object of your anger and your fear in an instant. That's why Mother Moss had to take me: I would have killed again and again because they would never have stopped hunting us."

"That was then and this now, Mother Nightshade."

"I know, dear heart, but the world was beautiful then even for us Mothers and those men had families and loved ones but, at my command, the universe destroyed them utterly."

"But the Order's killed *billions*..."

"I am *not* the Order!" Nightshade snapped. "I am Wiccan but my parents gave unto me a soul and a conscience and their words of love shaped my heart. I never spoke to them again nor my new sisters though I watched them from afar. I used to go to Accyngate in disguise and sit in the malls and bazaars hoping to catch a glimpse of them till I thought my heart would shatter like thin glass. Mother Moss eventually stopped me going as I would weep for weeks and fail in my tasks at the Retreat. So we built our coven and awaited the End of all Things though Mother Moss would leave us often, following this vision or that vision. The Plague came, and thanks to Professor Farzad and our friends in Exodus, we had access to the vaccine and we gained immunity."

"Was the Retreat the place that the Light-Father spoke of? The Hill Where It Never Rains? I wish I could've seen it."

"It was wonderful even after the Plague and the long rains began then one day Mother Moss left her staff with us. This is unheard of for a Wiccan but she only told us what she needed us to know and we accepted that. We'd argued bitterly with her about curing the Ferals and why she was obsessed with you Scatterlings."

"I'm glad she was. We only live because of her."

"We missed her and I was sorrowed to hear you children blamed us for abandoning her. Just as your sister knew when and how her end would come, Mother Moss knew her cruel fate well. I think she saw that if we came to her aid then the Retreat would have been attacked by the whole Order. There would be no Mothers left nor would you Scatterlings have survived if that had come to pass."

"She was strict with us. What was she like with you?"

"She was *tyrant* to us Daughters," Nightshade grimaced. "It may have been the guidance of her visions but she was brutal and merciless in our training. Every waking moment we studied and meditated, learning lore and ancient tongues and practising control of both craft and emotion." She laid her hand on her staff. "It was the proudest moment of my life when she presented this to me yet she'd just killed Clover so I hated her with all my heart. It was only years later that I understood why she had to do it and why she'd made our lives so miserable. She gave me visions of the Plague, Tally-men and strangely, dear heart, a vision of the two of us standing here, watching Gaia rage above our heads."

She grasped her staff and used it to get to her feet, wearied by her remorse. She smiled down at Mouse and laid a hand upon her head. "Bless you, little Mouse, for Mother Moss was right: I needed to remember Bordan and Kendra and the love they had for me and to come to terms with all the terrible things I've done since then. At the Abbey I killed many Brothers and we forced those men to shoot their brethren yet I must *never* become indifferent to the suffering of others no matter how cold and corrupt their hearts are."

"You'll never forget those three policemen, will you?"

"Nor should I, Mouse," Nightshade nodded. "I think you must be stealing a little magic from the Light-Father," she smiled, laying a hand upon her breast. "My heart feels lighter somehow."

"And the storm is almost over," Mouse noted.

"Yes, you're right. Come, let us rejoin the others. They must have a fire going as I can smell our fish roasting on a grill. Let us eat something and get some sleep. I fear we may have yet more fighting to do before this day is out."

"I'd rather eat double-chocolate ice-cream," Mouse said mournfully. "And make daisy-chains in the sunshine..."

"One day, we'll do that together, Mouse, I promise."

~~~~~

Harold looked up at the ceiling. "The hail has stopped," he observed. "It's still raining hard but the thunder is moving away so this storm should be gone by dawn and then the fun begins."

Michael knocked the door. "May I have a word?" he said.

"You can say what you need to in front of Fern and the Scatterlings," Harold frowned. "Then get some sleep. I want to hear what the children have to say about the Great Abbey."

"It's a little... uncomfortable in there. I..."

"Your younger brother survived the Redemption Cells," Fern said sharply. "We know. Look elsewhere for forgiveness."

Michael looked at the floor for several moments. "Aye, it is both boon and bane. Marc's told me in gruesome detail how my family, the Onderhelms, suffered in the Plague and how he survived with his rare immunity. He told me of the unimaginable horrors he's witnessed: the giant rats feasting on human flesh and dog packs hunting the survivors down and killing them one by one. He watched young children warp into Ferals and he's asking me over and over why I let this happen; why I stayed in my beautiful chambers toying with my computers and radios and Angels while the world drowned in blood and rain."

"What did you expect?" Harold said sarcastically "Flowers?"

"No," Michael said wearily. "I tried to explain the rapture we all experienced and how I shut out the truth from my mind then watched the endless rain for six years within the walls of the Great Abbey whilst dreading sleep. I have no excuse other than my

186

weakness and cowardice so there is no answer or solace I can give him. I do not deserve his forgiveness, but God praise him, I *will* dedicate the rest of my pathetic life to protecting him and the Children of Exodus. I will earn his forgiveness."

"We'll see. Be seated," Harold said with ill grace, indicating an armchair. "How are the others doing?"

"My brother and the others are asleep," Michael reported, lowering himself gratefully into the chair. "Shield and Saul remain awake and - *ahem* - we need to give them some privacy."

"Noted now be quiet and let Peter and Rabbit finish their story and we can all get some sleep. Surl predicts we may have to fight our way back to Milverburg tomorrow."

"Certainly, Light-Father, only I overheard how Ignatius helped them. The children hadn't mentioned him to me as we were being hunted but I always had a liking for the old rogue. I was also surprised to learn of Ondine's confession, I must admit."

"Ondine?" Peter asked. "Who's Ondine?"

"She looks after the Sisters."

"The Abbess?" Peter exclaimed. "She told Surl that she lost her family and hates what the Order did to the world."

"So I heard but if they find out that she and Ignatius helped you they'll be in grave peril from Schimrian and Pious."

"I hope they won't be punished," Peter said anxiously.

"I hope so too as I hold Ondine to be one of the purest souls I've ever met. On with the rest of your story, Scatterling, I'm curious to know how you all survived those two weeks of sabotage."

"You and me both," Harold said impatiently.

~~~~~

The first day had gone well: they'd followed the north-eastern branches of the sewer system and crawled underneath the Exodus laboratory building. The smell of chemical, oil and smoke grew stronger and Peter was first to realise that it was coming from the fuel stores that were still ablaze above them. They were relieved to finally find the inspection chamber under the enclosed courtyard that Ignatius had carefully marked upon their map.

Surl slowly lifted the manhole cover and looked about the yard which was surrounded by former stables that had been converted into modern toilets and shower rooms for the Brothers-Technician and Exodus scientists. Unknown to the Scatterlings, they were in the very complex where the Plague virus was first cultured. She could see biohazard warnings on the walls and corpses everywhere but no sign of life. "It's safe to come up," she assured them but she was anxious that no fluttering moth had been there to guide her. "I think the Brothers are all fighting the fuel depot fire."

They emerged into a fine drizzle and the sound of distant thunder rumbling to the north. They could see smoke billowing up from the depot fire into the dank overcast sky to form a vast ominous smudge. Beyond the eastern wall, they could hear the desperate shouts of Brothers, novices and postulants fighting the blaze. There was a concussive thump and gouts of flame belched into view as another oil drum exploded adding to the chaos.

They had to step over the bodies but the torrential rain had washed most of the blood away. Surl gagged as she realised that she'd washed her bucket out in that run-off water. There were Brothers and Tally-men entangled in their death-throes and several white-coated Brothers-Scientist lay with gaping wounds having been trapped in the courtyard and run through with spears.

They soon found the laboratories but on Ignatius's map was a stern instruction in red: '*Do NOT open any of the refrigerators or sealed flasks in the laboratories.*' Surl found a small storeroom in one of the corridors and lit a candle. She set it on one of the shelves and made sure that it couldn't fall over or get blown out then she led them back into the laboratory which was strewn with corpses, smashed equipment and broken furniture.

"Now turn every gas tap on full," she told them and they complied until the sound of hissing gas was almost deafening. Following the instructions on the map, she did the same with the hydrogen and oxygen cylinders. "We have to run! When this gas reaches the candle the whole building will explode."

They needed no urging as they clambered over the dead in the entrance and scuttled down the rungs and into the inspection chamber with Surl heaving the manhole cover into place behind them. They frantically crawled down the narrow sewer with Surl struggling to keep the lantern and map dry above the gushing and contaminated rainwater. Suddenly a surge of rainwater scooted them down the gentle slope and out into the chamber pool by their Keep in the nick of time: a gargantuan blast shook the walls and a ring of smoke puffed into the chamber. "That was *fun*," Pup grinned as they clambered out of the pool. "Let's do it again!*"*

188

Surl looked at their wet, soiled clothing and remembered the advice on the map: *Wash your clothes and skin: there may be toxic chemicals in the sewer from Exodus and the depot fire.* She led them into the cellar and found four large bowls of water on the floor, bars of soap and some towels. There was even a tub of lice powder. She slumped onto a chair in sheer relief and let the reaction and adrenaline release in a fit of quaking and trembling. She pondered briefly at how unaffected they all were by all the bodies they'd stepped over and sighed deeply, bowing her head.

"What's the matter?" Peter asked, stepping out of his clothes "Ignatius is right; my skin is *itching*. We've got to wash this chemical kack off us quickly or it might make us ill."

The four children washed themselves thoroughly and Surl made sure the lice powder was applied. She got them to wash their clothes in the bowls but there was nowhere to dry them in such a dank cellar. She started at six knocks on the door and all four children scrambled for their weapons. She opened the door carefully but again Ignatius was gone leaving them a pile of night-garments that obviously belonged to the postulants so all four of them could settle down to eat in dry clean garments.

And so it went for thirteen days.

~~~~~

"That first day was the worst," Peter explained. "We itched for days afterwards but Ignatius seemed to know even though we never saw him. There would be the six knocks and a jar of zinc salve or lantern batteries or food or a flask full of hot tea. We wouldn't have survived without him." He counted off their attempts at sabotage on his fingers: "We set fire to the library by leaving candles against the drapes. We did the same in the armoury which was badly damaged and parts of it were still on fire. Ignatius believed that no Brother would enter a burning armoury but we got in through a hole in the wall, piled up all the begiullers we could find on top of the last crates of the plasma-grenades…"

"Those grenades could have gone up at any moment!" Michael exclaimed indignantly. "Ignatius should've warned you…."

"Hush! Let him speak," Fern said sharply.

189

"He *did* warn us," Peter said resolutely. "On the map, he wrote: '*if on fire, there'll be no Brothers but things might explode so be careful.*' We may have but a few years compared to you but we do know what peril is." He shrugged: "It was no different to what we faced every day in Crawcester: in this world *you* helped create."

Michael raised his hands: "Point taken. Please ignore me."

Peter frowned at the mutilated cleric then shook himself and continued: "We found a metal canister of cleaning fluid which we threw over the crates. We got to the hole and threw some burning rags at the liquid and *whoosh*: they went up quickly. We got back into the sewer just in time as the explosion was huge and some of the bricks flew out of the wall *and* we had to wash all this oil and chemical kack out of hair and clothes again," he shuddered.

"We went back to the library complex the next day and we found a store of fuel for the heating boiler serving the library and all the other buildings around the memorial gardens. Ignatius wrote down how to pull the fuel pipes out and to leave candles burning on the floor: the fuel didn't explode but the flames spread through the classrooms and refectories. We almost got caught: some Brothers and novices fighting the library fire came into the gardens to get buckets of water from the fountains!"

Surl yawned and rubbed her eyes. "The manhole cover was in the gardens beneath one of the classroom windows so we thought we were trapped and poor Pup and Rabbit were panicking. The Fates saved us: there was a crash from inside the library and the Brothers ran back inside to see what was happening. I think the roof was starting to collapse. That's when we saw *him*."

"You saw *who,* dear heart?" Fern prompted.

Surl and Peter paled at the memory. "Pious!" Surl burst out, gagging on the name. "The gardens were covered with holes and there were bodies and coffins piled up next to them in the rain. Pious came through the south gate into the gardens and he was angry with these postulants who had but twelve years by the looks of them. He wanted them to dig more graves but one boy said they were tired and threw his shovel to the ground. He lifted the boy off his feet and threw him into a coffin, slammed the lid shut and kicked it into a grave then he ordered the other postulants to throw earth onto the coffin until it was completely buried!"

"He's a *monster*!" Peter snarled, baring his teeth. "We could see the postulants crying and shaking and wetting themselves then

Pious went into the library. After a while, they started digging more graves then one of them noticed the fire spreading into the building behind them and they all turned to watch the flames. We climbed out of the window and into the manhole and they didn't see us or hear us as the fires were making so much noise!"

Surl closed her eyes again. "It was faint because of the earth on the coffin but we could hear that boy screaming only the other postulants pretended not to hear him. It was *horrible*. I am so *tired* of the Order's cruelty!"

"Ignatius later told us that he survived," Peter fumed. "But his mind was destroyed. Pious…"

"Forget about him for now," Harold urged. "We have to get some sleep soon. What happened next?"

"Let's see," Peter said, counting on his fingers again. "We stole parts from the Tally-men relays and the radios then we set fire to some fuel drums stacked in the generator rooms. There were two Brothers asleep on the floor when we did that!" he said proudly. "We had to stop Rabbit from axing them."

"She was terrified they'd wake up," Surl explained.

"We put sugar in all the half-track fuel tanks but best of all was when we got into the Angel compound and found those fuel drums they'd stacked behind the barracks because of the fires in the hangers," Peter continued. "They were working on the Angels in the burnt-out hangers so we set candles against the curtains on the ground floor of the dormitory and set a trail of fuel from the windows to the drums."

"The manhole was out of sight behind the dormitory so they couldn't see us from the hangars," Surl added excitedly. "But we almost got caught by the fire. Even though it was athidol, it spread so *fast* to the drums which then spat fireballs everywhere!"

"We got the manhole back in place just as the first drum exploded," Peter said. "And when we got back to the Keep, there was more food from Ignatius and towels on the table waiting for us and a note saying to come and see him urgently."

Harold nodded approvingly. "It seems you four did a good job, Peter. Was there anything else left to sabotage?"

"Not much," he grinned. "So we went to see Ignatius."

~~~~~

"Ah, Ondine!" Ignatius said brightly after opening the tower door. "Come upstairs and dry yourself out by the fire. I raided the coal bunkers today so I can make you some tea and toast."

"I'd rather you not call me by my birth name, Ignatius, but these are the darkest of times, I suppose."

"They are indeed," he agreed over his shoulder as he led her up the stairs to his beloved study at the top of the tower. "I enjoy being invisible: even Camus and Pious don't notice me as I potter about with my buckets of coal. Please be seated," he said, guiding her to one of the two comfortable armchairs set by the ancient tiled fireplace. "Luckily, you've just missed two postulants who were forced to bury that poor boy alive last week."

"That's one of the reasons I came to see you," she said as she sat down. "That boy is *still* under the ground in his mind but Pious just laughed at me when I asked that he be sedated." She shuddered. "It was more like a snake hissing than a human laugh. I saw the black veins in his neck and on his hands: is he one of the walking dead as my Sisters claim? What news of Abbot Michael? I heard Schimrian still has imprisoned him in one of the Redemption Cells."

A kettle was steaming gently on the hearth so Ignatius patiently made them tea, pouring the aromatic brew into some bone china cups. "I have but three packets left of Indian tea and two of a rare Chinese blend then civilisation truly falls, I'm afraid."

"You look nervous," she noted bluntly. "Are you expecting company? Perhaps our little sewer trolls perhaps?"

He looked taken aback: "What do you know of them?"

"I'm not one of my poor Sisters, you know. Ah, this is *so* good," she said contentedly. "It's been so long since I've had real tea."

"Well?" he prompted nervously.

"They're beneath the main kitchen in that wine cellar that only you and I know about. I actually bared my soul to one of them through crack in the old door leading to the cellar. The child said nothing but I sensed a youngling maybe having eight to twelve years. I know you're helping them because you frequent that cellar every day to partake of its bounty." She laughed at Ignatius's faux umbrage and pointed to the large box by the door containing dozens of empty bottles. "You can't fool me! Your poor liver must be the size of an ox. Ah," she said, cupping an ear. "Six sharp taps on the courtyard door! Now that's strange as it has *such* high walls around it. Shall I go down and let them in?"

192

"No, I'll go," he grumbled, getting to his feet. "It's lucky you have keen ears. The back door is open as there's no point in locking it and I doubt Ferals could climb the walls."

"They climbed the outside of the South-West Tower easily enough," she reminded him. Six knocks sounded at the study door. "That was quick: our little trolls found their way through your unlocked door easily enough it seems."

Ignatius paused by the door with his hand on the door knob. "Please sheathe your weapons before you enter, children. I have a welcome guest here who knows of your presence and I don't want any accidents or misunderstandings."

Ondine stood up to formally greet the four nervous Scatterlings as Ignatius introduced them to her. "This is the Abbess," he announced formally. "This is wonderful," he added, rubbing his hands with glee: "So many guests! Oh, how it reminds me of my youth in the villages! Please pull up those stools around the fire, children, and dry yourselves out."

Ondine fanned at her face. "Saints preserve them," she gasped. "The dear hearts absolutely *reek* of smoke and worse."

Surl glared at her. "Perhaps it comes from us crawling around in sewers beneath burning buildings, Abbess," she said sarcastically. "Did you mean what you told me about hating the Order and sensing that evil presence in the Great Abbey?"

"So it was you I confessed to! I meant every word. I sense a similar evil in Pious. He is not of this world any more. He..."

"Pup saw him bury a boy alive," Pup chipped in. "His friends pretended they couldn't hear him screaming. Pup hates them!"

"His friends were scared to death of the Abbot," Ignatius explained, stoking the fire. "I had two here earlier who had soiled themselves and were too scared to go back to their dormitory where they would be punished again by their House-Father. They've been forced to dig graves, build pyres and haul corpses by hand. They're completely traumatised, all of them."

"And we're not?" Rabbit seethed. "Oh, sob, sob! We've lived with Tally-men, Brothers, rats and dogs trying to kill us for *six* years while they've been coddled up in here in their nice warm beds. Mother Moss tried her best but we had rot and fleas and lice from being wet all the time and risking our lives every time we opened a tin. They lured children out of hiding so they could be *killed* so they can eat kack and drink piss for all I care!"

Ondine raised her hand. "A child is still a child, dear heart. They were forced to act as Judas-goats as you well know and they're as innocent of Revelation as my poor Sisters are."

"Drink some tea, children," Ignatius insisted. He poured them a mug each and added some milk and sugar. "There's very little left in the world now. Would you like some bread and jam?"

"Pup would," Pup grinned hugely and took the plate but the others declined. "Pup's always hungry!"

"Why do you want to see us?" Surl demanded.

"Ah, I'm concerned about you," Ignatius said after sitting back down in his armchair. "As is the Abbess it seems," he added after a nod from Ondine. "We consider ourselves to be *not* of the Order yet we're trapped here, the Abbess to aid her Sisters and I remain to help the postulants and novices who confide in me."

"And the endless supply of wine," Ondine teased.

Ignatius reddened but did not rise to the jibe. "We stay because there is no alternative but there may be now that this Light-Father of yours has appeared. The postulants say he is ten feet tall and can rip a man's head off with his teeth. They say he's not of this world. What say you? What's he like? Is he really a human being?"

Peter told them of the appearance of the Light-Father and their adventures as the two adults listened in silence and a growing respect. "My life and soul," Ondine exclaimed. "Could that evil will I've sensed be from another plane as well?"

Ignatius pursed his lips. "It has to be. Abbot Camus told me last year about an alien device at the core of the Great Computer which they thought came from a parallel world. He mentioned that they used living brain tissue to activate it and he suspected it came from Schimrian's very own brother, Abbot Breostan. He was the only other nominee for the throne when Great-Abbot Cystig died suddenly after only a year in office."

"Looking back, I see the hand of Schimrian in the untimely demise of both Cystig and Breostan," Ondine said thoughtfully. "Breostan was not mourned: he was a most unpleasant man who sexually and physically abused Sisters, novices and postulants alike whenever he could get access to them. I had to lock my poor lambs away whenever that beast visited the Great Abbey."

"Anyway, children," Ignatius continued briskly. "Schimrian has fallen into a stupor and speaks in tongues after being attacked by the Wiccans and you have…"

194

"No!" Surl said angrily. "I saw in my vision he was attacked by Azrael, the demon he bought to life with that machine. It was Azrael that took over the Tally-men and made them kill Brothers and Sisters because when Fierce destroyed the machine at the core of the Great Computer, all the Tally-men dropped dead."

"Ah," Ondine gasped in morbid fascination. "Azrael? I heard tell of a winged body being cremated! So Schimrian tried to create an angel but his madness spawned a devil instead. So I was right! The evil I'd sensed in the Great Annex all this time was real! O, thank the saints! I thought I was going insane!"

"If it was spawned from a corrupted alien technology and Breostan's brain, no wonder it was such a powerful and monstrous being," Ignatius pondered aloud, intertwining his fingers and staring into the flames. "I presume Azrael brought those dead Brothers back to life during the fighting because like the Tally-men they ceased to move after the explosion. All but one: *Pious!* He revived and controls the Great Abbey now. Camus is his lapdog through sheer terror whilst Schimrian wanders about raving like a madman. With the fires all but extinguished, it's only a matter of time before Pious finds you and puts you to a cruel death."

"I fear Pious could still resurrect that demon," Ondine added, making the sign of the Cross, "God save us!" Her eyes widened suddenly and she sat upright in her chair. "You said you saw this creature in a *vision* just now, Surl! Have you the craft?"

Surl nodded reluctantly and Ignatius smiled: "I guessed as much seeing as you destroyed the generators and found that cellar. That wasn't just blind chance. Can you foresee anything now?"

"No, I can't," Surl sighed, massaging her eyes. "I think I've overtaxed my craft. I only see the colour red when I try to pierce the 'veils' as I call them to see all the paths of the future. I have no other craft manifest and no mark that I know of."

Ignatius frowned and suddenly knelt before Surl, surprising her. "Open your mouth and stick out your tongue as far as you can," he commanded with some urgency. "Hoi! There it is: faint but definitely a mark of the craft on your tongue! Oh, I *do* so enjoy being right!" he exulted, returning to his chair.

"A real live *Daughter*," Ondine gasped. "Bless! I never expected to meet someone of the craft in my lifetime."

"Be that as it may," Ignatius said forcefully. "It's almost time for you to leave the Great Abbey. I've one more mission for you now you've managed to sabotage the garages and the smithies. Pious and his Inquisitors have butchered all the Unworthy prisoners apart from the five he's keeping in the Redemption Cells directly beneath Schimrian's chambers. He was furious that some had escaped dressed as Brothers and claims that the Order no longer needs new Tally-men but I fear he may be keeping those five poor souls alive for his perverted sport."

"I'm so glad Ken Glascae and his friends escaped but we didn't know about all the other cells," Surl admitted sadly, her eyes downcast. "We thought they were all in that one corridor."

"How could you know, Surl?" Ondine said kindly. "It's a large building and there are over a hundred cells. I take food and water to the surviving five when I can but it's not enough and when this crisis is over they'll be guarded again. Unless we help them they'll die and I'll have yet more deaths on my conscience."

"And there's one more thing," Ignatius added. "I heard that the Wiccans... sorry, this Azrael mutilated my friend, Michael, so they call him the Naked One for that reason. Pious is threatening to kill him so I'd be grateful if you could help me free him as well."

"I'm allowed to give him food through the service hatch," Ondine explained. "But I'm not allowed to see him. Pious and the others blame him for the success of the attack on the Great Abbey and many say he's been punished by God and not this demon; this foul Azrael that we speak of *but*," she warned, raising a finger in emphasis: "I still sense Azrael's presence within the Great Abbey: it's faint but it's definitely there. We must be on our guard."

"Maybe you have the craft as well, Abbess," Surl suggested.

"I doubt it but some of us lesser mortals *can* be sensitive to the paranormal but that's not the point. Pious is to be feared: Azrael's black craft lingers in him for some hellish purpose. Schimrian has all but anointed him as his successor and when he recovers his wits, his inhuman lapdog will be despatched to scour Britannia to find and kill your precious Light-Father."

Ignatius poured the Abbess some more tea in the silence that followed. "I was glad to hear that Kai fought alongside your Light-Father. He was a protégé of both Michael and I," he said proudly.

"We still don't trust him," Rabbit scowled.

"That's understandable but if he's found sanctuary with your Light-Father, then both the Abbess and I would like the same opportunity for as many Sisters and postulants as we can save."

"Are there any other Brothers who would renounce the Order?" Peter asked hopefully. "We could do with more fighters."

"None I would trust in the Great Abbey," Ignatius said sadly. "Many were hand-picked by Schimrian for their blind loyalty and they welcomed this rapture that engulfed us all six years ago. They *rejoiced* in the Plague's release and volunteered to spread the Virus. But in places like Bede and Norton Abbey and in outposts across the globe, I suspect some must now question the whole purpose of the Revelation Virus especially now their stupor has dissipated with the death of this demon. They'll see the promise of a New Jerusalem was nothing more than a deceit of Satan designed to make them accomplices to *genocide*."

"If this Light-Father can indeed offer them salvation," Ondine suggested. "We can bring many back into the light. If we are to rebuild this world then we'll have need of them. Brother Kai might be the first of many to surrender to his healing magic but I hope he won't be the last. From what you say about his powers, I would give my life to meet him."

"So what say you?" Ignatius prompted. "Will you help us free Michael and the others before you flee westwards?"

Surl gasped as a death's-head moth emerged from the flames. It fluttered across the room to settle on her upturned palm only to vanish in a puff of dust. "I think we have no choice," she said.

~~~~~

197

Howlings

"Well, Pious," Schimrian said, setting aside his glass of brandy. "Forgive me for summoning you again but I heard some pitiful bleating through the floor beneath my feet so may I take it that you were Inquiring of our treacherous lamb?"

"That I was, Excellency," Pious said, his voice a dry graveyard whisper. "He tried to break my skull with a fire-iron at his tower so I have some respect for his fighting spirit but not for his years of dissolution. He has such a low threshold of pain that he keeps fainting on me, no doubt as a result of his incessant intoxication. He's an utter disgrace to the Order."

Schimrian yawned and stretched. "Indeed, my friend. Did he confess his sins to you?"

"I'm afraid not. I suspect he is protecting someone at the Great Abbey whom he holds in high regard. It's helping him to resist my Inquisitional arts. He's such a Philistine: he has no appreciation of the time and skill I lavish upon him."

"Whom is he protecting? A Father? It can't be a lowly novice or a postulant. Could it be Camus?"

"Absolutely not, Eminence," Pious frowned. "Camus was with me when the Exodus laboratories were destroyed. What troubles me most is that just before he passed out, he mumbled something about *saboteurs* infiltrating the Great Abbey."

Schimrian's eyes blazed and he slammed his fist down on the desk. "So there *were* saboteurs and he'd known about them for weeks, damn his eyes! I will *personally* Inquire of him tomorrow! He shall face my full wrath for his treachery!" He glared up at the impassive chalk-white face of his old ally. "May Saint Saul curse me for my indisposition: I might have deduced that saboteurs were at work here but I cast no blame, my son, for you and Camus were hard put to it during the crisis but nevertheless these saboteurs have cost us dear. We need to find them!"

"If there were any saboteurs then they fled with the Naked One taking my five prisoners with them because there have been no further reports of missing parts or mysterious fires since then and those prisoners could not have escaped without their help."

"It could also mean that there were no Unworthy here at all and that Ignatius and his vile accomplice are simply lulling us by ceasing their sabotage after freeing Michael and the others."

"I agree that's possible but consider this: Ignatius is old and stiff of joint. He could not possibly have crawled through the smaller sewers in the northern reaches of the Great Abbey. Many novices and postulants think well of Ignatius and visit him often so they may have been corrupted but I've had my hands around the throats of all of them: children who soil themselves in front of you cannot lie. No, I'm beginning to think that there were some accursed Exodus brats left behind by that Light-Father. I also fear that our postulants and novices might have innocently given Ignatius information that he passed on to these saboteurs."

Schimrian ground his teeth in impotent fury: "It makes sense but it doesn't rule out the possibility that we have one or more serpents still walking freely amongst us. When I raised Brothers Theo and Edward to the Fatherhood today, I told them in my arrogance, that I had deduced that the Light-Father would *not* leave any of his followers behind but I was a fool: Lord, grant me some sense and humility! Do you see this revolver upon my desk?"

"Yes, a fine Prussian weapon, Eminence."

"It's a treasured possession of mine as it once belonged to my grandfather, a knight of the Holy Prussian Empire. I have been contemplating why I never thought to draw this on entering the Great Annex and simply shoot the Light-Father." He indicated the Austro-Hungarian sword with a badly damaged hilt next to the revolver. "No, I wanted to test him in combat, sword to sword, and redeem him personally," he laughed bitterly. "Was it witchcraft, aesthetics or a sinful arrogance about my swordsmanship that drove all thought of this revolver from my mind, hmmm?"

"I cannot say, Eminence," Pious shrugged. "Maybe the Wiccan cast a spell upon you as that old Harlot did at Crawcester when you Inquired of her. I was engaged in the Cathedral so I did not witness your swordplay with the Light-Father and his Wiccan nor did I witness the final emergence of your archangel."

"Ah, sweet Azrael," Schimrian sighed, his eyes shining. "He was *magnificent*; everything we imagine an angel of the Lord to be." His face became a mask of fury: "That *Wiccan* bewitched him! Even with all those begiullers screaming at her, she worked her dark craft and through him, she corrupted our Tally-men! Her arcane devilry had already impaled every Brother-Technician in the Annex. The other witches defiled and raised our Brothers from the dead and then that Exodus *brat* destroyed my beautiful Adonis! He had strategy, Pious. That thrice-accursed Light-Father had *strategy*. We must *never* underestimate him again!"

Pious looked sceptical: "By that logic, Eminence, I owe my continued existence, such as it is, to their arcane arts."

"No, no, *no*, my friend," Schimrian insisted, emphasising each syllable with a chopping motion of his hands. "In his death throes, Azrael filled *you* with his holy spirit to enable you to serve our great purpose: to build our glorious New Jerusalem in his stead! You were chosen by God to return victorious from the Gates of Death: *know that I would have your heart beat again and the blood surge warm into your limbs so that we may rise up as brothers and cast down the Queen of Babylon.*"

Pious raised an eyebrow. "Thomas Tythe? The Ruin of Reason? Act two if I'm not mistaken. How appropriate."

Schimrian smiled wearily: "I see you are astute as ever, old friend. The Wiccans have taken much from us but with you by my side, we'll reclaim our prize in the fullness of time. Now that I've repented and acknowledged my human frailties in such matters, let us return to Ignatius and his villains."

"I failed you, Eminence, and beg your forgiveness," Pious said, his hand upon his cold and silent heart: "I did not see the sabotage amongst so much carnage and then I thought that Ignatius must have acted alone but I must caution you: we only have his ramblings as proof that there actually were any saboteurs. It may be a desperate ruse on his part to escape Redemption and protect his accomplices here at the Great Abbey."

"We are not flies ensnared in Pyrrho's web, my friend: the Great Abbey *was* contaminated by the Light-Father," Schimrian seethed, running a finger along his sword edge. "Are you sure there are no more vermin running loose beneath our feet?"

"None, Eminence, but whether there were or not, any Brother or Father who assisted Ignatius is still a threat to the Order."

"I think you may be correct in this analysis, my friend," Schimrian sighed, massaging his eyes. "Nevertheless, I want the sewer systems searched for evidence. Use every Father and Brother if you have to - except for our new Fathers, Theo and Edward. Let them work on the generators your Inquisitor found for us."

"Father Aten is efficient *and* loyal, Eminence."

"He is. I visited Theo and Edward earlier only to find them asleep at their desks. Poor Camus was taken to his chambers after

200

collapsing as he repaired an Angel. Camus and all the others need to rest in order to focus on repairs whilst you prepare the Brothers-Martial tomorrow for our Inquisition of Milverburg."

He gave vent to another jaw-cracking yawn. "In fact, we shall suspend all morning services until our holy task has been completed. I envy you for no longer requiring sleep, my friend, nor are you afflicted by the need to take repast or toilet – ever the thieves of our precious time upon this sweet Earth."

"It has its disadvantages, Eminence, as I know not what sustains me," Pious hissed with a hunger animating his dead eyes. "I feel no thirst or hunger yet this Holy Spirit; this blessing fills me with such divine strength. It means I can exact my revenge on that Exodus upstart who robbed me of my life. How dare he pierce my heart! I shall redeem him most *exquisitely*."

Schimrian held a hand for silence and listened intently. "This storm is abating," he declared. "Have we heard from Father Ursaf and his Angel crews? I would have them bury Father Beorcraft and his Brothers rather than leave them as carrion for crows and dogs to feast upon. We also need to recover their half-tracks as we have few left that are serviceable."

"Alas, the athidol tanks had been filled with sugar but we assumed that this was done during the initial attack. We've heard nothing but static from Ursaf's Angels according to Brother Matthew and he tells me that Bede cannot raise them either. We have yet to hear from our outposts and retreats up there but I fear all our Scotian and Eirann Brothers and Fathers are dead. We must have electrics soon else all our battery-packs will be depleted and we'll lose contact with everyone across the globe."

"Our two new Fathers are confident we'll have the electrics restored to the Manse and the Great Cathedral by Compline tomorrow. We'll keep trying to contact our bases in Scotia and Eirann: I won't accept that we've lost them all!"

"Neither will I, Eminence," Pious agreed, adjusting his sword belt and the machine gun he perpetually carried upon his back. "But there has been no contact. If any had survived then they would have been here in person to report to you. We must investigate once the Inquisition is done. However Burslen will send us eighty stout Brothers-Martial under Father Hvretsope."

"Ah, as ever, you bring me solace and glad tidings my old friend but I mourn the loss of loyal Abbot Damien at Burslen. Now there was a Worthy soul and a true stalwart of the Conclave. Hvretsope is loyal to me and a fine Father-Martial so he will take Damien's place at Burslen after our Inquisition. We have no Fathers-Martial left here and but forty Brothers-Martial while none were left alive at Bede. What news of Wyehold?"

"They were sore depleted but they can still muster four Fathers-Martial and sixty-five Brothers-Martial. I regret I must bear grim news: Abbot Amalgan of Wyehold, another of your supporters at the Conclave, succumbed to his wounds this morning."

"Ah, this is grim news indeed," Schimrian grimaced. "I shall pray for his Worthy soul. By all the fires of Hell, I could lose my majority in the Conclave unless I add new Abbots to it!"

"With respect, Eminence, that's a bridge we'll have to cross when we get to it. For now, we have the Light-Father and his Wiccans to deal with. Camus agrees that we may need boats but if we man these with Brothers-Technician, they'll need firearms and begiullers yet you are loathe to countenance this."

Schimrian chewed at a thumbnail: "You know I am, old friend," he fretted. "Fathers who've earned my trust can carry them but *not* Brothers. A Brother at the Great Abbey could easily kill me with a firearm and I *reluctantly* acceded to their possession of plasma-grenades at *your* insistence! Even now, I will *not* change that decision. We'll hold those boats in reserve and only issue firearms *in extremis*. Instead we shall pray to God to send us calm weather so that we may advance along the viaducts with our Angels guarding both the air above and the estuary below."

"You've read our minds, Eminence," Pious nodded approvingly. "It's a blessing to see your wits fully restored. Meanwhile, we'll deploy our brethren at the end of each viaduct while Angels sortie when they can across Uppermost and use searchlights at night to sink any vessels fleeing our glorious Inquisition."

Schimrian reached for his brandy glass and downed it in a single gulp. A rare smile touched his thin lips: "Ah, my friend; my solace; my shield, you've laid out sweet comfort upon my brow to salve my woes and bid me sleep. I bid you goodnight, my friend, but tell me: what will you do in the dark watches before dawn?"

"I will meditate and pray for the Blessings of the Lamb upon our mission," Pious said, getting to his feet. He bent to kiss the ring of the Order upon Schimrian's finger. "Then I might drag a postulant or two from their beds at cock-crow and watch them soil themselves. I find it instils obedience and discipline."

"So you claim but I beg you, just don't render them incapable of assisting the Sisters about their tasks as you did with that postulant you buried," Schimrian said as he poured yet more brandy into his glass. "They will be Brothers one day and I want soldiers of the Order to build our New Jerusalem not trembling bedwetters. I am still unconvinced about your decision to slay all but five of the Unworthy in the Redemption Cells."

"As I've said before, the Tally-men are redundant as we cannot trust them, Eminence, and we were wasting scarce rations keeping them alive. As for the postulants, I will find some other activity with which to pass the time. Perhaps I might read The Ruins of Reason as Tythe echoes well our current dilemma."

Schimrian watched him depart in silence and sipped at his brandy, savouring both it and the call of a dreamless sleep creeping over him; a man who had engineered the deaths of billions. Within and without the Great Manse swirled a billion angry shades unseen while a billion vengeful voices howled unheard.

~~~~~

The thunder had ceased and the rain reduced to a dull soothing roar upon the tiles. Peter was starting to nod off in his chair when Michael returned with dry blankets he'd found wrapped in plastic in one of the cupboards. Surl, Pup and Rabbit were in a snoring but contented tangle on the sofa whilst Fern and the Light-Father were sleeping relatively quietly in the other armchairs. He placed blankets upon them all and then placed his hand on Peter's head. "You did well, brave boy. Sleep well. I shall watch over you all till dawn for I need little rest and what sleep I get is filled with hateful ghosts. This is ordained by God to give me more time in which to pray for His forgiveness for my countless sins and failings."

"I don't think God had anything to do with that," Peter yawned. "Mother Moss preferred to call it *karma*. If God did that to you after He let billions die then why pray to Him at all?"

Michael shrugged. "It's all I know. It's all I have." he whispered as he tucked the blanket around Peter. "I can do naught else."

"Do what you will for I lie here with your hand atop my head when I would lie in the arms of my parents but for your Order."

Such was the hate in his eyes that Michael withdrew his hand as if scalded. "That, Scatterling, is something I cannot undo."

"Then leave me be for I need no comfort from a *butcher*," Peter snarled, turning his face away and drawing the blanket over his head. "Mother, be in my dreams, I beg you, *please*."

Michael pinched out all but the one candle at the dining table by the window and sat upon a dining chair to listen as Peter's muffled sobs slowly transformed into gentle snoring. He arose and checked upon the five sleeping men in the bedrooms and gazed down at the face of his brother as he twitched and muttered in vivid blood-red nightmares about Redemption Cells as did the other four: time and again the names of Pious and Aten passed their lips until an anger stirred in his heart and he clenched his fists. "I am finally on the right path," he whispered up at the ceiling. "Lord, I thank thee for tearing away the veils about my empty heart. Bless me and aid me as I guide them all into your Holy Light. Amen."

The next bedroom which had two beds with the slumbering forms of Ibrahim and Bas huddled together on one as were Shield and Saul upon the other. Another long-unfelt feeling stirred in his heart: love; a pure and overwhelming love for these precious children as all woe and fear had vanished from their faces in such a deep sleep. "Thank you, Lord, for granting me this vision. Again, I vow unto you, Father of All, that I will be their shield and defender unto my dying day. This I swear."

Tears flowing freely, he doused all but one candle in the kitchen and returned to his chair at the dining table where he beheld a book covered in dust and cobwebs. He opened it and found photographs of the family whose house this was and various notes from the children lovingly affixed to the pages. He now knew all their names and whispered them one by one ending with: "May God have mercy upon your souls and grant you eternal peace amongst his heavenly hosts. Forgive me as I strive to atone for your untimely deaths and hold you in my soul forever. Amen."

He closed the book as an overwhelming weariness claimed him. He laid his head upon his arms was asleep instantly, dreaming of drinking wine with Ignatius in his study, discussing art and poetry whilst eating cheese melted upon thick toast. He felt the warmth of the coal fire upon his face as he laughed at a joke being poorly told by Ignatius and for the first time in six years, his dreams were free of the hate-filled, faces and voices of the dead.

~~~~~

Burslen Abbey was being hammered by the storm with giant hail smashing onto the flagstones along with stone fragments torn from statues and masonry. A lightning strike had blown one of the spires apart sending half of it crashing through the roof of the nearby dormitory killing a novice and three postulants. A young Brother was watching the lightning from the refectory two floors above the large garage housing the half-tracks. He turned to the muscular, blond cleric next to him: "This is the worst weather I've seen for six years, Father Hvretsope," he said nervously.

"Is this is the Wrath of God, my son, or the Devil hindering the righteous?" the impassive Father shrugged. "It matters not: there's nothing we can do about this tempest except hold true to our faith and endure it. Schimrian is counting on us to move our Brothers-Martial south to that abomination of a city to Inquire of this monster they call the Light-Father and his coven."

"They say Wyehold and Bede will help us but what news of our barracks and brethren in Norton?"

"As you know, there were but a handful of Brothers-Technician left alive and they've been ordered to abandon Norton altogether and assist Abbot Camus at the Great Abbey."

The Brother looked doubtful: "They say they can still reach our brethren overseas on the radio but our brethren in Scotia and Eirann have fallen upon the spears of their Tally-men."

"This is correct, my son, and we can't trust those we have left."

"Burslen will be undefended as Bede is. If this Light-Father struck northwards after you've headed south, he could overrun us as our perimeter walls are only eight feet high at most."

Hvretsope was silent for a moment as he appraised the young Brother. "Valour ripostes when the Devil lunges, my son. You have your spears and plasma-grenades and I will leave two begiullers. If the walls are overrun then retreat to the Sister's Enclave or the Infirmary and barricade the doors. Fear not, Brother Ionas, we'll be back in two days or three at the most to assist with repairs."

"We lack the masons to restore the spire and the statues and Father Thomas is struggling with the injuries from the falling masonry. Eight of the youngest are badly injured. With the Tally-men killing so many of us and Abbot Damien and now this storm, it feels like God is forsaking us, Father. We..." His voice was cut off by Hvretsope clamping a large and powerful hand about his throat.

205

"Never *ever* blaspheme in my presence, my son," he hissed.

"Urk! Gahah! I-I a-apologise, Father," Ionas choked out, massaging his bruised throat. "I meant no sacrilege. We *will* see our New Jerusalem built one day!"

"Apology accepted, my son, and we *will* restore the Twelve Tribes in the decades to come with the help of our blessed Sisters. Look how white the ground is in this strange green storm-glow! It reminds me of a blizzard I saw one Christ Mass before I became a novice and began my martial arts. I made snowmen... hoi, what is happening to the electrics? Are the generators failing? Go to the generator room and see what transpires there, my son."

The lights were flickering badly as the young Brother hastened away. A few minutes later, the lighting was restored but Ionas returned drenched and with a panicked look upon his face. "The athidol in one of the tanks was low," he explained. "I refilled it myself as Brothers Argent and Tayte were nowhere to be found but then I beheld a trail of blood smeared upon the floor leading towards the rear doors. I fear someone has taken them!"

"Impossible!" Hvretsope snarled, checking his firearm. "These Blessed Isles are empty but for dogs, wild pigs, dying beast-children and this so-called Light-Father at Milverburg! We need to let the Brothers-Martial rest for tomorrow so go and gather five Brothers-Technician you can rely upon, get them to take up their spears and meet me at the generator room. We Martial always err on the side of caution, my son, but they are most likely to be in the infirmary adding to the woes of Father Thomas."

After Ionas had gone, Hvretsope ambled downstairs with gun in hand and suppressed a yawn. If the two Brothers were slacking or asleep somewhere, he'd make them regret it. He opened the rear exit door and immediately stepped back across the threshold for against the eerie sheen of the hail he could see black, fleeting shapes running silently to and fro as if hunting. Some were clearly canine or wolf but there were other silhouettes resembling apes yet capering at great speed across the carpet of ice and broken stone.

He watched as the hail ceased and the lightning paused creating an unnerving silence but for the susurrus of the rain. For a moment, he thought he could hear Ionas desperately screaming for help in the distance. Then the howling began.

~~~~~

Strange Dawns

The Ferals twitched in dreams of lost childhoods on makeshift beds alongside the railway carriages as were Fria and Amos, still hand-in-hand. Nightshade was lying across four seat cushions in the cabin of the Phoenix with Mouse snuggled up to her, smiling in her own dreams of happier days - mostly due to the herb infusion Nightshade had given her. Warm sun played upon her face as she ran pell-mell around the family garden during a summer solstice party playing tag with her sisters and cousins. Their huge garden was full of family, guests and marquees; wine glasses clinked, people laughed and sang as meat sizzled on outdoor grills.

She frowned suddenly: her parents were sitting in a rowing boat on the small duck pond but nobody else in the garden seemed to notice them doing this. They were beckoning to her.

Nightshade stirred and whispered: "You cannot go, Mouse: they sail the lakes of Avalon beyond the Gates of Death. This is not your time. Dream not of dark museum halls or of rats and death but of daisy chains and summer days. Be at peace, dear heart."

Mouse stirred and muttered: "Fierce wasn't in the boat; why wasn't she in the boat?" before slipping into meadow-dreams.

Nightshade removed Mouse's mouse-ears headband and stroked her hair before she, too, drifted back to sleep but her meadow-dreams were not so tranquil. She was lying on the blue-green grass of a strange world where a gas giant planet could be faintly seen hanging in the sky beyond the cumulus clouds. The sun had just risen above the hills casting long shadows as iridescent, six-winged dragonflies swarmed about her and a breeze scented faintly with strange spices and honey gently swayed the wondrous and exquisite flowers about her. Beyond the distant hills, she could see the golden and silver towers and spires of a colossal city.

"Welcome, Mother Nightshade," said a female voice behind her. "I'm so happy to meet a Wiccan again!"

Nightshade rolled over to sit cross-legged and behold a young Caucasian woman sitting upon the grass. She seemed to have but twenty-five years or so but Nightshade felt instinctively that this woman measured her span in millennia not in mere orbits of the Earth about the Sun. She seemed solid enough but she was surrounded by a nimbus of faint neutron-blue as plasma filaments radiated away from her, vanishing into thin air.

She was dressed in blue trousers and leather boots and wore a leather jacket over a patterned T-shirt with a slogan in Romanic letters that Nightshade could not read. Her long blond hair was tied back into a ponytail and her tanned elfin features bore a small, sensuous mouth and a slightly-upturned nose. There was a butterfly tattooed on her left cheek. Nightshade sighed at her ethereal beauty but it was the eyes which were truly unsettling: they had a slightly oriental look but the whites were a brilliant blue and two small blue sparks glittered where the irises should have been.

"Am I dreaming?" Nightshade demanded, running her hand through the grass. "I can't be: I could never dream texture like this nor, ah, smell these peculiar fragrances. Ach…" She had to avert her eyes from the heavens as that gas giant hanging above them gave her waves of debilitating vertigo as if this world was a moon falling upwards to its inevitable destruction.

"You are not dreaming: this world does not exist in your reality. I've simply drawn forth your astral form to speak with you."

"This is my astral form?" Nightshade gasped, staring at her hands. "Some of us can project our consciousness when we far see places and events but not as completely as this! *Dreistkred*!"

The woman simply smiled, crossed her legs and laid the backs of her hands upon her knees as if in meditation. There were now six plasma streamers emanating from her and if they'd been arms, Nightshade thought she could be in the presence of a Hindu avatar – not that she knew much of their religion: the Wiccans had such a cluttered and contradictory pantheon of their own gods that it precluded such study. "Are you Gaia?" she asked, awe-struck. "Diana? Helen? Verdandi?"

"None of them and all of them," the woman said enigmatically, speaking in a voice with a thousand faint harmonies. "I suppose you could say that I am One of the Powers That Be but I do favour this form more than the others as I was born of human parents."

"So you are not a god?"

"No but I have been worshipped as one if that impresses you."

"A priestess then?"

"I suppose you could call me that but guardian and harbinger would be a better description of my purpose."

"Is this why you've summoned me, priestess?"

"We wage a war eternal against demons across the whole of Creation and beyond. A demon seed entered your world centuries ago and lay dormant until it was revived by fools who did not know of its compulsion to exterminate sentient life. We did not sense its presence on your world until it was too late as even we cannot be everywhere and *everywhen* but with my help you destroyed the physical form of this creature - as foretold by Mother Moss."

"What? She knew you?"

"I brought her here as I've brought you. She was remarkably wise for someone of such few decades but that's the price of prescience: you can live a thousand lifetimes in just one."

"You said you helped us. How?"

"Ah, Mother Moss begged us to give you the Light-Father."

"The Light-Father?"

"Yes. Without his presence at *that* key turning point your world would have been stripped of all sentience by now." The woman's outline suddenly faded until there was nothing but a network of glowing nerves. Her body slowly reformed but her face was contorted in agony: "Ah, the Enemy *moves*..."

"But why have you summoned me? Who *are* you, priestess?" Nightshade demanded, shaken by the images.

"I have so many names that I cannot recall the first name my mother gave me. I am called Ormuzd in worlds such as yours. I brought you here to warn you; to *prepare* you."

"What do you mean? We fought the Order and they number thousands yet we defeated Azrael and killed many of them at the Great Abbey. Are you saying if we die at their hands then we can die content knowing that we kept Hell from manifesting?"

Ormuzd shook her head. "No, you see: there is a Divine Design governing each and every Creation but there must also be a Divine Balance in all things. For life to evolve there *must* be conflict and challenge; there must be good and evil..."

"My world has evil in abundance! Where was this precious 'Balance' of yours when four *billion* of us died?"

"That happened because the Balance is being destroyed by the Enemy; the Greatest of All Satans. These ancient parasites gorge upon the divine spark in all living things and they bring entire Creations down in ruin and dissolution. Be warned: the One you fought may rise again in many forms before your world is cleansed of evil and the last sagas are acted out."

"Azrael will rise again? No!" Nightshade moaned, holding her head in her hands in despair. "Oh, I am so *tired*, Ormuzd!"

Ormuzd leant forward and placed an index finger on the centre of Nightshade's forehead. "As am I," she said. "But we brought the Light-Father to you and instilled your language into him as best we could. We cannot aid you any further for we alone face the First of the Fallen Angels who strove for Heaven in their arrogance but fell into the void between Creations. There they festered and became envious of all sentient life and resolved to wipe it from the face of Existence. That is their fell Purpose." Ormuzd tapped Nightshade's forehead. "Be thankful you have but *one* of these demons to deal with but now it's time you got some rest, little Ellete."

Nightshade blinked and was floating naked but unharmed in a sea of burning stars and fiercely glowing nebula. She could see her body was emitting a pure white light but she was but a spark above a blue giant star.

She blinked again only to find herself as a child in Kendra's arms drifting down a well of peaceful, dreamless sleep.

~~~~~

"Jesus and Mary spare my shriveless soul!" Spero cursed as his spear was seized again and he had to use all his strength to recover it. "I can't tell if one of these things is a Feral or a wolf!"

Hneftal looked over his shoulder as he pointed his spear down the hallway. "If it's a wolf with hands, it's a Feral," he shouted. "And if it's a Feral with claws, it's a wolf."

Ursaf and Marcus still braced the door but the last two bolts were beginning to fail. Ursaf had already fired two shots killing two Ferals in the hallway and one through the hole in the ceiling killing something but he wasn't sure exactly *what* he'd killed. He knew he had to conserve his bullets but at least the shots had caused the attackers to withdraw from inside the farmhouse for now.

Hneftal and Piamadet had acquitted themselves well and a score of wolves and Ferals lay dead in front of their makeshift barricade. Both men had been raked badly during the fighting but were elated at having survived thus far on sheer adrenaline and good fortune. "I think they're climbing back into the other rooms," Piamadet said. "Come!" he shouted. "Come and meet your Redemption! Come at us if you dare, thou Hell spawn!"

"What of the begiuller, Brother Gudflan?" Ursaf panted. He and Marcus were exhausted by the constant assaults upon the door.

210

"The battery is almost drained, Father," Gudflan grunted. "The electrics gauge is reading twenty percent: enough for another two short blasts I reckon then our throats get torn out."

Ursaf checked his watch and then wiped the sweat from his eyes. His clothing was saturated but it wasn't rain. "Three hours," he grated. "How many plasma-grenades do we have?"

"Three remain, Father," Gudflan said, trying to peer into the darkness beyond the broken window frames. "It's keeping most of them away from the kitchen windows but that won't last. I think they'll come at us down the hallway and the ceiling next and then attack the kitchen door again. What say you, Father?"

"There is a pattern," Ursaf wheezed, trying to draw breath. "They attack and withdraw then rest and attack again after a two-howl signal. What of your dart guns, my sons?"

"We've emptied them, Father, and no doubt the ones we've darted are already waking up out there," Spero muttered, clutching the spear Marcus had given him. "Oh, thank you so much, Great-Abbot Schimrian! I would trade my soul for a rifle right now!"

"Cease your blasphemy!" Ursaf bellowed, his face turning a mottled crimson. "We *will* survive this as true brethren of the Order and defenders of the Faith! Be careful what you wish the Devil for, Brother Spero, as such…"

Marcus had his ear to the door. "Two howls!" he cried out. "They're coming again. Fire the begiuller!"

Gudflan pointed it out of the window and pressed the trigger and again they felt a silent pressure in their inner ears. Outside, a shrill yammering broke out but this time it did not recede. "It's not powerful enough to drive them away!" he cried in despair.

There was a massive impact on the kitchen door and the bolts failed completely and to their horror, both Ursaf and Marcus were pushed back inch by inch. With his left shoulder against the door, Ursaf managed to fire a shot through the gap and the pressure eased and they could shut it once more.

"The accursed begiuller has died!" Gudflan shouted, throwing it across the kitchen in frustration. "I'm going to try a grenade!" He primed the fuse and threw it through a broken window pane. The explosion was almost instantaneous but the concussion caused the door to twist on its hinges and cast Ursaf and Marcus cursing to the floor. Gudflan and Spero were cut by flying glass shards but it had bought them another lull in the attack.

Marcus clambered to his feet and glared at Gudflan. "You mule-brained kack-spewing *troll!*" he roared. "Why in Saint Peter's name didn't you throw it further than two yards from the wall?"

"Bind your mouth, Brother! I cast it a goodly distance but they must've thrown it back towards the door before it detonated."

"Enough! Brace the door!" Ursaf said curtly. "The hinges have failed and we have only our strength to protect us, my son. All of you: you've made me proud this night to be your Father. Dawn is almost upon us and dawn oft brings hope..."

He never got to finish the sentence as the attack was swift and brutal. A wolf smashed straight through the shattered window frame into the kitchen as Gudflan was turning back to his station and clamped its jaws about his throat as more shapes swarmed through the window and brought him down.

Shadowy forms appeared at the hole in the ceiling and there was a rush down the corridor only Hneftal was ready and had grabbed a grenade. Simultaneously, the door shattered into fragments sending Ursaf and Marcus crashing into Spero as a tide of teeth and fang burst through the doorway sweeping Hneftal over the barricade and to his doom in the hallway. Piamadet managed to leap aside and gore a large dog with his spear but he could not stop the others from attacking Hneftal and savaging Durwyn's body.

Ursaf, Marcus, Spero and Piamadet hastily retreated to the far corner of the kitchen. Marcus grabbed some kitchen knives from a wall rack as Spero and Piamadet readied their spears. All the candles had been snuffed out in the attack except for one guttering on a work surface but they could clearly see the kitchen was filled with over fifty silent shapes. The pale green phosphorescence in those eyes unnerved Ursaf immensely for it revealed an intelligent, murderous intent that regarded them as *prey*.

Hneftal shrieked: "Forgive me for I have sinned....*aieee!*" The thrashing of limbs ended and there was silence but for the tearing of flesh from three corpses. The Ferals and beasts watching them did not move a muscle as these gruesome sounds continued.

"How many bullets have you left, Father," Marcus demanded.

"Four I think, my son, but not enough for all these fell things."

"They're for us, Father! Grant us a swift death, I beg you."

"Another mortal sin you would have me commit?"

Piamadet laughed incredulously: "Sin? The true sin of the Order stands before us, Father, these monsters are *our* creations; *our* sin.

212

Hoi! Look through the windows, Father! We are blessed to see another sunrise after all."

Ursaf saw the unmistakable ruddy glow from the sun ascending a cloudless sky and heard the avian chorus heralding its arrival in the nearby trees. "Aye, my son, we've survived but let us pray for the souls of Gudflan, Durwyn and Hneftal. Grant them divine mercy, O Lord, and receive them into your heavenly host. Amen."

"Amen," Marcus echoed quickly. "*Why* are they just staring at us? What *is* it about the dawn that troubles them?"

"Ah," said Piamadet, jabbing with his spear as a wolf slunk towards him. "Hoi! Have at you, beast! I'll not die today!"

The wolf began growling as did the others in the room etching the scene into their memories. The wolves and large dogs were bad enough but the Ferals had more wolf traits than human and they were adult-sized, barely upright and muscled massively across the shoulders. Their fangs were formidable and saliva foamed at their mouths and it was obvious that they were *hungry*.

Ursaf's eyes widened. "These Ferals are from Erdethric!" he exclaimed in horror. "I heard a dark rumour that Professor Farzad was breeding such chimerae in the Exodus laboratories on the island after consulting with the Great Computer and the Fathers-Surgeon. It must've been true because these lupine abominations are definitely not Ferals!"

"And now they're on the mainland, Father," Marcus grimaced. "Our divine retribution writ large! Shoot us now! Quickly, before they tear us apart!" he yelled, frantically slashing one wolf across the muzzle with a knife causing it to yelp and retreat a few feet. "Look at them: they're toying with us; watching us panic!"

Ursaf came to a decision and fired at the nearest four Hybrids killing two outright and wounding two others which were then set upon by their starving fellows. There were more than enough left to press the four clerics further into the corner. Suddenly, there was a fusillade of shots outside and the hybrids and their wolves flinched, sinking to their haunches, their hackles rising.

"Is that Pious or some of our Brothers come to rescue us?" Piamadet wondered joyfully as he jabbed his spear at a wolf causing it to yelp in pain as the tip dug into its shoulder. "Fly, you damned animal! Back to Hell with you!"

Like an ebbing tide the pack turned and flowed out of the door leaving the survivors to sink to their knees in relief and exhaustion to offer up private prayers of thanks for their deliverance. More shots rang out to be met by wordless screams and howls of hatred followed by the crackling of automatic weapons. Then there was a heavy silence before the dawn chorus resumed and then came the sound of booted feet approaching the doorway. Five heavily armed young men entered the kitchen only they were not of the Order.

"Who are you?" Ursaf demanded querulously.

The man who was obviously the leader of the group stepped forward and his blue piecing eyes were full of hatred and contempt. He was gaunt with long dank black hair and dressed in a green quilted hunting-jacket and corduroy trousers and muddied walking boots. Like the others he wore numerous ammunition belts and strange black goggles hung around his neck.

As he spoke they realised that he was Scotian: "My name is Ken Glascae," he said as all five of them pointed their weapons at Ursaf. "Stay on your knees, *aglaecen*! Only three weeks ago we were all being tortured in your Redemption Cells. How in God's name can you claim to be of God and do such evil? Who gave you the right to kill innocent women and children? Who ordained you to take a knife to a man's brain to destroy his personality and make him a mindless drone? Where in the Holy Scriptures did all that cruelty and arrogance come from? Gah!" he spat copiously at Ursaf. "I am minded to send your souls screaming to Hell."

"Then kill me but spare the others," Ursaf begged. "As a Father of the Order I bear the full burden of guilt for our monstrous crimes. We at Bede have torn the veils from our eyes; we have unchained our hearts. We accept that we were the agents of a great evil and I can blame no other here more than myself. Let my Brothers live. Let them atone for their sins, I beg you."

The three Brothers looked at Ursaf in astonishment: they had all thought him utterly incapable of such a selfless act.

"Pathetic *and* ironic," Glascae snorted. He spat again. "Pah! To think we thought you *scaernae* were refugees being ambushed by those monsters and thus risked our lives to save you! Now what shall we do with you sinners, hmmm? I remember the favourite adage of my murdered father: *out of the skillet and into the flames.* Rather appropriate in your case, don't you think?"

~~~~~

At the end of the quay closest to the harbour entrance of the Merchant Docks, Ivy watched the faint red-gold glow of dawn tinting the wavelets and the massive harbour walls were slowly becoming visible through the open dock gates. In the artistic excess typical of Milverburg there were two gigantic and ingenious marionettes of Neptune and his wife, Amphitrite, each with a hand upon the edge of the harbour gates so that when they were opened it looked as if both god and sea nymph were pulling them apart.

"It's a shame we're facing west," she sighed aloud. "I would love to see the sun rise unfettered after all these years." An obscure poem came to her lips: "*As Sol sheds the sleep of Selene or Arctic night, how does it happen that birds sing, that ice melts, the rose unfolds, the red of blood; of birth renewed grows lighter, whiter behind the silhouettes of trees and hills to blush the Spring Maiden's cheeks as her lips draw near to those of the Summer Youth whose scent of apple wood enticed her...*"

Kai had fallen asleep on their bed of sacking after telling her of his youth spent under the various House-Fathers who had stalked their dormitories at night singling out the comeliest of their helpless charges. He'd told her of beatings and casual brutality and how his heart and spirit broke as he was forced to act the Judas-goat, leading Unworthy children to a brutal death at the hands of the Order. Better a quick death, he'd told her, than what awaited them at the hands of the more fanatical Abbots and their Fathers-Surgeon in the Abbeys of Britannia and beyond.

Again, he'd relived Cora's death, shuddering at the memory and crying helplessly. She had cradled him until his sorrow was spent and made him recall how Brother Ignatius had been there for him; how the old man had slowly restored his soul, giving him the strength to break free of the Order when the opportunity arose in Crawcester. He was too indoctrinated to let go of his faith, she'd realised as she studied his sleeping form, his head resting upon her lap, but he'd awakened to more than just blind dogma thanks to Brother Ignatius and the science of Abbot Camus.

She laid more sacking over him as she felt no need of sleep herself as she drew sustenance from the ever-growing light. "I know you're behind me, little *déathscufan*," she whispered. "If you keep pointing those arrows as me I will become *vexed*. You fired arrows at me once. You will not be able do so again."

There was a faint scraping as the weapons were laid upon the flagstones. "We do not fear thee, Wiccan," said a blond-haired girl as she sat next to her upon the sacking. "But we fear the Order. They will come in their thousands. They will kill us."

A black-haired girl sat down in front of Ivy and stared angrily at her before taking the hand of her blond companion. "We have talked long in our nest. We weary of hiding in shadow and fear and listening to the cursing of rats and mice."

"We hear of the magic of this Light-Father," said the other.

"We wish for his enchantments upon us."

"We wish to run in green fields and sail the seas once more."

"And feel the sun again. There is a strange day upon us: there are no clouds and the sea-birds soar high into the blue."

"We have played too long amongst bones and statues."

"It's made our hearts harder than a gargoyle's."

"We are so..."

"*Lonely...*"

Ivy smiled as she stroked Kai's hair. "Perhaps it's because you feel you are of birthing age and need a mate," she said suggestively. "I knew you would not hide from us for long."

"We need no mates. We have each other. You caught our arrows so we were curious of your craft."

"We wished for them to strike your heart as we did with Tally-men and Brothers uncounted as they hunted down Plague survivors in the ten towns who were not as we were."

"Stupid as sheep and easily slain."

"Not us. We knew their tricks and we taught them to fear the dark places beneath Uppermost and lo, after three years they did not climb the Stairways again and we were free of them."

"Milverburg was our home."

"Until you came."

"Yes, until we came, dear hearts," Ivy sighed. "I wish it were otherwise but they will attack us here and we will fight them as we did in the Great Abbey. We will defeat them and make the whole of Britannia our home and not just Milverburg."

She studied the two girls. They were both strong and dressed identically in plain khaki cotton shirts and trousers, short sleeveless jackets and stout leather boots. Their hair was hacked short and both had two knives in sheaths on their leather belts but what caught her eye were the amulets they wore. The black-haired, brown-skinned girl's amulet was a black Yin symbol while her fair-skinned blond cousin wore a white Yang symbol – obviously gifts from the Japanese Empire traders. "What are your names?" she prompted. "As you know, this is Kai and I am Mother Ivy."

The two girls looked at each other sheepishly and intertwined their fingers. "I am Pomona," said the black-haired girl. "Pomona Regina of the Regina merchant clan and my sweet Yang-chan here is Kayleigh Burr of the Scotian Burr merchant clan and we are cousins by wedlock as our clans often intermarried."

"The Beomodor is the fastest boat owned by our clans yet your Light-Father would steal her from us," Kayleigh said angrily.

"You are being foolish: you cannot sail her and there is nowhere to sail *to*," Ivy said bluntly. "Stay with us. We shall be your new clan; the clan of the Scatterlings. Stay and tell me of your life in Milverburg and how you 'wish' your arrows to strike the targets. Do you bear the mark of the craft?"

The girls held up their palms and there they were: one upon the right palm of Kayleigh and one upon the left palm of Pomona. "The merchants knew of the mark," Pomona explained. "But it mattered not as we were always at sea and our fathers bid us wear gloves ashore and they forbade the crews to speak of it."

"We could move things with our minds and one captain called it te-le-kin-es-is," Kayleigh added proudly. "We could wish things to move and so we were often paid a silver coin apiece to rig the dice games. They would get so vexed with us."

"But we were such *kawaiee* little girls," Pomona laughed. "They couldn't stay mad at us for long!"

"I met merchants who were tolerant of the craft," Ivy nodded. "The longer the open road walked, the more open the mind."

Kayleigh pressed the palms of her hands to her eyes. "Even with the mark, they loved us and we miss them."

Pomona wiped at her tears. "An Exodus scientist called Edric Olafson came to see my father when the Plague began. He knew my father well of old and gave him two vials. He said it was the only vaccine they had left and then he told Da how the Order had betrayed their work and infected them and their families and that everybody in the world was going to die. His wife and daughter died quickly but the vaccine had saved his son and he'd hidden him in Crawcester. Even though he was dying he knew of our mark and felt compelled to make one last journey to see us."

"He was shaking and coughing up blood," Kayleigh sniffed. "Then he left saying he was going to speak to God in some tavern. Da and everyone talked about the vials then they injected us with the vaccine and then, one by one, the Plague took them."

"We couldn't save them," Pomona wept. "We tried talismans and apothecary powders and nothing worked. They gave us the vaccine knowing they would die and we would live. They said we had to remember them and then they'd live on in us."

Ivy pushed a basket towards them. "Here. Eat. This is cooked fish seasoned with roots, herbs and spices from Uppermost. I put this aside for you as I knew you two would come especially if we sat here patiently far away from my poor Ferals."

Ivy had planted a compulsion in them to seek her out but it had not really been needed: their loneliness and fear had overcome their mistrust of strangers. Thus the tide slowly ebbed, the daylight grew stronger and as the two girls relished their food, they told her of their clans, their life at sea as small children and their battle for survival for six long years in Milverburg. Their words poured forth in torrents and breathless cascades as they'd not spoken to a living soul since they'd nursed their dying clans.

She marvelled at the happenstance that had revealed two able Daughters unto her whilst the presence of Kai's head in her lap stirred a passion deep inside her that any man would have been hard put to quench. A death's-head moth fluttered into view to land briefly upon the heads of the two curious girls and then it settled upon Kai's brow only to vanish in a puff of dust.

"Ah, I see I have your blessings upon all three," she said and to consternation of Pomona and Kayleigh, she placed a hand across her eyes and gave vent to her decades of sorrow and grief.

~~~~~

Second Skirmish

"In the midst of chaos, there is also opportunity." – Sun Tzu

"It's past Eight Bells, Light-Father," Rabbit said, shaking him vigorously by the shoulders. "Wake up! There's blue sky! Blue *sky*! There are no clouds!" she gabbled breathlessly and climbed onto his lap to bounce up and down all but winding him.

"Oof! My God, you're full of beans," he muttered, wiping the sleep from his eyes and stretching luxuriously. "I thought you all hated the sun when you were in Crawcester because the rain kept the Tally-men away from the Keep."

Rabbit frowned quizzically and put her face close to his; almost touching noses. "That was before you came, Light-Father and why would I be full of beans? I'm a girl not a sack of beans."

"It's just a saying in my world," he sighed wearily. "It just means that you're full of energy for some reason."

"I slept deep and long. Mother Fern said she'd placed herbs about us to chase away the nightmares and here I am: back with my very own Light-Father," she gushed and hugged him tightly.

It was a full three minutes before she would let him get up. "What's that smell?" he wondered. "It is! I can smell *bacon*!"

"Bas went out hunting before dawn and killed a young boar in the woods. Fern and Ibrahim gutted it and chopped it up while Michael went out and found edible mushrooms and wood sorrel, chickweed, wild garlic and even dandelions. He's cooking some more just for the two of us. Fresh bacon! Oink, oink!"

"Ow! So that's why you're jumping up and down on me!" His eyes widened and he set her down on the carpet. "Wait a minute, he's *cooking*? The smoke will give us away!"

"Not so, Light-Father," Michael said from the doorway. "This cottage has a modern gas range. Apparently being a wood-master was a profitable occupation. Everyone has eaten except for you and the young kit there who wanted to break her fast with you."

Harold had to look twice at the sinisterly-robed and cowled cleric. It was as if Death had exchanged his scythe for a spatula and an apron with 'Welcome to Thamesmead' emblazoned upon it. It was so incongruous that he could barely suppress an incredulous chuckle. Michael drew himself up imperiously: "There's no mirth in this. Cuisine is the practical application of *science* after all."

"Forgive me, Michael. You are full of surprises. In a way, it seems you are beginning to regain your humanity."

"If you say so; I have a long road to walk before that. However, I do feel curiously refreshed as do all the others. Some of them say it's due to Mother Fern's herbal lore and the others say that it's your magic that calmed their dreams. Either way," he said, bowing. "I am eternally grateful. For the first night in six years, I saw no Gates of Hell opening beneath my feet and a great weight has been lifted from my soul thanks to you, Light-Father."

Harold kept his doubts to himself and followed Michael and Rabbit into the kitchen. He was astounded by the change in the five escapees as they sat on chairs in the corner of the kitchen drinking black tea and talking quietly to each other. They'd shaved, washed and found clean clothes to replace the soiled robes that Surl and the others had brought them before helping them to escape. Even the Scatterlings had found some garments similar to their own which had been irrevocably fouled by their sewer exploits and the seven days on the run from Beorcraft. He was struck by a sudden sense of déjà vu: as a student he'd gone to an environmental encampment and this could be the exact same communal kitchen prior to a strenuous day of coppicing in the forest.

Fern was braiding her hair by the door and smiled at him having pried into his thoughts: "We are where we are, Light-Father," she laughed and indicated Rabbit who was sat at the kitchen table with a knife and fork in her hands. "You're harder to wake than one of the gargoyles in your tower so we sent in the heavy ordnance."

Harold sat down and Michael placed a breakfast in front of him and another before Rabbit who almost impaled his hand with a fork in her haste. It was indeed a feast that he and Rabbit ate with relish and not even the sound of Ibrahim sharpening his battle-axes and Bas maintaining her quiver and weapons could distract them from the task in hand. There was even some black tea which Shield insisted on pouring for him.

Replete, he sat back to marvel at the fact that some in the kitchen had fought a savage hand-to-hand battle in Wealthorpe only yesterday while the others had been hunted mercilessly by Beorcraft. He turned to Fern: "There must be other Brothers out there searching for us. As Surl said, we'll probably have to fight our way into that village again before we can return to Milverburg. We need to use the boat – I don't want to abandon it."

Fern finished braiding her hair and put her arm around Surl's shoulders. She closed her eyes and concentrated: "I cannot sense any Order search parties to the east. Maybe they've returned to the Great Abbey after losing Beorcraft. I honestly don't know: my craft is not accurate over such large distances."

"Beorcraft led the main party hunting us," Michael explained. "There were smaller scout groups and the Bede Angels searched for us as well. They knew we had to follow the main roads through Fosskeep and Thaneton so they set ambushes but thanks to Surl's visions we avoided them. He had half-tracks and could always get ahead of us but we still covered over thirty miles a day."

"We could have covered more if not for the short rations and torture, brother," Marc observed bitterly. The other four men nodded enthusiastically. Michael said nothing as he put the dishes and pans into the large sinks and strapped on his two gun holsters. Having already searched the cottage and its outhouses, he handed them a variety of weapons: two large lumber-axes and three large knives. "Now that your strength is returning," he said bluntly. "You should be able to wield them without injuring yourselves."

"I'm afraid you'll have to fight," Harold told them. "We have to get to our boat at Wealthorpe and get back to Milverburg. As soon as everyone has finished going to the toilet, we'll get going and... what's so funny, Pup?"

"It's just that Shield keeps telling Pup that heroes in sagas don't need to go to the toilet," he giggled.

Michael surprised them all by laughing out loud: "They do, young one, but nobody writes about the mundane necessities of life. I'm sure you don't want anyone reading the Tale of Pup the Mighty to know about your bodily functions, now would you?"

Before Pup could answer, Surl's face went blank and she shuddered, grasping Fern's hand hard. "We must hurry," she gasped, closing her eyes. "I see half-tracks to the east and to the north and ships in the Milverbore and... something else in the red shadows in the north, something *terrible*..." She retched a little. "I am sorry, Mother Fern, my craft is still weak. I cannot see anything but I *feel* a great evil is moving towards us... it's... it's..."

"Shhh, dear heart," Fern said soothingly. "You have but few years and have yet to awaken fully into your craft. What..."

Bas stepped forward and raised her hand. "When I was hunting, there was something in the air that made the animals nervous. The wind set north for a short while before setting south-west and there was a faint scent I've never smelt before: an animal I am not familiar with but my instincts tell me it's a threat to us."

"Some animals from zoos and menageries survived," Michael suggested. "Maybe a large cat is hunting in the woods."

Bas shook her head: "No, not a cat but something *different*; something *foul*. The scent was faint yet the badgers and foxes were hiding underground in mortal fear." She shook herself. "Be not afraid: my brother and I will take care of it should it attack."

"Good, let's get ready to leave," Harold said firmly, strapping his katana sheath to his belt. "Um, where *is* the toilet?"

"It's outside but you may want to defecate in the woods," Saul said delicately. "Unless you have no sense of smell."

Harold looked at the grinning Pup. "No," he laughed, wagging a finger. "That's *definitely* not going in your saga!"

Ten minutes later, after Harold had completed his toilet - and won the battle to keep his breakfast down - they were on the road back to Wealthorpe with Bas and Ibrahim scouting ahead of them. The road was covered with hail-shredded foliage and fragments blasted from the roadside trees by countless lightning strikes during the storm. A few huge pines had but charred trunks remaining and the smell of scorched pine-sap was a torture to the senses especially to those of poor Bas whom they could hear coughing, sneezing and cursing fluently in the distance.

The smell of pines faded to be replaced by a gentle westerly carrying the salt-sea air of the Milverbore. Before them lay the rail-tracks leading to Milverburg and they headed a little south to the place where they'd crossed over it when fleeing Wealthorpe. From the cover of the trees to the east of the tracks, they could see the corpses and the crows, ravens and seagulls which were already at work upon them and bickering over the spoils.

"Ugh, I see rats as well," Saul grimaced. "I never wanted to see such a sight as that again even if they were of the Order!"

"Your vision is much sharper than mine," Harold said somewhat enviously. "But it looks like we'll be able to get to the boat without a fight. Finally, we have some good news!"

He was about to break cover when Surl put a hand on his shoulder: "There's a large boat rounding the headland and keeping close to the shore," he said urgently. "There are over a dozen aboard and they wear the field robes of the Order."

"They're hardly likely to be anyone else," Harold said grimly.

"Ah, my inner demon rejoices," Ibrahim grinned before carefully removing that grin at a glare from Fern. He ran a finger along the edge of one of his axes. "He is still naught but an imp, Mother Fern, but he relishes the coming battle as I do."

"Shhh, everyone, get down!" Harold hissed. "They're at the quay and they can see us from there." He watched carefully as the Father and his Brothers made their vessel secure and three of them investigated the Ellendaed. He could see one of the Brothers pointing towards the village having spied the crows upon the bodies. After a short deliberation, the Father led eleven Brothers towards the ruins while four were left upon the quay to guard the boats with their spears at the ready. "We need to deal with those four at the same time as the others but how do we do that?"

Bas looked offended: "Shield and I will see to them, Light-Father. There is cover to the east of the causeway almost down to the water's edge. We'll climb the stonework from the east and that will put us above the Brothers so that we can fire down upon them and take them by surprise. I'm sure Saul and my brother can deal with most of the others," she grinned, showing that the points to her canines had indeed grown. "Remember to clean your sword afterwards, Light-Father! We'll wait until you start your attack then we'll join you once we've killed the four Brothers."

"Just be careful, dear heart," Saul urged.

Shield briefly kissed him and followed Bas into the overgrowth, keeping low and moving silently. Harold turned to Fern and Saul as the Brothers began checking the bodies and chasing away the vermin. "That's a lot of ground to cover and that's not a rifle the Father's carrying: it looks like a machine-gun!"

Saul shaded his eyes. "It's strange that they did not bring Tally-men with them. Hoi! One of the Brothers is standing guard with the Father and he has a begiuller ready. That Father is not making the mistake that the others did yesterday by keeping it in the half-track. They're retrieving shovels, Light-Father: they could just be a burial party and maybe they'll leave after burying them."

"I doubt it," Harold said thoughtfully. "They've seen our boat and they're very alert so they must have a radio and know we're close by. I think it's an advance party sent to seize this causeway. I bet Schimrian is sending others to seal off the other two causeways to prevent the Phoenix leaving across the viaducts. They'll probably use boats and Angels to stop us taking to the Milverbore as well. This is not good. We have no choice but to fight these Brothers then we'll go and get the others and escape northwards. Beorminghas might be a good place to go. Those towers could be the perfect place to hide."

Surl shook her head: "I don't think we can make it there, Light-Father. More Brothers are coming and we only have time to make a stand in Milverburg." She winced and put a hand to her nose and wiped away the fresh blood. "Ah! I cannot see any more!"

Fern put a hand on her head and stared into her eyes. "Do *not* use your craft again!" she said forcefully. "You're starting to haemorrhage. Any more of this and you'll have a stroke. Rest here with Pup, Rabbit and Peter. You've done more than your share already. I will try my geis: I think I might be able to cover us up to the village but there are three times as many minds there to glamour than in the Angels yesterday. Keep close behind me so I have a smaller area to camouflage. Follow me and tread as quietly as you can! If you make the slightest sound, my illusion will be shattered and we will lose the element of surprise."

They drew their weapons and crept in a tight formation towards the ruined cottages. The Father and the Brother next to him were scanning the woods as they approached but it was obvious that they couldn't see them at all. Michael and the other escapees were in awe of the power of the craft she was displaying.

They were ten yards away when the Father's eyes narrowed and then widened. "Fire the begiuller, Brother Abraham!" he screamed. "A Wiccan is upon us!" He raised the barrel of his own weapon but before he could pull the trigger, Michael had shot him neatly between the eyes. Fern, however, was pole-axed by the begiuller and Harold's knees buckled briefly beneath him. The pain was short as Ibrahim swung his axe and the Brother's head was almost cleaved from his shoulders. Ibrahim then shattered the begiuller with two tremendous blows from his bloodied axe.

Fern was totally incapacitated so Harold had to carry her away to a safe distance from the fighting before rushing back into the fray. These were well trained Brothers-Martial and they all handled their weapons expertly but Michael had the sense to stay apart from the fighting and whenever a Brother tried to prime a plasma grenade, he shot him. The Brothers were possessed by a righteous fury at the attack on the Great Abbey and did not yield, screaming their hatreds of the Unworthy and the Harlots of Satan with *'revenge Abbot Amalgan'* as their battle-cry.

Two of Marc's companions were gored by spears as they tried to use their knives. They fell to the ground, clutching at their mortal abdominal wounds in agony, one screaming for a mother six years dead. Eight Brothers remained and two charged at Michael who managed to shoot one but then his gun jammed. Before he could draw the second weapon from its holster, a spear tip penetrated deep into his shoulder. He grasped the shaft with both hands so that the Brother could not withdraw it and was thus left vulnerable as Harold swung his katana with all his strength.

Michael sank to his knees and yanked the spear free. "Ah! I will recover," he hissed. "Leave me! Help the others!"

The surviving Brothers could see that their boat was lost to them so they slowly retreated westward in a tight formation keeping their spears jabbing at their foes so that Saul and Ibrahim could not close on them until Ibrahim was almost incoherent with frustration. Two stepped behind the others to prime plasma grenades but a crossbow bolt and an arrow put paid to their endeavours and their lives. The survivors broke and fled wildly but like sprinters bursting from their blocks, Ibrahim, Saul and Bas were upon them whilst Marc brought down one himself then began stabbing his fallen enemy repeatedly until Harold was forced to drag him off the corpse.

"It's over, Marc," Harold said gently. "Come on, son, you can stop now. They're all dead."

Marc got to his feet and flung the bloodied knife away: "It'll never be over, Light-Father, not until every stinking *sweflennic* one of them is dead and their bones crushed to powder!" He glared at Michael: "Better him than you, eh, *brother?*"

Michael came up to him to stare into his eyes. "You're right, Marc, better me than anyone else," he said quietly. "But that man you killed and the others from Wyehold were the most fanatical of the Order. Abbot Amherus held sway there before Abbot Amalgan was appointed so their loyalty to the Conclave was *absolute* which is why Schimrian distrusts them. Whatever the Light-Father may do or say, there's no way he can break their conviction. We will have to kill many more of them before this is over."

"Then I'll relish every death," Marc grated through clenched teeth. "Now I'd like to say farewell to my companions: they were named Wyne and Rowan - not that *you* would care!"

Michael shook his head as his brother turned from him. "No, you're wrong, Marc. I shall mourn them whether you like it or not." He looked at Harold who was supporting the badly-dazed Fern. "He hath need of thy magic, Light-Father, as do I, I fear."

Harold left Fern's side only after she'd assured him that she was not about to die and handed a shovel to Ibrahim. "Saul, recover that machine-gun for me and get spears for Marc and the other two. Shield and Bas, search the bodies for plasma-grenades and find a bag to carry them in. Ah, here they are!" he grinned as Surl and the other three children ran up to join them.

"Pup would've helped," Pup huffed. "They can't write a saga about Pup if Pup hides in the wood like a frightened rabbit."

Rabbit cuffed him: "I wasn't frightened!"

"Pup meant hoppy rabbits! Hoppy rabbits!" he whimpered.

"Enough!" Harold said wearily. He was about to sheathe his katana when Saul seized his wrist. "What? Ah, hell. I'm sorry, Saul, I almost sheathed it without cleaning it! Damn it," he sighed, wiping the blade on the field robes of a dead Brother. "A month ago I was cleaning centrifuges not bloody *swords*!"

He and Ibrahim set to the grave digging whilst the four younger children eagerly helped Bas and Shield search the bodies, oblivious to the gore and the fact that most of Beorcraft's party had lost their eyes to the crows and ravens. Harold paused in his task to study the macabre scene and rue the fact that these children were so immune to such slaughter and carnage. He smiled ironically: no more so than the African child-soldiers of his world. Determined anew to save them, he resumed his digging with a will.

Despite Marc's protests, they allowed Michael to lead a prayer over the two graves punctuated by everyone except Pup responding with: "*In manus tuas, Domine.*"

As they approached the quay, Harold pointed to the sleek Wyehold vessel which was obviously once a military craft. "Would you kindly scupper that?" he said to Ibrahim who leapt to the task with glee. It took eight mighty blows before the reinforced hull gave way and it sank. They boarded the Ellendaed and to Harold's immense relief, the engines started at the first turn of the ignition key. He edged the boat out to get the feel of the fast ebbing currents of the Milverbore before opening the throttles wide. The Ellendaed surged towards the vast bulk of Milverburg whilst its passengers shaded their eyes from the unaccustomed sun.

Bas was the first to hear them. To the east, through the arches of the viaduct they could see two Angels keeping close to the surface of the Milverbore and approaching at high speed. "Damn!" Harold cursed. "They'll be on us before we make the docks! Fern? Can't you hypnotise the crews like you did yesterday?"

Fern was sat upon the decking, clutching her staff with her head upon her knees and a pool of vomit between her feet. "That begiuller has completely drained my craft," she groaned. "It was too close to me when it fired: I'm as helpless as a babe."

"Does anyone know how to use that machine-gun? What about you, Shield? Do think you can knock them out of the sky like you did in Beorminghas?"

"I'll try, Light-Father, but I was affected by the begiuller as well," she said grimly, holding on tightly to the gunwale as the Ellendaed ploughed through the estuary waves. "I can't aim a bolt at them: the boat is rocking too much."

The Angels roared over their heads and then swung round in a leisurely arc to attack, their chain-guns beginning to spin up. Shield concentrated and began an arcane chant patiently taught to her by Mother Moss but she quailed as from the north came two more Angels moving fast and low towards them. "I can't focus on them all," she despaired. "I can't! Saul! I'm so sorry, dear heart!"

"Damn them! I will *not* let them get us!" Harold bellowed and swung the steering wheel over hard to try and reach one of the gigantic viaduct arches to use the piers as cover but he knew they would not make it. Time itself seemed to slow to a crawl as the two incoming Angels opened fire.

~~~~~

"Brother Simon, have you raised the Great Abbey on the radio yet?" Abbot Amherus demanded, his fingers drumming on an ancient Vatican table in what had once been the Pope's personal chambers. His contempt for the Papacy and the fact they had brought the Seven-Headed Lamb upon the face of the Earth had led him to vent his fury on the antique furnishings and tapestries during the long years of the European Inquisitions. A tenth-century hand-illustrated gold-bound Mass written on rare vellum was transfixed to the table-wood by an ornate Romanic sword.

Simon seated himself slowly. "I apologise for my presumption, Eminence, I was poisoned in the Venetian Enclaves. The nuclear reactors there still spew their toxins."

"They were the powerhouse of the continent at one time and we failed to shut them down in time so you are forgiven, my son, even for coughing up blood during Vespers. Luckily, we are well versed in treating radiation sickness or at least that's what I'm told by the Fathers-Surgeon that God spared from the catastrophe."

"They are well-skilled, Eminence. I have but few years and the vitality of youth so I mend quickly in their care. As you know, the Great-Abbot assigned me to that cruel task personally because of a minor indiscretion on my part. I regret I now owe him no loyalty or trust, Eminence. I tried my best after the Tally-men malfunctioned but it was pointless. The few Unworthy creatures that crawl upon the ground there are diseased or mutated and not worth redeeming so I sailed here with the last of our Adriatic Brothers and Sisters on my own initiative and abandoned the last of our Tally-men. They were easily poisoned by the radiation and too stupid to seek shade during the hottest part of the day and thus they died."

"This is why I know I can count on you, my son. Though you are but a youth you have intelligence and motivation. So, have our Brothers-Technician raised the Great Abbey today?"

"No, Eminence, they have not. I am told that the losses in Britannia were significant with but three dozen Sisters left alive at the Great Abbey. Brother Theo knows me well and told me last night that the Scotian and Eirann abbeys and outposts were also lost due to the Wiccans seizing control of our Tally-men."

"So I understand, my son," Amherus said, steepling his heavily bejewelled fingers. "Now here are my doubts about the corruption of the Great Computer: something rings the bells of falsehood. I have known well the covens of old in the Russias and Iberia: they were craft-wise but completely unskilled in computers."

Simon consulted a note from his pocket before responding: "I have but few years and little experience, Eminence, but I must agree. According to Theo, Abbot Pious was in charge after the attack and according to the radio operators, Brother Theo also let slip that Pious was brought back from the dead and that they are all absolutely terrified of him and his Inquisitors."

"I see, my son, but he cannot be a reanimated corpse though the craft of Wiccans is both dark and deep. No, we are blessed by the foresight of the Order so no doubt our genes pulled him back from the Gates of Death but, I regret to say, some of us may wish otherwise. He and his Brothers-Inquisitor were here in Italy some weeks ago and they shamed me with the number of Unworthy creatures they winkled out from the cellars and catacombs beneath my feet; fey scraps of flesh that we'd overlooked in all our years of scouring Europe. No doubt Schimrian revelled in our shame. How dare he belittle me so! I was once his staunchest ally in the Conclave and deliberated with him upon the creature bred within the so-called Holy City! We of the Conclave were the trumps of God: we brought forth Revelation upon a world of sinners."

"Hallelujah, Eminence," Simon said carefully. He had quickly seen that Amherus was vain, capricious *and* a fanatic: one of the men who had calmly signed the death warrant of humanity. "I was told that Abbot Pious assaulted and seriously injured three Fathers here for their failures without discussing it with you."

Amherus's handsome face darkened and he clenched his fists: "I will never forgive that insolence though he is of my rank. He ruled the Great Abbey briefly in the Great-Abbot's name until Schimrian recovered his wits and is said to be still as loyal as a dog to that fool. I fear him: when he was here, unholy motivations were plainly at work in him as he gloried in butchery and torture. Tchah! Had I been Great-Abbot, no Unworthy scum would've come within ten leagues of our spiritual heart! It's no wonder that they continue to forbid the Conclave from returning to Britannia to hold them to account. This is madness of course when they have but four hundred souls left in the whole of that blessed realm!"

"How are you sure of the numbers, Eminence? I am told the Great Abbey was tight-lipped about what happened there."

"Father Silas reckons that is an accurate estimate based on our losses as the corrupted Tally-men were most thorough without much variance across the entire planet."

"Some of the Brothers claim it is hotter here than Hades, Eminence. If they sortie out at midday, they invariably get heatstroke and some are beginning to die despite our genes. They crave the cool, perpetual rains of the northern climes."

Amherus beckoned to a Father who was waiting by the door for an audience. "Come and sit with us, Father Silas," he beamed at the newcomer, indicating one of the ornate and gilded chairs set before his desk. "I need to rally the Conclave across the globe. What news have you obtained for me in this regard, my son?"

The short, stocky Father kissed the ring of office on the Abbot's finger and sat down to mop at the copious perspiration on his face.

"I apologise for my appearance, Eminence, but bless these marble halls: it is so cool in here! The temperature and humidity climbs once again, Eminence. The surviving Tally-men are failing because of the heat and the damage done to their barrack computers across the globe. Without direction, they stand in the sun until they die and we dare not trust the ones we have left. The weather and communications satellites we access are starting to fall out of the sky but it's the Equator that's become my main concern."

"What do you mean, my son? You tell me of the equatorial storms making landfall from time to time in Africa and the East and how they inconvenience us by destroying port facilities but we still manage to get our vessels through even now, do we not?"

Silas opened a folder and laid out satellite images across the desk showing the entire equatorial band of the planet. There were six vast hurricanes girdling the entire equator all equidistant from each other and all interconnected with their eyes at least fifty miles across. Silas pointed at them in turn and swept his hand across the images. "The sea temperatures are so high that these storms now appear to be permanent, drawing in heat and moisture from the seas to the north and south. I've never seen anything like it but this bizarre equilibrium is due to the atmosphere trying to distribute the global energy surplus. The equatorial desert temperatures are above the boiling point of water and the equatorial seas are aflame from the methane rising from the depths. I have no idea how long this will last but the temperate rain bands have moved further north and are becoming unstable with huge thunderstorms and vortices constantly forming on their southern edges."

Amherus rubbed at the bridge of his nose: "So what are you saying, my son? Our ships and aircraft can no longer cross the Equator? What of our brethren in the South, in Australasia, Southern Africa, the Incandean States, the Antarctic coasts?"

"They cannot reach us, Eminence, and we cannot reach them as long as these storms last. We could see the climate either stabilise once the heat has dissipated or it could become ever more chaotic and dangerous. Already, Italy and Iberia burn under this accursed sun and now southern Frankia and the Urals. We…"

"Enough," Amherus said wearily, raising a hand for silence. "It's clear they are lost to us for now. We must tell all our surviving brethren in the north to cease these endless and fruitless Inquisitions and gather at the Bocage Abbey. The Great-Abbot has need of our Inquisition having suffered the Great Abbey to be decimated by the Unworthy and their Wiccans."

"The brethren in Italy are with you, Eminence."

"Thank you my son. Our new crusade shall be the cleansing of Britannia and restoring the rule of our Order upon those hallowed isles. We cannot build a new Jerusalem while we are chasing half-beasts and the handful of Unworthy left upon this miserable Earth." He clenched his fist and a fire burned in his eyes: "Given the scale of this disaster, the Conclave intends to Inquire not only of the Great-Abbot himself but all those who failed him as well."

"Such as Abbot Pious?" Silas ventured hopefully.

"*Especially* Abbot Pious."

~~~~~

Tower of the Sun

Harold despaired as four lines of erupting fountains from heavy calibre rounds plunging into the Milverbore advanced towards them then passed the Ellendaed spraying them all with seawater. Rounds then impacted the two original Angels and tore through the cockpits blasting out expanding haloes of windscreen shards and worse. Gouting fire and smoke, the stricken rotorcraft tumbled down into the estuary. One rotor-blade sheared off on impact and everyone on the Ellendaed involuntarily ducked as it whirled over their heads making a fearsome thrumming sound.

He let out an expletive as he narrowly avoided ramming the Ellendaed into the base of a viaduct pier. One of the rescue Angels rose up a hundred yards to act as sentry whilst the other hovered a few feet above the estuary waters. A man dressed in a green quilted hunting-jacket and corduroy trousers with goggles hung around his neck, stepped out onto one of the huge chain-guns bolted onto the landing skids and held onto the rim of the cockpit doorway. He had a loudhailer and waited for Harold to bring the Ellendaed as close as he dared. Despite the engine noise there was no mistaking the broad Scotian accent of their saviour.

"Well met, Surl of Crawcester!" he called down and she literally bounced up and down in the boat with relief and joy, waving at him with both hands above her head. "I told you we'd meet again! We're glad to return the favour and it looks as though you've freed another three prisoners. Well done, little Scatterling!"

Harold cupped his hands to yell a reply but it was pointless as his voice was whipped away by the rotor downdraft.

"I can't hear you!" Ken Glascae continued. "I presume you're this Light-Father we've heard about. We have some new recruits for you and you now have an air force! I'm told there's a large public park on Uppermost near the Tower of the Sun so we'll land there and wait for you. We owe your four younglings there our lives so we want to repay that debt."

Surl was ecstatic as he looked so much healthier than when they'd freed him but she'd foreseen a different reunion and that worried her on so many levels. Fern raised her head: "Prescience is never accurate," she advised blearily. "You'll learn to accept that and make allowances for it." She vomited a little again. "By Gaia's paps, Harold! Get me to solid ground now, *please*!"

He nodded and gestured for Ken to follow them. He gunned the engines making the Ellendaed surge forward through the gentle swell causing Fern to retch noisily. Ken saluted them and climbed back into the cockpit then both Angels rose swiftly and headed towards Uppermost. Harold looked around the deck at the varied expressions of surprise and relief on everyone's faces and realised that he was the only one trembling like a leaf from yet another near-death experience. "Well, I did not see that one coming," he admitted then he saw Surl looking downcast and worried.

"Neither did I," she said. "I'm sorry, Light-Father!"

"Don't worry, Surl," he reassured her. "You'll grow into that power of yours, I'm sure of it, but for now could you help Mother Fern? You and Shield need to get her away from all that puke. People's faces are not meant to be that shade of green!"

"But you're as white as a sheet," Shield pointed out.

"Having bullets and rotor-blades miss us by inches has that effect on people," he replied grumpily. As the girls dragged Fern to the gunwale, he noticed that the other Scatterlings were chattering excitedly with Marc and the other two escapees but Michael sat cross-legged at the stern with his hands clasped together in prayer. He wondered what was going through the mutilated cleric's mind and noted that the spear wound had already stopped bleeding but his movements were restricted.

He recalled the image Fern had relayed into his mind. The Naked One: Azrael had somehow made Michael's skin completely transparent so that all the muscles, capillaries and veins could be clearly seen in all their raw red glory. This was no doubt done to add to his torment at Azrael's feet; every reflection exquisitely enhancing the psychological torture…

Surl tugged at his sleeve, derailing his thoughts. "Mother Fern says we *can* trust him," she reported. "I had a vision last week that showed me he has a hard road ahead - he'll be tempted to betray us but I don't think he will. I couldn't see much more as there are too many twists and turns ahead for every one of us."

"I understand," Harold said, throttling down as they passed through the gateway and coast into the dock area. They moored the Ellendaed but, as the tide was low, they had to use the dockside ladders with Harold assisting Michael up the rungs. His hand came into contact with Michael's forearm flesh as he heaved him up. The skin felt normal to the touch but as soon as he saw the muscles and blood vessels pulsing, a powerful gag reflex almost made him spew. "Jesus! No wonder she fainted," he gasped.

Michael shrugged as he sat upon the flagstones. "Imagine how I felt when Father Aten first brought me a mirror. The cruel bastard actually found this *funny*! He and the rest of Pious's Inquisitors survived because they held back from the fighting. I was told brave Father Aten actually hid under a pew in the Great Cathedral."

"Typical thugs," Harold grunted sourly. "They're not used to their prey fighting back."

Michael pointed to Fern who was still prostrate on the boat with Surl, Saul and Shield tending to her. "Your place is clearly at her side," he advised. "She should recover quickly now the other Wiccans are here. Ah, the Ferals are here as well. I'm glad they survived the Great Abbey. Wait... *What?*"

Harold had to stand in front of Michael to block ten Ferals who had scooted around Ivy and Nightshade, clearly intending to attack Michael dressed as he was in the robes of the Order. "No, you will not!" he roared, holding his arms out wide as they bared their teeth. Such was the force of his voice that they halted in their tracks and stared at him in puzzlement. "He's with us! He's *disfigured*."

The boldest of the Ferals, Godwin, came up to Harold and put a hand on his chest. He looked up quizzically. "Arrrrrhh wee naht disssfighered tooo?" he asked. "Heee Orhhduhr. They khill ahr famleees. They whaarrp usss. They khill efreethiiing!"

Kai strode forward to stand over Michael, hands on hips. "Have you truly repented?" he demanded. "Why do you skulk beneath that cowl? Why did they turn on you and call you the Naked One?"

"Godwin and Kai need to see what Azrael did to you, Michael," Harold insisted. "Otherwise they won't believe you."

Michael struggled to his feet. "Very well, Light-Father, but first," he said, turning to Ivy and Nightshade. "Your fellow Wiccan in the boat needs you. You've probably far-seen this but she caught a begiuller blast at point blank range in Wealthorpe. It was far worse that the begiullers she endured at the Great Annex."

Ivy brushed past him and began to descend the rungs to the boat. "I'm not surprised she's ill," she said angrily. "It's like having every nerve in your body set on fire. That weapon was designed to torture Wiccans as we hear such a wide spectrum of sound as part of our craft. As we suffer from your infernal devices it's only fitting that you show Kai the true price of serving the Order!"

"There's something else you all need to know as well," Nightshade announced. "I received an insight while I was asleep. I was shown what's *really* behind this nightmare and I was given a warning that Azrael could rise again."

"Rise again? What do you mean by that?" Harold demanded. "Are you a seer as well?"

"No, Light-Father, but my astral form met a goddess," she said excitedly. "She told me that Azrael is part of a fathomless ancient evil that's near impossible to kill so it won't end with the Great Computer or its manifestation in the Great Annex…"

"Then he might be the cause of this new evil coming from the North, Mother Nightshade," Bas chipped in. "The animals were terrified of a new scent carried on a northerly breeze."

"I'm aware of it," Nightshade nodded. "I scanned Ursaf's mind as the rotorcraft flew into Uppermost. "Light-Father?"

"Yes?" Harold said, watching Ivy tend to Fern in the boat. "So how will Azrael rise again?" he asked, completely distracted by his concern for his lover.

"I see I'll have to discuss my vision with you later," Nightshade said pointedly. "Ursaf and his Brothers were attacked by human-animal hybrids that have escaped from Erdethric. That's what Bas detected: creatures like her! There may be hundreds of them to the north and they have packs of wolves running with them as well. Bas and Ibrahim's father had something to with breeding these chimerae and I fear they can *procreate*."

"This is getting to be a sick joke," he groaned. "There won't be anything left alive in this bloody world at this rate."

"That's Azrael's true purpose, Light-Father."

"So they're hybrids like us?" Bas demanded angrily. "These wolf-children from Erdethric?"

"They're nothing like you, Bas. Whether this dark will is guiding them or not, they're killing *everything* they come across."

"Well, there's a bonus if they're attacking the Order as well," Harold noted ironically. He turned to Michael who had Godwin and Kai standing impatiently before him. "For God's sake hurry up, Michael, before they throw you into the dock."

"As you wish, Light-Father," Michael conceded reluctantly. He pulled back his cowl and slowly peeled away his bandages.

Godwin gaped and sat back on his haunches in shock while Kai's reaction was unexpected: he pushed Michael hard in the chest

235

sending him backwards to land heavily on his behind. "No!" he screamed. "You aren't Michael! He's twice your size!"

Michael started rewrapping the bandages around his face. "I *was* twice my size, Brother Kai, but Azrael ripped the fat from my bones in his resurrection machine *without* anaesthetics and made my skin transparent because it amused him."

"I'm no Brother," Kai fumed, glowering down at Michael.

"Then why do you wear the field robes of the Order, my son?"

"He has a point," Harold observed dryly.

"I've told you, Light-Father: it's to remind me of my sins!"

"No. It has to stop, Kai. You need to move on."

Kai's shoulders sagged. "If you insist, Light-Father."

"I do. It serves no purpose. Dress in camel-hair shirts or sacking if you wish to scourge yourself but those robes offend everybody. I want you to become one of the Scatterlings not a distraction."

Michael drew the cowl about his head again and stared down at the flagstones but Godwin closed his jaws and crawled forward to press his forehead gently against Michael's. "Jussteess. Jussteees," he growled softly, almost purring. "Ahr whull fahrgeeve youuu, Mmmarkhell.. Justesss ees sseee..." he ended on a low gurgling sentence that nobody but Kai could decipher:

"He said justice has been served," Kai translated. "He forgives you for being of the Order, for killing his family and turning him into a half-beast. He takes no pleasure from it but he does take comfort from seeing a punishment befitting the crime."

"Indeed it does, young Kai," Michael laughed wryly. "Ach! The wound reopened. Damnation! I'm bleeding again!"

"He fought with us, Kai," Ibrahim interjected, joining Marc to help Michael back upon his feet. "He shot several Brothers and took a spear in the shoulder. Bas and I don't look like you so we don't care what he looks like to us because we trust him and you should too. You say you're still a Christian so where's all your Christian sympathy and forgiveness?"

Kai reddened and looked away. "He did try to look out for me and protect me from the House-Fathers," he relented. "But we were both enraptured when the Plague was released. It's only since the battle at the Great Abbey that my mind's been truly clear."

Peter joined them. "The Abbess reckoned that an evil will was affecting your minds to varying degrees before it took physical form in the Great Annex." He paused on seeing two new faces peering from behind Nightshade. "Light-Father! Look! I think Nightshade has two new Scatterlings with her!"

Bas immediately scampered forwards to sniff at them but they recoiled at her sharp teeth as she grinned. "The stone ghosts!" she gloated. "I know their scent! You've finally enticed them out into the open, Mother Nightshade! What are their names?"

Nightshade placed her hands on the girls' arms and drew them and their bows and quivers of arrows into plain view. "This is Pomona Regina and this is Kayleigh Burr. They're from the Regina and Burr merchant clans who owned the Beomodor and many buildings on nearly every level of Milverburg."

The two girls ignored Bas, much to her chagrin, and stood before Harold, bobbing a courtesy at him. "You can call her Yang-chan," Pomona simpered, grasping Kayleigh's hand tightly.

"And you can call her Yin-chan," Kayleigh declared lovingly. "You're our Light-Father now."

With that, they both launched themselves forwards into his arms almost knocking him off his feet. They hugged him and kissed him on the cheeks repeatedly making Bas emit a little involuntary hiss of jealousy. Her ears and tail drooped as Nightshade wagged a finger at her: "Jealousy has no place here, dear heart."

"So you're our mysterious stone ghosts, eh?" Harold smiled, guessing that this was the first physical contact they'd had in six years apart from each other. "Welcome to the Scatterlings, Pomona and Kayleigh of the merchant clans." He looked over at Nightshade who'd coughed discretely to get his attention.

"It's unlikely that they'll ever take a mate," she advised him, having read his thoughts. "But that's not all: they bear the mark of the craft upon their palms."

"They're Daughters?" he exclaimed. "What're the odds?"

Nightshade shrugged. "Pretty good given that they've survived alone in this place for six years. No normal human child could've done that so they either had to be Children of Exodus or possessed of the craft. They're very proficient with the bow and almost succeeded in sticking two arrows into Ivy and even our brave warriors, Fria and Amos, were no match for them."

"The little vixens nicked my ear," Fria growled, grasping a knife hilt. Nightshade frowned and concentrated. "Ow! Not fair! A geis!" Fria squealed, dropping the knife and rubbing the palm of her hand vigorously. "You made it red hot!"

"You imagined the heat but be at peace, child, we've no time for silly vendettas!" Nightshade admonished. "You and Bas must not be jealous of them as they had to watch their entire clans die before spending six years with corpses and rodents for company. Light-Father, you need to help Fern up the rungs then you must go: you have to work out how we're going to defend this place!"

"I know. I should've given it more thought before now."

"You were too busy brooding, *Harold*," Fern said waspishly, ignoring his outstretched hand as she hauled herself slowly up the rungs with Ivy's assistance. She crawled up onto the Wharf to lie on her side in a foetal position. "Now I'd like you to go away," she groaned, clutching at her stomach. "Just leave me be!"

"Huh? What did I do?"

Nightshade laid a hand upon his shoulder in sympathy. "You must understand what's happened to her, Light-Father. She loves you but she knows that if you touch her in this condition, she'll lash out with her craft and probably blow you and this entire dock apart. Go to Uppermost! We'll take care of her."

"Very well," he agreed doubtfully. "Just make sure she's okay. Can you get the Ferals to watch the docks and the viaducts?"

"Of course," Nightshade assured him. "We can far-talk with you to keep up to speed or if we see any movement on the banks or in the air. Ivy and I can counter any sorties along the viaducts so make haste," she urged, shoving him gently in the back.

"We have some ideas, Light-Father," Pomona volunteered.

"Yin-chan and I know every inch of this place," Kayleigh chipped in brightly. "They can only attack each level from the Four Circumference Stairs so you can booby-trap them as you retreat. We know all the air ducts, chimneys and vents so you can ambush them anywhere on every level at any time!"

"We know where all the apothecaries and gardening stores are as well," Pomona added. "We can show you."

"Huh?" Harold exclaimed, looking at her with a puzzled frown then the penny dropped: "Oh, of course! Nitrates and chromates; charcoal powder and sulphur! We can make more pipe-bombs – damn, we should've been making them weeks ago!"

"Have some faith in us, Light-Father," Nightshade said in a peeved tone. "We've made thirty or so, and we can easily make others if these two really do know where to look for the ingredients. They need to go with you for now but Surl must stay with me as her visions have almost destroyed her health. She'd be tempted to scry for you and could suffer permanent harm. She must rest."

"Anyway, Pup is hungry," Pup said, looking meaningfully at a basket full of cod. "Can we stay and eat, Light-Father?"

"Pup is always hungry," Harold laughed. "Fine, you stay with Surl, Peter and Rabbit and see if the Mothers can grill you some. Everyone else, come with me. We've a long climb ahead of us as we can't use the lifts to go up without power."

"I can sort that out," Michael offered, gazing around the dimly-lit dock. "Those generators over there are known to me. I am sure I can rewire them or any others on the docks level to power at least one set of lift motors and maybe the dock gates too."

"That's good to know. I've started servicing them but we'll all have to climb for now," Harold said in martyred tones as they all headed in to the Central Core to find the passage leading to the Northern Circumference Stairs.

"I can carry you," Ibrahim suggested with a mischievous grin. "If you're not up to it, that is."

"Show your elders some respect!" Harold grumbled. "I can make it under my own steam, thank you."

"Of course we respect you, Light-Father!" Bas smiled sweetly. "When you aren't puffing on those foul cigars of yours or trying to rip my ears off!"

"They are indeed curious ears," Marc observed, walking in step beside her. "What's that word that Japanese Empire trader used to describe cat-girls? That was it: *neko*."

"The Japanese word for cat," Harold explained as Bas frowned at Marc who stepped back a pace, raising his hands defensively.

"Don't take offence. I've never met a chimera until I met you and Ibrahim today. I really do think you look amazing," he grinned. "I know your tail is real too. It's so *kawai-ee*."

"What *is* he babbling about, Light-Father?" Bas demanded.

Harold rolled his eyes. "In my world, Japanese boys had a fetish for cat-girls so I guess it was the same here. Kawai-ee is Japanese for cute as in a cute child or a kitten."

"I'm no kitten!" Bas hissed and executed a breath-taking leap over Marc's head to land behind him with her arm around his neck and her knife-point pricking his throat before her discarded bow and quiver had landed upon the ground. "Don't you *dare* patronise me again or I'll gut you like one of those fish!"

"Hoi! I'm sorry! I'm sorry!" Marc apologised hastily. "I just find you a very attractive young *human* girl despite the cat attributes. I was only being chivalrous."

Ibrahim slowly prised Bas away from Marc. "You weren't being chivalrous, idiot! As children we were paraded naked by our father, Professor Farzad, at scientific conferences as an example of how to splice genes," he explained with exaggerated patience. "I had ape genes spliced into me but it was worse for Bas because they would pet her and make her lap milk from a saucer. Calling her cute or a kitten just brings those unbearable memories back so if you disrespect her again, *lecher*, I'll rip your head off."

Harold stepped between them. "That's enough, both of you. Save it for the Order," he said curtly, pushing them apart. "Bas is just a child for all her maturity, Marc, so I'd appreciate it if you respected that otherwise I'll throw what's left of you into the Milverbore." He turned to the other two escapees and half-drew his katana. "The same goes for you two. If you disrespect any of my Scatterlings, you'll answer to me. Understood?"

All three men bowed deeply, thoroughly chastened. "Yes, Light-Father," they said in unison. "Forgive me, Bas," Marc added, displaying his left hand which was missing its fingernails. "I was trying to forget this by being insensitive. I apologise."

Mollified, Bas nodded at him and sheathed her knife. "I accept your apology but think before you speak in future."

"Good. I'm glad we've cleared that up," Harold beamed, slamming the sword back into its *saya* making Saul cringe at the abuse of such a skilfully-crafted weapon. "Let's get to Uppermost before someone else says something stupid they'll regret."

The climb progressed in near silence and near darkness but for the window slits allowing a little northern light to filter through the fifty-yard thick outer wall. Harold had to fall back as Michael was struggling and called for Ibrahim to assist him.

Ibrahim demonstrated that his genetically-enhanced strength was no idle boast as he unslung his axes, giving them to Harold to carry, and hoisted Michael into a piggy-back position to ascend the last two flights with little apparent effort.

They found the two Angels in the park near the Tower of the Sun and to their surprise they saw a portly Father and three Brothers sat upon the rough overgrown grass with their hands upon their heads and five heavily-armed men armed standing guard over them.

Harold recognised the man who'd used the loudhailer and correctly assumed him to be the leader of the group.

"I take it you're Ken Glascae?"

Ken grasped his hand and shook it fiercely: "Aye, I am. It's good to meet you, Light-Father. I've heard so much about you from these four *scaernae* and what you did at the Great Abbey. They actually think you're some kind of demigod! They're from Bede but we saved them from a pack of wolves and those weird hybrids thinking they were refugees like us..."

"They're chimerae created by Professor Farzad at Erdethric," Ursaf interrupted. He would have had a gun butt slammed into his face but Saul had quickly intercepted the blow and pushed the man aside. "Thank you, my son. We want to warn you..."

"We already know about these creatures," Harold replied. "Farzad spliced wolf genes and God knows what else into those children just as he did with his own. The man was a *monster*."

Ursaf's jaw dropped as he beheld Bas and Ibrahim. "Ah, I've seen these two before! They're his most accomplished creations!"

"We have souls and *names*," Bas hissed at him and again Ibrahim had to restrain her. "We're not experiments any more, you stinking pile of *kack*!"

"I apologise, child," Ursaf said, bowing as best he could in a sitting position. "I can see that but those things that attacked us were your father's handiwork and they showed very little of your awareness or humanity. They broke free of their cages and killed everyone on Erdethric some years ago. The Order hoped that the seas would contain them but, as ever, they were wrong."

Harold sat down to face the cleric after asking their names and those of Ken's companions. "I want to know what you plan to do now," he said urgently. "Are you free of this power that affected your minds or will you simply attack us again if I set you free? Should I let Ken and his men kill you right now?"

"They're cowards, Light-Father," Ken observed. "They opened fire on their own brethren simply because we pointed a gun at their heads and threatened to shoot them."

Ursaf glowered up at him. "You deliberately misunderstand us, Glascae," he said angrily. "We retain our faith but we are *not* of the Order now. May we be permitted to stand, Light-Father?"

Harold nodded and all four men got to their feet and within moments, they were standing naked but for their somewhat grubby

241

underwear feeling the hot sunlight prick the pale skin of their backs, having cast their field robes away. Ursaf placed a hand upon his flabby chest: "We pledge ourselves to you, Light-Father. Be mindful: we are not Brothers-Martial but Brothers-Technician yet we will fly the Angels for you. We won't return to an Order run by Schimrian and his fell servant, Pious, who would gut us alive for our failure at Wealthorpe. All four of us want to bring this madness to an end. We can persuade others at Bede to join us…"

"We've had years of this *darkness* whispering inside our minds and now we have a million dead screaming for our souls every night, Light-Father!" Piamadet pleaded. "We beg you to work your magic upon us! We'll fly the Angels and defend this Queen of Babylons for you as best we can. You have our word."

"So you see the dead every night now that the thrall has been lifted?" Michael interjected before Harold could reply.

"I know that voice! Well met again, Abbot Michael!" Ursaf enthused. "Is what they say about the Great Abbey true?"

"Yes," Michael nodded. "There was a demon within the Great Computer and it took shape as an angel called Azrael: beautiful but deadly to look at. He slew Schimrian whom he placed in the machine I was in and it brought him back to life. I can confirm that this demon also commanded the Tally-men to slaughter everyone for his pleasure. I too would cast aside my field robes as you have but you would retch and vomit as Camus did and flee screaming. However, I intend to serve the Light-Father in the battles to come and save as many of his Scatterlings as I can."

"Bless you, Eminence," Ursaf said formally.

Michael forestalled him with a raised palm. "I am Michael Onderhelm *not* Abbot Michael. As with young Kai here, I reject the Order and all its works and declare it to be my enemy."

Ursaf bowed reverently. "Then I am no longer a Father of the Order and will henceforth be just Ursaf Unwin of Accyngate and the answer to your question is yes: all of us at Bede see the dead at night only more so during these last three weeks now this demon's seductive *fog* no longer dulls our senses."

"Camus and I have seen them for six years," Michael said thoughtfully. "Probably Azrael did not apply the geis to us as strongly as he did to you and the rest of the Order."

"We can discuss this later, gentlemen," Harold urged. "We have work to do! Ken, can your men please stop pointing their guns at

Ursaf and his Brothers? They're hardly likely to attack us in their underpants, now are they? We'll go into the tower and find you all some clothes then we'll go up to the Northern Library and decide what to do about defending this place. There's water and some food up there if you're hungry."

"What about you, Kai?" Saul asked pointedly. "Are you going to follow their example as the Light-Father requested?"

"You have your path and I have *mine*, Eldest," Kai seethed through grated teeth. "I'm less than a beast in the eyes of God." He pulled at his field robes. "These remind me of how I led countless children to their *deaths*. I do not deserve fine garments until I find forgiveness and absolution for my sins. If you'll excuse me, I will rejoin Mother Ivy and my Ferals."

Michael stepped forward to stop him leaving but Harold raised a hand. "Let him go, I'll talk to him later."

"I should take that responsibility, Light-Father. I did mentor him as a postulant and novice after all."

Ken shielded his eyes from the glare of the Tower of the Sun. "What a waste of gold," he murmured in disbelief. "Sometimes I think the world deserved to die when so much obscene wealth was in the hands of so few. Tell me, Light-Father, what are those strange white towers in the centre of each quadrant?"

"The Towers of the Moon," Harold replied. "They used to house the four global banking clans until they moved their operations to Beorminghas to build even bigger towers."

"Bankers!" Ken scoffed disdainfully as they crossed the Tower drawbridge. "Trust me, we never had any of this revolting Sasana opulence in Scotia when I was a child!"

Harold smiled, taking a deep liking to the young Scotian: "We have the same injustices and disparities where I come from." He paused at the doorway to gaze at Uppermost shimmering and steaming in the rare hot sunlight. "How can I defend all this?" he wondered aloud, waving a hand at the hundreds of luxurious mansions and imposing civic buildings. "We can't flee anywhere so we *have* to stay and fight."

"I'm sure you'll find a way, Light-Father," Shield assured him, placing a hand on his arm. "We have faith in you."

"That's good. I just wish I had some faith in myself."

~~~~~

243

Council of War

"Fall now, sweet irony; like rain upon a desert dune;
a brief oasis then a cruel mirage for thirsting souls." – Thomas Tythe

Camus rapped on the door to Schimrian's chambers. "It's Ten Bells Eminence!" he called out nervously. "Can you not hear the Great Bell tolling the hour? We have news! Fathers Theo and Edward are with me! We have grave news, Eminence!"

The door opened and they beheld the Great-Abbot, unshaven and still in his night-clothes. "Ah, my sons; forgive my slothful appearance," he yawned. "Cancelling Matins meant I slept the deep sleep of the truly righteous. I hope the three of you are similarly refreshed?" He looked at Camus with a raised eyebrow. "Hmmm, perhaps not so in your case, my son; I take it the vengeful shades of unwarranted guilt still terrorise you in the night?"

Camus rubbed at his red-rimmed eyes. "Aye, Eminence. It's been worse since the attack but I managed a few hours after a bottle of rum I'd prudently set aside. It dulled the wraiths for a while." He bared his right forearm and displayed four deep scratches. "But they appear to be gaining some form of corporeal presence."

"Unlikely, my son," Schimrian assured him, placing a hand upon his shoulder. "You claim to be a man of science: these marks are more likely to be self-inflicted in the throes of a troubled sleep, wouldn't you agree? The subconscious is our own worst enemy in times of great stress. I'm aware of how overburdened you are, my son, but the Order is *eternally* grateful to you."

Deep within the recesses of his fracturing mind, Camus thought that the Great-Abbot was far more dangerous when smiles like this crawled across his normally humourless face. Controlling the shrieking fear in his soul and a debilitating urge to flee, he bowed his head and murmured: "You do me great honour, Eminence."

Theo, by contrast, was desperately eager to ingratiate himself with the Great-Abbot and genuflected: "Thank you for your blessed concern, Eminence! Like you, Brother Edward and I also slept the sleep of the righteous at our desks so we could be up at cock-crow, restoring the electrics to the Manse. If you throw the light switches, all your chamber lamps should now come on."

Schimrian did so but there was a bang and a shower of sparks as one of the lamps above his bed exploded making Edward and Theo quake inwardly at the withering look of contempt directed at them. Luckily the rest of the lamps and lights dealt with the power surge and the shadows in the chambers were finally dispelled.

There was a pause, pregnant with retribution, reducing the two newly-appointed Fathers to a quivering shambles. "Wait here while I shave and get dressed," Schimrian ordered curtly. It was a full ten minutes before he admitted them into his chambers and he appeared to be in a much better mood. "Behold, my sons! You've freed my beloved ceiling angels from the Light-Father's chains of shadow," he beamed, raising his hands heavenwards.

Theo and Edward grinned to each other in relief at the reprieve then they made the mistake of looking upwards: both immediately thought that the carved faces of the angels had somehow subtly altered during the night so that they appeared to be leering down at them in unholy appetite and expectation.

They could not avert their eyes from the corrupted angels until Schimrian sharply bid them to sit in the chairs before his desk so that he could gaze benevolently upon them. They noted that there were nine chairs set in a neat line before the imposing desk. Schimrian pre-empted their questions about the seating: "We have Abbot Pious, Father Aten, Father Dreorman and their three Brothers-Inquisitor joining us for a conference soon. I suggest your 'grave news' can wait until they arrive."

There was a faint wailing cry of pain and despair from beneath their feet that made the blood of all three run cold for they knew who was being tortured. Schimrian sighed deeply and steepled his fingers, looking imperiously at Theo whose robes were already damp with copious nervous perspiration. "Well? Are the internal communications restored, my son?"

"Aye, they are, Eminence," Theo responded quickly. "The Redemption Cells beneath you can be reached by entering…"

"I am *not* some postulant!" Schimrian snapped, entering the code into the intercom unit on his desk. He leant close to the microphone: "Pious, cease your Inquisition and bring yourself and your Inquisitors to my chambers *immediately*."

He punched in another intercom code. "Abbess? I would welcome food for ten brethren in my chambers and some tea if there is any left. What's that? I appreciate that you have but three dozen sisters and the postulants to help you but, thanks to this Light-Father and his Harlots of Satan, there are a great many less mouths to feed. Fifteen minutes? Ah, it will have to do. Thank you, my daughter." He disconnected the intercom with a flourish then relaxed on hearing a respectful knock at the door. "Come in, my sons," he called out. "I have no need to lock my door."

Pious was the first into the chambers and bent over the desk to kiss the ring of office upon Schimrian's right index finger. "Given the infiltration and the betrayal of Brother Ignatius, Eminence," he wheezed, seating himself next to Camus. "I think such confidence may be premature. Because of the sparseness of our brethren, we cannot guarantee that we can prevent further infiltration by the Unworthy. You are our guiding light, Eminence: we cannot risk losing you at this most critical of times."

"Well said, old friend," Schimrian nodded in approval. "As ever, I bless your divine resurrection in our times of need."

Pious placed his black-veined hand upon his cold dead heart and bowed his head: "Bless you for your confidence in me, Eminence. Permit me to formally introduce my colleagues of old: Father Aten and Father Dreorman, you already know." He paused as the two Fathers bent to kiss the ring of office and sat down. "This is Brother Feris," he began, as the hulking, bearded torture specialist kissed the ring. "He was demonstrating some interesting Inquisition techniques just now upon our traitor."

"So I heard. I still wish to Inquire of him *personally.* I would be grateful if he is left relatively intact to appreciate my displeasure regarding his slothful and decadent treachery."

"He's pathetic, Eminence," Feris grunted sourly as he sat down. "You only have to breathe on that traitorous rat and he swoons like a maiden. I'm surprised that my cousin, Father Bucheort, failed to sniff out his foul deceits before now."

"Ah, I thought I recognised a family likeness in you!" Schimrian exclaimed delightedly. "Then you'll know that my ever-faithful Bucheort was as dear to me as if he were my own son. I mourn his loss every day as no doubt you do yourself."

"Thank you, Eminence. I will make the Harlots of Satan pay thrice over for his unseemly and blasphemous demise."

"This is Brother Cwellor from the Mentougou Abbey," Pious continued. "He is our best projectiles specialist. His mother was of Beorminghas but his father was a member of the Royal Conclave of Architects chapter in that province. He has shown me much fervour and loyalty these last six years."

The half-Chinese Brother bowed deeply before kissing the ring. "Abbot Pious does credit me overmuch yet for all my flaws, I serve the Order and *you*, Eminence. We cannot risk internal conflict now that we are but One Tribe in number."

Camus noted Cwellor's ice blue eyes and shock of striking blond hair contrasting his dark Asian features. Like Father Dreorman, he was reputed to be an excellent shot and as utterly ruthless as Pious. He reckoned it was a miracle they ever brought back any Tally-men recruits to the Redemption Cells at all.

"Last but not least, Eminence: Brother Brodiglede, our ordnance specialist," Pious said as proudly as his bellows-wheeze of a voice would allow. "Don't let his slight frame deceive you: he's the most accomplished Brother-Martial in the Northern hemisphere."

The elegant, almost foppish Brother kissed the ring. "I'm sorry we have not been introduced before, Eminence, but we've been out hunting down the Unworthy these last three weeks. We cannot bear to be idle knowing that scum still stalk these Hallowed Isles."

Camus restrained his tongue: not only had these brutal men failed to fully engage the invaders, except when they managed to corner a few Ferals, they had refused to assist in the repairs and rebuilding although Father Aten had located the generators now powering the lights. They had taken half-tracks out on Inquisitions but when they were despatched to help hunt down Michael and the escapees, they had refused the authority of Father Beorcraft and swung northwards into the Middle Cities - apparently at the behest of Pious. Consequently, the postulants, novices and many survivors at the Great Abbey detested them but they all avoided them as best they could for they were known to be utterly merciless towards anyone who showed them even the slightest disrespect.

They were heavily armed with rifles, machine guns, handguns and swords which clinked and rattled as they sat bolt-upright in their chairs whilst giving the Great-Abbot their utmost respect and attention. "Thank you for your courtesies, my sons. Alas, your brethren here were not as respectful upon entering my chambers," Schimrian began sarcastically, displaying the ring with the seal of the Order. Theo and Edward paled visibly as they'd forgotten to do this and squirmed with fear and embarrassment as the three Brothers-Inquisitor smirked at them.

Camus kept his counsel and his face impassive though his heart beat a fierce tattoo. Schimrian steepled his fingers and stared at him over his prince-nez glasses. "Abbot Camus, you all know and these are Fathers Theo and Edward whom I trust implicitly. Well, my son; now that we all know each other let us begin with the grave news you so calmly announced at my door earlier, hmm?"

Camus coughed to clear his fear-clogged throat: "Ahem! We've lost contact with Father Ursaf and his two Angels. I assumed that the storm had damaged the rotors and the radios but we've also lost contact with the two Bede Angels I ordered out to search for them this morning. They came upon a boat full of Unworthy near Milverburg and went down to destroy it but we lost contact at that point. I fear the Light-Father and his Wiccans may have destroyed them both. We've lost *four* Bede Angels, Eminence!"

Schimrian's brows knitted with fury as he drummed the fingers of his right hand on the desk. "Ah, grave news indeed, my son: Bede has failed us *again*," he snarled. "You always questioned my suggested appointments to Bede but I respected your judgement and *this* is the payment I reap for that blind trust! The Brothers-Technician there have been left to their own devices for far too long! Father Aten? Bede has need of an Abbot of your obvious calibre. Are you worthy of such a post, my son?"

Pious clasped a hand on Aten's shoulder. "Eminence, forgive me but I had hoped that Father Aten would accompany me on the ground assault upon the Queen of Babylons."

"Indeed so. I value your request, old friend, but I sense Bede is morally adrift and losing focus and that's where our remaining Angels are gathered! If the Light-Father strikes there, he will find an undefended target and you'll have no air support for your Inquisition tomorrow."

Pious considered this for a moment and acceded: "You are of course correct, Eminence: if I were this damnable Light-Father, that's *exactly* where I would strike next. I therefore congratulate my fellow Abbot here on his elevation…"

Aten raised his hand. "If I may beg your indulgence, Eminence, but I will need Brother Feris and Brother Cwellor with me to instil discipline there if what you suspect is true. I've heard that they're in their cups from Matins to Compline since the invasion and seem to share the same night terrors as poor Camus here."

"Then I do pity them," Camus muttered. "But if we are to succeed in our endeavours, we'll need all the remaining Angels to take to the air tomorrow…"

248

"Exactly how many Angels have we got left?" Cwellor interrupted, deliberately foregoing Camus's title of Eminence.

Camus bristled at the insult until he saw the thin smile on the dead white face of Pious and the disdain in his lifeless eyes. "One is now airworthy here and fully armed," he reported through clenched teeth. "There remain eleven at Bede but I understand from my radio conversations with Brothers Thanewell and Gerald that three of them cannot fly due to engine faults."

"Nine should be enough," Theo ventured, eager to make a mark. "Three to cover Uppermost and two to cover each viaduct in support of the Brothers-Martial crossing them."

He swallowed nervously as Schimrian glared at him. "Just concentrate on restoring the electrics to the rest of the Great Abbey, my son," Schimrian said dismissively. "You and Father Edward also need to fully restore our global communications as quickly as you can. Leave the strategy to your elders, my son."

"Y-yes, Eminence," Theo stuttered. "Pardon my presumption." If looks could kill then Edward's glare would have turned his oldest friend's body into a pile of smouldering soot.

"I want you and Edward to remain here and monitor the radio traffic of our brethren abroad," Schimrian continued, jabbing an index finger onto his desk in emphasis: "Especially those transmissions between Abbot Amherus and the Conclave."

"We shall, Eminence," Edward pledged quickly. "Is there anything else you require of us?"

"No but it is fitting you remain here and listen to our decisions as you will be the ears of our last great Inquisition. Now be silent as I need to hear more of this 'grave news' from Camus…"

"Burslen Abbey was attacked last night as was the convoy from Norton, Eminence, losing half the Brothers that set out last night," Camus reported slowly, mopping at his brow. "The survivors are being tended to by the Brothers-Surgeon as we speak. Father Hvretsope is setting up camp at Wealthorpe but he reports that they sustained losses at Burslen."

Pious turned to Camus: "What's this?" he demanded. "Has the Light-Father the capacity to reach *that* far?"

"No. Hvretsope told me the same story as the Norton survivors: they were attacked by wolves sweeping down from the north and there were human-animal hybrids amongst them that they'd never seen before. He's fortified the inner compounds at Burslen but he can only spare thirty Brothers-Martial to secure the causeway to the Eastern Viaduct at Wealthorpe. He's creating a walled compound around several of the less ruined cottages to serve as a base but he and I agree that Ursaf may have also been attacked by these same hybrids as they weathered the storm."

Schimrian scowled and turned to Pious. "You do not seem particularly surprised at this news, old friend. Would you care to enlighten us as to what you know of them, hmm?"

"I keep no secrets, Eminence. They're obviously Farzad's work," Pious replied with a shrug. "Erdethric was where Farzad and our most loyal Exodus scientists worked on hundreds of orphans to perfect the gene-splicing techniques that we used to create the Virus of Revelation and to engineer our longevity."

"Ah, yes, I recall visiting there," Schimrian noted thoughtfully. "I was present when he began creating his ape-child and cat-child abominations. It was a pity he harboured later doubts about his great works for the Order - he would've made a fine Brother."

"As you recall, Eminence, all contact was lost with our facilities on the island during the Year of the Rats…"

"And now they've made it to the mainland," Camus interjected. "But that's not all. They mature rapidly and they can reproduce!"

Schimrian's eyes widened as the implications registered. "So they mature as quickly as the animal genes spliced into them?"

"Yes, Eminence," Camus answered. "His own spliced children matured at a *human* rate but these prototypes do not. They could breed us into extinction if we fail to exterminate them."

A deranged half-smile formed on Schimrian's lips. "Did not my beloved Azrael warn me of the risk of Ferals procreating like the beasts they are? Did he not advise me to destroy them all?"

"But these are *not* Ferals, Eminence," Camus protested, uncaring of the consequences such was his foreboding. "Farzad had eighty or so male and female specimens at Erdethric. Assuming they reach sexual maturity when they have three years and bear a litter of four then they could easily number nine hundred or more by now."

Pious placed his hands on his knees and drew in a rattling lungful of air. "No doubt Hvretsope significantly reduced those numbers last night, Eminence, but we must focus on the Light-Father who I deem to be the greatest threat."

Schimrian drummed his fingers on his desk for a minute. "Hmm, I tend to agree with that logic, old friend, but these chimerae worry me. They may aid the Light-Father in the long run if they keep on attacking our outposts and convoys."

"There's more news from Wyehold, Eminence, both good and bad," Edward ventured hesitantly. "Father Vance led fifteen Brothers-Martial by boat from the Wyehold docks at Balnan to secure Wealthorpe but the Abbey has lost contact with them."

Schimrian removed his prince-nez glasses to massage his eyes. "May the Holy Lamb forgive me my frustrations this day," he fumed. "We must presume that the accursed Light-Father wiped them out before he took to the Milverbore in that boat! What of the other expeditions from Wyehold, my son?"

"They are still in contact, Eminence. Father Urthayne is at the village of Drytenham overlooking the Beorminghas line and the causeway to the Western Viaduct. Similarly, Father Stilnatus has secured the village of Cwiclasc and the causeway of the Southern Viaduct. With Father Hvretsope now at Wealthorpe, the Unworthy cannot escape by rail using that train of theirs."

"Ah, Father Edward," Schimrian said benevolently. "My faith in you is indeed thrice rewarded! This is a rare and welcome glimmer of hope in the darkness that is this so-called Light-Father. I am revitalised, my sons," he added decisively. "Father Aten, you and your Brothers hasten to Bede to restore purpose to our wayward brethren. Fathers Edward and Theo, go to the communications rooms but oversee the continuing restoration of the generators when you can. Pious, you and Camus will find boats and man them with novices and any Brother we can spare from repair duties."

"Can I arm them all, Eminence?" Pious enquired patiently. "You can't stop a vessel with just spears and dart guns."

"Yes," Schimrian agreed reluctantly, his face looking as though he was biting into a particularly bitter lemon. "Issue rifles and radios and pray they don't shoot each other. See if you can train them today to at least point the things in the right direction."

Pious bowed his head: "Blessings be unto you for your trust in me, Eminence. The boats need to blockade the Small Harbour and the Great Harbour and the eight docks – ten vessels in all."

"With but a handful of lambs in each boat," Father Aten pointed out. "They'll be wiped out by any vessel escaping Milverburg."

"They're not supposed to engage the Light-Father," Camus explained patiently. "We deem that they only need to alert the Angels as to the fleeing vessel and let them take care of it."

251

"Like the two Angels we've just lost?" Cwellor sneered.

Camus could barely contain his loathing for this supercilious Brother-Inquisitor. "We'll mount a co-ordinated assault along all three viaducts once the boats are in position at the dock entrances. The Bede Angels will ferry the Brothers-Martial from the Great Abbey to seize the Circumference Stairways. The Wiccans number but three: they cannot be everywhere at once so we will assign two begiullers to each stairwell party. We have but twenty begiullers left in Britannia so we must use them wisely."

"It will be the Devil's own job to hunt and search each level with so few of us," Dreorman fretted, chewing at a nail. "Do we have detailed maps of each level here at the Great Abbey?"

"We did have them in the Library," Theo said dejectedly. "But they've been lost to the fires. All we have are tourism brochures and there's not much useful detail in them."

"It will have to do, my son," Schimrian said. "Your first task then is to get them to Abbot Pious and Abbot Camus."

"Ah, I took the trouble of securing them before this meeting, Eminence," Theo said obsequiously, drawing out a wad of tourist maps of Milverburg and laying them on the table.

Edward muttered a derogatory expletive as Theo smugly took his seat once more, ignoring the barb completely.

Pious took one of the maps to study it. "Ah, this is all but useless but I do have one more item for our agenda, Eminence: a gift for you. I sent my inquisitors north to the army depot near Stepperton to secure ordnance. We've salvaged five heavy-calibre machine guns and three pieces of field artillery. As I said before, we shall reduce this decadent city to smoking *ruins*."

Schimrian was not impressed. "I would've appreciated being consulted on this 'gift' because your presence at Wealthorpe could have saved Beorcraft *and* Father Vance *and* all their Brothers from death at the hands of the Light-Father at Wealthorpe. Yes?"

Pious bowed his head again: "Eminence, I prostrate myself before you and humbly beg your forgiveness for my hasty tactical decision but for all my transformed state, I do not possess the gift of foresight. I did not expect Beorcraft to be taken unawares nor did I know of Wyehold's plans to secure the causeway villages. Perhaps, having instructed Camus and I to plan the assault you might have consulted us in that decision beforehand and we could have prepared reinforcements."

Schimrian reddened at the implied rebuke and grasped his sword scabbard. "I thought it prudent, my son, as both of you were not available at the time," he countered darkly. "I had to get things moving and pre-empt your commands so I, in my turn, apologise for taking the initiative at Four Bells this morning. Nevertheless, we have secured our first objective though I admit that we are few in numbers. Therefore, I beseech thee: go forth, all of you and ready those boats, the radios and the Angels. I want all of Milverburg's docks blockaded at first light tomorrow!"

Pious stood and bowed deeply. "It shall be done, Eminence," he wheezed. "But what of these chimerae that attacked Burslen? Are you sure we should ignore such a potent threat to our northern flanks? Hvretsope could be overrun at Wealthorpe for as the old Celtic proverb goes: *tragedies come a-calling in threes*."

Dreorman patted his powerful sniper rifle. "It sounds as if these creatures could provide us with *sport*, Eminence!" he chuckled excitedly. "I look forward to seeing them in my sights."

Schimrian raised an enquiring eyebrow at Pious: "Sport or not, I suggest you join Hvretsope at Wealthorpe, old friend, and let *Abbot Aten* ready his forces at Bede then at midday tomorrow we'll synchronise our attacks upon this Unworthy redoubt."

"Midday tomorrow it is then," Pious agreed, turning to look down upon the white-faced Camus. "Come, let us gird up our Brothers-Technician, our novices and our postulants for battle. I'll make these lambs ready for the assault while you liaise with Wyehold to bring ten boats to the wharf at Wealthorpe."

"Aye, I'll see to that," Camus consented reluctantly. "Though I can't guarantee they'll have ten that are seaworthy."

Schimrian raised his hand for silence. "This council of war is at an end, my sons, I am sorry that the Abbess was unable to bring us refreshments quickly enough. Blessings be upon you all."

They all rose to bow deeply to Schimrian who was pleased at the deference and respect being paid to him. Pious was last to leave the chambers but he paused by the door.

"Was there anything else, Eminence?" he asked. "I fear that I may have lost some of your trust this day and that vexes me."

Schimrian waved a hand in negation: "No, my son. You are my rock and my shield as ever, old friend. As God has resurrected you and filled you with His holy strength to do His holy works, I too was reborn and invigorated anew with our holy destiny reaffirmed.

Beneath my angels who watch over me, my mind is crystal-clear and full of purpose once more. I concur with you that we must communicate more freely with each other and we can do that now that power is being restored."

"Aye, *a silent tongue oft spreads the deadliest discord.*"

"Chenikov! Touché in both our cases," Schimrian smiled thinly. "There is one more thing however," he added, standing up and drawing his sword from its scabbard. "This glorious morning, I am resolved to leave my throne untended for a while and personally do battle with this Light-Father. I'm coming with you, my son, and we shall fight side by side as we did of old."

"Hallelujah, Eminence!" Pious grinned, clenching his fists. "This is welcome news!" He paused as a respectful pattering sounded upon the doorframe behind him. "Ah, Abbess!" he grinned, turning to savour her displeasure at seeing him. "I see you have brought sustenance though somewhat too late for my brethren. It's a shame that I have no need for such worldly necessities otherwise I would no doubt wax enthusiastic about your culinary arts. If you'll both excuse me, I've mewling lambs I must forge into tigers before Matins tomorrow."

She paused at the doorway, transfixed by fear and loathing, to watch him stride down the corridor to the stairwell before wheeling the service-trolley into Schimrian's chambers. Schimrian was once more sat at his desk with his naked sword before him and holding out his ring hand for her to kiss the symbol of his power. She said nothing but kissed it then laid a plate of sandwiches on the desk and poured him some tea.

"Thank you, my daughter," he said gently. "I have a favour to ask of you, if you would be so kind."

"You have but to name it, Eminence," she said carefully.

"Take the rest of this food to the communication rooms and then I want you to feed that traitor Ignatius. I want his strength restored so that I may Inquire of him this evening. I have much need of exercise and he has much need of confession. Why do you tremble so at this? Do you hold this traitor in such high regard?"

"No, of course not, Eminence," she spluttered. "It's just that I was dismayed, nay, devastated to learn of his treachery."

Schimrian ran a finger along the keen edge of his sword. "We suspect other traitors are among us but rest assured, we'll find them and make them rue the day they were born."

Ondine feigned shock and put a hand to her mouth. "Dear God! We have more traitors at the Great Abbey?"

Schimrian nodded, sheathing his sword. "Dear God indeed, Abbess! Some of us have strayed from the path; gnawed by doubt and beset by phantoms at night but damn them to hell! This is not a time for faint hearts and those who lack belief in our New Jerusalem!" He curtailed the rant and gazed at her sympathetically. "I apologise, my daughter, a man can only bear so much misfortune in one day before his demeanour becomes somewhat uncivil. Forgive me. Ah, this is excellent tea, thank you."

Ondine felt the evil presence she'd sensed before but she could see nothing in the ceiling space above her head yet from the corner of her eye she was convinced that one of the angels had turned its head to glare at her. "You're welcome, Eminence."

"Good. Is there anything you'd like to discuss with me before you attend to your tasks? There clearly seems to be something on your mind, my daughter."

"I just worry for my poor Sisters, Eminence," she lied quickly. "They've lost so many of their friends that I'm hard put to keep their spirits up and motivate them when they won't go anywhere near the Tally-men without collapsing into hysterics."

"There's nothing I can do about that, my daughter," he replied, sipping at his tea. "Only time and your gentle touch can heal them. Are you sure that's all?"

"Um, what are you planning to do with the traitor?"

"Ah, gentle heart that you are; you worry for his immortal soul! We are truly blessed by your presence." A deathly chill enveloped her as he looked up at her from under his eyebrows and a cruel, macabre grin disfigured his face. "He will of course be put to death in view of all at the Great Abbey before we Inquire of Milverburg. An example must be set. Are you shocked by this?"

"N-no, Eminence," she stammered. "He all but destroyed our Great Abbey and b-brought our Order low."

"He has that, Ondine," he said, surprising her with the use of her birth name. "You'll attend to his last rites because I want you to watch as he is brought to atonement for his sins."

She could feel the malice of that vast, disembodied will pressing down upon her soul, corroding every fibre of her being like psychic acid: "As you wish," she whispered helplessly.

~~~~~

255

Defend Ten Towns

Harold sat at the head of the table quietly appraising the others in the North Library as they chatted to each other, waiting for Ursaf to return from an attempt to raise Bede on the Angel radios. To his immediate right sat Michael who now wore a stout black leather jacket, black trousers and army-style boots. He turned to Harold on sensing that he was being stared at. "Does this Noh mask disturb you, Light-Father? Your shield-maiden over there found it in one of the collections in this tower. With this military head cover it means I don't have to swathe my head in filthy bandages."

"It's a bit unnerving, I'll admit," Harold smiled. "But better than looking at red muscles and blood vessels. I'm not familiar with Japanese theatre but you look like a ninja."

"An apt choice of word given my complicity in genocide but this character is not a ninja but a Kishin Shuju according to the label," Michael replied, tapping the ruddy-complexioned mask of a young grinning man with his teeth slightly parted. "Shuju is a sea spirit that loves drinking alcohol so it would be more appropriate for Brother Ignatius but it allows me a good field of vision and the mouth gap is wide enough for me to breathe easily."

To Michael's right sat Fria, retying her ponytail whilst listening intently to Amos whispering about Pomona and Kayleigh who were sat opposite them. The girls were oblivious of their animosity preferring to share stories with Mouse and Shield. Saul was seated between Harold and Shield yet he was silent, brooding deeply whilst toying with a lock of his long, black curly hair. Like the other Scatterlings, his weapons were upon the table before him. He'd said little except to hint of his fears about the oncoming battle so Harold was concerned: Saul had been Eldest of the Scatterlings for six years yet now that mantle had passed to him and he wondered if that was preying on the young man's mind.

Ibrahim and Bas to the right of Amos were deep in discussion about the two battles at Wealthorpe and gently bickering about their fighting techniques as only true siblings can despite their artificial dissimilarities. Linden, one of Ken Glascae's men, sat to their right and next to him was Ken and both men had turned their chairs around to talk to their three companions; Seainare, Beorstahl and Naeglin. Harold noted that they all still bore the marks of torture at the Great Abbey but they'd fully recovered unlike Marc and his two fellow escapees, Olias and Stunnal, who would need a month or more to regain their full strength having suffered the attention of Pious and his Inquisitors for two weeks.

Saul suddenly placed a hand on Harold's left forearm, startling him. "Patience, Light-Father, my father used to quote Sun Tsu to me all the time and given the sunshine in Uppermost this quote came to mind: *With regard to precipitous heights, if you are beforehand with your adversary, you should occupy the raised and sunny spots, and there wait for him to come up.* In other words; we have the heights and all we have to do is wait for our enemy."

Michael leant forward to talk across Harold. "Well said, Scatterling, your father was a wise man but we must prepare a strategy to defend the ten towns."

"My parents were both well-educated and well-travelled," Saul retorted, displaying his saya. "The swords that I and the Light-Father wield are a pair he bought for the cost of a small house from a merchant here in Milverburg. It might have been one of Pomona's clan but he was extremely satisfied with his purchase."

"May I look at it?" Michael inquired. He drew the katana from its saya and studied it closely. "What superb craftsmanship and skill," he sighed genuinely moved. "Can you imagine the smith folding and refolding and quenching the shingane, hagane and kawagane steels in this blade thousands of times right down to a molecular level? This ridge here is called a hamon and requires meticulous handling and covering with clay to modify and control the tempering. I've never seen a hamon so precise and uniform – these katana are the work of a master."

Saul took back his katana and sheathed it. "Another skill lost forever to the world," he declared bitterly. "Thanks to your damned apocalypse. No doubt the jungle is reclaiming the bones and forges of the man who created these as we speak. All that's left of him is the soul he poured into these blades."

Michael said nothing and Harold was glad the awkward silence was broken by the bustling return of Ursaf and his three men to take their seats at the other end of the table. Unlike Kai, all four of them were now dressed in comfortable civilian outdoor clothes and looked completely different; as though a massive spiritual weight had been lifted from their shoulders. Ken and Linden turned their chairs around eager for news but they and the others had to wait for Ursaf to regain his breath after climbing so many stairs.

"We managed to contact Bede," he gasped finally, savouring the deliciously cool air of this marble-floored oasis after half an hour under the relentless sun in the park. "I spoke to Brother Thanewell. Camus has warned him on their private frequency that Aten was elevated to Abbot. He and two of his brutal Inquisitors are on their way to take control of Bede. He says they're all terrified."

Michael shifted in his seat. "I'd hoped Camus would've defected by now but he's too much of a coward."

"I don't know, Michael," Ursaf disagreed. "He's playing a dangerous game. He revealed that Schimrian plans to lead the attack on Milverburg at noon tomorrow. He told Thanewell to tell me that the Order has *already* secured the three causeways to prevent us escaping along the rail tracks and boats will take to the Milverbore at dawn to block the dock entrances."

"I confess to being pleasantly surprised," Michael approved. "When he ran from me screaming, I thought he was lost to that shadow-geis forever. On the other hand, I can't believe Schimrian would ever leave the Great Manse let alone lead an assault. I think this Azrael-Satan is still manipulating his puppet's strings. What was it that Wiccan was saying? Something about a vision telling her that Azrael is actually part of an ancient enemy intent on destroying all life in God's Creation?"

"That's what she said," Harold confirmed. "I'd find it hard to believe but for the fact I'm from another world myself."

"So, Michael, this Azrael was more than just a 'program' or an 'artificial intelligence' as you believed yesterday," Shield observed shrewdly. "That machine was his *ship*!"

"I believe that this 'ship' arrived *centuries* ago," Michael agreed reluctantly. "It all makes sense now! From the moment that sphere entered this world in Heofland, the Order has been gently moulded in His image. I see it all so clearly now: how my thoughts and feelings and those of others in the Order were subtly altered and manipulated. I now feel completely different: my mind is free from doubt and paranoia for the first time in *decades*."

Harold laughed contemptuously: "This is all so convenient, Michael! Where I come from we've always had that old defence for sin and murder: *the Devil made me do it*!"

Michael slammed his fist on the desk. "Don't you think for one second I'll *ever* hide behind that excuse, Light-Father! None of us, not even Amherus and Schimrian, were controlled like Tally-men and some fled the Order as the Great Plague was unleashed though where they went I know not. Azrael could not nurture and influence every individual in the Order as perhaps he did with the Conclave but he found in us the perfect clay: corrupt and paranoid because of our *arrogance*. We thought we were the Chosen Ones of God but Azrael was that doubt; that fear of the Unworthy; that dream of a New Jerusalem eroding reason and compassion. But, Dear Lord, I ask myself: how can such an incorporeal creature *exist*? It denies every tenet of science I hold dear."

"You believe in an invisible God even though you say you're a scientist," Ibrahim interjected bluntly. "So why is a Satan capable of achieving such power over your soul so hard to believe?"

"A good point well made. I think the Light-Father and I need to talk to the albino and see what else we can learn," Michael conceded thoughtfully. "If this creature is incorporeal then perhaps we can only kill it if it takes physical form again."

"Mmm, let's focus on the corporeal for now," Harold decided. "What else have you got for us, Ursaf?"

Ursaf looked at him with some sympathy: "I have bad news for your little saboteurs, Light-Father: Brother Ignatius is now being tortured for helping them then he is to be executed immediately after Matins tomorrow. Pious will do it front of all the novices and postulants as a warning of what will happen to them if they fail tomorrow. Camus is in charge of organising them and the Brothers-Technician into manning the boats blockading the docks: if a vessel leaves they are to call down the Angels to destroy it."

Harold slumped back in his seat. "That's what I would do in their place but they won't know that we have two Angels on our side unless this Thanewell tells them? Will he betray you?"

Ursaf shrugged. "Thanewell and Gerald are actually in one of the three Angels about to take off to join us but they report that nobody else will join them through fear, blind loyalty to the Order or intoxication. They have an hour at most before Aten and his two butchers arrive then they'll be forced to prepare the remaining six Angels to land Brothers-Martial in Uppermost. The Bede crews will be there on sufferance now that the dark geis is lifted. They'll be slow to react and they'll make mistakes."

"Why doesn't Thanewell destroy those accursed Angels after he takes off?" Ken demanded, his face reddening with frustration. "It makes no sense just to leave them intact!"

259

Ursaf held his hands up in a gesture of apology: "Three were in hangars and three were being serviced by Brothers. Thanewell refuses to open fire upon his brethren."

"I hope that changes when he gets here," Harold said icily. "They'll have to fight or be killed by Pious and Aten!"

"The five of us will lie in wait for the enemy machines," Ken Glascae growled in disgust, indicating his men. "There are only three parks on Uppermost where they can land from what I've seen from this tower. As you can see we took a lot of equipment from the army base we came across. These three weapons here are high-powered sniper-rifles so we'll kill the pilots before they can land and pick off anyone surviving the crashes."

Piamadet raised a hand and Harold bade him speak. "I'm all for fighting a guerrilla war in Milverburg, Light-Father, but why not escape? If we attack along one of the viaducts using the two Angels we have now, we can overwhelm the causeway defenders. There can't be more than thirty or so Brothers and about twice as many Tally-men holding each of the three causeway villages."

"That will not be easy," Ursaf cautioned him. "Schimrian has finally acceded to Pious and all the Brothers have been allowed to carry rifles and the Fathers all bear machine-guns. Even the novices and postulants in the boats will be issued with rifles."

"Then Azrael must be overriding Schimrian's paranoia," Harold reasoned aloud. "But if we flee, we would be out in the open either on foot or on the train and once more open to attack by Angels or run down by half-tracks. We're in a fortress so we can meet the onslaught on our own terms. What's the matter, Michael?"

"You're right," Michael replied thoughtfully. "Schimrian is so paranoid that only Azrael could force him to leave his throne unguarded. Azrael is free of the device but he was weakened by losing his corporeal form at the Great Annex which is why his geis upon the rest of the Order has waned. I fear his power will be restored when he has more souls to feed on after Amherus and the rest of the Conclave return to the Great Abbey."

"There's no point in second-guessing a disembodied demon," Harold pointed out. "The Wiccans will do what they can but it's up to us to defend this place. Yes, Pomona?"

"You know that all the towns but Uppermost and the Core are in permanent darkness, Light-Father?"

"As black as black can be!" Kayleigh added brightly.

260

"Yes, I know this," Harold replied patiently. "There's some light from the slit windows on the Circumference Stairways during the day but I've only managed to get the emergency lights working on the Core Level and in the docks. Someone switched the lighting off in the Core when the Plague struck but not on the eight levels between the Core and Uppermost so all their emergency lighting batteries were drained. So what's your point, Pomona?"

"We know the vents," Pomona shrugged. "We can find our way through them in the dark…"

"And the Brothers will need torches," Kayleigh grinned.

Saul's eyes widened at the implication: "Ah, I see. If any Brothers start searching those levels then we can find them easily by watching their torches from the vents and ambush them."

"I will go," Bas offered. "I can see in the dark as well as any Feral and if I can't see, I can *sniff* them out." Harold heard the bloodlust in her voice and it worried him deeply: was it a sign her animal genes were starting to dominate her humanity?

"If Ken and Ursaf can defend Uppermost with snipers and Angels," he said, rising to collect a large coffee-table book from a nearby shelf. "We can fight a rearguard action all the way up to Uppermost. If they aren't engaging enemy rotorcraft, our Angels can strafe the viaducts and attack the boats on the Milverbore and free up more escape routes. Ursaf? Could you co-ordinate that? Will you be happy attacking your former comrades?"

"That's a good point, Light-Father," Ken Glascae chimed in. "Thanewell obviously couldn't. Will you four be able to pull the triggers on your chain-guns if you have to?"

Ursaf rose to address them all. "I understand Glascae's scepticism but we are free of Azrael's bane so the answer is yes, Light-Father. Those who attack us may also be free of him but they will seek revenge being fanatically devoted to the Order. We have no choice but to kill or be killed. It's as simple as that."

"We'll hold you to your promise to heal us, Light-Father," Spero intervened, rising to his feet. "And we'll hold to ours. We've brought these hand-phone sets for you to use."

"We have others," Marcus added despondently, displaying the four sets. "But their radio signals won't penetrate stonework this thick. They probably won't even penetrate a single level."

Harold opened the book in the centre of the table and carefully unfolded a map from the centre section that depicted a detailed

261

cross-section of Milverburg and its ten towns. They all rose to gather around to marvel at the sheer scale of the citadel and the engineering required to support all the nine towns above the Core with the titanic central pillar, aptly named Yggdrasil, rising and tapering to form the base of the Tower of the Sun. Four similar pillars rose at the centre of each quadrant to form the bases of the four Towers of the Moon and each of these had a name taken from Norse Mythology: Nidhug, Surtr, Vili and Ve – the latter two being the brothers of Odin. These were central to a complex arrangement of flying buttresses and ribbed arches that transferred the immense weight of the citadel onto these pillars and the outer wall.

Harold pointed to the Core which was also called Niflheim by the original builders as winter fogs used to roll in through the dock entrances and linger for days. "We need to close the dock gates and lock them all bar the Merchant Dock where I have the Beomodor fuelled. It's the only boat large enough to take all of us if we have to retreat into the estuary. My main problem is I don't know how to defend those three railway entrances."

"We could destroy the viaducts," Saul suggested.

"I would like to find a way to keep them intact because this world will have need of this city again," Harold declared, savouring the surprise on every face around the table. "That's right: I'm thinking about what we do once the Order has been defeated and Azrael is finally exorcised from this world."

Ken tapped a viaduct shown on the cross-section: "There is too much heavy masonry in each arch to be destroyed easily. We can make pipe bombs from any gunpowder we find in the armouries and from ingredients in the garden stores on the level below but they won't be enough to destroy arches of this size. You need demolition charges or military explosives to do that."

"What can we do, Light-Father?" Linden asked anxiously. "If they attack along all three viaducts at once we're finished."

"We'll push wagons and carriages into the tunnel mouths," Harold said decisively. "Lock their wheels then jam dock trolleys and trucks into the spaces between them to form defensive barriers. We'll hold the Core as long as we can then retreat to the Northern Circumference Stairway after booby-trapping the others. We'll mine or bomb the stairway as we retreat but we need to make as many trip-wire bombs as we can today. *Ahhhh...*" He winced and closed his eyes, placing his fingertips to his temples. "Ow!"

"Are you ill?" Michael asked, placing a hand upon his shoulder. "Shall I go and summon a Wiccan?"

"No, no, I'm fine," he assured them all hastily. "In answer to Marcus's concerns about communication, the city's phone system doesn't work but we have Wiccans who can use telepathy or 'far-speaking' as you call it. Nightshade has just used it to tell me that Kai and twenty of the Ferals are already at work closing the dock gates. The other Ferals and the little ones are already pushing carriages and wagons into place in the Loki Tunnel."

"So they're 'far-hearing' our discussion," Ursaf noted. "I'd love to know how telepathy works as with all their other gifts."

"As would I," Michael agreed wistfully.

"The Wiccans already know about the groups on the causeways – at least that's what Nightshade told me," Harold replied, tapping at a temple in emphasis. "Fern is recovering already so they'll each take a barricade tomorrow and slow down the attacks. However," he added, turning to Ursaf and Ken. "That means they can't take out enemy Angels if they're down in the Core."

"I'll join Ken in that case," Shield declared, brandishing her crossbow. "With my craft, this is as lethal as any sniper rifle."

Ken beamed. "Ah, I get to see a Wiccan in action! What an interesting day tomorrow promises to be!"

"I hope I get to kill Pious again," Saul said, gripping his katana. "This time I'll remove his *balanith* head from his body."

"What else did the Wiccan tell you, Light-Father?" Spero demanded anxiously. "What will you do if the Brothers spread out into the levels below us? They may find other ways to access the upper levels. I suppose you'll be able to see where they are from their torches but how will you see in the dark?"

"As I said, we'll retreat up the Northern Stairway so they'll have to follow us and be concentrated there as it's unlikely they'll spread out across the towns *unless*," Harold announced thoughtfully, raising a finger in emphasis. "Pomona, Kayleigh and Bas and whoever is on their teams can plant torches as decoys to draw them into ambushes. You could even come at them from the rear as they climb the Northern Stairway. Who'll go with them once the railway tunnels are breached?"

"Olias, Stunnal and I will fight rearguard on the Stairwell," Marc declared. "We know how to use firearms from our years ambushing Tally-men but we need to find these armouries first."

263

"We'll take you," Pomona and Kayleigh pledged in unison. "Then we'll show the Light-Father all the garden stores in Midgard and the places where the fireworks are stored in Alfheim," Pomona added, grasping Kayleigh's hand.

"The gun shops and the armouries are down in Svartalfheim," Kayleigh continued. "They have lots of rifles and shotguns!"

"This is excellent news," Olias approved, clenching a fist. "My father bought his hunting rifles from Svartalfheim but pipe-bombs will be the most lethal in the confined spaces of the Stairways. We'll need hundreds of them. Perhaps the Wiccans can instruct us how to make them. But," he added cautiously. "As Spero pointed out, we'll be fighting rearguard in total darkness as any light we use will make us easy targets for Brothers storming the stairways."

"They'll be easy targets too and the dark is not a problem for me or the Ferals," Bas assured him. "But it will be for you and the others if you panic and start shooting blindly."

Ken and his men placed their goggles on the table. "These are night-vision glasses," he explained proudly. "We found them at the army base. I just wish we'd brought more now. If the rear guard uses these they won't need any torches but there won't be enough for anyone setting ambushes in the towns."

"The other three Stairways will have to be mined and barricaded," Marcus fretted, jabbing at the map. "They could send up a sortie to outflank us otherwise."

Harold sighed. "That's my worry as well but we can only do so much in the time we have left – about twenty four hours. Let's see: Saul and Ibrahim, you'll join the rear guard. Ken?"

"Aye, we'll show them how to use guns and rifles."

Harold nodded in approval. "The Wiccans will retreat with me and try and confuse the attackers with their illusion-geis. Fria and Amos, what would you two like to do?"

"And me!" Mouse chipped in. "I want to fight!"

"You and the little ones will stay with me," Harold said sternly. "I abandoned four of you once. It'll never happen again!"

"We'll go with Yin and Yang over there," Fria said firmly. "We'll show them what real Scatterlings can do."

"Amos?" Harold asked pointedly. "Remember what we've told you about keeping focused in battle?"

Amos looked sheepishly at Fria. "Now I have something besides Surl I want to protect, Light-Father, I'll think of others first."

"Fine," Harold nodded, unconvinced. "But you must spend some time with Surl this evening. Right, you all know what you need to do: barricades, guns then pipe bombs."

"What will you do first, Light-Father?" Marc asked.

"I'll wait with Ursaf and his men to see if these Bede Angels make it but we'll post a lookout in top of this tower in case the others attack today. We'll all meet here at Six Bells to distribute the weapons. Nightshade and Ivy already know what we plan to do," he said, wincing at the two voices in his head. "The Ferals say they want to join Bas and the others ambushing the Brothers in the levels below us. She says their senses are so sharp that they won't need night-glasses. She thinks they'll prove to be even more deadly than they were at the Great Abbey as they will have the advantage in the pitch dark. That's all for now: good luck everyone."

Michael applauded, his gloved hands making a dull thumping sound: "Well done, *General*. Sun Tsu lives on in you."

"I'm no general," Harold replied, somewhat embarrassed by the compliment as the others began to file out of the library. "It's just the best I can come up with as there's so few of us. I'm confident, given the numbers that we can hold out..."

"But when Amherus and the fanatics of the Conclave return, it'll be a different story," Michael reminded him.

"I know but I can only focus on one impossible task at a time."

"Excuse me for a moment, Light-Father," Michael apologised. "Shield? Mouse? Could you join us? I have something for you. One of the postulants found in the wreckage in the Great Annex and Ignatius bid him bring it to me. He thought I was the only one who would know what it is and he was right. I think you should see this before I pass it on to the Wiccans to work their craft upon it."

He unwrapped a glistening ovoid object and placed it upon the wrapping-cloth so that it would not roll about the table. "Look at the mark here: this is the ancient symbol the Wiccans use to denote the element of water..."

"Mother Veneris had water as her element!" Harold exclaimed incredulously. "Are you saying she created this?"

"It was found *exactly* where their brave sister sacrificed herself so I have a theory, based on my research, that this is a Wiccan Egg. I have no idea what material it's made out of but, Shield and Mouse, look closely at the surface and tell me what you see inside? You have to almost touch your nose to it."

Mouse went first and her eyes were as wide as saucers as she peered through the Egg's translucent sheen. "I can see a foetus moving inside it!" she gasped. "Look, Shield!"

Shield followed suit then glared suspiciously at Michael. "What is this Wiccan Egg and what has it got to do with us?"

Michael reached out and held it aloft in his hand to study it. "It defies science like so many things that the Wiccans do. There's an ancient tale of a noble Celtic warrior who sacrificed himself to save his king in battle. He was brought back to life by an arch-druid who captured his essence inside such an egg - a powerful symbol of rebirth amongst the Druids and the Wiccans. I believe your Mother Veneris achieved something similar to create this."

"What do you mean by capturing an *essence*, Michael?" Shield demanded angrily, clutching at a knife-hilt. "By Saint Peter's heart, I warn you: you'll pay a heavy price if this is a cruel jest!"

"I make no jest but you both needed to see the Egg before the Wiccans do because if I'm right then inside this wondrous object resides the soul of your sister, Fierce!"

~~~~~

The Worms Turn

Ondine returned to the parlour at the Abbess Manse and looked anew at its opulent busts and paintings of saints and former Great-Abbots and found the bile rising in her throat. Despite the warmth of this rarest of sunny days, one of the Sisters, Frances, had set a fire blazing in the hearth as she always did without a thought for the sweltering heat now rippling through the high-ceilinged room adorned with intricate plaster mouldings depicting the seven ranks of angels. The ones that disturbed her most were the six-winged seraphim with two of their wings hiding their faces.

The electric lamps flickered fitfully as an indication of the Brothers-Technician attempts to connect the new generators to the power grid. Large telseiean lamps shone brightly enough in all the recesses to highlight the magnificent and sumptuous representation of Christ Ascending painted by a master on the high ceiling. It was based on the statue that the Wiccan had destroyed in the Great Cathedral and Ascending with Him was depicted a heavenly host including the thirteen disciples and Mary Magdalene.

A momentary spasm of anger at such Pagan defilement of her beloved Lord filled her heart but she set it aside instantly. "No, Azrael!" she snarled aloud, making a sweeping gesture with her right hand. "I feel your fingers clutching at my heart again! Jesus would care no more than a humble carpenter would about a carven image. Your evil has ensnared Schimrian but not me!"

"I'm sorry, Abbess, but who are you talking to? Who is this Azrael you speak of? Is he not the Lord's Angel of Death?"

"Ah, Sister Frances, forgive me," Ondine gasped in surprise. "I didn't see you there. I was just talking aloud in a brief crisis of faith, nothing more. Why aren't you preparing the midday meals?"

"I was but I've brought you some tea," Frances said shyly, pointing at the teapot, milk jug, cup and saucer set upon the tea table by Ondine's favourite reading chair. The chair was set in a corner that boasted ornate bookshelves crammed with hundreds of classical books that Ignatius had procured for her. "I know how hot it is today but I heard you were upset after visiting the Great-Abbot and I thought some tea would soothe you."

"Thank you, dear heart," Ondine said gratefully. "I am moved by your charity and thoughtfulness. What's really troubling you?

I've cancelled Midday Prayers with the Great-Abbot's approval so is there anything else that concerns you?"

Frances blushed, clutching the tray tightly to her chest. "Father Aten molested some of us this morning and encouraged Brothers to do the same. They tried to r-r-ra…" she spluttered to halt and looked at the fire, her eyes glistening with tears. "I can't say it!"

Ondine instinctively took the trembling young Sister in her arms and comforted her. "Be at peace and tell me what happened."

"I was d-delivering breakfasts to the Fathers' Lodges after Matins when Father Aten and Father Leo suddenly dragged me into a cloakroom near the entrance. Aten p-pushed me against the wall and forced his hand between my legs. He made Father Leo grab my breasts and told him I was nothing more than a toy to play with… I-I tried to push them off but they were too strong. Father Leo's face kept changing: one second he was remorseful and the next he was a demon pawing me *everywhere*. I feel so… so *dirty*."

"You are not dirty, my lamb," Ondine crooned gently into the distraught Sister's ear. "Now tell me what happened next."

"They… they were trying to tear off my habit when Father Aten was summoned to attend Pious in the Redemption Cells. He forced a kiss on me then told me to attend his chambers where he would fulfil his most holy mission of restoring the Twelve Tribes. He laughed in my face, Abbess, groped me *there* again and left. I felt faint and fell to the floor. Father Leo apologised and helped me to my feet then he bade me promise not to say anything to you."

"So Azrael is reaching out," Ondine sighed whilst staring up at the picture of Christ while holding Frances tightly as she shuddered and wept. "It was a terrible experience for such an innocent as you but this is no time for tears, dear heart! You've brought me the resolve I need to face this Satan moving once more amongst us. Dry those eyes and get me Abbot Camus. He's either in the Angel Compound, repairing rotorcraft, or he's in the communications rooms. Find him and bring him to me."

Frances disengaged from the Abbess reluctantly and took out a handkerchief to wipe her face and blow her nose. "I shall, Abbess, but we're so *frightened*. The Brothers and novices made lewd comments yesterday but this morning their faces are so full of hate and lust. They used to be so kind to us but they've all changed. What have we done to deserve this? Why did the Tally-men kill three Houses full of us Sisters? Have we sinned?"

268

Ondine held the Sister's face in her hands: "Sweet child," she said soothingly. "You have all done *nothing* except be the sweet young lambs I am sworn to serve and protect." She kissed Frances gently on the forehead. "The Devil entered their hearts long ago but now their hatred of women is being revealed. Such has always been the nature of men in this world who see women like us as nothing more than mere possessions. Be of stout heart, my daughter, and when you have found Abbot Camus, bring the Sisters here into this parlour. Can you do that for me?"

Frances nodded. "Yes, Abbess, but not Sister Persephone."

"Why? Oh, sweet Lord, what's happened to her?"

"She won't come out of the baths in Saint Agnes," Frances explained, her eyes downcast. "She was seized by many novices after Matins this morning and we found her almost out of her mind and tearing out her hair in the Northern Processional near the North Gate. She was trying to flee into the woods for shame. They all took turns to ra... ra... to *violate* her."

Ondine went white with fury. "The word is *rape*, my daughter. Satan prowls the Great Abbey and has ensured that our piety and innocence is no longer a shield against the base instincts of these corrupted Brothers. With his myth of New Jerusalem dispensed with, the Devil has no need of brood mares..."

"I'm sorry, Abbess. What are brood mares?"

"Nothing, dear heart, nothing," Ondine reassured her quickly, waving a hand in dismissal. "Go and get me Camus! I will see to Sister Persephone. Is there anyone with her?"

"Sister Freya and Sister Geraldine."

"Good: they are the two best suited to comfort her." She went over to her tea table and swallowed the cup of tea in one gulp and wiped her mouth with the back of her hand. "Thank you for the tea. Don't just stand there gawping, my daughter. Go!"

Frances stared wide-eyed at the Abbess like a bewildered rabbit for a full ten seconds; time enough for Ondine to reflect and curse how the Order had limited the intellect of her lambs deliberately for generations. Finally, the cogs meshed and Frances left the parlour drawing the door shut behind her only to reopen it a moment later. "I'm s-sorry to disturb you again, Abbess," she stammered. "But His Eminence was already in the corridor. Shall I show him in?"

"That's why I sent you to get him, dear heart," Ondine replied patiently. "Now go and bring the Sisters here."

"All of them?"

"Dear Lord, give me strength! Yes, all of them!"

Camus entered without invitation and the flustered Frances bowed deeply then pulled the door shut. There was a used teacup and saucer on another table so he took them to make himself a cup of tea. He then drew a chair up to the tea table and at down, hands on thighs and tilting his head back to gaze at the ceiling. Ondine sat in her reading chair and poured herself another cup of tea. She thought Camus looked dreadful with vivid dark rings under his eyes and a grey pallor to his skin. He was dressed in stained overalls and his hands had already left oil smudges on the arm-rests. Normally she would have scolded him but those times were over.

"I've just heard that there was a serious incident in the novice refectory where a Sister was attacked and others have been harassed. Something new is happening to the Brothers at the Great Abbey and to me and I need to know what. This is why I've come to see you. I know you saw Schimrian just after our little council of war earlier. I must ask what you sensed in the Great Manse."

"What do you mean?"

"You've confided in me often enough, Ondine. I know of your sensitivity to otherworldly phenomena. Michael, Ignatius and I have often discussed you and your forebodings. Even I felt something evil looking down at me from the ceiling in Schimrian's chambers earlier. So tell me: did you sense anything?"

"Yes, something profoundly evil: Azrael."

"But that damned angel was destroyed in the explosion."

"Only his physical form was. He was there in the Great Manse pressing down upon my soul, mocking me until I imagined the angel statues were moving and staring at me. His shadow has wrapped itself around Schimrian and Pious and so I fear for my Sisters for this Satan is amongst us."

"I see. You know that here was an alien device at the core of the Great Computer?" Camus ventured.

"Yes, I heard as much plus the fact it was possibly centuries old and that the Great-Abbot found it in a cave in Heofland. He claims that the voice of God told him where to look but now…"

"But now you think Azrael was speaking to him," Camus interrupted shrewdly, his eyes narrowing. "My Brothers all spoke of a veil lifting from their souls so they've been wrestling with their consciences these past three weeks but fear and faith kept them chained here. As you've sensed, Azrael is gaining strength and another darker veil is descending upon them."

"Yes. Azrael's influence is growing. I can feel it."

"So you share my belief that this is why the Brothers and novices are suddenly harassing the Sisters?"

"It has to be," she replied, pursing her lips in thought. "Ignatius told me that you thought this alien device came from a parallel universe. He said that Schimrian's own brother, Abbot Breostan, was the donor for the brain tissue needed to activate it. He often abused postulants and Sisters as the Brothers are doing now so this vile behaviour of theirs carries his *stench*."

Camus ceased studying the ceiling artwork and turned to stare at her: "As soon as he gained physical form, Azrael wielded his full power; controlling the Tally-men and resurrecting the dead. Wiping out so many of the Order proved to me that he truly desires the end of all conscious life in this world but if Breostan is a part of him, as you say, then he's a very *human* demon; bringing death yet delighting in torture and sadism. We were fortunate, if you can call it that, in that we had no Tally-men in the Angel Compound but..." He trailed off into an anguished silence.

"What ails you, Camus? You look dreadful. Are you still seeing the dead at night?"

He rolled up his sleeve to display the scratches on his forearm. "I see millions of them," he groaned. "Millions! They now include the tortured souls that the Wiccans forced me to shoot in the Compound. The dead have gained corporeality enough to injure me thus. Since that infernal meeting just now, I see them swarming around me whenever I shut my eyes even for a second. They are in here with us now," he said, waving a hand at the parlour ceiling. "They're begging us to rescue Ignatius who is due to be executed tomorrow after Matins. They say he's important. They want me to find the Light-Father - they feel he has the power to turn the whole world onto a new course. He also has with him a child that they desire bearing the strangest of names: *Surl*."

"Surl?" she gasped. "She was one of the young Scatterlings left behind when the Light-Father..." She clamped a hand to her mouth and looked away, fearing Camus would betray her.

"Don't worry, Ondine," he assured her, correctly guessing her concerns and doubts about him. "Now I'm listening to them, the dead have told me how you helped Ignatius and his little saboteurs.

Ignatius has not betrayed you despite the torture and neither will I. It's obvious that these Scatterlings were Children of Exodus to be able to wreak such havoc across the Great Abbey."

"Yes, the four of them were of Exodus but Ignatius found the mark of the craft upon Surl – she's a *seeress*."

"Really? A seeress? Like those Panchen Lamas?" he exclaimed, blinking in disbelief. "Ah, that explains why they were able to escape detection for so long even with your help." He rubbed at his unshaven jaw, deep in thought then yawned. "The dead say she is vitally important for the future of mankind but they won't tell me why or how. They also say they can't move into the light as they don't want their deaths to be in vain. They want to stop the Order and end this Satan that killed them all but they have no corporeal power. Perhaps this Surl can give them that?"

"She's an extraordinary girl but her power of foresight may be what they're referring to. It could be the salvation of us all. What's this?" she exclaimed as death's-head moth landed upon the back of her hand only to dissipate in a puff of dust. "Did you see that?"

"Peculiar," he nodded. "It has to be an omen. Schimrian said he was plagued by them during his bout of madness. I expect without Azrael sustaining him, his sanity collapsed but now, as you fear, Azrael is recovering his strength. However, I wonder why Azrael allowed the dead to torment Michael and me all these years."

"Maybe it simply amused him," she suggested, shrugging her shoulders. "Or by focusing their collective will, the dead could target individual minds and break through his barriers to get inside your dreams. Perhaps Azrael couldn't block out so many souls when they were focussed on just two targets."

Camus slumped even deeper into his chair and drained his tea before replying: "Perhaps but to seek out the Light-Father will be hard for me given how many of my brethren I was forced to slay. They crowd around me venting their anger towards me but the others come and tear them away and threaten to cast them *and* me into the Pit. I have no strength left to resist them any more."

"I understand," she said sympathetically. "It may be that you and Michael were the only truly open minds in the Great Abbey but enough speculation about Azrael: how can I save my lambs?"

"It's why I came to see you. The final straw breaking the donkey's spine: as well as the incidents I've heard about, when I got back into the hangars, all the Brothers would talk of nothing else but copulating with Sisters, willing or otherwise, as their holy duty to repopulate the Gross Thousands. They would not listen to me or focus on the repairs. I found their voiced intents disturbing and, shall we say, extremely *explicit*."

"Yes, we're just the brainless brood mares of the Order," she snarled, clenching a fist. "I utterly *despise* this cruel misogyny. In hindsight, I think I, too, must've had my mind lulled for decades by Azrael to so blindly accept the putrid elf-dust fed to me that my Sisters were taken in by the Order as an act of *charity*."

Camus rubbed at his eyes and smiled guiltily. "It was always covertly accepted amongst the brethren that this would be so to maintain the holy number in our New Jerusalem for all our vows of chastity. This was why utmost respect for you and the Sisters as saviours was programmed into us as novices but now that respect is disintegrating at just a whisper or two from Azrael no doubt. They are slowly being consumed by lust and obsession: I predict they'll storm this Enclave before sunrise tomorrow."

"I fear this too, Camus. We must flee this place as soon as we can. New Jerusalem was but a myth that corrupted their souls yet it held their base desires in check. We had to be revered as chaste and sacred in order to preserve that fantasy but now that veneer has been stripped away revealing the beasts within."

He mopped his brow with a cloth and stared at the fire. "The Gates of Hell are opening beneath our feet, Ondine, but I will listen to these siren voices beseeching me in my dreams. They hint at my salvation but I need to be careful: I told my Brothers I was coming here to ensure their evening meals would be on time and there would be some *meat* in the broth," he smiled wryly.

"What do you mean by *that*?" she demanded, outraged.

"I'm sorry: that was the only excuse they'd accept in that frame of mind," he explained, grimacing. "Theo and Edward are spying on me for Schimrian which, to me, along with Schimrian's anger towards me, confirms that my life will shortly end if I remain trammelled here. He plans to lead the attack on the Light-Father tomorrow but," he added brightly, raising a finger in emphasis: "I've also heard that three Angels have just defected from Bede and the rest may follow! Aten has been despatched to Bede to bring them into line but I'm hoping he'll be too late."

"Are there any other Brothers here who can resist these primal urges and flee the Order?" she asked him. "Ignatius didn't think there were any worth approaching when we discussed trying to save my Sisters and as many postulants as we could."

"Mmm, none that I can think of in the Great Abbey," he replied sadly, drumming his fingers on the armrests. "Not even the ones newly arrived from Norton. Schimrian chose them for their loyalty to him and their blind devotion to his New Jerusalem."

"Then Azrael does not need to do much for us to see their true faces then," she sighed resignedly. "Ignatius told me how so many of them *volunteered* to spread the Virus."

"The Conclave wants to return here and I suspect most of them will be of the same mind as Amherus but how many Brothers abroad will desert the Order, I cannot say. I promise you that I'll save you and as many Sisters as I can but how can we free Ignatius? What condition has Pious left him in?"

"He's weak and passes out before they can do any real damage from what I saw when I took him a meal on Schimrian's orders. He wants me to *watch* as they butcher him tomorrow."

"Ach, yet another reason we must leave this nightmare," Camus snorted in disgust. "I've repaired and fuelled the surviving Angel. If we can get Ignatius into the Compound, we can escape by air."

"What about my Sisters?" she snapped. "I will *not* leave them to be raped and molested like Persephone!"

"Persephone? Ah, no, she's such a sweet innocent!"

"Innocent no longer you mean! How can I save them all?" she demanded desperately. "They'll not survive the night if the Enclave is attacked."

There was a gentle tap on the door which opened when Ondine rang the small silver bell she kept on the table. Frances poked her head around the door: "I-if it p-pleases you, Abbess, Eminence, there are thirty-three of us here. Sister Freya and Sister Geraldine cannot get poor Sister Persephone to stop scrubbing herself. They fear for her, Abbess: she's howling like a banshee."

"She needs sedating," Camus said decisively, reaching into a pocket in his overalls and extracting a small bottle of white pills. "Make her take two of these and bring her here. Don't look so worried, Sister: they're just sedatives. I use them to give me a few hours of sweet oblivion every night and they'll do the same for her. Come, Sister, don't be shy. Take them!"

"Sister Frances!" Ondine ordered curtly. "Do as His Eminence bids but only give her two, do you understand? Two!"

"Y-yes, two, Abbess. I understand," Frances whispered as she crept across to Camus and gingerly took the bottle of pills from his hands. "Thank you, Eminence," she said, bowing deeply and left, once more shutting the door behind her and cutting off the querulous, frightened babble of the Sisters in the corridor.

Camus wearily massaged the back of his neck. "Ach, by the Holy Trinity, it's clear that Michael and I are nothing more than a conduit for the dead but I'll lose my sanity if they don't let me rest for just a few hours."

Ondine stood up with her arms outstretched. "Enough, dear hearts!" she said sternly. "Leave him be for now. You've won: he hears you at long last and he will do as you bid as will I. If you must burden him then burden me for I share his mortal sins!"

A look of horror formed on Camus's haggard face and he reached out a hand to stop her. "Wait, Ondine, you don't know what you're doing! You're opening the Gates of Death!"

She shrugged and turned to look down upon him. "I cannot sense them for all that I sensed the evil in Schimrian's chambers. *Aieee!*" she screeched suddenly and clutched at her chest, struggling for breath. "I see them! I see them! The dead are before me." She pressed her hands to her ears and whimpered: "I cannot shut out so many voices. So much hate!" She crumpled to her knees. "How can you and Michael endure this?"

"Please," Camus begged the invisible horde swirling about the parlour. "You must not press upon us so otherwise we cannot serve your desires! She's a sensitive! In the name of God, you're killing her! Let her go and let us save Ignatius and her Sisters! Let us find the Light-Father and this Surl-child for you!"

She was struggling to breathe as he helped her to her feet. "They've gone for now," he assured her. "I think it's only because we're communicating with them instead of trying to block them out with drugs and alcohol as I've done for six years."

"So many furious souls," she shuddered, grasping his arms for support. "They want revenge upon the Order but they fear Azrael above all else yet they are determined to do battle with him. How they can do that, I know not, but we must help them!"

"Indeed but what else did you learn?"

"They've been doing this to the Brothers in Bede and elsewhere all across the globe. They say they're trying to weaken Azrael's influence but they say he's shielding the Conclave as he needs them to ensure his resurrection." She drew a deep breath before sitting down to drink the rest of her now-tepid tea. "There's one more thing," she whispered, wide-eyed. "Something *terrible*."

"What could *possibly* be more terrible than four billion dead?"

"They call Azrael a *Soul-Eater*. They fear that if he extinguishes sentient life from the face of the Earth then it will be as if mankind and even the Earth itself had never existed! He will absorb all the souls of the dead then move on to other worlds until all of Creation is destroyed and the last star is snuffed out."

"By the Souls of Thirteen Apostles, agnostic philosophers often posited, to much scepticism, that reality exists because of sentience and vice versa. In other words, they saw observation as an act of creation. To think they may have been *right*!"

"I can't understand it any of it," she sighed, placing her hands on her cheeks. "For fear of insanity, my mind recoils from accepting that we're less than insects in the Scheme of Things."

He sat down and ran a hand through his hair in frustration. "Whether or not all this is true, we insects must focus on the tasks in hand: the only way we can get three dozen Sisters out undetected is through the overflow tunnel under Ignatius's tower. It leads to the River Elver to the south and we can strike west along its banks until we reach the forest. Is Ignatius guarded? Where are Pious and his Inquisitors?" He paused as a fusillade of shots echoed and re-echoed about the Great Abbey complex. "Ah, they're training the postulants and novices how to use rifles by the sound of it. Do you have keys to the corridors? Since the Light-Father's attack they've taken to keeping the doors locked."

"Of course we do," she replied, displaying ten large brass keys on a rusty metal ring. "We feed the prisoners, remember?" She selected one. "This opens the corridor door below Schimrian's chambers. Given that Azrael's presence is in those chambers, will you be able to withstand his spiritual pressure?"

"Possibly," he grimaced. "An entity like Azrael must be able to read minds as the Wiccans do so I can only conclude that the dead have shielded me and I pray they will do so again."

"You need to go now," she urged. "Schimrian is setting aside several hours to torture Ignatius *personally*. Find an excuse to go to the Manse and free him. Take him along the south side of the Abbot's lodges and south along the Eastern Cloisters as Tally-men don't patrol there. Go to the Chaste Gate at the east of the Enclave which I'll leave unlocked. We'll wait for you in the main kitchen under the pretence of finishing the midday meals. There's a door to the main sewer which leads to the overflow tunnel."

"Ah, that's a good strategy. We'll meet there at First Bell. That should give me enough time to get Ignatius to the kitchens."

"He's barely able to walk as they've torn out the poor man's toenails and two teeth," she warned him. "But, praise God, they haven't broken any bones or damaged his eyes yet."

"Thank goodness. Gather bundles of food and flasks of water and as many torches as you can find," he advised her. "Get the Sisters to put on trousers and jackets under their habits then they can shed them as we flee. Can you organise this?"

"Of course I can!" she replied haughtily. "This Manse houses the seamstress rooms and the laundry on the ground floor so there are novice and postulate clothes aplenty that will suffice."

"Excellent. Remember to take knives," he told her, brandishing the small handgun he kept in an inside pocket. "This will not be enough to protect us but I can't return to my lodgings to get my other weapons as I'm being watched. I won't have time to sabotage the Abbey Angel either – I pray we won't regret that."

He wanted to tell her about the packs of wolves and Erdethric hybrids sweeping south but he knew that the Sisters would be too terrified to leave if they learned of them. It was truly the proverbial devil and deep blue sea situation but he knew that they stood a far better chance of survival out there than they would at the mercy of the Brothers at the Great Abbey.

"We have no choice, Camus," she insisted, echoing his thoughts. "I couldn't bear it if he died after all that's happened."

"Neither would I," he assured her, listening carefully to the crackle of small arms fire. "It sounds like everyone is in the library gardens – it's the only open space large enough for target practice." He made a face. "I'm sorry but it means we can't rescue any of the postulants. We'll have to pray that God will protect them."

"I understand but my Sisters are in far greater peril than they are right now." She took his hands in hers. "May God protect you!" she said impulsively.

"It's about time He protected *someone*," he replied.

~~~~~

277

Azrael Strikes

"Where are they going?" Harold demanded of Ursaf who was sweating copiously in the afternoon sunshine beating down upon Uppermost. The air was sultry; wisps of steam spiralled upwards as the pavements and tarmac of the merchant town dried out for the first time in six years. The three Bede Angels had hovered briefly above them whilst Ursaf had spoken to the crews on the radio then they'd banked sharply and sped south-westwards.

"They're going to the armouries in Brigstowe," Ursaf explained. "I was wrong about the place being empty. There are still some drums of aviation fuel and chain-gun magazines hidden in one of the warehouses there. I thought I knew Thanewell but when he worked at Brigstowe, he set aside secret stores of ammunition without telling the Fathers there. He confessed that he didn't believe the Conclave would release the Virus and planned to sell them to a notorious clan of weapons merchants."

"So his greed and treachery worked to our advantage then," Harold said sarcastically. "I trust him already."

"You've killed people," Ursaf countered bluntly. "You're in no position to judge Thanewell's morals."

"I *am* in a position to judge. I was dragged into this world and left with no choice but to kill in self-defence and to protect my Scatterlings whereas your Order killed billions without cause. Azrael couldn't cloud all your minds: many in the Order *wanted* to exterminate the Unworthy and did so for *six years!*"

"Not at Bede!" Ursaf protested. "We had *nothing* to do with the Virus, the Inquisitions or the Tally-man program. It was Amherus who decided to convert Unworthy prisoners into slaves so that Brothers could be freed to Inquire of the world. Even saying this is difficult, Light-Father - each word I utter is a needle of guilt in my heart because we did *nothing* to stop it."

Harold grimaced. "There's my problem with Azrael and his geis influencing minds: all he had to do was reinforce a willingness to hide from the truth at Bede. He fostered a belief in the moral and intellectual superiority of the Twelve Tribes whereas the Unworthy were reduced to being less than human; mere laboratory animals to be experimented on or disposed of. This is the classic propaganda theme of the *untermensch;* dehumanising your victims exorcises any remorse you may have about killing them."

"You've told me a little of your world," Ursaf said pointedly. "It's plain your world suffered wars and genocide too."

"Yes, we did. We had fascist regimes and two brutal world wars that killed millions. Given what's happened here, I suspect another Fallen One was at work in my world but, thank God, we didn't have anything as efficient as the Order – at least not yet."

Ursaf mulled this over for a while. "Thanewell and the others are keen to meet you. They apologise for failing to persuade the others from joining them but something happened as they were about to take off..." he fell silent, gazing southwards.

Harold did likewise, shading his eyes. He could not see the hills and moors of the Southern Lands from here as the perimeter walls obscured the view, but the sky was the deepest cobalt blue he had ever seen and utterly cloudless. Here, near the centre of Uppermost, you could imagine those walls marking the finite boundaries of the known universe. Fern had quoted a Milverburg poet at him when he'd mentioned that feeling to her one night: *'From the bowl of merchant gold, fifteen pillars rise like spears, pinning Nut to her blessed hold, as her stars cascade like tears.'* He also knew in his bones that a violent storm-line was forming over Southern Europe fuelled by the moisture and furnace heat of the Equator.

He saw Ursaf's face was grim: "So I take it that Thanewell only managed to escape by the skin of his teeth?" he prompted.

"Another of your strange sayings, Light-Father, but yes, they were lucky. As they boarded the Angels, those others not addled by alcohol had gathered to watch them depart with some berating them and the rest beseeching them to stay and protect them from Aten. As they started up the engines, Thanewell noticed that nine of the Brothers staring blankly at him like Tally-men awaiting instructions from a barrack-computer. It made his blood run cold, he said, when they walked towards him as the blades began to spin up. He said that he and the others in the Angels felt that their willpower was draining away as it did six years ago. They also saw images of sexual violence and depravity; a primal lust stirred in their loins until it became difficult for them to think rationally."

"It sounds as though Azrael was trying to distract them by going for their baser instincts this time round."

"I agree, Light-Father, but you don't understand the full horror of it. These were brethren I've known all my adult life from when Bede was a world-renowned medical-relief airport. These were men who travelled the world on aid programmes, helping others devastated by natural disasters and wars. There were no Unworthy back then just *people*! We had no extremists at Bede but, enthralled as we were, we did not weep when our relatives died or when the winds carried the smell of death from the Southern Cities and rats swarmed across the runways. I fear Azrael will strip away the last shreds of their humanity and turn them into beasts."

"Then how did Thanewell and the others escape if everyone was affected? How did they resist Azrael's compulsions?"

"Ah, Thanewell said they suddenly felt and *heard* the presence of billions of souls about them, shielding them from Azrael's dark will. They were almost overwhelmed by the dead but they rallied quickly when they realised they would be torn apart for there was no way for them to get airborne in time."

Harold noted the misery and grief on Ursaf's face but persisted: "So how come these Brothers failed to stop the Angels from taking off if the blades were still spinning up?"

"They didn't duck."

"Ah," was all Harold could say as the gruesome penny dropped.

"Ah, indeed," Ursaf echoed, wiping at a tear. "I mourn for them: they were reduced to meat-puppets. I suspect it amused Azrael to see their skulls smashed open." He placed his fingertips to his temples and closed his eyes. "I can hear him even now whispering at the edge of my consciousness like a shadow out of the corner of my eye but he has no power over me."

"The dead protect you," Fern said. Both men jumped because it looked as though she had simply materialised out of thin air in front of them clutching her staff and a tray with food set upon it.

"Jesus, Fern!" Harold spluttered. "I wish you wouldn't do that!"

"Forgive me," she grinned impishly. "I was using my illusion-geis to camouflage my approach – I need the practice and I wanted to eavesdrop on your conversation. I can clearly sense a psychic pressure in the direction of Bede. It's been too weak and subtle for us to detect before but now it's powerful. Like a candle becoming a supernova. I fear your Brothers are lost to you, Ursaf."

"Aten will no doubt kill anyone who resists that vile geis," Ursaf seethed, chewing at his lower lip. He clenched a fist: "I will make Schimrian and Aten pay for their deaths!"

"*And so, even in the world of the dead, death still begets more death.*" Fern sighed heavily.

Ursaf smiled and bowed as she laid the tray upon the grass. "I humbly deserve that Tythe quote," he said formally. "But I cannot comprehend how bodiless souls can protect us for all that they've haunted our dreams of late. We thought them to be *gescyldgrimen* – apparitions conjured forth by heavy hearts!"

Fern brandished her black mahogany staff so that he could see the raven set upon it. "This was a gift for Mother Rosemary from the Eirann as she could speak to the dead. The Eirann called her the *Wibrana* – a Bearer of Souls as represented by this raven. You and Michael claim to be empirical men of science yet you hold to the 'reality' of a Holy Spirit on faith alone. Similarly, I believed I had a little of her craft as I've seen the dead on the Paths of Mag Mell for six years *but*," she added, looking sheepishly at Harold. "This day, I've realised that they weren't the dead at all but my own tortured mind conjuring up gescyldgrimen because I failed to save my Ferals and everyone else in this Order-forsaken world."

"About time," Harold declared; the relief evident in his voice.

She rewarded him with a weary smile. "But, even if we cannot see them, the dead are indeed with us. If only Mother Rosemary was here: she could converse with them as a Heliodrammus, standing before the Gates of Death itself."

Ursaf looked at Harold with his eyebrows raised. "I'd heard the Wiccans could do this but I thought it was simply a myth they'd woven about themselves to befuddle the weak-minded."

"But now you think your *ges*- ah!" Harold winced, screwing his eyes shut. "Ah, I must stop doing that!"

"What ails you, Light-Father?" Ursaf asked with some concern, placing a hand on his shoulder.

"Whatever Moss did to program your language into my brain was crude, Ursaf," Harold grumbled, massaging his temples.

Ursaf turned to Fern in some alarm: "Why is he speaking gibberish? Can your craft discern what ails him?"

"What the hell happened to me?" Harold demanded bleakly.

Fern frowned and placed a hand on his forehead. "There is some foul presence at work, Ursaf! I…" She gasped as her arm was flung back, causing her lose her balance. "Azrael!" she cried.

Ursaf took a pace back as a blue light briefly engulfed Harold who was clutching at his head in agony. Faint tendrils of writhing smoke erupted from his ears and nose to be pursued by streamers of blue light intertwining like snakes locked in a death-struggle.

281

Mesmerised, Ursaf reached out a hand to touch the astral forms as the light about Harold faded and he fell to his knees but Fern seized his arm in the nick of time.

"Don't touch them!" she cried out. "Unless you wish to become a psychic battleground! Azrael tried to disconnect the Light-Father from us but he's been driven out by that blue light."

Ursaf helped Harold to his feet as the bizarre combat drifted away from them, fading until nothing was visible. "Then our struggle tomorrow will be physical *and* metaphysical!" he exclaimed. "I wish I could understand Azrael's power; that blue light or the powers you witches wield to bind the senses." He put his lips to Harold's ear: "Are... you... all... right?"

Harold pulled away, scowling. "Don't bellow in my damned ear," he grunted. "Or talk slowly to me as if I'm an *idiot!*"

"He's back to normal," Fern laughed. "As for my illusion-geis: you saw me clearly enough; I simply persuaded your brain to ignore the concept of Fern. Without the concept of ground, for example, what's holding the both of you up?"

Both men staggered as a massive wave of vertigo struck them and they fell down upon something *solid* but they could not remember what it *was* until Fern said simply: "I release you." Suddenly the grasses and soil of the parkland reappeared beneath their bodies. She sat down beside them, enjoying their chagrin and the sun upon her upturned face. "Ah, by the grace of Diana, I hope we have more days of sunshine. I'm so tired of the rain."

Shield and Ursaf's men joined them. Shield had brought them their meals as they'd finished checking several bullet-holes they'd discovered in the fuselages. They listened intently as Ursaf related what had happened at Bede and it was obvious that they shared Ursaf's desire for revenge. They looked at Harold with a new respect when Ursaf explained what had just happened to him.

"How do you feel, Father?" Shield enquired anxiously. "You've just had a Satan inside your head!"

"I feel pretty violated, that's for sure," Harold replied after swallowing some beautifully-cooked fish. He noted with some humility that she'd dropped the 'Light' prefix. "I had this vision of a beautiful transparent being, full of light and sailing from star to star yet being denied Ascension and dragged, full of rage, into a strange kind of *void*. Then I had something *else* inside me fighting him. It's not the first time I've felt those kinds of presences...

spirits or whatever we're going to call them. A sphere similar to the one that brought Azrael here came into my University. It was made of a type of white metal that emitted a blinding light – like a huge arc-welding spark with black swirling shadows around it. It got into my mind telepathically and projected the faces of dead relatives and vile emotions until I could feel its hate like acid eating away at my brain. I could hear its programming - it was definitely insane alright but in a *human* way like Azrael is…"

"The machine here had a canister filled with human brain tissue attached to its processing core," Ursaf pointed out. "So the same may have been true for that device in your world."

"Maybe but it told me it was going to '*purge the world of deviation*' and projected this music into my mind that sounded like whales being tortured until I thought it would blow my head apart. It attacked me but it vanished in a blue-white flash the same colour as those energy ribbons we saw just now."

"I think Nightshade's vision may explain it," Fern interjected.

"In hindsight, the shadows *around* the machine's arc-light might have been a Fallen One like Azrael and it told me, not in *actual* words, that I have this 'fulcrum of destiny' that it could not allow me to fulfil – whatever that means. It told me that there was no God, no Devil, no Allah, no Buddha, no good, no evil, only sentience which it regards as a kind of *disease* to be eradicated. I've had nightmares about that day ever since."

"Then Nightshade's vision *was* right," Fern said brightly. She related the details of Nightshade's astral meeting with Ormuzd and what Azrael's original purpose was in controlling the Order. They all sat in stunned silence, looking at each other in horror.

"How can we fight demons?" Piamadet exploded. "This Ormuzd or whatever she is fights a horde of Satans of which Azrael is just *one* who used us to destroy all mankind!"

"So he really is a Fallen Angel in the true Biblical sense," Spero snarled, clenching a fist: "I'm terrified to the core of my being, Light-Father, but I want to fight him!"

"Ormuzd sent her astral form to save the Light-Father just now," Fern replied. "So we know that she'll help us when she can."

"Mother Moss didn't bring me here then," Harold concluded, somewhat disappointed. "She simply asked Ormuzd who brought me across the planes by using one of those machines. This 'goddess' did it by using plain old science and not magic!"

283

"Perhaps only these machines can cross the veils between worlds," Marcus suggested, finishing the last of his meal with relish. "The devices must adapt to the physical laws of the new reality otherwise they'd break down on an atomic level."

Ursaf exhaled heavily: "Given the existence of such entities, it's no wonder the dead are able to fend off a creature as powerful as Azrael – there are four *billion* of them unable or unwilling to ascend. Perhaps they want revenge above all else."

"I don't pretend to understand the physics of it: I'm just grateful they can help us," Harold stated firmly. "I hope they can hear me say thank you to them because, finally, we know what we're dealing with: we are part of a universal war that spans the whole of Creation. It scares the hell out of me but at least I know what my 'fulcrum of destiny' is: saving what's left of this world so that the dead can finally be at peace." He massaged the bridge of his nose and chuckled ironically. "Hah! No pressure, then!"

"Father, Mouse and I need to talk to Fern about... the *thing* that Michael gave us," Shield pleaded anxiously. "We need to know if what Michael believes about it is true or not."

"Fine," Harold said sympathetically. "But please don't get your hopes up. Let's sort out all the pressing mundane matters first. How are things going down below?"

They listened intently to Fern as the shadows of the nearby Angels slowly crept towards them and their radios crackled faintly. She reported first on the bomb-making and the progress of the intensive searches of the gunsmiths and weapon-shops in the Svartalfheim level. "Marc and Ken report that they will have an arsenal of weapons ready for us by Six Bells."

Harold shielded his eyes to gaze up at the dazzling apex of the Tower of the Sun. "Who's taken first watch up there?" he asked.

"Kai volunteered then Ivy joined him," Fern replied.

"She'd be more useful making bombs or reinforcing the barricade," Harold said with some surprise. "Does she really need to be keeping watch up there with him?"

"Yes," Fern smiled enigmatically. "In a manner of speaking."

Piamadet grimaced suddenly. "Ah, here's a bleak thought, Light-Father: that machine in the Great Annex withstood the explosion and the electrics could be restored at any moment. Unless it's destroyed, Azrael could rise again!"

~~~~~

284

"Why are you here, Mother Ivy?" Kai demanded, his face flushed and his heart pounding. "I volunteered to keep watch up here so that I may reflect upon my sins and the downfall of Abbot Michael. Why are you not down there with the Light-Father?" He could not meet her candid gaze and an image of a faun before a tigress came to mind. "With all due respect, I fear you are here to distract me once more from my vows and my faith."

"The Light-Father is truly extraordinary," Ivy agreed with a smile, laying her staff upon the bed and joining him at the window from where he had been scanning the eastern shorelines with powerful binoculars. "Yet he is but an ordinary man and therein lies the enigma. I am curious. What do *you* see in him?"

He shrugged. "The same as you, I suppose. He seems to salve my soul somehow. I can't explain it but for all that he mourned the young ones, even the Ferals revere him as he talks to them as human beings and not the deformed creatures they are. The Scatterlings also told me of how he came to them in a blazing halo of light and in a few short days, he rekindled their hope enough to attack the Great Abbey with you Wiccans against impossible odds so that Fierce could destroy Azrael. That to me is miraculous."

"It was miraculous. It's no wonder Fern is besotted with him. We could have stayed behind our illusion-geis at our sanctuary in the woods for some time but we knew from Mother Moss that hope would arrive and we had to act. He surpasses us yet he wields no magic but when we summoned his soul to our circle, we saw a soul free of deceit and hatred with a heart large enough to encompass us all – a rare thing in a man. We knew he was of the Seventh Degree; a Herald of Saturn who would save us all."

Kai nodded in agreement. "I know nothing of these pagan Wiccan labels; all I know is that he gives me a reason to live, atoning for my sins by fighting alongside him." His eyes narrowed suspiciously. "So why have you joined me?"

She smiled innocently, clasping her hands behind her back. "Oh, no reason, dear heart; I merely wanted to view this magnificent bedroom before returning to the making of pipe-bombs."

The topmost room of the Tower of the Sun was the sumptuous master bedroom of the matriarch of the leading merchant clan of Milverburg. It had survived the Apocalypse intact with little mildew or rot evident upon the drapes, portraits, gold leaf-covered mouldings and the ornate but decadently decorated ceilings.

"I may have few years, Mother Ivy, but I am aware you desire me carnally. I respectfully decline. I know nothing about the ways of the flesh and you are a Wiccan; a Harlot; a *seductress* that the Fathers warned us about morning, noon and night," he glanced at the clothes neatly folded upon the bed. "Why have you brought those for me? I had hoped that even you would respect my decision to retain my robes as a symbol of my penitence."

"Dear heart," she said, coming close to him and tugging at the fabric. "This does not earn you respect from the Scatterlings even though you acquitted yourself well at the Great Abbey. The Light-Father is right: your decision just brings pain to everyone here who would otherwise welcome you into their family with open arms. There's no excuse: you insult every one of their dead relatives and friends by this misguided obsession that you should eternally repent for events you had absolutely no control over."

He placed the binoculars to his eyes and resumed his searching for enemy Angels. "I can't accept absolution from you in this, Mother Ivy," he said archly. "You yourself admit that you are not of God and regard the Holy Scriptures as *fiction.*"

"No, I never said that," Ivy murmured, taking the binoculars from him. "The Bible and other holy texts contain the Words of the Creator but they're written down by the hand of Man through the distorted lenses of politics and history. I don't need these to keep watch," she whispered, placing the binoculars on the sill and drawing him into her embrace. Her lips drew close to his. "This is as good a time as any to complete your education." He tried to draw away but his will crumbled before a tsunami of desire. "How I feel your heart quicken," she smiled, drawing his robes over his head, leaving him bare-chested and helpless.

She followed suit and his eyes bulged as he beheld her naked breasts. He did not protest as she hurled his robes through an open window where they fluttered from view on the southerly breeze. Neither did he protest as she gently drew him onto the bed where a tiny part of his mind registered that the sheets had been freshly laundered and wondered how this could possibly be so. She removed his boots and trousers and enticed him to remove the last of her clothing and explore her body. History affords them a little privacy regarding their passionate love-making but it notes that Kai felt his all-pervading guilt dissolving like morning mist and he was truly at peace for the first time in his short life.

He lay beside her in a blessed, wondrous post-coital daze, gently caressing her body when she stiffened, her left hand groping for her staff. "What's the matter, Mother Ivy," he asked nervously, snatching his hand away. "Have I offended you?"

"No, dear heart," she assured him, her eyes focussing upon something through the walls. "I sense something down there," she hissed, rushing to the easternmost windows. "I am far-speaking with Fern: Azrael attacked the Light-Father but he's been driven off by the same creature that summoned Nightshade's astral form! Diana save us: there's truly one of the Powers That Be amongst us! Ah! There!" she said, beckoning him to join her. "There's an Angel hovering to the east. Can you see it?"

He grabbed the binoculars and adjusted the focus. "I can see a Father using a telescope. I'm not sure but I think it could be Father Aten. He's a vicious brute of a man."

"So I sense," she grimaced, clenching her right hand. Her brow furrowed with the effort. "I am trying to reach into his mind but there's a mist… a *distortion* about him. *Ahhh!*" There was a silent concussion and she flew past Kai across the room to slam into the quilted headboard of the bed. She landed heavily on the mattress but rolled off and back onto her feet in a fluid motion holding the staff before her. "Azrael! I *deny* thee!" she snarled.

Kai felt the heat drawn from the room and his breath misted. A faint image of a huge floating head composed of billions of tiny human faces in torment formed before the window. A voice composed of soul-searing harmonies spoke: "I despise thee, *insect*," it grated, forcing Kai, cowering, to his knees, his hands covering his ears. "I have Purpose to which thy will *succumb!*"

The Moon symbols on her pendant and atop her staff flared with a searing white light that tore into the apparition. "I deny thee, Fallen One! As a Wiccan; as a *woman* and by the new life now seeded within me!" Embers guttered on the head until a fierce white fire consumed it and it was gone leaving wisps of foul smoke and a necrotic stench. She gasped, leaning on her staff for support. "Ah, I am spent, Kai! Help me to the bed. I must rest!"

He did so and watched her lying there, spread-eagled, gasping in huge lungfuls of air. "You defeated him!" he said, utterly awestruck. "But, um, what did you mean by new life within?"

She placed a hand upon her belly: "Nothing and *everything*."

~~~~~

287

Flight of the Sisters

Ondine looked at her flock aimlessly milling around the kitchen in bleak despair. If any of the Sisters started bleating, she thought savagely, it would not seem out of place. Why had she wasted her life protecting them? For what reward? These endless blank looks and vacuous ninny smiles; orders kept simple without a hint of ambiguity otherwise disasters would inevitably occur. She was so far above these creatures intellectually yet she'd been cajoled, seduced, bamboozled in spending her adult life trammelled in a cage of prayer and duty to these... these *imbeciles*.

Just getting them all to undress and put on shirts, stout work-jackets, trousers and field boots had been an ordeal taking nearly an hour and now they all moaned and whinnied about being too hot with their habits over these clothes. She'd tried and tried to explain clearly and simply that they had no choice but to escape but they just twittered with fear and indecision:

"We can't go down there, Abbess. It's *unclean*!"

"It's so hot and smelly down there!"

"Why aren't we finishing the meals?"

"Do we *have* to carry these bundles of food?"

"Why weren't you taking midday prayers, Abbess?"

"How do these torches work, Abbess?"

Ondine realised that she was grinding her teeth as a speechless, relentless fury boiled in her heart. Where the hell was Camus? It was ten minutes to First Bell and there was no sign of the fool. Who cares about Ignatius? He's old. He got caught too easily! She quailed at the notion of leading these cretins into the woods as they'd probably wander off witless in all directions. She was leaning against a table with a chopping board and she realised that her left hand had reached behind her, almost of its own volition, to grasp a long knife that settled sweetly into the palm of her hand as if it was destined to become an extension to her body.

Her mind was full of images of that knife rising and falling; rising and falling bringing forth a beautiful rain of crimson *silence*. All she had to do was stab thirty-six times and she would be free of this brainless babble for ever. A sharp cry of anguish snapped her out of her black trance and she hastily released the knife, clutching at her chest, almost doubled over in shock. She bared her teeth: "Azrael!" she hissed. "How *dare* you violate me!"

She saw Sister Persephone sitting, huddled in a corner with her arms around her knees despite the patient coaxing and cajoling of Geraldine and Freya. She was still naked, refusing to touch male garments and her limbs clearly covered with bruises from blows and restraints. Her anus and vagina were still bleeding.

"There," Ondine growled under her breath. "Is thy legacy, O Fallen One! The extinction of innocence and the extinction of life itself: is this what brings you comfort in the Void? How *petty*! Begone from my mind, demon, for I *deny* thee."

Like viscous tar she felt that vile presence slough away from her and she almost collapsed, clutching onto the table for support. She turned to see Persephone staring at her, her eyes as wide as saucers. "A shadow," she gasped, pointing. "Abbess, there was a dark shadow all about you and it was *whispering* to me: telling me how I deserved to be raped and how worthless I am. It said I deserved death then I saw you pick up that knife!"

Ondine shuddered. "*He* was trying to possess me, my daughter," she said through clenched teeth. "Trying to fill me with his hatreds but I've driven him from me. Ah, I feel so *tainted*, dear heart, but he's made you suffer far more than I. Come, let me tend to your wounds. It's going to sting but I must apply salve and antiseptics to your injuries then I will dress you. Will you comply?"

She held out her hand but Persephone laid her forehead on her knees. "Take up thy knife, Abbess, and slay this Unworthy vessel. I am no use to God and Jesus like this! They did not save me from defilement as they clearly think me Unworthy!"

Ondine was brutal: she stepped forward and hauled Persephone over to one of the sinks where there was a medical kit she'd opened earlier to check the contents. "I have no time for this, my daughter," she insisted. "This has always been the lot of countless women in this patriarchal world for millennia so you are not the first but, as God is my witness, you *will* be the last!"

The kitchen fell silent as Ondine saw to the cuts and abrasions, rubbed salve into the intimate wounds, and a healing gel on the developing bruises. She dressed the trembling Sister until she looked like a postulant as all the Sisters kept their hair short. She cupped Persephone's face in her hands and kissed her forehead. "You'll survive, child," she assured her firmly, almost nose to nose. "You'll never forget this violation nor should you for it is now part of you. With your sisters and I beside you, you'll grow stronger than the memory; you'll grow strong enough to forgive those who sinned against you and become whole again. It will take time but we will be with you on this journey! Do you understand?"

"Yes, Abbess," Persephone whispered, her voice hoarse from hours of screaming and her skin raw from the scrubbing. "I will escape the shadow of the Evil One. I will survive."

"Good! You must be a sensitive to have seen his presence, my daughter," she said softly. "What is it, now?"

She followed Persephone's fear-stricken gaze and saw, standing in the corridor portal, two Brothers bearing rifles and spears - the same two that had almost caught the Scatterlings in the bell-tower. Her heart almost stopped from sheer dread. It was so *unfair*. They were going to be killed or worse before they'd even had a chance to escape. "God, why hast thou forsaken us?"

Cyrus smiled a predatory smile at the cowering Sisters: "*I give them eternal life,*" he intoned, stretching out a hand. "*And they will never perish, and no one will snatch them out of my hand. My Father, who has given them to me, is greater than all, and no one is able to snatch them out of the Father's hand.*"

Luke nodded approvingly. "Amen," he said.

~~~~~

The door to Redemption Cell corridor had opened easily enough after a bowel-loosening mistake with the wrong key. Camus had his handgun at the ready but he'd slung several rifles and filled a shoulder bag with spare ammunition from the Manse armoury by the corridor entrance. He now rattled and clanked alarmingly as he tiptoed down the corridor where all the cell doors were open bar one. He noted with revulsion the blackened pools of blood on the floors of the corridor and the cells and the bloody finger-smears of injured and dying men upon every wall.

The neon strip-lights flickered and buzzed like swarms of angry bees adding to the hellish nature of the place. He could feel a monstrous spiritual weight pressing down upon him, his knees buckling as he approached the door. He was nothing but an insect, a crawling defecator upon the virgin earth...

He shook himself free of the thrall but a quote from Revelations surfaced in his mind as he fumbled with the cell key and he spoke aloud: "*But the beast was captured, and with it the false prophet who had performed the signs on its behalf. With these signs he had deluded those who had received the mark of the beast and worshipped its image…"*

A quavering voice within answered: *"The two of them were thrown alive into the fiery lake of burning sulphur."*

"Ignatius! Thank God you're alive!" Camus exclaimed, rushing to untie the naked old man from the Inquisition Table.

He was stained with blood and faeces and covered with welts and bruises innumerable but his voice was strong. "Bless you, Eminence, but you'll have to carry me as my circulation has been somewhat compromised by their enthusiasm. Unh! I apologise for my toiletry shortcomings but they cared little for my hygiene. Father Aten and Abbot Pious are such uncouth fellows."

"I care not, old friend," Camus said, weeping openly. "We stood idle while Hell formed around us but now there's hope!"

"It's a pity," Ignatius croaked, as Camus carried the old man in his arms down the corridor. "I understood Great-Abbot Schimrian was coming to share afternoon tea with me. I so love scones."

"You need to stop rambling, Ignatius," Camus urged as they reached the armoury. There was a sink and using paper towels and cloth he cleaned the shaking, swaying Brother as best he could. He dressed him with clothes from several Unworthy victims that he'd found in a large storage space behind the weapons-racks and laced boots upon his feet then he made Ignatius drink as much water as he could stomach. Despite retching pitifully, he kept it down.

Camus froze as a spear-tip was tapped upon his shoulder when everyone was supposed to be practicing at the Library! There was a chuckle as Brother Luke set his spear upright then he too selected a rifle. "We were sent to fetch more rifles but Father Theo told us to follow you if we saw you so we did."

"We had dreams," Cyrus explained, foregoing his usual penchant for quotations. "My mother came to me and told me that she and the rest of my family were watching over me and they wanted me to help this Light-Father. We've seen the same ghosts you have, Eminence. I'm sorry we didn't believe you."

"I saw my dead family, too," Luke nodded, handing Cyrus a rifle and an ammunition belt. "They've only been able to break through into the Great Abbey after Schimrian's monster was defeated in the Great Annex but this devil is slowly regaining its strength."

"It's our only chance to escape," Cyrus added.

"We could feel him trying to poison our souls," Luke continued, steadying a grateful Ignatius. "But the countless dead that you and Abbot Michael could see are shielding us. There was dreadful talk at the Library of storming the Sisters' Enclave once that undead abomination, Pious, was satisfied with their weaponry progress. Far from decrying such a sin, he told them it was their reward; their holy duty to impregnate the Sisters before they set out upon the Last Great Inquisition at dawn tomorrow."

"Azrael controls them just as we corrupted and controlled the Tally-men," Camus grunted as he and Cyrus half-carried Ignatius down the stairs. "Thus irony and karma are the twin pillars of our nightmare." The exit was next to his office which gave him such an incongruous pang of nostalgia that he laughed out loud.

Cyrus smiled as if reading his thoughts: "*Godly sorrow brings repentance that leads to salvation and leaves no regret, but worldly sorrow brings death. We, too, are leaving all we've ever known. We know not if we tread the Path Righteous or a bridge built of crumbling bones set high above the Abyss.*"

"Corinthians *and* Parsifal," Ignatius chuckled as the Great Bell tolled once. "I taught you two well as postulants, did I not?"

"Seeing you abused like this dispels all doubt," Cyrus declared fiercely. "New Jerusalem was but a deceit that made us murderers and now, out there before Pious's dead eyes, *they howl as one for blood and flesh. They are demons all bar hooves and horns.*"

"Tythe again," Ignatius chuckled as they went as fast as they could down the Cloisters. "How the echoes of civilisation stir my aching bones! I must meet this Light-Father!"

"It was a relief to see you, Eminence," Luke admitted. "We thought we were the last free souls in the Great Abbey. We were going to arm ourselves and steal a half-track but we found you by happenstance. I presume you have an escape plan?"

"Yes," Camus said, wisely keeping the details to himself. "There's no such thing as happenstance in this brutal dystopia, my son. The dead must have guided you to our meeting."

Luke unslung the loaded rifle he was carrying and held it one hand and his spear in the other. "Possibly but it's lucky that the Light-Father failed to destroy the Manse armoury - these spears are all but useless in battle."

They were through the sturdy oaken doors of the Chaste Gate but Camus suddenly felt a powerful urge to turn back and lock them then pocket the key. As they headed past the Abbess Manse they heard dozens of novices hammering on the doors as they'd slipped away from weapons training having decided not to wait for nightfall. Camus could hear their demands and pleas for entrance mixed with chilling threats of physical and sexual violence. "Dear God," he shuddered. "Cyrus was right."

He entered the kitchen, still supporting Ignatius, a few moments after Luke and Cyrus had entered and saw the mortified expressions on the faces of the Sisters. "I'm sorry we startled you, Ondine," he apologised quickly. "Fear not, Luke and Cyrus are with us. The dead have reached out to them and warned them to leave before Azrael regains control of their minds."

"The stupid bull-pats could have said so! They nearly gave me a heart attack!" Ondine fumed then she saw Ignatius and immediately guided him to a chair. "He needs calories! Freya, dear heart, put honey on some bread and butter. We can't leave until he has energy inside him. We can't carry him in the sewers."

"Ah, off the skillet and into the kack!" Luke groaned comically. "We were going to steal half-tracks," he pointed out.

Camus saw Persephone trembling by the sink, propped up by Geraldine. Instinctively he went over to comfort her but she pulled away, cringing and weeping uncontrollably. Geraldine held up a field-calloused hand to forestall him. "Forgive me, Eminence," she frowned. "She knows you mean well but countless men and boys forced themselves upon her and you are a man, after all."

"Ah, this might be a problem," Camus said to Ondine as he stepped back. "We can't have her shrieking like that as we flee. I need to give her a stronger sedative, Sister Geraldine. He fished out a red vial from the medical kit. Make her swallow this pill. She'll be sleepy for a few hours but still able to run if needs be. Ondine, novices are clawing at the Chaste Gate already but the doors there are stout enough to resist them for now."

"I've already locked and barred the other two Enclave gates," she assured him. "They'll need battering rams."

"The walls can easily be climbed," he reminded her. "We need to buy as much time as we can."

She nodded and barred the kitchen door then locked the main door at the end of the hallway. Luke carried several tables and jammed them between the porch inner wall and the door under her direction. She returned to the kitchen to brusquely order the Sisters to discard the habits that they now no longer needed. She carefully dragged the narrow corridor table to one side so as not to topple the lit candlesticks. At her command, Luke shoulder-charged the door and the props and wedges Peter had placed there failed easily. Camus had just finished bandaging a gash in Ignatius's arm when he noticed that the shooting had stopped.

"We have to move NOW!" he roared. "They must know we plan to escape. Either they've found the Redemption Cell empty or Azrael is influencing them but there's a foul wave surging towards us. Hurry! Hurry!" he urged, literally hurling the Sisters and Ignatius through the door. "They're coming!"

He drew the table into place, taking care not to disturb the lit candlesticks. He and Cyrus dragged everything off the shelves and piled the heavier shelving units up against the door before descending the steps to the wine cellar.

Luke had already notice the makeshift beds in the torchlight and the stale bread upon the table. "Aha!" he crowed. "Here's the nest of our saboteurs!" then he shone his torch upon the wine-racks. "So you did help them as they say, you old rascal! It was selfish of you to keep this place secret: there are some excellent vintages!"

"I know," Ignatius said sadly, patting a bottle like an old friend. "Perhaps, one day, we'll come back and reclaim them."

"Let's move!" Ondine barked. The cellar was crowded with frightened Sisters clinging to each other and a smiling, drowsy Persephone declaring her undying love for Freya. "I'll take the lead with twelve Sisters including Persephone and Geraldine. Eminence, you take Ignatius and the next twelve then Cyrus with his twelve and Luke at the rear. Is that acceptable?"

"Aye, Abbess," Luke grunted sourly. "The rearguard is always the first to get killed in all the war sagas but I'll give a good account of myself: you have my oath on it."

"Thank you," she said gratefully.

Despite the foetid darkness, they felt their spirits lighten the further they got from the Great Manse. It was difficult to herd the disoriented Sisters up the four feet of rungs into the overflow tunnel that opened out onto the River Elver a mile to the south but once in the tunnel, they made good speed despite Persephone's rambling euphoria and Ignatius's injuries. Camus swore that the old man was regaining his stamina at an amazing rate as they scuttled along the cylinder of dancing and flaring torch-shadows.

The old man smiled at him as if reading his thoughts: "The beatings and losing my toenails was bad enough but that thing was in my *mind*," he explained, tapping his temple. "He drew pleasure from every moment of agony. A despicable creature but strangely, for all his ancient hatreds, I told him that I pitied him. He did not like that," he chuckled. "But his grip upon my soul weakened at that point as if he had nothing to hang onto. I think a mind free of hate, revenge and desire is a poison to him."

"So when he has no physical form, he can only magnify the existing flaws in a heart to control that person. That's useful to know," Camus assured him, pointing ahead. "There, Ignatius! It's the proverbial light at the end of the tunnel!"

"Um, I think I can hear rushing water behind us," Ignatius noted fearfully. Others behind them had also heard the dull roaring sound which was rapidly growing in volume. "It can't be a flash flood as there's no rain so what's making that sound?"

Camus gasped as the awful answer struck him: "They've opened the sluices of the Abbey Reservoir! Everybody! We need to fly as fast as Hermes!" Even as he said it, he felt the first three inches of water impacting his boots followed by a dull whoosh of air as the waters in the sewer submerged the mouth of the overflow tunnel. "Everyone!" he cried. "Sit down and put your hands on the back of your heads and take a deep breath: we're going for a ride!"

~~~~~

"Shield?" Harold said. "Can you bring it down from here?"

"No, Light-Father," she replied, reverting to his formal title in front of Ursaf and the others whilst aiming her cross-bow at the distant Bede rotorcraft. "It's at least another three furlongs beyond the perimeter walls. It's too far. I can't reach it."

Pity," Spero said. "If only we had Glascae's sniper rifles, we could at least make them back off. It has to be Aten on a reconnaissance flight: he's supposed to be as smart as he is vicious. By the time we fire up the engines, he'll be long gone."

"What about you, Mother Fern?" Piamadet asked hopefully. "You Wiccans took out our rotorcraft in Beorminghas and Crawcester easily enough. I'd love to see how you do it!"

Fern did not reply as she was staring up at the Tower of the Sun with a worried expression on her face. "My nerves are still jangling after that begiuller hit me so I can't reach into the pilot's mind," she explained. "Either I'm still too weak or Azrael is shielding their minds from me but I do sense they're full of hatred and... darker things but not Aten: he is, as you say, a monster by his own design." She put her fingertips to her temples and concentrated then gasped in awe: "Ivy tried to read Aten's mind but Azrael attacked her. She drove him out of the tower somehow!"

"Does she need medical assistance?" Ursaf enquired.

"No it was a psychic assault not a physical one but young Kai is with her. He's now... um, seeing to her needs."

Despite the danger and the enemy rotorcraft to the east, Harold found himself smiling at Fern who was blushing furiously with a hand to her cheek. He wrapped his arms around her waist and kissed her tenderly on the other cheek. "I think you need to stop eavesdropping on them. Talk to Ivy later and see what she found out about Azrael. As you said, she managed to drive him off: I'd like to know how she did that."

She kissed him briefly on the lips. "As would I, dear heart."

Harold turned to Ursaf. "Get on the radios and warn Thanewell and the others not to approach until that bastard up there is gone. He's seen the two Angels and us clearly enough but I want them to think Thanewell has deserted to one of the Southern Cities. His rotorcraft will come in very useful tomorrow."

Shield shaded her eyes. "It's moving south now I think."

"Damn it," Harold fumed. "They'll be checking on the Brothers guarding the causeways and they'll probably scope out the dock gates as well. It's what I would do: look for a weakness. Fine, let them see the barricades!"

"Shall I go to one of the towers, Mother Fern? If he comes too close, he might be vulnerable enough for me to take him down."

"No, Shield," Fern said firmly. "You'd be alone if Azrael lashed out at you. See? The Angel is retreating eastwards now."

"Trust me, Shield," Harold grimaced, rubbing at his forehead. "You don't want that *thing* inside your head! I saw something warping these huge star-creatures, dragging them into this..." he shrugged, at a loss for words. "Void I suppose. There were billions of them all crushed together and resenting their fate. I have no idea why Azrael showed me this. It doesn't make sense."

Ursaf sucked at a tooth thoughtfully. "Might be a race memory," he suggested. "Perhaps they were trying to ascend when something went horribly wrong and they were cast into the Abyss."

"As it says in the Book of Peter," Marcus intoned, folding his arms. *"For if God did not spare sinning angels, but thrust them down into Tartarus, and delivered them into chains of darkness, being reserved to judgement."*

"Yes, that's exactly the 'feeling' I got as if he was trying to justify cosmic genocide," Harold nodded. "We'll have to trust the Wiccans to keep him at bay tomorrow as we'll have our hands full dodging spears, bullets and all sorts of *physical* death. Marcus? Can you let Thanewell know it's safe to return?"

As Marcus complied, Harold fretted about the Angels. "If they attacked this evening or at dawn they could catch the Angels on the ground and wipe us out. Does anyone have any ideas? Fern, Ivy and Nightshade have to defend the viaducts."

"I'll be with Ken Glascae and the snipers at dawn," Shield confirmed. "It may be difficult to stop them strafing Uppermost once they clear the perimeter walls but at close range I can destroy them as my element is air and I am awakened unto it."

"We need more lead time," Ursaf reminded them. "We could keep one Angel airborne at all times but we're low on fuel. We can't use the athidol here; it has to be aviation grade fuel."

"Can you 'far-see' yet?" Harold asked Shield.

"No," Shield admitted gloomily. "I cannot 'far-talk' either. I don't know how. Mother Fern? Can you teach me?"

"You are of the craft, dear heart," Fern assured her, grasping her by the shoulders. "Close your eyes and imagine the Milverbore in your mind. Can you see it? Concentrate. Shut off all physical senses and let your mind soar like a bird. What do you see?"

"Sea birds," Shield gasped. "I can feel the wind beneath their wings, *my* wings. Oh, I am one with a bird! Now I'm moving east. I see the Angel heading for Bede. There's a darkness shrouding the Great Abbey that's *watching* me. Azrael! I'm moving south. I see trees and something in the River El... *ulp!*" She opened her eyes in horror and began vomiting copious amounts of clear water, sinking to her knees and struggling to breathe.

"Fern! Do something!" Harold cried out. "She's *drowning!*"

~~~~~

Revelations

Pious stood silently before Schimrian's desk flanked by the stony-faced Father Dreorman and the diminutive, effeminate form of Brother Brodiglede. It was obvious the Great-Abbot had availed himself of several brandies as a ruddy glow suffused his high-boned cheeks but, nevertheless, his eyes were as cold as ice. Brodiglede swallowed nervously as he thought he could sense another presence superimposing itself upon Schimrian's physical form. He'd glanced up at the ribbed ceiling on entering the chambers only to find every carved angel's face was now a demonic mask of hatred glaring down at him.

He had to shake his head as he thought it was a trick of the restored electric lighting but a second glance confirmed that the desecration of the angels was *real*. He felt as though the nervous perspiration trickling down his spine was solidifying into a glacier as Schimrian finally spoke, his left hand resting upon a revolver. A drawn sword was also laid upon the desk before him.

"What happened out there, old friend?" Schimrian demanded of Pious. "Father Leored reported to me that you've willingly aroused the lustful desires of our novices and younger Brothers against our beloved and chaste Sisters! Sister Persephone was assaulted and *raped*! This is an insult to every tenet of the Order!" Spittle flew from his lips. "Then I find the Redemption Cell empty and Camus missing! I have also heard via our restored communications systems that the Sisters' Enclave has been barricaded shut! Can you enlighten me as to these events? Hmm?"

Pious gazed up at the ceiling for several seconds as if listening to a radio before returning his attention to the Great-Abbot. "We must restore our Holy Number, Eminence," he said, his voice evoking sensations of graveyard breezes. "Forgive me if I inflamed our young brethren by reminding them of the sole purpose of our Sisters in that endeavour. I personally went to console Sister Persephone as soon as the training was concluded but, as you've heard: the gates to the Enclave were locked and barred as were the doors to the Abbess Manse and the kitchens. I've ordered Fathers Theo and Edward to lead a search of the Enclave but they've not found a trace of Camus, the Abbess, Ignatius or the Sisters."

"This is not what I want to hear. Why did you send Father Dreorman through the North Gate to empty our reservoir?"

Pious sighed patiently, the sound uncannily reminiscent of handfuls of dried leaves being crushed and rubbed together. "Forgive me for acting precipitously, Eminence, but given the damage caused out by those saboteurs, I assumed Camus and Ignatius and whoever else is with them would resort to further treachery so the simplest solution was to flush away the infestation from beneath out feet."

"Why wasn't Ignatius guarded?" Schimrian seethed. "I gave *specific* instructions that he be guarded at all times!"

"It was Father Leored's domain but in his defence, you also *specifically* instructed us to train every single novice and Brother, Eminence," Pious retorted. "And in that regard, we have succeeded. The Brothers and novices appear to be free of doubt and fear for the first time in my experience. They are of firm resolve and thirst for revenge against this Light-Father tomorrow."

"So along with the kack, you've also flushed away the Abbess and all the surviving Sisters! How is that master-stroke supposed to populate our New Jerusalem, hmm?"

"We haven't finished searching the Enclave yet," Father Dreorman nervously explained. "We may find the Sisters hiding in the Manse. Of course, we must find a way to protect them from the excess of passion stirring amongst our Brethren. We could house them within our Redemption Cells, Eminence, to be guarded by the most mentally, um, *disciplined* of us."

"Pray that they are unharmed, my son," Schimrian snarled making the bearded Dreorman pale visibly. "Or you will personally retrieve their bodies from the sewers and inhume them."

"I p-pray that I will not need to do that, Eminence," Dreorman stammered, sweating profusely. He too became acutely conscious of the disfigured angels above his head. "I am sure we'll find them safe and sound... apart from poor Sister Persephone, of course."

"Of course," Schimrian said icily. He steepled his fingers briefly than laid both hands upon the blade of his sword. "I order the three of you to dissuade our brethren from any such lusts and desires in future until such a time as I deem appropriate. Then I shall arrange with the Abbess that such affairs are conducted with due respect for her lambs. Do I make myself clear, my sons?"

"Yes, Eminence," they chorused, bowing their heads.

"Good. Now please update me as to Bede. Has Abbot Aten and his two Brothers bolstered their wavering hearts?"

"Aye, Eminence," Dreorman responded quickly. "However, he regrets that twelve Brothers have deserted to the Southern Cities in three Angels after callously slaying nine of their brethren. All of Bede's Tally-men were confined to their barracks and he found secure cells with ten completely deranged Brothers confined within them. He has five Angels and twenty Brethren at his disposal and has already flown a sortie to the Queen of Babylons as Cwellor sobered up the drunken Brothers and novices. He found two intact Angels in the park at the centre of Uppermost. He saw Ursaf and several other Brothers with the Light-Father alongside them. He surveyed Milverburg, Eminence, and reports the dock-gates are closed and the entrance tunnels barricaded."

"Traitors all!" Schimrian hissed, shaking his fist. "Why did he not open fire upon treacherous Ursaf and his new master?"

"He perceived the influence of Wiccans in his mind and did not want to be bewitched into crashing the rotorcraft so he withdrew. They believe the two Angels that Camus sent to Wealthorpe were shot down by Ursaf's two rotorcraft and their crews lost to us."

Schimrian massaged his eyes. "Please, God, give me strength to endure this torment! If only we could have saved my beloved Azrael from that Unworthy brat! They have taken Azrael and our New Jerusalem from us, my sons but we'll have revenge on this foul creature that calls himself Light-Father! We leave at Five Bells tomorrow so what news of the arrangements, hmm? Will these Erdethric hybrids be a problem, my sons?"

Pious nodded at Dreorman who answered: "No, Eminence. Even though half our Norton brethren were overwhelmed en route and Burslen Abbey attacked, Father Hvretsope at Wealthorpe reports no sign of them along the northern shores of the Milverbore but he is fortifying the hamlet in case they come at him in the night. He has begiullers and he found that they are effective at keeping them at bay. He claims that he and all thirty Brothers-Martial are looking forward to commencing your Great Inquisition tomorrow."

"Ah, finally I have some good news to assuage the doubts and turmoil within my heart. What of the other causeways?"

"A half-track with two of our Brothers-Martial has already been sent towing a field-artillery unit to Cwiclasc and another to Drytenham. Wyehold lost a Father-Martial and fifteen Brothers-Martial at Wealthorpe but they've still mustered two Fathers-Martial and thirty Brothers-Martial at Cwiclasc. They also have

Father-Martial Awrecai and twenty Brothers-Martial at Drytenham but they've added another twenty armed novices and Brothers-Technician to reinforce their numbers there."

Pious tore his gaze away from the ceiling. "I believe we should send all our Angels in half an hour before midday to see if we can destroy Ursaf's machines on the ground before ferrying our Brothers-Martial into Uppermost. We'll have our Wyehold brethren feint along their viaducts just before midday whilst we four lead the main thrust from Wealthorpe after destroying the barricade in the entrance tunnel. Is this satisfactory, Eminence?"

"Yes, I endorse this plan," Schimrian said, pursing his lips. "But I *will* be taking Compline this evening so please ensure *everybody* is there! My sermon will be focused upon the sins of carnal desire so I expect three of you to be in the front pew!"

They bowed without reply and turned to leave after Schimrian had waved a hand in dismissal. As Dreorman reached the door, the Great-Abbot called after him: "As I said, my son, if no Sister is found alive, you *will* spend the night searching the sewers."

Dreorman's shoulders sagged as a sudden and murderous rage burned in his heart at this unnecessary humiliation: "As you wish, Eminence." He glanced up at the angels to find their expressions were now ones of sadistic mirth and he retreated from the chambers quickly, his heart hammering wildly in his chest.

He found Pious waiting for him in the corridor.

"Azrael is with him, my son, yet he knows it not," Pious said, with an ironic half-smile. "He's sustained by the spirit of our archangel as am I although I cannot fathom the craft of it."

Dreorman collected his thoughts quickly as his natural sadistic demeanour returned. He grinned maliciously: "Yes, I was aware of his presence in the chambers as are so many Brothers and novices yet I crave this Inquisition, Eminence. I wish to prove myself to you, to the Great-Abbot and to Azrael who watches over us. I care not what the weak-minded Brothers say; our New Jerusalem *shall* be built upon the bones and ashes of the Unworthy."

Pious placed a hand upon the shoulder of his most trusted Inquisitor causing Dreorman's knees to buckle briefly. He wheezed in two lungfuls of air to speak in a voice as desiccating as a Saharan simoom: "Then your heart beats for the two of us, my son."

~~~~~

301

Fern knelt next to Shield as she sat upon the grass spewing endless gushes of water that erupted like fountains from her mouth. Fern placed her hands upon her temples and chanted repeatedly in a forgotten tongue which grated upon the ears: "*klew mewe workomendw gentisc: adsoro kwu tu askornane!*"

"Where the *hell* is all that water coming from?" Harold cried, placing his hands on top of his head in impotent despair.

Shield arched her back briefly, gazing sightlessly up at the blue sky then she coughed up the last of the water from her lungs and slumped backwards. Fern laid her gently down upon the long, coarse grass and repeated the chant making Harold's skin crawl as he felt as if his brain wanted to leave his skull via his eye sockets. He knelt down by the unmoving, unresponsive Shield and took her pulse. There was none. "Ah! Damn it all to hell, Fern, why'd you let her do this? She's had no training!" he snapped, pressing the palms of his hands down upon Shield's sternum and pumping.

"The Wiccan soul goes where it wills," Fern said helplessly. "If only Mother Rosemary was still alive: she could have saved her! I'm sorry, Harold: she's already passed beyond the Gates of Death. I can't bring her back as we did with Mouse!"

Harold uttered a searing profanity before inflating Shield's lungs and after what seemed like an eternity of pumping, she gasped and drew a great shuddering breath and blinked her eyes. She sat up, clutching at him and shaking violently. "I was drawn to them for a *reason*, Light-Father!" she cried out. "I was drawn to them as flood water hurled them down a tunnel and into the River Elver!"

She released Harold to grip Fern by her forearms: "We have to rescue them, Mother Fern! They're being washed up on an island in the river but some of the Sisters have drowned! That's all I know. I feel so peculiar; like I'm not fully back in my body!"

"That will pass, dear heart," Fern assured her as Harold and Ursaf hovered nearby. "Harold," she insisted, looking up at him. "We need to take the Angels to that island and rescue them."

"If we can," Harold replied coolly, still fuming at her for giving up so easily on Shield. "I want to save them too but we'll have the Bede Angels to contend with."

"They could still die here," Ursaf pointed out. "They may have a better chance of surviving there than we do here." He flinched as Fern stood up to glare at him and brandish her staff. "I can sense Thanewell and the others returning from Brigstowe. The three of us

302

will come with you in case you're intercepted by Aten. I know you'll have to fly far to the south to avoid detection by Bede and I know that will use up your precious aviation fuel but we will *not* abandon refugees from the Great Abbey."

Ursaf shaded his eyes and gazed to the southwest. "Yes, you're right: here they come now. I'm sure Thanewell will want to rescue the Sisters anyway. He's related to the Abbess, apparently."

"How many survivors did you see, Shield?" Harold asked her.

Shield looked up at him. "At least thirty Sisters and four men I think, Light-Father. I can't be sure as this is the first time I've ever done this. It was chaos: I was in one mind and then another and then another as they were fighting the current to get to the island. This is how Mother Moss described astral projection to me but I never thought it would be this strange and this dangerous." She shuddered, pressing her face into her hands. "I was drawn to a Sister as she was drowning so I felt I was drowning with her yet I was here as well. It was horrendous! All her life memories flashed before my eyes and I experienced her fear as all the Brothers turned on them this morning. They were like animals; pawing at them, groping them and one Sister was *gang-raped.*"

Ursaf made a wry face at the news: "Thirty-four altogether. Each Angel can carry ten people so it shouldn't be a problem," he ventured thoughtfully. "It sounds as though they were flushed out of the main sewer overflow tunnel leading south underneath the Angel Compound. I know this island downstream where the Elver divides: there's a large house with lawns upon it so we should be able to land there if they're not too overgrown." He paused to look down at Shield: "If what you far-saw in that poor Sister's mind is true then no wonder they were forced to flee. Dear Lord, the evil festering there is beyond belief... beyond mere *words...*" he trailed off, shaking his head slowly in bewilderment.

"I sensed Azrael at the Great Abbey, Mother Fern. I think he was aware of me but he was unable to stop me."

"Ivy weakened him somehow," Fern explained, glancing at Harold with a deep sadness: she did not need to read his thoughts to know how displeased he was with her – no more than she was with herself: "Did you see anything else along the River Elver? Were there any Brothers on the banks of the river?"

"No but I saw wolves on the north bank and I saw some strange Ferals with them," Shield said, closing her eyes and searching her mind for those images now fading as fast as a dream at daybreak. "They were shrouded in this... this *shadow*. There's nothing in their hearts but a desire to kill every living thing by fang and claw. They're Azrael's creatures, I'm sure of it. I saw deer, foxes and boars torn to pieces in the woods behind them. I saw..."

Harold raised a hand to silence her as Thanewell's Angels clattered above them and made ready to land. "That's enough, Shield," he shouted as rotor downdrafts whipped the long grasses this way and that and tore the heads from the wild flowers about them. "I promise you we'll save them from those creatures."

As Ursaf and Spero guided the three Angels in to land, her expression became somewhat hysterical and she gripped his hands: "I far-saw, Light-Father, I did it! I astral-projected! I really am a Wiccan! I really do have the craft!"

"That's wonderful," Harold said, straining to be heard above the noise of the Angels. "But it almost killed you! Remember that! I have no idea how all that water got into your lungs so we need to work out how that happened before you try it again. I can't advise you but even a dull technician like me knows that being inside the mind of a dying person is an incredibly bad idea."

They watched the Angels land and Ursaf, Piamadet, Spero and Marcus greeting Thanewell and his eleven companions with open arms. Harold smiled at the vigorous camaraderie and back-slapping that was going on: his little army was growing quickly! He turned to see Fern staring at him intently. "How did you bring her back, Light-Father?" she demanded. "I could not sense her essence on this side of the Gates of Death! How did you do it?"

"Seriously?" he demanded incredulously. "You don't have CPR in this world? You're kidding me! It's a basic technique to keep a heart attack victim alive until the ambulance crews arrive!"

Fern looked deeply puzzled and pronounced the acronym with difficulty: "Ch-pr-rurr? What is that?"

"Cardio-pulmonary resuscitation," he explained patiently, hoping that it translated well. "The compressions pump blood through the heart and oxygen into the brain. Usually, a young drowning victim like Shield will recover quickly even though her heart had stopped. Honestly? You Wiccans have never heard of this?"

Ursaf had approached to report and overheard them. "You can't blame her for thinking Shield was dead, Light-Father; the Order kept most of its medical knowledge and techniques from them and the rest of the world. One whole Tribe of us were surgeons of the finest calibre so we created a medical monopoly and held entire governments to ransom. That's how we grew so powerful."

"Well, thank you for that, Ursaf," Harold smiled coldly. "It just makes it even harder for me to forgive you all."

"That's your prerogative," Ursaf sighed heavily. "I know it's not my place but I think you owe her an apology."

Harold turned to Fern and thought that if looks could kill, he'd be a pile of soot right now then a little voice chimed in: *she's a Wiccan so it's not an idiom in her case.* "I'm sorry I was angry," he began lamely. "I thought you'd given up on her too soon."

She turned from him pointedly and uttered a single "*Hmph!*" making his heart sink as that was the exact sound of his marriage breaking up after the death of little Naomi. Cot death syndrome: such an impersonal sanitising label for something so devastating to any parent. His hands clenched until the knuckles were white and he shuddered, remembered vividly how his wife picked up their daughter who had such a gorgeous smile upon her face only she was cold and lifeless. Andrea kept turning from him and uttering that sound again and again until he could bear no more and left the house never to see or hear from her again.

Fern twitched as she detected his thoughts but she still had her back to him so he was a loss as to what more he could say until he heard a chuckle from Shield who was still seated upon the ground. "I'm so grateful you saved me again, Light-Father, but she's not really angry with you," she grinned. "It's just that she can't cope with the fact a lowly *normal* human male like you could bring me back through the Gates of Death when she, a mighty Wiccan, could not. What was that phrase you used last week?" she wondered aloud, placing a finger to her cheek. "Yes, that's it; she's definitely up her own backside at the moment."

Ursaf laughed out loud then apologised as Fern stiffened but remained silent, facing away from them. "I'm sorry," he said carefully. "I'll go and see to the refuelling and re-arming the chain-guns. It should take only fifteen minutes at the most."

"It's a pity you can't attack Bede on the way," Harold said.

"It is but I made sure that there's a working radar system there so they would all be in the air ten minutes before we reached them. The hills to the south create a radar shadow so they can't see any low-flying rotorcraft. Will you be coming with us?"

"No, I need to stay here to brief Thanewell's men, introduce them to the others and get them oriented as to what we plan to do. We really need their help in making more pipe-bombs."

"Good!" Fern said icily.

Ursaf shot Harold a time-honoured look of sympathy. "They're all good technicians so they should pick up quickly enough," he said aloud. "They may even add some refinements as they hate the arrogance of the Brothers-Martial. Now, if you'll excuse me, I'll help to get these Angels ready for your rescue mission."

As Ursaf's and Thanewell's men bustled about the chain guns, Harold felt isolated in that tableau beneath the hot westering sun with Shield, still too weak to get to her feet and Fern still standing resolutely with her back to him. Shield closed her eyes and concentrated. She gave a sudden small yip of pain and opened her eyes with a sheepish look upon her face.

Fern whirled around and glared down upon her, her face white with indignant fury. "Daughters," she said imperiously. "Do *not* invade the minds of Mothers! Know your place, child!"

"Child?" Shield retorted sharply. "What happened to 'dear heart'? You, Ivy and Nightshade read people's minds all the time without their permission, even ours!"

Harold thought to himself: '*Ha, she has you there! You read my thoughts like dipping into a sweet jar whenever it suits you.*' He was rewarded by another ferocious glare. '*I love you but then you already know that,*' he added for good measure.

Shield gazed up at Fern defiantly: "The main reason she's like this is because of what happened to your Naomi, Father. She's been trying to tell you for days but she's afraid to stir up more of those painful memories because she loves you and besides, you were too busy brooding in your tower or the docks weren't you?"

"Tell me what?" Harold demanded, perplexed.

"By Saint Peter's teeth, Father, you can be really slow in the pate at times! She's *pregnant*!"

~~~~~~

"Sweet Lord Jesus, I've failed them!" Ondine wept inconsolably. "Six lost to the river because they knew not how to swim!"

Camus stared upstream and shaded his eyes from the late afternoon sun. "Some were knocked out by others landing on them in the water so it cannot be your fault," he assured her. "Opening the reservoir sluices has got to be the work of Pious but on the plus side, there's no pursuit along the northern bank," he added with some relief. "They'll concentrate on Milverburg and the Light-Father which gives us until the day after tomorrow to find somewhere to hide. Hoi, this is odd: I don't feel Azrael's presence any more. Do you?"

Ondine chewed at her lower lip as she searched the river waters without hope for her lost charges. "No," she murmured distantly. "Now we are out of the Great Abbey, it's like a cloud has been lifted from my soul. He almost had me in the kitchen; I wasn't conscious of picking that knife up and, oh, how I wanted to be free of the burden placed upon me!"

The Sisters were sat upon the mud and gravel of the shoreline and bewailing the dead now drifting towards the Elver Estuary that opened out into the Drowned Lands to the east. Poor Persephone was lying in a patch of river sediment making mud angels like a child and cooing: "Blue sky! Pretty! Blue sky! Pretty!"

Camus looked at her and felt that his heart would break. Nobody deserved what she'd been subjected to and he silently vowed, unknowingly echoing Ondine's conviction, that nobody else on this desolate planet would suffer the same fate. "You'd best get her out of that slime and clean her up," he suggested. "If I remember rightly, this island was owned by a banking family, the Fitzgeran Clan. With any luck, their mansion has survived so let's see if we can find somewhere to regroup and dry our clothes."

It was arduous getting the Sisters moving through the trees that covered most of the island especially as the Sisters would not go near Camus, Cyrus or Luke although they tolerated Ignatius as he was looking exceptionally haggard. Sister Geraldine actually leant him a shoulder for support as Persephone skipped on ahead.

They emerged onto a huge lawn that looked as though it had just been mown due to the goats they saw grazing upon it. The ivy-clad mansion was so imposing with its three stories and countless windows that they all fell silent as they approached it. Camus and Ondine climbed the steps and opened the main front door which swung inwards on oiled hinges. They looked at each other in astonishment: somewhere, deep within in the spacious cobwebbed interior, *they could hear children singing.*

~~~~~

307

The Nick of Time

Thanewell had never seen a Wiccan before but Mother Ivy, with her Persian heritage and long brown hair set in pearls, was the most exotic and intriguing creature he'd ever seen in his cloistered adult life. He felt a stirring of arousal as he cast sidelong glances at her slender profile despite her clothing that mocked the Conclave of Architects. Her knuckles whitened as she sat in the co-pilot's seat of Bede Angel Eight, grasping her ebony staff. She looked at him from the corner of her eye and adjusted her headset microphone. "Pardon me, Wiccan," he apologised quickly, turning his head away. "I fear Azrael was infiltrating my thoughts."

"You're not an unhandsome fellow now that you've discarded those robes," she replied magnanimously. "The urges you feel are perfectly natural and flattering up to a point bearing in mind how misogynists like you have persecuted Wiccans like me for centuries. Even without the urgings of the Beast, your predecessors would have me stoned to death or burnt at the stake."

Thanewell chewed at his lower lip and reddened. "This I must concede, Mother Ivy: a mere few weeks ago I would've thrust a brand into your pyre and counted myself blessed by God but..."

"Why did I kiss young Kai in front of you all before we climbed into the Angels? I wanted to show you and the Light-Father that we can all move on; Wiccans and Brothers alike. We can shed our fear and hatred of men and you can shed your fear and hatred of women. Kai was foolishly punishing himself for the sins of the Order so I bedded him to absolve him of those sins."

"Using one sin to absolve another?" Thanewell spluttered and then he grinned bashfully being painfully aware that the Wiccan had the ability to pluck the very thoughts from his head. "What a curious reason to justify corrupting a young, *former* Brother."

"Pah! Think what you will of me, Thanewell, I'm no crib-thief and Kai is no child." Ivy shrugged, staring through the windows to enjoy the spectacular views of meadows and forests basking in the unaccustomed sunshine below. "This is the first time I've ever flown in a rotorcraft. It's somewhat unnerving yet wonderful."

"You get used to it and it's probably a lot more comfortable than a broomstick," he chuckled nervously.

"Ah, a joke oft foretells the flourishing of an open mind," Ivy nodded approvingly. "There's hope for you yet."

"What about you, Piamadet? How are you faring?"

"Don't be concerned about a gun-monkey like me, Thanewell," Piamadet grumbled through his headset microphone. "You get used to the permanent kinks in your neck and back."

"How much further is it to this island?" Ivy enquired. She smiled as a childhood memory fragment surfaced: she was in the back of her parents' car endlessly whining: *are we there yet?*

"Another five leagues or so," Thanewell replied, checking his fuel gauges. "About ten minutes flight at this speed." He glanced at her. "Thank the Virgin Mary we have you with us as we must maintain radio silence. Even though we're on different frequencies, there's no guarantee that Aten won't think of this and scan the airwaves for us. Speaking of which: can you detect *him*?"

"Azrael? Yes. He's brooding in the Great Manse as far as I can tell. I fought him off earlier at the Tower of the Sun after I tried to scry Aten's thoughts but I'm not sure how I managed it. I discussed it with Fern and Nightshade and we think it's because he cannot bear new life being created in his presence."

"Whatever it is," Piamadet added with heartfelt sincerity. "I hope you can do it again. I've never thought this clearly in my life: I don't want to be overtaken by that miasma again. Hoi! Look at that scenery down there! After years of rain, this is the perfect metaphor for me: sunlight representing a sense of being reborn."

"I'm glad to hear that. You claim you had nothing to do with the Great Plague or Tally-men," Ivy reminded them brusquely. "But you all have to live with the fact that you've flown countless missions in support of brutal, bloody Inquisitions. You've killed dozens if not hundreds of people with your chain-guns."

Thanewell gritted his teeth until the veins on his temples stood proud. "Their deaths will always be on our consciences; you have but to read our minds to see that! Don't forget we had no choice: a Brother-Martial was *always* on board directing the strafing of any defences erected by survivors. One of the advantages of being removed from your target is that you rarely get to see the blood and body-parts flying everywhere but fear not; our imaginations fill in the blanks. I rue every day, every single death."

"As do I," Piamadet echoed. "We're above the Elver now. I can see the Great Abbey from here. Get lower, Thanewell, otherwise they'll spot us from one of the towers. They must have heard the noise of our rotors by now. Look! On the northern shore there's movement. Hoi! It's those bloody-handed devil-hybrids we fought! Can you see them? By Saint Stephen's arrow-heads, how can those things move so fast? They can't be natural."

Thanewell banked the Angel slightly. "Yes, I see them. The hybrids are easily keeping up with the wolves! They're not even looking up at us as they're fixated on something.... Ah!" he exclaimed, his eyes widening. "They're going after the Sisters but how would they know they're on the island? They can't possibly track them by scent as they were thrown into the river!"

"It has to be Azrael," Ivy answered grimly, staring through the windows at the running packs that seemed to flow along the banks like a black river. "Both the wolves and the hybrids down there are full of the same malice infecting the Brothers at the Great Abbey. They carry the same psychic stench as Azrael did when he attacked me in the tower: an insatiable hatred of sentience. I only defeated him because he could not bear witness to the *creation* of life."

Thanewell looked grim. "You've told me how this monstrous entity controlled the Order for centuries yet you also claim to have defeated a Fallen Angel described in the Bible itself. I can't believe that you Wiccans are *that* powerful." His brow furrowed. "But tell me: how can a disembodied will actually exist?"

Ivy sighed then patted her abdomen. "Azrael's will survives because I suspect his real body is embedded in the Void. If he can transfer to another physical form in *this* world, he will become infinitely more powerful as when he seized control of the Tally-men and resurrected those dead Brothers. We only defeated him by the sacrifice of a young Scatterling and our good fortune in that he was still attached to the Great Computer by those umbilical cords." She fixed him with a penetrating stare: "Had we not done so, all Gaia would be lifeless bar those tortured souls begging for death in his Dark Jerusalem."

"You said the creation of new life repelled this devil so are you saying you're pregnant by Kai?" Thanewell gasped. "How can you possibly tell in just a few short hours?"

"I see you're just as shrewd as Ursaf claims you are. I couldn't tell but Azrael could. New life must be an unbearable torment to creatures cast childless into the Void by their Creator. Anyway, let's discuss this later - there's the island ahead of us."

"That's an impressive mansion! The lawns down there look level enough to land but we must hurry!" Piamadet urged. "Wolves and hybrids were entering the Elver and swimming out into the current - they'll be all over the island in minutes!"

"I can't see the Sisters," Thanewell fretted, craning his neck to search the mansion and the grounds. "Did they really make it to this island as your Scatterling claims they did?"

Ivy put her fingertips to her temples for a few moments. "Ah, I have them. They're hiding in the cellars as they fear we've come to take them back or kill them in cold blood."

"Of course they would," Thanewell sighed. "Brace yourself: I'm going to set down as close as I can to the main doors."

One by one the Angels landed and Ursaf broke radio silence to instruct Thanewell and the other pilots to keep their engines on standby. "Everyone else," he added. "Keep your rifles trained upon the surrounding trees until the Sisters are on board."

Piamadet pushed himself into the cabin on the roller bed and got up to grab his rifle. "We've fought those beasts north of Wealthorpe," he told Thanewell. "They're vicious beyond belief. They tore Gudflan, Durwyn and Hneftal to pieces and both wolf and hybrid *ate* them!"

Thanewell blanched and turned to Ivy: "I have to stay here so you'll have to persuade my cousin, Ondine - that's the Abbess if she's survived – and the others to get to the Angels otherwise we'll all be overrun by Farzad's abominations. Oh, and get everyone to keep their heads down when they get close to the Angels." He shuddered: "I don't want a repeat of what happened at Bede: Azrael made those poor fools *jump* into our rotor blades!"

"I understand," Ivy acknowledged, removing her safety belt. She clambered down to the ground and waved to Nightshade and Fern who had joined the six crew members forming a defensive ring around the Angels. As she entered the mansion doors, she could hear the first of the wolves howling on the island shore. "Diana, preserve us," she whispered, scurrying along one of the dusty corridors to a cellar door where she knew the Sisters and the others had taken refuge. "This is going to be close!"

She was about to open the door when a premonition gripped her and she stepped aside in the nick of time as a volley of bullets tore through the wood and smashed into the plastered wall opposite destroying a large, priceless Grecian vase. Part of her mind had noted the sumptuous furnishings, ornaments and gilded mouldings of the mansion and the ceramic fragments somehow symbolised the

311

shattering of the world. "Hold your fire!" she screamed, mortified that her haste had almost got her killed. "I'm a Wiccan! The Light-Father has sent us to rescue you. Quickly! Something evil is on this island and it will kill you all unless you move!"

A male voice demanded gruffly: "How do we know you're a Wiccan? You could be a Sister from Burslen sent to deceive us!"

Ivy ground her teeth in impotent fury then she concentrated. Several men screamed out and she could hear their rifles clattering down the cellar steps and onto the flagstones below eliciting thin shrieks and screams from the terrified Sisters and what sounded like children. "Now do you believe me?" she yelled out. "That was an illusion-geis making you believe your guns were hot!"

The door bolts were thrown back and a middle-aged woman dressed in male clothes stepped into the corridor to embrace her. "Bless you and the Light-Father, Wiccan," she said gratefully. "I am Ondine and Abbess to my thirty beloved Sisters. I have Abbot Camus and three Brothers with us and two children of the Fitzgeran Clan who've survived here alone."

Ivy gave Ondine a reassuring squeeze. "We must hurry. Azrael's Erdethric monsters are already on the island and they will kill us unless you hurry! I release my geis: now pick up your rifles!" she shouted down the cellar steps. "Trust me, you'll need them!"

Ursaf appeared at the end of the corridor. "They're here!" he bellowed, panic-stricken. "They're emerging from the trees!"

Ivy was glad that Ursaf had come to warn her because what awaited them was the stuff of nightmares. The former lawns were roughly circular and close-cropped by goats that were huddled against the mansion wall, trembling and bleating pitifully. From the western arc of trees and undergrowth, black wolves were emerging along with dozens of shambling powerfully-muscled ape-like hybrids with hunched shoulders and arms almost touching the ground. They were advancing from the lengthening shadows into the bright sunlight whilst keeping a dreadful, focussed silence.

"What are you waiting for?" Ursaf cried as he herded the Sisters through the doors. "You three fill the gaps in the defence," he ordered, virtually hurling the bemused Camus, Cyrus and Luke down the steps. "Don't let them near you! They'll rip your face off! Come on, Abbess! Let's get the Sisters into the Angels."

Ivy was relieved to see the resolute look on Ondine's face as she took command and divided the Sisters and the two boys into groups but it was difficult as the Sisters were terrified out of their wits as the first shots rang out. Ondine had to resort to slapping the most hysterical as she forced them to climb into the cabins. Ignatius used the last of his strength to crawl aboard as Ivy joined Nightshade and Fern to face the creatures who, unfazed by their comrades being killed and injured, were still pressing forward implacably.

"You are in *my* domain!" Ivy cried out suddenly, raising her staff at the advancing packs. Piamadet and the others stopped firing at the sound of her voice which carried unearthly harmonies that made their teeth itch. They stared in awe as the ground beneath the hybrids and wolves undulated then thick vines erupted vertically ten feet into the air with leaves budding and growing upon them at an unbelievable rate. The wolves howled then yelped in agony as the vines seized their bodies and crushed them to the ground. The hybrids however slashed the vines apart with their talons and teeth or simply tore themselves free by sheer brute force.

Sporadic panicky fire broke out as Camus and the others quailed at the sheer remorseless fury on those warped and bestial faces. Only Piamadet and Spero made their shots count, crying out the names of their three fallen comrades.

Fern raised her staff. "My turn I think," she said decisively and brought it down hard upon the ground which bucked beneath their feet. Glass panes shattered in several mansion windows as seismic shock waves radiated away from the point of impact. The earth and rock beneath the feet of the hybrids heaved upwards tossing them twenty or more feet into the air to land heavily amongst the overgrowth and tree branches.

Ursaf looked up at Ondine who was standing on the struts of Bede Angel Eight having recognised Thanewell. She had her mouth open. "Impressive, aren't they?" he grinned. "Yet for all that craft, they obey the Light-Father without question."

Ondine pointed southwards as more shapes burst into view from the brambles, willows and overgrowth. "Thank God for the Wiccans but those beast-men are mostly unhurt!" she groaned. "And there are others trying to outflank us!"

"Everyone!" Ursaf roared, cupping his hands. "Get into your Angels! We can't fend them off: there's too many of them!"

More wolves erupted from the trees but Ivy raised her staff again and the goats bolted forward to intercept them. The wolves, presented with easy prey, immediately fell upon them, clamping jaws about throats. The screams of the goats as they were torn apart echoed those of the two Fitzgeran children who'd raised them.

Everyone, including the three Wiccans, needed no urging and clambered into the cabins as another wave surged towards them with a few pausing to feast upon the dead and mortally-wounded. As the Angels rose, chaos reigned as hybrids leapt up and grabbed the landing-struts of all five machines. Several tried to claw their way through the cabin doors only to be shot in the face by Piamadet and the other gunners but many more clung to the struts so that the Angels could not gain altitude and two were already slowly sinking towards the trees with their engines labouring.

Nightshade bared her teeth, growling as the bestial, alien thoughts of the hybrids overwhelmed her mental barriers. She screeched in an ancient forgotten tongue that made everyone without headsets flinch and cover their ears: "*dawje gentin kommaljho mallostillnyae*! I am Mother Nightshade of the Fourth Degree, Servant of Leo and Wielder of Fire and I *deny* thee!"

The five Angels suddenly gained altitude and Ondine risked leaning out of the open cabin door to watch as screaming hybrids, limbs flailing and bodies ablaze, tumbled into the trees and the River Elver below like fiery meteors. Piamadet drew her gently back into the cabin and closed the door as the Angel picked up speed. "What do you think of the Wiccans now?" he asked, with a wry smile. "If they hadn't been here, those abominations would be tearing the flesh from our dead bodies right now."

Ondine gave him a relieved grin and received a reassuring pat on the shoulder in return then, cursing and grumbling, he wriggled onto his roller bed and slid forward into the nose-cone.

Ivy was weary to the bone and slumped in the co-pilot's seat with her eyes closed remembering little of the journey back to Milverburg apart from a few hopeful shots fired at them from the Cwiclasc causeway. She was last to leave Bede Angel Eight and skirted the excited melee that had gathered after the last of the rotor-blades had come to a stop.

All three Wiccans were not party to the hubbub and chatter as Ondine tended to the Sisters with the help of the Scatterlings especially Surl who seemed to bond instantly with the befuddled, distraught Persephone who would not let Amos approach her. Amos was about to protest but Ondine placed a hand upon his shoulder and whispered into his ear. A look of shock and then outrage crossed his scarred face. "Tell her I'll kill the next man that lays a finger on her!" he pledged.

As they could bear no men to be close to them and Bas terrified them on a primal level, Ondine decided to lead her Sisters into the Tower of the Sun assisted - as instructed by Harold - by Mouse, Fria, Surl and Rabbit as well as Kayleigh and Pomona who were exceedingly curious, bombarding Ondine with endless questions about the Sisters and their life at the Great Abbey.

Camus helped Ignatius get to the ground and was immediately embraced on alighting from his Angel by Michael. The two men hugged in silence, watched by Harold, Ursaf and Thanewell, for a full minute before Michael finally said: "I forgive you, old friend," – a simple statement that moved Harold immensely.

Ignatius had to be supported by Thanewell and Camus but he extended a veined and shaking hand to Harold who took it and shook it gently. "Well met at last, Light-Father," he smiled, looking Harold up and down. "I'm honoured to meet you though I must admit I expected someone a little more... *imposing*."

Harold laughed ruefully. "I used to get that a lot in my world, Ignatius. What you see is what you get, I'm afraid. I really want to thank you for saving Mouse, Peter and Fria and for finding the sign of the craft on Surl's tongue of all places."

"They helped to save others including Michael here as Camus, Luke and Cyrus saved me. Surl is an extraordinary girl, Light-Father. Look after her well. I cannot help but feel her craft may be the saving of us. You must excuse me but I will be of little use to you for a while - Pious and Aten were most proficient in their Inquiring of me and I think both my feet are bleeding again."

Harold beckoned to Amos who was examining a chain-gun and to Saul who was talking earnestly to Shield some yards away about her far-seeing attempt - it was plain to see that he was deeply upset. "Yes, Light-Father?" he said. "What do you wish of us?"

"Ignatius, this is Saul Dis, the Eldest of the Scatterlings and this is Amos, Surl's older brother. They'll take you to an unused bedroom on the fourth floor that has books in it as I understand from the young ones that you're a scholar." He turned to Saul and Amos. "Ignatius was badly tortured by Pious and Aten. Can you see to his wounds and make sure he eats some food, please?"

Saul's face became grim and he rubbed at the scar upon his chin. "Amos and I am pleased to meet you, Ignatius and we, too, praise you for helping the little ones. So Abbot Pious likes to torture old men," he added darkly. "Well there's another reason for me to chop that *balanith helrúna's* head off!"

Ignatius bowed to the tall, black-haired youth. "Thank you. I hear some of the Old Tongue in your speech, my son. When I am well and this hellish nightmare is done, I would be honoured to be a tutor to you and the Scatterlings. Oh, I am so looking forward to exploring the libraries here once I am rested."

Harold watched Saul kiss Shield briefly on the cheek but she remained impassive, her eyes upon the ground and did not return the kiss. Saul sighed then he and Amos supported Ignatius as they walked towards the tower. They had to physically carry the old man up the flights of stairs, laying him gently on the bed as he was in considerable pain. Sunlight and a fresh sea-scented westerly streamed in through the open window. He gave a contented sigh, muttering: '*ah, this is bliss*' and fell into a doze before Saul and Amos could return with water, food and a medical kit.

Meanwhile, Harold was introduced to Camus who also shook hands with Ursaf and Thanewell as Shield went to talk to the Wiccans and question them about astral projection. He noted sadly that Fern had difficulty meeting his gaze then he listened attentively as Camus related what he knew of the planned attack.

"We guessed it would be coordinated," Harold told them. "But we still don't know which viaduct will carry the main thrust or how their Angels will be used in Uppermost. If those bastards use that field artillery, those barricades won't slow them down for a second unless the Wiccans can stop them."

"If what I witnessed today on the River Elver is anything to go by," Camus laughed incredulously. "I think we have a fighting chance. I've never seen anything like it, Light-Father, and I certainly don't understand the physics of it."

"Neither do I," Michael interjected.

Harold smiled. "One of the Doctors at my university, Doctor Smith, always used to say that an inexplicable event was just something waiting for science to catch up to it."

Camus watched as the shadow of the Tower of the Sun crept across the park and the mansions beyond. "Somehow, between Azrael and their craft, it'll be a *very* long wait."

Michael placed a hand on his old friend's shoulder. "Come now," he said kindly. "Let's rid you, Cyrus and Luke of these filthy robes and find you apparel as befits free men. Then we have to go down to the lowest level where we've set up a factory of sorts. We have a lot of pipe-bombs to make before nightfall!"

After they'd gone and the Angel crews had left for the Core after refuelling the Angels, Harold spoke at length to the two shy blond Fitzgeran boys, Eric and Deorth, who were twelve and fourteen years of age respectively. They were whisper-thin and undersized for their age but they seemed healthy enough so Harold placed them in the care of Ibrahim and Bas who took to them immediately. As they ambled towards the Northern Circumference Stairway, the boys bewailed the loss of the goats they'd raised from kids then they begged permission to fluff Bas's tail and stroke her ears. To Harold's immense surprise and a wink from Ibrahim, she knelt and stoically endured the humiliating petting for a full minute and a half before baring her teeth and hissing like a cat, making the boys laugh out loud in delighted surprise.

Finally, only Shield and the three Wiccans remained. Fern, Ivy and Nightshade were all exhausted and stood silently, leaning upon their staffs, gazing expectantly at him as he removed his cap and ran his fingers through his thinning ginger hair.

"Well done," he said.

~~~~~

Such Calm Before

Nightshade was observing the Brothers occupying the Cwiclasc causeway through her binoculars. She was concerned to see Tally-men with them given the information from Ursaf and Camus about them being killed or confined. "This is not good," she murmured to herself. "Azrael must've purged their suspicions."

A barrier of rubble, felled trees, beams and girders had been heaped across the causeway to ensure that any train emerging from the Mouth of Freya - as this railway tunnel was called - would be derailed. She imagined them staring back at the immense carving of the warlike face of the Vanir Goddess of the Valkyries surrounding the entrance as the setting sun threw deep shadows across her snarling features. She could not see the field ordnance but she knew in her heart that it was there; waiting to blow the ramshackle barricade she was standing on to gledes and smithereens.

She remembered entering Milverburg as a young Daughter with Mother Vervain on the Brigstowe train, imagining it all being devoured by Freya's maw now gagged with carriages, trolleys and all manner of dockside items by the Ferals and Scatterlings. They'd left a gap at the top of the tunnel so that lookouts could climb up and observe the viaduct through Freya's upper fangs. The ad hoc barricade shifted ominously beneath her weight and she knew it would offer scant defence against their besiegers.

Despite her exhaustion, she let her mind roam around all three causeways but she could only 'far-see' the one field gun at Wealthorpe surrounded by excited Brothers and novices consulting a manual or unpacking artillery shells from padded transportation crates. Dozens of Tally-men guarded the camp perimeter with their spears upright and standing to attention like statues.

She returned to her body but the effort of astral projection had drained her and she trembled a little from fatigue. Adjusting the binoculars, she could just make out the village of Cwiclasc nestling to the right of the causeway. Unlike Wealthorpe, the imposing houses were all two or three stories high as befitted the village of the legendary engineering clans who had designed and built the mammoth causeways and viaducts. The mildewing white-washed walls and sharply-sloping roofs glowed ruby-red from the setting sun and here and there window panes reflected crimson laser-flares of light. She smiled as she recalled the old rumour that the villagers

318

had evolved cast-iron noses being the only folk in Britannia unaffected by the foetid reeks of the adjacent Dead Marshes.

"What are you smiling about, Mother Nightshade?" Mouse asked as she scrambled up to join the albino Wiccan.

"Oh, just memories from when I visited Milverburg," Nightshade replied wistfully, placing a hand upon Mouse's cheek. "Mother Vervain brought me here whenever they caught me sneaking off to spy upon my family. Like Fern and Clover, I was mesmerised." She swept out an arm to indicate the vast spaces of the Core beyond the tunnel mouth. "There were incredible sights and scenes back there to captivate a fanciful young maid like me: merchants shouting at stevedores to unload their cargo; the Dock Masters screaming back at the merchants; the peculiar Duct Masters strutting about in their black uniforms as if they owned the place. Diana bless their souls," she sighed. "We'll never see such a spectacle again."

"Were the towns above just as busy?" Mouse asked, trying to imagine the scenes then she gasped as they came to life before her mind's eye. "Oh! You're sharing memories with me!"

"I am," Nightshade chuckled. "These people were enlightened if somewhat curious about albinos but they made us welcome as they often sought Mother Vervain's advice and assistance. The level above us was Muspelheim where the tedious money exchanges and international barter houses were. Despite the rise of Beorminghas as a global financial centre they still thrived because merchant clans never trusted bankers and would not deal in stocks and shares like the Beorminghas traders did."

"So merchants were more like pirates then?"

"Pretty much," Nightshade agreed. "But I loved the town above that: Folkvangr or Freyaheimas as some called it and that's where spice and textile trading took place. Mother Vervain used to spend all day shopping for herbs and spices but I never got bored of all the incredible shops and busy bazaars. The town above Folkvangr was Helheim and I hated that bleak place where all the hospitals, prisons and funeral directors were sited. It was so *quiet* compared to the clamour and clatter of the other levels." She counted the towns off on her fingers: "And then you had the smithies and weapons-masters of Svartalfheim."

"That's where that Marc, Ken and the others were, wasn't it?"

"Aye, they've found more than enough weapons," Nightshade said, peering through the binoculars again. "They distributed them

319

all at Six Bells so everybody is armed to the teeth but we've run out of gunpowder to make any more pipe bombs."

"We've worked really hard helping the Ferals today," Mouse wheedled. "So tell me about the rest of Milverburg!"

"Well, the town above Svartalfheim was called Alfheim; the Town of the Artisans. Oh, I *loved* exploring the galleries, studios and workshops where they made the statues and the gargoyles and so much more. Let's see now: ah, yes, Vanaheim was where all the trading in electrical and ceramic goods took place then above that was Jotunheim where the goldsmiths and jewellers worked. Mother Vervain once dragged me out of there by my collar and beat me when I tried to buy a brooch for my mother!"

"Then the last is Midgard where the servants who worked for the rich people in Uppermost lived," Mouse concluded brightly.

"Correct but you didn't climb up here just to badger me for a geography lesson, now did you, little Mouse?"

Mouse looked guilty and toyed with her spear: "No, Mother Nightshade. It's the Wiccan Egg that Michael gave us. Mother Fern has it but Shield and I want to know if Michael was telling the truth: does it really hold my sister's soul?"

Nightshade embraced Mouse and hugged her tightly: "We can't promise anything, dear heart. We did not think Mother Veneris was capable of such a feat as it was but a legend amongst us. Mother Rosemary was adamant, even as a Heliodrammus, that she could not do such a thing but Mother Veneris spent years studying the old ways in the grimoires at the Retreat. We had the greatest collection of incantations and lore in all Britannia so we may need to go back to the Hill Where It Never Rains to read them."

"Well? *Can* she be brought back?" Mouse demanded tearfully.

Nightshade's smile faded. "There is a way: a ceremony we call *kwenkanatikitu* or The Five Soul Fold in the modern tongue. Do you know why we never have a coven with five Wiccans?"

Mouse shook her head, wide-eyed. "Is it because five is an unlucky number for Wiccans?" she suggested hesitantly.

"You used to find covens of three easily enough in the old days," Nightshade explained, turning to view Cwiclasc through her binoculars once more just as Fern was watching Wealthorpe and Ivy was watching Drytenham. "They reflect the Triple Goddess and Life itself as bound to the Three Fates but centuries ago we found six to be a safer, more powerful number incorporating the elements and our powers as our craft and knowledge grew. You see, five is the thaumaturgical or magical optimum number in this reality. When five of us far-talk to each other at the same time, something both wondrous and perilous happens: our minds quickly 'fold' together until we are but *one* mind living in *five* bodies. Whole covens were lost to the sheer erotic bliss of such a union as their neglected bodies died yet their co-joined minds survived decaying into malicious, vengeful sprites before fading away as if those five Wiccan souls had never existed."

"Un-*geh!*" Mouse breathed. "So they became monsters?"

Nightshade turned to smile down upon Mouse once more. "Not at first. The Five Soul Fold is powerful enough to touch the very stars but as the ecstasy grows, it becomes fey and seductive. This is why there must be a *sixth* Wiccan present to disrupt the Five Soul Fold once its task has been completed. We've never done this in Britannia for over a century but even *if* we were willing to take the risk, we may not be strong enough to draw your sister back into this reality and you must accept that, Mouse. I'm sorry."

"Yes, I see, Mother Nightshade," Mouse said glumly. "Would that Five Fold thing be strong enough to ward off Azrael? Shield told me that he attacked the Light-Father and Ivy but how can he do things like that without a body?"

"His true form lies in the Void but he astral projects his will, part of which rode that machine into our world as a 'seed'. I doubt we'll defeat him as he's of an ancient and powerful race that stormed the very Gates of Heaven. I think the goddess Ormuzd aided the Light-Father but," she added thoughtfully. "Ivy fended him off alone because she and Kai had just lain together in the Tower of..."

"What?" Mouse exploded, blushing furiously. "You mean a Wiccan has just mated with a *Brother*?"

"Technically, he's not a Brother any more," Nightshade pointed out delicately. "Tch! You all know how new life is created. Mother Moss taught you Scatterlings well enough."

"What do you mean....?" Mouse probed. "Is she...? I mean how can... lying together in a bed stop a demon like Azrael?"

"Mother Nightshade! Mouse!" Saul called up to them. "It's almost Eight Bells! It's time to meet with the Light-Father and the others in the Town Hall in Uppermost. He says this is our last chance to discuss tomorrow's tactics before the twilight fades. Is there any activity out there in Cwiclasc?"

321

"Not much; they're settling down for the night," she reported, glad of the distraction. They began descending the rickety jumble of trolleys, cases and dockside equipment that creaked and shifted alarmingly with each step. "There's field artillery at Wealthorpe as well as Tally-men and the same in Cwiclasc."

"Ah, far-seeing again," Saul noted with the doubt plain in his voice. "The Light-Father really needs to know of the Tally-men as Ursaf said they'd locked them up at Bede after the massacre. In my heart of hearts, I knew they would use them to attack us."

"I sense you also wish to ask me a favour."

"Aye, I beg you to talk to Shield. I don't want her to scry again – it's far too dangerous but she won't discuss it with me," he added sadly, offering a hand to assist Nightshade down from a tall cargo trolley. "I need your help to convince her."

She leapt nimbly down after declining his assistance leaving him flustered and barely able to catch Mouse in time as she jumped gleefully into his arms, almost braining him with her spear shaft.

"You should never, ever ask a Wiccan to deny another's craft! I advise you to let her become what she needs to be," Nightshade told him with a steely edge to her voice. "Would you be happy if I took that katana from you by force?"

"No, I wouldn't," he sighed, setting the exuberant Mouse upon her feet. He reached over his shoulder to draw the blade and for a brief moment, Nightshade sensed his frustration emerge in a desire to slice clean through her staff. He ran two fingers lovingly along the *hi* and *hamon* of the blade then he sheathed it. "After all that time together in Crawcester I thought I knew her well but I don't." He looked stricken, prompting Mouse to hug him sympathetically. "I'm so afraid of losing her, Mother Nightshade!"

Nightshade closed her eyes for a moment then opened them again, grinning from ear to ear. "Ha! Foolish boy!" she laughed. "As the Light-Father has told you countless times: she's grown into a strong, complex and beautiful woman as well as a powerful Wiccan and you must accept all those facets of her not just the one you want. You must give her time to explore her craft but know this: she loves you from the deepest depths of her heart so the only thing you're going to lose, dear heart, is a little dignity."

Mouse giggled on cue: "She loves you, Eldest! You're all she ever talks about, you know. She's grumpy, tired and frightened right now but you'll always be her honey-*numpkins*!"

322

Saul looked mortified. "Dear God, kill me now," he groaned in martyred tones. "I didn't know she'd told anyone about *that*!"

~~~~~

Fern sat upon the window sill of their bedroom in the Tower of the Sun, combing her hair. It had been a pleasure to wash it as the ends of her tresses were normally intricately beaded and a chore to maintain. They hadn't bothered drawing the heavy bedroom drapes to hide the candlelight and lamplight as there was no longer any point. A bloated full Moon had just risen in the east between two perimeter towers with a leprous yellow hue to it. Nevertheless, she enjoyed seeing it for the first time in six years and softly sang an old lament about the Lunar Goddess in welcome.

She turned to Harold who had shed his overalls and was pacing up and down the bedroom in boxer shorts and a singlet. "Come here," she said, beckoning him to the window. "We should both be dancing naked in a sycamore grove to welcome Selene."

"It's just a lump of dead rock," he grumbled but nevertheless he sat on the sill to enjoy the view. Along the southern horizon was a band of thin, high stratus that flickered faintly from the lightning discharges of distant storms but he felt the weather was betraying them somehow as those storms could have frustrated their attackers and lessened their fighting abilities especially the Tally-men now deployed on all three causeways. "It looks like this north-westerly wind is keeping those storms at bay for now."

He studied the Moon and inhaled sharply. "The face is not the same as the Moon in my world!" he exclaimed then he sighed: "Of course it wouldn't be! The general process of formation is the same but the asteroid bombardments would be different. You know, that Moon really does make me feel like an alien."

"Your world had no hold on you so you're of Gaia now," she assured him, squeezing his hand. "Whether you were brought here by Mother Moss or Ormuzd doesn't matter: the Fates meant you to be here to save us. None of the Scatterlings, none of the Brothers out there, none of *us* would be alive but for you, dear heart. You are the pebble setting off an avalanche; a pivot about which the destiny of this world has lately turned."

"Well, I don't feel very pivoty right now," he sighed, taking her hand. Suddenly a brief chorus of a dozen blackbirds in the park trees below sounded as a counterpoint to the sombre tone of his voice. "Who the hell asked you for your opinion?" he shouted down to them, making Fern laugh.

"You are more in tune with our world than you realise," she explained then she concentrated, closing her eyes. He gaped at her as one by one the blackbirds sang creating a complex harmony. "That's part of my craft," she smiled, releasing them. She listened as their territorial songs resumed. "But it pains me to know I'll never match their creativity."

"You spent some time with Surl earlier," he pointed out. "How is she? I haven't had time to speak much to our little saboteurs today. They were helping the Ferals build the barricades and there just hasn't been time to talk to them."

"She cannot use her prescience as she still haemorrhages when she tries but she is well enough to be jealous of Fria falling in love with her brother. Amos is enjoying being the centre of their attention. I've spoken to Fria but you may need to speak to Amos about the *male* side of their relationship. They're too young to be engaged in love-making as I fear Fria may not be mature enough to bear a child safely. We need to find them contraceptives and instruct them on how to use them properly."

"Fine," he agreed reluctantly, reddening slightly. "We're about to be wiped out yet you want me to teach a teenage boy how not to be a chauvinist and how to use a condom. I'm more used to fixing mass spectrometers than giving sex education talks."

"I've no complaints about your credentials, dear teacher."

"Don't try sweet-talking me, Fern. I wish you'd told me about the pregnancy before Shield blurted it out."

"It's just a late period, dear heart. I didn't want to raise your hopes or remind you of little Naomi." She tapped her forehead. "I try not to pry into your thoughts but powerful emotions are hard to filter out such as the love you once had for Andrea."

"You know how much I love you. Do I need words?"

"Words are good," she smiled, scooting along the sill to snuggle up to him. "An unvoiced thought is a leaf torn from a tree in a storm whereas a word is the seed that takes root, dear heart."

"I haven't read any books here yet so I've no idea who you've just quoted but he sounds like a very wise man."

"Woman," she corrected sweetly.

"Fine, woman," he conceded, blushing slightly and decided to change the subject: "Have you fully recovered your strength yet? I wish I'd been there to see the action, especially when Nightshade torched those hybrids. I had a lot to organise here but, all in all, that was quite the rescue on the Elver you pulled off."

"Yes, it was," she said archly. "But we expected a little more praise from you than '*well done*' you know. You have no idea how much Ivy and Nightshade respect you. All those men who joined us today also spoke of their loyalty to you as they laid the mines and traps on the Stairways. They see you as a natural leader, despite the overalls, and their only hope of salvation."

"I can barely remember their names," he noted despondently. "And many of them could die tomorrow. Why aren't they bedding down in the Tower of the Sun? There are plenty of bedrooms."

"Marcus told me that the Ferals make them nervous given what happened in the Great Abbey and they say they aren't worthy yet so they're sleeping in a Tower of the Moon for now. See their lights in the East Tower windows? Oh, and before you ask, we looked into their minds but we found no sign of treachery. The only one we couldn't scry was Ignatius as he's deeply asleep and dreaming of wine and literature," she chuckled. "Peter, Rabbit, Surl and Pup visited him earlier with two bottles of red wine and Ondine joined them. They really do love that old man! Given the torture he's endured, he's so forgiving and gentle."

"That's good to know. I'm sorry about the 'well done' earlier but my brain was still fried from having that bastard inside my head. I would love to meet Nightshade's goddess in person to thank her for whatever it was she did to get rid of him."

"She probably knows if she really is one of the Powers That Be. Ivy is still exhausted as that conflict with Azrael had weakened her to the core before the fighting at Fitzgeran Island. Kai is fussing about her in the bedroom above us at the moment," she chuckled, pointing up at the ceiling. "She's telling him that conception hasn't turned her into fragile glass and that he should lie next to her. She may be tired but, oh, by the Huntress, she's *insatiable*."

"You're like a psychic curtain-twitching old biddy. Give them some privacy," Harold insisted. "How are the Ferals doing?"

"They're determined to keep watch on the dock gates and the tunnels. Marc, Olias and Stunnal have joined Ken Glascae and his men and are using those grills to cook meals for them. They're learning to communicate with them and getting them to sleep in shifts in the beds by the Phoenix."

325

"Good. I didn't ask them to do that but Ken said they would find it hard to sleep on the 'eve of our revenge' as he put it. They really need to be rested and up here covering Uppermost at first light," he fretted. "They are Ursaf and Thanewell's only defence as the Angels are sitting ducks unless we can get them into the air. You can't give us an early warning if you're defending the tunnels."

"Yes, we need to be focussed on the viaducts," she admitted. "Even Wiccans can't be everywhere at once."

"Mmm, right now there's one place I'd like you to be," he grinned, getting off the sill and hauling her to her feet.

~~~~~

"Do you see them below us, Yin-chan?"

"Yes, six climbing men, Yang-chan."

"They can see the handholds in the moonlight."

"There are lots of handholds in these old stones."

"They're very brave to scale such walls."

"We did the same for fun before, remember?"

"I do. They must be here to sabotage the Angels."

"Most likely they want to kill the Light-Father."

"We can't allow that, now can we, Yin-chan?"

"No, Yang-chan."

Two bows sang as one three times.

~~~~~

Shield and Bas had tucked in Surl, Peter, Rabbit and Pup who had bonded together during their adventures and closed their bedroom door. Even though Pup gave her a goodnight kiss, Bas was so melancholy that her ears drooped forward as she put a hand to the sign taped to the door upon which was scrawled in a childish hand: *Do not disturb. Saboteurs at work!*"

"Pup has grown distant from me," she confided. "He didn't want a story from me tonight. I should've gone back for him and not fled the Great Abbey like some coward."

"Pup knows you would've been killed but it no longer matters," Shield said, grabbing her friend by the shoulders and gently shaking her. "He's alive and still has need of his mother. Who will protect him tomorrow, if you don't?"

Bas perked up and smiled. "True, like all mothers, I know he's growing up and will leave me but it hurts so much!"

"It's that pain that proves you've a human heart," Shield replied simply, desperately hoping that she'd said the right thing.

Bas raised an eyebrow. "Shield, you must be jesting with me! Me? Have a human heart? Don't let the shade of our cruel father *ever* hear you say a thing like that," she said bitterly. "He'd die once more from laughter. You have the Eldest in your bed now and even Amos and Fria have awakened to their feelings for each other. Even that Kai has found comfort with a Wiccan like *you*."

Bas had emphasised the 'you' with a poke to Shield's chest leaving her completely at a loss at what to say. It seemed to open up a chasm between them that she felt could never be crossed.

"Look at me," Bas continued, swishing her tail and flicking her ears. "Who would ever bed a freak like me? A tom cat? Where will I find love in this dead, empty existence?"

The door creaked open and Pup, dressed in a night-shirt, marched resolutely up to Bas with a determined look upon his face. "Wait for Pup to grow up and fall in love with you!" he declared. "You're the most beautiful thing in the whole world!"

Bas sank to one knee to embrace him and relaxed, her tears damp upon Pup's shoulder but he did not seem to mind. "You can tell Pup a story now if you like," he said.

~~~~~

Michael, Cyrus, Luke and Camus had returned to their Spartan quarters in the Eastern Tower of the Moon after seeing to Ignatius and keeping him company as he fell asleep after enjoying glasses of wine with them all. Cyrus opened a bottle of whisky and poured them shots in cut-glass tumblers. "Ignatius is impressive," he said. "He endured all that torment yet not a shadow clouds his heart. He puts me to shame: I just want to avenge him. I hope I get the chance to take down that bastard, Aten, and his butchers."

Luke shook his head: "Pray you never come across Brodiglede, Cyrus. If he doesn't shoot you first, your severed head will watch him sheathe his sword."

"The most fearsome foe shall not daunt thee, my Prince, for thy arm is righteous, thy cause noble, thy quest thrice blessed."

"Tythe," Michael sighed, sucking his whisky up through a straw. "What would he make of me, I wonder?"

Camus drained his glass "I was a coward once," he confessed. "But this strange man, this Light-Father, somehow inspires me."

Luke refilled their glasses. "What is it about him? He looks so unremarkable yet he commands so much love and loyalty. To the man from another world," he proclaimed, raising his glass. *"Though we dishonoured souls may falter and fall before the Gates of Chaos, may God and valour grant us salvation!"*

"Chenikov again," Michael muttered. "Appropriate."

~~~~~

Near dawn, Edward and Theo opened a second bottle at their table in the generator room to celebrate the fact that they were not scheduled to take part in the Inquisition. Four frightened postulates entered and approached them cautiously. "Ah, young Cashelm!" Edward slurred happily, patting one of them on the cheek. "Are you here to listen to more of my wondrous tales, my son?"

"No, Father, sitting on your lap makes me uncomfortable. Father Leored requests that you go to the Great Annex. The auxiliary computers have all come to life for some reason."

"What?" Theo slurred. "That can't be. We disconnected them as they cannot function without the Great Computer."

"Nevertheless, Father, they're all active now."

"Very well," Edward grumbled, hauling himself to his feet. "But you four are coming with us. If this is some kind of prank, we'll thrash the living souls out of you."

In the Great Annex, the ceiling lights were ablaze and the machinery thrummed. "It's true," Theo exclaimed. He turned to the four cowering postulants: "Did *you* connect these power cables?"

"No!" Cashelm whimpered. "We know nothing of electrics!"

"Look," Edward said, pointing at thin red pencils of light flickering randomly above their heads. "The communication lasers are operational. How can this be?"

"The largest door of the immortality-machine just opened," Cashelm pointed out fearfully. "Who's doing that?"

Curious, Theo and Edward skirted the wreckage of the Great Computer to peer into the open cubicle. The cables on the floor suddenly rose up and wrapped around their throats and bodies and dragged them into the machine. Theo reached out his hands to the postulants. "For God's sake, get help!" he croaked.

They tilted their heads to leer at them as the whites of their eyes turned black. *"Your flesh to my flesh!"* they hissed in unison.

~~~~~

Gambits

Harold was working in the maintenance bay at the university watching dumbfounded as a plug and flex attached to the small lab spectrometer in front of him began to slither slowly towards the socket like a living snake. He looked up at the sound of a discrete cough to see his faculty director grinning like a deranged Cheshire Cat whilst tapping the dial of a Geiger Counter with the needle in the red and making *tic-tic* noises with his tongue…

He jerked bolt-upright in bed, clutching at his chest and drenched in sweat. "Jesus! Bloody Henderson!" he gasped. "That slimy bastard is *still* in my subconscious!" He shaded his watering eyes as the sun had edged above the perimeter walls of Uppermost, flooding the bedroom with ruddy light. The park trees below were alive with the chirps and trills of the dawn chorus.

"I was plagued by nightmares too," Fern sympathised, handing him a towel and a glass of water. She was naked in bed beside him but he saw that her hair was newly braided and beaded so he knew that she'd been awake for at least an hour. "The Paths of Mag Mell were dark but our nightmares were not of Azrael's doing: they were conjured forth by our own fears, our own regrets."

He shrugged and placed the glass and towel on the bedside cabinet then leant over and kissed her tenderly. "I could do with more sleep," he yawned: the old adage: 'make love like there's no tomorrow' could not have been more appropriate and his lower back *ached*. "Have you contacted Ivy and Nightshade?"

"Yes. Ursaf and Thanewell are flight-checking the Angels while Ken Glascae and his men are setting up sniper-positions on the buildings overlooking the parks. Shield has just joined Ken. She's exhausted after a night of 'reconciliation' with Saul but she insists she can still focus her craft. She's learning to 'far-talk' with so little teaching! I spent five years mastering that discipline!"

"You're envious? You did say Mother Moss despaired of you."

"She did," she smiled ruefully, getting out of bed. Harold's heart skipped a beat as she was so breathtakingly *beautiful*.

She pirouetted in the rosy sunlight and laughed as she swept up her clothes from a nearby chair. "Why, thank you, dear heart. You grow ever more attractive too - as you lose weight."

"Here we go: damned by faint praise again. Still," he added, sitting on the edge of the bed. "I think I can dispense with the overalls today but I am wearing my Grateful Dead T-shirt for luck and this stab-vest Ken found in the gun-shops." He picked up a fancy-dress general's cap that Amos and Surl had found. "But I'm not wearing this! They were making fun of me."

"They meant no disrespect as they love you. It was a diversion from their fears of what might happen this day."

"I know, I know, but we could really use Surl's prescience today of all days. Any moment those field guns could open up and we... *ugh*, I wished I'd washed this," he confessed as he pulled the grubby T-shirt over his head.

"Why were those musicians called the Grateful Dead?" Fern frowned. "It's not a good talisman to take into battle."

"It's from a folk tale where a poor man gave his last penny to bury a corpse and the ghost rewards him." He looked at her candidly: "I'm doing the same thing here but on a much bigger scale so no, I don't think it's a bad omen at all."

She looked sceptical. "Hmmm, if you say so, *Harold*."

"Fine," he huffed. "Are Ivy and Nightshade in the Core?"

"Yes but they're angry that Ken Glascae and ten of the Ferals disobeyed your orders in the night."

"Jesus! What the hell did they *do*?" he demanded anxiously.

"At One Bell," Fern replied reluctantly. "They slipped into Wealthorpe hidden by the moonlight-shadows of the viaduct retaining walls and killed a dozen Tally-men and Brothers."

"What? Were any of them hurt?"

"No. They used knives and managed to get back unhurt and undetected. That man is a natural leader and Ivy said the Ferals told her that he and his men were smiling in their sleep afterwards. Marc, Olias and Stunnal wanted to go with them but he pointed out that they were still too weak from the torture so they stayed down in the Core. They're busy making breakfasts for everyone but Ivy says she's getting sick of eating nothing but fish!"

Harold grunted as he pulled on his boots. "Tough," he said somewhat callously. "When they've checked the Angels, I want those not flying with Ursaf to defend the Core with us."

Fern adjusted her hemp belt. "Luke, Michael, Camus and Cyrus have taken up arms and joined Ivy to defend the Mouth of Loki. Our Scatterlings are already down there waiting for you apart from our two new Daughters that is," she added, indicating the tapping at door. "They wish to confess to you. Come in!"

Kayleigh and Pomona entered, flushed and breathless from the ascents and descents of the vast Northern Stairway and from running halfway across Uppermost. "We killed six Brothers in the night for you, Light-Father," they declared in unison and bowed deeply, Japanese-fashion, clutching their bows tightly in both hands. "We're sorry we did not heed your wishes."

Harold attached his katana's *saya* to his belt and began to strap on the holsters for the two handguns Ken had found for him and taught him how to fire and reload. "Did I not tell you two to get some sleep?" he admonished. "So what happened?"

"We climbed the perimeter walls once," Pomona began.

"The stones have many hand holds," Kayleigh continued.

"We knew you had not thought of this."

"So we watched the walls in the bright moonlight."

"And there they were: climbing the walls like spiders."

"So we shot them with our arrows."

"They went *urk* and then *sploosh*!" Pomona grinned, miming the fall of the stricken Brothers into the Milverbore.

"We love you, Light-Father!" Kayleigh added. The pair of them put their bows over their shoulders and rushed across to embrace him. "Please don't be angry with us," they begged.

He placed his hands solemnly upon their heads. "I'm not angry with you; I'm just grateful that you were both alert to a danger that I'd missed but *please* talk to me next time, alright?"

The two girls beamed and released him then, hand-in-hand once more, they bowed to him. "Yes, Light-Father," they promised. "We're the Duct Masters! We'll make you proud of us!"

"I'm sure you will now head down to the Core and wait for me there. Make sure you get something to eat!"

"We will!" they beamed contentedly and were gone in a whirl of motion and excited chatter.

"They need to be trained," Fern noted, grabbing her staff. "But you have two new additions to your family, *Father*."

"O lucky me," he groaned theatrically. "I need a shave then we'll head down to the Core." He put his baseball cap upon his head and touched the visor brim before putting his guns into the holsters. "Get ready, little lady. Hell is coming to breakfast!"

Fern paused at the bathroom door, raising an eyebrow: "Why are you talking in that ridiculous accent? Are you ill?"

~~~~~

The engine laboured and the smell of athidol seeped into the driver's cabin and the rear compartment of the half-track. Father Leored was driving, conscious of the Great-Abbot sitting in the passenger seat with his arms folded, glowering at the mouldering spires and ivy-smothered academies of Fosskeep. "Are you well, Eminence?" he asked nervously.

"Well enough, my son," Schimrian replied absently. "I am contemplating the many failures and treacheries that vex me such as the loss of our dear Sisters and the fact that Fathers Theo and Edward have betrayed my faith in them and deserted us. We have none to replace those *snakes* in our communications rooms. Who will eavesdrop on the Conclave for me, hmm?"

Father Leored tapped the transceiver on top of the dashboard. "Fear not, Eminence, these have a range of thirty leagues so we don't need to use the Great Abbey radio relays."

"Good, good, but my main concern is the fact this Light-Father now has *five* Angels at his command as Aten has failed me."

There was a bellows-hiss from the back seat as Pious inhaled. "It was not his fault, Eminence." he wheezed. "He's about to attack Uppermost at your command so the Light-Father's Angels should be destroyed well before we get to Wealthorpe."

"I hope so, old friend, but if he fails me again, those Angels will disrupt my Inquisition! I'm also vexed that Hvretsope lost eighteen Brothers and Tally-men in the night. I ordered you to ensure no such action took place without my presence!"

"Um, Father Hvretsope has asked me to apologise for his initiative, Eminence," Leored interjected nervously. "He sent six Brothers skilled at climbing to sabotage the Angels but they were killed. Twelve perimeter guards were also killed during a raid early this morning. They had their throats slit. He fears that it was a sortie by Farzad's hybrids but he's keeping his Brothers from panicking while they await your arrival."

"Then I shall forgive him and confirm him as Abbot of Burslen," Schimrian declared imperiously. He handed the transceiver to Pious who was sat between Dreorman and Brodiglede. "Old friend, restore my faith in you: have our guns announce my Inquisition by firing shells into Uppermost before Aten attacks."

Pious stared at Schimrian for almost a minute then he nodded slowly. "As you wish, *Master*," he said.

~~~~~

"It's funny," Harold confided to Fern as the lift descended slowly through the pitch-black darkness of Milverburg, the ageing brake-wheels squealing and sparking against the steel hawsers as six of Thanewell's men were also in the lift with them. "I feel no fear even though I know this is going to be a bloodbath."

"We're glad to hear that, Light-Father," one of the men behind him said. "We've awoken from one nightmare only to face another but that's fine: it's no more than we deserve. Hoi! What's that noise above us?" he cried out staring fearfully up the shaft. Several small lumps of stone and concrete landed upon their heads and shoulders as they all cowered down with but two levels to go. "That sounded like an explosion up there!"

Before Harold could ask her, Fern already had her eyes closed and her fingers pressed to her temples. "Shield says shells are landing in Uppermost," she reported. "Ursaf and the others are starting up their engines as they fear a lucky strike may hit the Angels. He believes we have no choice but to attack the gun positions on the three causeways despite the risk."

"Damn it!" Harold spat. "We'll probably have an aerial assault when the barrage stops. Tell them to attack Cwiclasc then Drytenham and get back to defend Uppermost."

"She's relaying that to Ken who's passing it on to Ursaf who… who wishes you 'good luck', Light-Father! I'm beginning to like that man," Fern smiled, opening her eyes.

"He has his good points," one of the men agreed.

"If you can find them under all that flab," another joked.

They arrived at the Core and were met by Saul and Ibrahim. "There are ten Ferals to each barricade," Saul told him. "And ten by the dock gates. There's a boat blockading the Southern Harbour with Brothers and novices aboard all armed with rifles. They shoot at any Feral who shows their head around the gates. One had a cut arm from a ricochet about ten minutes ago." As if in emphasis, the faint sound of gunshots echoed around the Core.

Harold bared his teeth in frustration: "We need to keep that harbour open as long as possible in case we have to escape on the Beomodor." He turned to the Bede men. "Can you sink that boat for me?" When they eagerly agreed he turned to Ibrahim. "Can you show our friends to the dock-gates?"

Ibrahim had added two handguns to his arsenal and brandished one of his war-axes. "With *pleasure*, Light-Father!" he grinned.

As Harold, Saul and Fern walked quickly towards the docks, Mouse, Surl, Rabbit and Pup ran up to intercept them along with Bas and her two new charges. "We want to fight, Light-Father, we want to fight!" Rabbit babbled breathlessly as Surl unsheathed her machete and began practising with it.

He stopped to study these four Children of Exodus and the genetic engineering that had imbued them with keen senses and above-average physical strength. Within him grew an appreciation of the foresight of their parents who had worked so hard to give their children an advantage in the dystopia they knew would come. Forgiving them, however, would still take him some time.

"I have an important task for you four and it's dangerous. They're firing shells into Uppermost so I need you to protect Ignatius, the Sisters as well as Eric and Deorth here."

Deorth drew a large carving knife from his belt. "We don't need protecting by children, Light-Father," he protested indignantly. "We survived alone on our island for six years with our goats. Our parents bought enough vaccine for us but then they and all our servants died," he added tearfully. "We buried them."

Harold placed a hand on the trembling boy's shoulder. "So did many of the Scatterlings, Deorth. It's no shame to be afraid. Just help the little ones protect the Sisters. Can you do this for me? Uppermost is huge so the chances of a shell landing near you is small but don't take any risks, understood?"

"Yes, Light-Father," Deorth nodded, wide-eyed.

"Good lad. Now listen, all of you: there's a large government building on the south side of the park by the Tower of the Sun. Fern told Ondine to take the Sisters there this morning as there's a bomb-shelter on the ground floor with the entrance door in the foyer. Make sure they have water and take lamps with you as Ondine and Ignatius may not have enough light."

"Pup wants to fight with you and Bas!" Pup protested, clutching Bas's arm. "How can the Saga of Pup the Mighty end with 'Pup looked after some silly Sisters in a shelter?'"

Bas took his hands in hers. "Do as our Light-Father asks, little Pup," she pleaded. "I can't fight evil in the dark of the Ten Towns if I'm worried about you and the little ones." She leant forward and rasped her tongue up his cheeks making him squirm and giggle. "Please? Will you do this for me?"

"Yes, Bas, stop! Pup will protect the Sisters!"

"Thank you, Pup," Harold said as he knelt on one knee to speak to the others: "Rabbit, I know I haven't had much chance to talk to you but I'll make that up to you later, I promise."

She wiped away a tear and smiled bravely: "You'd better, Light-Father. Please don't die," she added, giving him a brief hug.

"And you, Peter, I'll make some improvements to the claw, I promise. Be careful. Some Brothers could land in Uppermost if Ursaf and Thanewell don't make it back. Understand?"

"Yes, Father," he nodded, pointedly omitting the prefix. "I'll kill them all if they try to harm us or the Sisters!"

"Surl, is your prescience back? I could really do with a heads-up," he smiled hopefully, placing a hand on her shoulder.

She glumly pulled out a white handkerchief and showed it to him and then to Fern. It was liberally spattered with blood. "I'm sorry, Light-Father, I only see the colour red when I try. I had a glimpse of you fighting Schimrian but that's all."

"Look, don't worry," Harold assured her. "You four have been my heroes and you've done more than enough but it's not safe on Uppermost. Listen out for incoming shells and get to that shelter. I have faith in you all and that means I don't have to worry about the Sisters when the fighting starts. Now, off you go!"

Saul thoughtfully watched them as they ran towards the Northern Stairway. "You are empathic, Light-Father," he began. "I admit I was jealous of you in Crawcester but you really do have a knack for inspiring everyone around you."

"He does," Fern teased. "I was certainly inspired last night as were you, I understand."

Both Saul and Harold glanced at each other and reddened as Bas bit down on her index finger to suppress a guffaw of laughter. "Oh, thank you for putting me in my place again," Harold retorted sourly. "Right, Bas? Are you and your team ready to take to the ducts once the barricades are breached?"

"Yes, Father," she replied, coyly tracing a circle in the dust with her right foot. "I hate to admit it but I've never been... *scared* like this. I need a... a..." she stammered to a halt.

Harold didn't hesitate and drew her into his arms. "Look, I'm frightened as well but I have faith in you. You're feeling uncertain because you're beginning to be a true parent to Pup and these Fitzgeran boys. You need to know that we all love you."

"What? Even a *freak* like me?"

335

"You're no freak, Bas," he said fiercely, grasping her by both shoulders and looking into her eyes. "You're as much a daughter to me as my little Naomi was. Never forget that!"

She shook herself free and stood proudly upright. "I and the Yin and the Yang will make them pay in every town they set foot in, Father!" With that pledge she turned on her heel and hared off to join Pomona and Kayleigh who were eating breakfast by the Phoenix. Harold noted with satisfaction that Marc immediately approached her with a welcoming smile and a plate of food.

He looked at Saul who immediately held up a hand. "No need to tell me," he smiled. "Make sure everyone knows what to do when the barricades are breached: get to the Northern Stairway and defend the barricade at Muspelheim."

"Good lad," Harold approved and patted him on the upper arms. "I'm counting on you."

"I won't let you down, *General*," he said, saluting before heading towards the Mouth of Freya to check on Nightshade and Mouse who had become attached to the albino Wiccan.

"Ha, yet another little dig," he smiled fondly as they headed towards Olias, Stunnal and Marc still stoically toiling over the grills surrounded by baskets of fish and six ravenous Ferals. "Fern? Can you far-see how Ursaf is doing? I think I can still hear chain-guns but I need to know what's happening."

~~~~~

Ursaf felt at home back in Bede Angel Seven with Spero at the controls and Piamadet grumbling over the headsets in the gunner's position though they'd agreed to change their call-signs to avoid confusion should Aten's Angels switch to their radio frequency. "This is Salvation One," he called as they rose a hundred feet above Uppermost. "Keep your eyes peeled as Aten could come out of the sun at us. We'll approach from the east and do the same to Cwiclasc. Make sure that field gun is destroyed!"

Ken Glascae and Shield were on the roof of the Central Milverburg Communications Hub, a tall incongruously modern building of steel and glass overlooking a large park and playing fields in the Southern Quadrant of Uppermost. They waved as the five Angels thundered overhead. "Good luck to the bastards," Ken grunted as he adjusted his heavy-duty sniper-rifle, having carved the futhric runes for 'god' into the stock. Hell will freeze before I forgive them. Have you got that far-seeing spell or whatever it is you witches do ready?"

"I think so," she assured him, shading her eyes as the morning sun was dazzling. "It didn't go so well yesterday. I can't sense Azrael at the moment but it feels like a thunderstorm brewing to the east only it's nothing to do with weather."

"All I see is this *haemedin* sun," he cursed. "So you'd better keep on your toes, witch."

"Witch? Am I making you uncomfortable, Ken?" she demanded curtly. "Are you afraid of us Wiccans?"

He pursed his lips as he lined up the rifle sights. "A little," he confessed. "I spent six years at the mercy of powers I couldn't control and now I'm at the mercy of powers I can't understand." He looked at her and smiled winsomely. She found him an attractive, assertive young man now that he was shaved and dressed in clean camouflage clothing. "No doubt my Grandfather would say something pithy in Old Gael," he continued with a sly grin. "About the seductive glamours and wicked wiles of witches but he was the first of us to die from the Plague spitting blood instead of his usual vitriol at the injustices of the world."

"We saw our parents die in Crawcester after they fought to free us from an Order halftrack," Shield replied coldly. "They hid us in the museum and trained us well before they left us."

"You have my condolences," he nodded, approvingly. "I think they'd be especially proud of your sister who destroyed that demon. I owe my life to her and those little ones."

"She may not be dead."

"Huh? What do you mean? She was blown to pieces!"

She told him of the Wiccan Egg that Michael had given her but he just made a scornful face: "Don't trust *aglaecen* like him. He's serviced the Order all his adult life!"

"Ah, listen! Chain-guns," Shield exclaimed, standing up and shading her eyes. "It's a pity we can't see them in action!"

She cried out in alarm as he dragged her roughly to the ground. "Get down, witch!" he barked as a shell whistled overhead and struck a building in the Northern Quadrant. "Unless you want a belly full of shrapnel! That was from Cwiclasc. Why are they wasting shells in Uppermost when they can't see the targets? Perhaps they're just trying to unnerve us."

"Not me," she said, prising his fingers off her upper arm.

337

He smiled with no contrition whatsoever and settled himself down into his firing position. "You're very comely for a witch. That Saul is one lucky fellow – if you don't turn him into a toad for forgetting an anniversary or your birthday that is."

She rolled her eyes heavenwards: "Mother Moss warned me about men like you: all penis and very little brain."

"Your Mother Moss had a sharp tongue," he grinned. "But it doesn't detract from you being a very *attractive* witch."

"May Saint Agnes protect me, I should have stayed with the Light-Father," she huffed, readying her cross-bow. "My name is Shield not 'witch', *Mister* Glascae!"

"My apologies, Shield," he said with a straight face, hand on heart. "For such petty gallantries. Listen. The shelling and chain-gun fire has stopped so what does that suggest?"

"Ursaf was successful?" she ventured. "Look! Here they come now," she cried, pointing at the five Angels slowly rising above the northern perimeter wall. Hoi! What are you doing?" she demanded as he swivelled around and studied the rotorcraft through his telescopic sights. "That's Ursaf and Thanewell!"

He grasped the radio and jabbed the transmit button. "So much for our witch!" he snapped. "The Angels to the north are from Bede. I repeat: the Angels to the north are from Bede! Get ready to open fire. Don't let them attack or land or we're dead!"

"What?" she gasped in horror. "It's not even Nine Bells yet. They weren't supposed to be *this* early!"

"Hello, Ursaf?" he shouted into the radio microphone. "Yes, the witch has failed us! Aten's flown in low from the north. They're above the Northern Quadrant searching for targets. Thank God you were in the air but where in Hades are you…? Forget Cwiclasc and get back here now! We must stop them landing in case they have Brothers-Martial on board!"

He lined up a shot at the first of the enemy Angels, his finger on the trigger. "That's it, you bastard: just a little closer. Hoi! What are you doing, witch? They'll see you if you stand up!"

"That first one has seen Surl and the others running through the streets," she said, her face grim. She focussed her fear and anger until a thrill ran through her body as she aimed her crossbow and fired, her very soul thrumming with the fletching of the bolt as it sped away. "I am Shield of the Second Degree, a Harbinger of Venus and I deny thee!" she screamed in defiance.

Ken cringed as a vacuum briefly formed around them then *something* erupted from Shield followed by a sudden inrush of air. "That's impossible," he exclaimed, using his telescopic sight to see the bolt smash through the pilot's windshield. Inside the cabin, the pilot blanched as the bolt tip hovered an inch from his forehead with coils of black vapour wrapped around the shaft. An aura of white light formed around the fletching as a narrow shriek of wind shattered the windscreen completely and the bolt plunged into the pilot's brain, killing him instantly. The machine tilted to one side then plummeted through the roof of a large mansion, demolishing it completely as it exploded within its Bath-stone walls.

Ken had to catch her as she slumped forward. "It's okay, Shield," he said with profound respect, laying her down. "Ursaf and Thanewell are here. They can deal with them."

"No," she gasped. "Azrael tried to protect that pilot. It took everything I had to break through! Ursaf and the others are almost out of ammunition and one Angel was shot down. You and your men have *got* to bring down Aten's rotorcraft."

"We will," he promised as she grimaced and closed her eyes. "I can't let you get the better of me, *witch*."

~~~~~

Hvretsope watched the Angels battling above Uppermost through his binoculars. "We can't wait for the Great-Abbot," he declared to his expectant Brothers. "Our brethren at Cwiclasc have been destroyed along with their field gun. We can't let them escape along that viaduct! Open fire!" he yelled to the gun crew on the causeway. "Destroy that barricade!"

A Brother handed him a transceiver and he placed the earphones upon his head. "Father Awrecai? I want all of you at Drytenham to avenge your fallen brethren at Cwiclasc," he ordered. "Destroy the barricade then send in your Tally-men as a vanguard and get into the Core. Yes, we'll be there to help you avenge Abbot Amalgan and those who died at Wealthorpe. We've lost many of our brethren when that so-called Light-Father sent Unworthy assassins and Ferals against us in the night like the devils they are..."

He turned to the Brother and covered the microphone. "Wyeholders!" he sneered. "Abbot Amalgan and Abbot Amherus coddled that Tribe of theirs too much. They still need an instruction manual to wipe their own arses."

The Brother nodded sagely. "True but their Brothers-Martial are more than competent, Father."

Hvretsope laughed out loud. "Not in our martial tournaments, they weren't. I had their strongest begging for mercy in twenty seconds." He placed a hand to one of the ear-phones. "What's that, Father Awrecai? You have wolves in the woods behind you? Ah, be careful then. They're the ones I told you about – the ones that attacked Burslen. I lost ten fine Brothers and novices there before we fought them off. They have a new type of Feral with them – chimerae from Erdethric; some of Farzad's monsters. If you see them, don't hesitate. Shoot to kill."

The field gun roared and he watched a distant puff of pulverised stonework appeared half-way up the vast walls of Milverburg. "In the name of the Holy Ghost," he roared up at the causeway gun emplacement. "Stop wasting shells! We have but a dozen more. Aim properly and take down that barricade!"

He returned to the radio: "Father Awrecai? As soon as you destroy your barricade, send in your Tally-men to draw their fire. The less we have of them, the less we have to worry about. No, you are *not* to feint as ordered by Abbot Pious! You have to breach that barricade and help us get a foothold in that abomination! The Great-Abbot is due here soon. He's in a radio-shadow right now but he would wish us to do this before he arrives. Remember, the Harlots in there caused our Tally-men to run amok so we have Abbot Damien *and* Abbot Amalgan to avenge!"

He sighed and covered the microphone with his hand again. "He's filling his pants at the thought of going up against Wiccans without waiting for the Great-Abbot," he sneered. "What did I say about them, Brother Mordecai?"

"Coddled," Mordecai agreed. The field gun roared but with the same result. "I think they've missed again," he observed.

"What's going on up there?" Hvretsope bellowed.

"What do you mean?" the gunner answered through cupped hands. "We scored a direct hit on the barricade! It's down!"

Hvretsope grabbed his binoculars and saw that the barricade in the Mouth of Thor was indeed destroyed despite Mordecai's protestations otherwise. "Father Awrecai? Our barricade is down. Yours is down as well? You know what to do! Why should Pious and his lapdogs have all the glory?"

~~~~~

Endgames

Harold was in the Mouth of Thor on top of the barricade with Fern, Olias, Marc and Stunnal as stone fragments cascaded down from the artillery rounds slamming into the masonry far above. He was studying the activity in Wealthorpe through powerful binoculars and could clearly see the puffs of smoke from the gun barrel. The crackling of gunfire echoed from the docks as Ursaf's men exchanged fire with the boats blockading the harbour. "Is your illusion geis working, Fern?" he asked nervously.

"We haven't been blown to atoms yet, now have we?" she gasped, her hair plastered to her head with perspiration. "Azrael is interfering: I can't reach them all. They're on the causeway: two dozen Order and twenty Tally-men. It's up to you, dear heart. Azrael has all but drained me. Ivy is still able to deceive the Drytenham Brothers but Nightshade tells me that none are left alive in Cwiclasc… and the Angels now battle for Uppermost."

"Oh, God, no! I sent the little ones up there! I just hope they made it to that bomb shelter in time. Tell Nightshade to bring everyone from the Mouth of Freya to the Northern Stairway. Where are Bas and all the Ferals?" he demanded, peering about the Core. "They have to go up to help Surl and the others!"

"Our two stone ghosts have already taken them into the ducts and vents along with Fria and Amos," she moaned, clutching at her head. "Damn Azrael: he's making far-speaking *painful*!"

Harold peered over the barricade and saw two-lines of impassive Tally-Men marching forward like robots, their spears at the ready. Through the binoculars, he saw a Father screaming at some of the gunners and pointing at the barricade. "Looks like they've seen though your geis, Fern: that Father is *seriously* ticked off! Get ready!" he cried, aiming his rifle. "Take out the Tally-men first! Open fire!" He winced at the report of his rifle but he was amazed at how quickly he adapted to the lethal rhythm of aim, fire, reload: aim, fire, reload. It was both a mercy and a slaughter as the Tally-men were advancing in tight formation and took bullet after bullet until a shot to head or heart brought them down.

With the Tally-man bearing the brunt of the defensive fire, the Brothers-Martial recovered from their surprise that the barricade was still intact and the opened up with machine-guns and rifles. Although they had no cover, the concentrated fire made it nearly impossible to shoot back. "Christ!" Harold exclaimed, wincing at the sound of the bullets striking and sparking off the metal in the barricade. "Those bastards know what they're doing!"

Olias cried out as Stunnal was struck in the forehead as he took aim and was killed instantly, his limp body tumbling down the ramshackle defences and onto the rails. "Fall back!" Harold ordered, physically gagging at the mess the bullets had made of Stunnal's head. "Fern, I know Azrael's at you but make sure Ivy can hold Loki as it's right next to the Northern Stairway."

She climbed down quickly to stand next to Stunnal's body and press her fingertips into her temples. "Yes, I got through!" she cried out in weary triumph. "I don't have the strength to cast a geis but Ivy has - she says she can hold them until we get there."

Olias lit a pipe bomb and hurled it through the gap as Marc held his rifle above his head and fired blindly down at the viaduct. "This is for Stunnal, you murderous scum!" Olias screamed above the sound of bullets slamming into the tunnel roof and striking sparks off the metal objects in the barricade. He and Marc scrambled down after Harold but both were clutching at shallow ricochet wounds to their shoulders. "We're okay," Marc panted as the pipe-bomb detonated with a dull thump sending shrapnel over their heads. "But I can't say the same for them. Olias made that one but I packed it with nails and ball bearings."

"Get to the Stairway now," Harold ordered, praying his hearing wasn't permanently damaged. "I just hope Ivy can buy us enough time. Ah, I forgot! Fern, tell Ibrahim and the others to close the dock-gates and retreat to the Stairway."

"Yes, general!" she puffed, placing her hands on her knees. "This is hard! Azrael is filling my mind with such horrors! He closed them two minutes ago and they're running to the Stairway. Ah! There's a begiuller out there!" she screamed, clutching at her head and sinking slowly to her knees. "Aiee! Not again!"

Harold saw that she was incapacitated so he quickly threw her over his shoulder in a fireman's lift and headed to the Northern Stairway with the others as Marc gingerly retrieved her fallen staff. They were joined by Ibrahim and the dock-gate defenders who ascended the Stairway at a flat run. Harold was struggling with Fern and was caught up with by Cyrus, Camus, Luke and Michael carrying the exhausted Ivy on his back. "She was magnificent," he said. "We killed the Tally-men and at least ten Brothers!"

They set Fern and Ivy on their feet behind the barricade then turned a truck-length metal trolley onto its side and jammed it into the gap in their defences. The barricade stretched right across the topmost steps which were some thirty feet across as they had once carried the bustling pedestrian hordes of all ten towns. Pale shafts of northern daylight from deeply-set windows in the perimeter wall did little to dispel the gloom in the broad Stairway but the lower half was bathed in the eerie blue glow of the Core's extensive emergency lighting around the Mouth of Loki.

As Harold's eyes adjusted, there was just enough blue light reaching this entrance platform to see that everyone bar Stunnal had made it. He was hoping that any Brothers charging up the Stairway would be silhouetted against the Core lighting and become easy targets for the defenders shooting down from shadows above them. They would be at serious disadvantage as there was no cover at all but for the gentle curve of the Stairway walls.

He beckoned to Ibrahim as Michael, still wearing his Noh mask, Cyrus, Luke, March, Olias and Camus joined Ursaf's men to take up firing positions behind the barricade. "Do you have my night-vision goggles?" he asked.

"Yes, here they are but we only have two more. Amos and Fria took the other two for the ambushes. We'll certainly need them if we have to defend the barricade on the next level but we'll be at a serious disadvantage if the Brothers them as well."

"I damn well hope not! How's your inner demon?"

"Impatient," Ibrahim growled, pointing at Fern. "The Wiccans don't look well, Light-Father. What are they doing?"

Out of the line of fire and virtually invisible in the murk of Muspelheim, Fern, Ivy and Nightshade had linked hands with their staffs laid at their feet so as to make a triangle. They had their eyes closed and were swaying and chanting in an ancient tongue: "*Biwon, neibo a Gaia abwa nasro-skeito...*"

"I guess they're trying to keep Azrael at bay," Harold concluded. "That bastard got into my head yesterday and we can't allow that to happen to any of us again. They can't use their illusion-geis but they're giving us a fighting chance. What's that noise?"

Ibrahim cocked an ear: "My inner demon believes our booby traps on the other Stairways have just blown up some boobies." He placed a hand on his broad chest. "Ah, I believe he's dancing a little jig of joy right now," he sighed contentedly.

343

Harold frowned at him then approached Ursaf's men as they waited nervously for the onslaught. "I'm sorry I haven't learnt all your names yet," he apologised. "But thank you for defending the docks. I can't think of anything inspirational to say right now as we lost poor Stunnal at the Mouth of Thor, except to say I don't want to lose any more of you, understand?"

"I'm Templein," the nearest man said. "We lost Carrus at the dock gates but we gave a good account of ourselves: few were left alive in those boats when we'd finished with them! This is Elias, Job, and Glensalic," he added, pointing to each in turn.

"Ah, I'm sorry to hear about Carrus," Harold said bitterly. "But it looks like we've all taken a heavy toll upon those bastards - the Mothers made them think they'd knocked out the barricades! Let's make sure their deaths are not in vain, shall we?"

"What of the battle in Uppermost?" Saul wondered aloud. "If they land Brothers-Martial up there, they could come down the Stairway and attack us from behind."

From the gloom to their left, Fern's voice came: "The Angels have landed after running out of ammunition. We've lost one and they've lost two but their last two were forced to land. Their pilots and Ursaf's were not very skilled at fighting in the air."

"Ah, damn it!" Harold spat. "How many enemy Brothers are in Uppermost? Can Glascae's men fight them off?"

"We can't say," Fern admitted. "There are about eight from Bede but they're heading straight for the Sisters! Azrael is guiding them! He wants to destroy them utterly. Shield is struggling to keep him out of her head as well - she's as exhausted as we are."

"Well, do *something!*" Harold cried.

"There's one thing we can try," Fern said hesitantly in a tone that warned Harold immediately that it was perilous.

Nightshade spoke next, her voice breaking from the stress. "It's called the *kwenkanatikitu* or The Five Soul Fold, Light-Father. But it's dangerous. We've never tried it before…"

"Just do it!" Harold insisted. "They're coming up the Stairway and you need to help Surl and the others on Uppermost."

"You don't understand the risk," Ivy groaned.

"We all have a serious risk of dying if you don't stop Azrael controlling these bastards so do it! Here they come!"

Eight Brothers were charging up the Stairway as the others gave them covering fire. Olias lit the fuse of a pipe bomb and hurled it at them with all his might. It bounced and clattered to the bottom of the Stairway where it detonated followed by the screams of four injured Brothers who were dragged to safety by the survivors. "That'll teach them to get ahead of themselves," he crowed.

There was a lull followed by the clatter of small metal objects bouncing *up* the stairs. Harold had seen enough movies to know what they were. "Plasma grenades! Get down!" he barked. The trolley was knocked back several inches by the concussions that left everyone's ears ringing. "Marc? Do the honours, will you?"

Marc nodded and took a pipe bomb with a long fuse from the stockpile they'd prepared the previous evening. He lobbed it down the Stairway where it detonated in the entrance hallway killing two Brothers who thought they were safe and injuring two more.

Olias gave a whoop of glee then stared over Harold's shoulder: "Hoi! By Saint Peter's teeth, Light-Father, look at *that!*"

~~~~~~

Even with the door of the reinforced-concrete room closed, they heard the sound of the Angels roaring overhead and the rattling of their chain-guns. The Sisters all sat on the floor, huddled together and most of them had their hands over their ears, trembling at every noise. Ondine had armed herself with two handguns and had briefly practiced using them under Naeglin's tutelage. She was confident she could use them even though she baulked at the thought of bullets tumbling and tearing through human flesh. She looked at Persephone as she whimpered with her face pressed to the wall and remembered the Sisters drowning in the Elver. Her resolution hardened: she was *certain* she could kill!

Surl stood before her as Pup gave a cup of water to Ignatius who was resting in a chair. "I think the air-battle is over," she observed. "I hear rifle-fire out there so the enemy must've landed. If they come in here, we know how to defend ourselves."

"That's good to know, dear heart," Ondine smiled. "You did so well at the Great Abbey. It's hard to believe that four children could bring the place to its knees but you did it."

"I'm glad you're with us," Ignatius assured them. "And young Deorth and Eric here look like fierce warriors to me."

"We know how to fight, Ignatius," Peter assured him, displaying the blade now attached to his stump. "Even Pup here is lethal with his catapult. He's taken out Tally-men with it."

345

Rabbit was listening at the door. "Shhh, all of you!" she whispered urgently, drawing her hand axes. "There's someone in the foyer. Two I think. No!" she cried in sudden panic, grabbing at the gear-wheel that moved the door bolts into the steel doorframe. "How is this moving? There's nothing on the other side of the door! Unh! Help me, Ondine, I can't stop it turning!"

The door swung outwards to reveal the slight athletic form of Brother Cwellor dwarfed by the bulk of the adjacent Brother Feris. "Ah, Ignatius," Cwellor said pleasantly, holstering his two hand guns. Brother Feris here was so disappointed: he was really looking forward to entertaining you. Abbess, *please*, lower those weapons before you shake them to pieces. You have the safety catches on in any case." He stepped into the cellar to study Surl: "Ah, you must be one of our little saboteurs. Well played, little ones! Schimrian almost burst a blood vessel because of you but," he shrugged, wagging a finger. "I'm afraid I'm going to have to kill every single one of you. Sad I know but it *is* an Inquisition! The Sisters we'll take back to the Redemption Cells." He leered at Ondine and sensuously licked his lips. "Where I'm sure they'll all willingly live up to the expectations of the Order."

Eric grasped his knife and ran at Cwellor only for Feris to swat him half-way across the room with a back-handed blow. Pup let fly with a volley of ball-bearings but Cwellor easily dodged them all. Three struck Feris in the head but the hulking Brother didn't bat an eyelid. Ondine felt her innards turn to water as she stared into those two merciless faces as their eye-whites and irises became black and their faces contorted with predatory grins. They tilted their heads to the left and hissed: *"Time to die, Ondine!"*

The atonal grating harmonies in those voices caused the Sisters to scuttle and crawl to the far wall where they cowered in abject terror and despair but Ondine stood her ground, fumbling at the safety catches of her guns. "I am *not* afraid of you, Azrael!"

Peter was about to attack them when he gasped, drawing Ondine's attention to Surl who was staring at the two possessed men defiantly. *"We are now One,"* she declared in five voices as a white nimbus formed about her. *"I am Surl, Servant of the Sun, Bearer of Souls and Wielder of the Light of Creation."*

The macabre expressions on the Brothers' faces faded to be replaced by ones of incredulity. *"You cannot deny me, child,"* they snarled but they could not move a muscle as embers formed upon their clothes. Grotesque crackling and popping sounds filled the shelter as their skin charred and splits formed in flesh releasing brilliant beams of yellow light. Pup fired at them again only this time their heads shattered into smoking fragments. Ondine thought she would faint as the outline of a demonic face etched in writhing black smoke hovered above Cwellor's smouldering shoulders. "*I am Eternal, Ondine. Fear me. Worship me.*"

Surl raised a hand at the apparition: "*We are the Five-Fold Soul, Azrael. You have no power over us!*" A silent concussion of white light obliterated that mocking face and radiated out through the walls and all ten towns to dissipate across the Milverbore. Surl smiled in rapture and hugged herself. "*Oh, the ecstasy of the kwenkanatikitu!*" she cried, enthralled, in that multiple-voice.

Ignatius jerked to his feet like a puppet being yanked upright by its strings. Snatching up Eric's knife, he raised it and ran at her. "*I have my Purpose! The Balance will be destroyed!*" he screeched in Azrael's unearthly harmonies but Peter barred his way and received the knife thrust intended for Surl's heart in his crippled shoulder. Doggedly, white-faced and hissing with pain, he held onto the knife hilt as Ignatius tried to pull it free.

Surl raised her right hand with the palm facing Ignatius. "*Leave him be!*" she commanded. An intense white glare enveloped Ignatius and he sank to the floor senseless. Foul black vapour poured from his mouth, ears and nose only to vanish in a galaxy of crackling sparks leaving behind a vile odour worse than any Dead Marshes reek. As the arc-bright light about Surl grew in brilliance, Rabbit, acting on instinct, raced forward to slap her as hard as she could across the face. The blinding aura vanished instantly. Surl blinked myopically for a few seconds. "Thank you, I think," she whispered then she crumpled to the floor unconscious.

Ursaf appeared at the door with Spero, Beorstahl and Naeglin close behind. "What in the Trinity happened here?" he demanded, staring at the two headless, smoking corpses. Curious, he prodded them and they crumbled into mounds of soot, charred flesh and bone making Rabbit rush to a corner to be violently sick.

"How goes it out there?" Ondine demanded, shaking from the adrenaline. "Are we safe? We heard so much gunfire!"

"Yes, we got the last of the Bede crews but these two slipped past us. I'm sorry about that," Ursaf apologised, unable to take his eyes off the smoking remains. "Father Aten and these two butchers were almost too good for us. Aten actually put a gun to my head when mine jammed but Naeglin here saved me."

"I got him with a head shot," Naeglin shrugged as if it was of little consequence. "He led the Inquisition that killed my sister three years ago so it was most gratifying."

"Apart from me being covered with bits of his brain," Ursaf grimaced, wiping at his bloodied jacket with a rag. "They killed two of Thanewell's men and Thanewell was shot twice but he'll live. Marcus got a bullet in the leg when these two raced across to this place. It was as if they knew you were here."

"Azrael was with them," Ondine explained. "He wanted to kill Surl for some reason. But for Peter he would have succeeded as he possessed poor Ignatius there to attack her."

Peter let out a low moan as he sat down upon the floor, shuddering from the shock of his injury. Beorstahl rushed into the room to examine the knife still deeply embedded in his shoulder. "Naeglin, see to Ignatius, would you? We were Brothers-Surgeon at Bede, Ondine," he told her. "It's not too bad, Peter, isn't it? There will be some muscle damage but it should heal." He took hold of the hilt. "Now, Peter, I want you to count to five," he said. "Then I'll pull the knife out. Are you ready?"

Peter nodded bravely. "Yes. One… *owww!*"

"There, well done. This is a field medical kit so I'll sterilise the wound and stitch it up," he said removing Peter's jacket and cutting away the shirt fabric from around the wound. "I'm sorry, but there's no local anaesthetic. Bite on this piece of wood. Ondine? Can you quieten the Sisters down? I need to concentrate!"

"Ignatius is coming round," Naeglin reported, helping the dazed old man into a sitting position. "Can someone get him and Peter a drink of water, please? They'll all need painkillers." He saw Deorth lifting his dazed brother off the floor. "Ah, another hero, I see! Bring him here and let me have a look at him."

"So the Wiccans defeated Azrael," Spero observed as Ondine sat down to cradle Surl who was twitching and drenched in sweat. Pup knelt beside them to anxiously hold Surl's hand. "How is the little one doing?" Spero asked. "She's of the craft so she must've smoked those two jackals." He smiled triumphantly as Ondine nodded. "I thought so! That young Wiccan, Shield, glowed like a nova on the roof before she keeled over. Glascae and Linden are carrying her down now as she's still dancing with the elves."

"Will you all be *quiet!*" Ursaf roared at the babbling Sisters. "I need to think about what to do next!"

Spero sighed gratefully as the hubbub abated. "We have to hope that the Light-Father and the others are still alive down there, Ursaf. We need to get the Angels back in the air so that we can strafe the boats and viaducts and break up any attacks."

"Ursaf? Naeglin and I will guard the Sisters and the young ones," Beorstahl offered. "Ask Ken, Seainare and Linden to take our machineguns and go down the Northern Stairway to aid the Light-Father. We'll keep the sniper-rifles to hand in case Bede gets the other two Angels working so we can cover you."

"I'll go down too," Rabbit insisted, wiping her mouth.

Pup grabbed her arm. "No, no, no! You'll *die!*" he pleaded. "Pup needs Rabbit to help Surl and Peter and Ignatius! Pup needs Rabbit! Surl needs Rabbit! Peter needs Rabbit!"

"You've done more than enough, dear heart," Ondine assured her firmly. "I'll need your help with the Sisters and these three injured souls. I'd be grateful if you could stay with me."

Rabbit sat down heavily next to Pup. "If you say so," she said wearily, laying her hand-axes on the floor next to her. She wrapped her arms around her knees and hid her face from Ondine. "I think I've had my fill of death."

Ondine stared open-mouthed and teary-eyed as Persephone wordlessly turned away from the wall to crawl across the room and enfold the quietly sobbing Rabbit in her arms.

~~~~~

Checkmate

Ten Bells came and went but luckily for the defenders, the plasma grenades thrown at the barricade bounced back down the stairs to explode harmlessly, making their ears ring. There were also distant detonations echoing across Muspelheim as luckless Brothers sent to clear the other Stairways made fatal errors in dealing with the complex webs of trip-wires.

Hvretsope ground his teeth in impotent fury having learnt that the substantial barricades blocking the Stairways were also seeded with pipe-bombs whose fuse-caps were triggered by the slightest tug on near-invisible threads. They were almost through into Muspelheim but they'd paid a heavy price.

From the Wyehold and Burslen Abbeys only he, Father Awrecai and twelve able-bodied Brothers remained to regroup at the entrance to the Northern Stairway now littered with corpses. He could hear the groans of the nine wounded Brothers on their makeshift stretchers nearby then his nightmare was compounded by Awrecai urgently tapping him on the shoulder.

He turned to see that thirty armed Brothers with Schimrian, Pious, Brodiglede and Dreorman at the fore had closed upon them in utter silence. "Ah, Eminence," he grovelled, trying to kiss Schimrian's seal of office only to have it snatched away. "You've arrived just in time. We breached the defences as Aten attacked Uppermost. Only the Light-Father and a handful of Unworthy remain at the top of this Stairway. I, um, thought it best to wait for you to lead the final stage of your Inquisition, Eminence."

Schimrian smiled thinly. "We've lost contact with Abbot Aten, my son. He clearly failed to secure Uppermost while you defied my implicit order to await my arrival to coordinate *my* Inquisition. Thanks to your precipitous action, *this* is all that remains of your Brothers bar those few in boats full of novices floating aimlessly about on the Milverbore. I was going to ordain you Abbot of Burslen but I see my faith has been sorely misplaced yet again. Old friend," he said, addressing Pious. "I despair of my trusting nature. Will you please restore my faith in *you,* my son?"

Pious strode forward and clamped his left hand around Hvretsope's throat and effortlessly lifted the large and muscular Father-Martial off his feet. Hvretsope's eyes bulged as he frantically lashed out with fists and feet to no avail until with one final squeeze and a crunch of bone and cartilage, Pious released him and his lifeless body flopped to the ground. Awrecai and the others retreated, watching helplessly as Dreorman and Brodiglede casually snapped the necks of the injured Brothers, blessing each of their helpless victims in Latin as they did so.

Schimrian grabbed a loud-hailer from one of the quaking Brothers and approached the Stairway. "Light-Father, this is Great-Abbot Schimrian. I wish to parley with you!"

"Just crawl away and die, Schimrian!" Harold shouted down the Stairway. "There's nothing to parley with, you maniac!"

"How disappointing," Schimrian replied urbanely. "Here we are at the end of your blasphemy yet where are all the *bon mots* and the badinage I was hoping for? This is the Last Great Inquisition: surely it should merit something a little more memorable from you - especially when I'm allowing you to beg for the mercy of a swift death for your Unworthy *brats*!"

"You genocidal bastard, Schimrian! Don't you *dare* threaten my Scatterlings!"

"It's not a threat but a kindness on my part considering your desecration of the Great Abbey and the death of my beloved son, Azrael. How I wish I'd killed you then, Light-Father! Heed my words: Fate and God will not deny me twice!"

As he spoke, Pious and Brodiglede were organising the cowed Brothers into three teams. Twelve were to remain with Awrecai, Leored, Dreorman and Schimrian while Pious led fifteen to the Southern Stairway which was now largely clear of booby-traps but not the blood and body parts of their brethren. Brodiglede, with his munitions and weaponry experience, quickly led his own team of fifteen Brothers towards the Eastern Stairway.

"Azrael isn't dead, Schimrian," Harold retorted angrily. "Only his corporeal form was destroyed."

"Impossible!" Schimrian snarled, almost incoherent with rage. "We cremated his body and his glorious wings. Nothing can live without flesh. That Scatterling bitch of yours destroyed him!"

"Yes, she destroyed his body but his *presence* remains at the Great Abbey and he's free of that device! Can't you remember what he said to you? What he did to you? He told you he was going to give you *his* New Jerusalem: a never-ending Hell with that resurrection machine bringing you all back to life over and over again! You can't say that I'm lying to you – you were *there*!"

"You cannot escape redemption with cheap deceptions, Light-Father! I... do remember... that *machine*..."

"Yes, it resurrected you!" Harold cried triumphantly. "Think! Remember how he claimed he had three fathers?"

"Azrael had acknowledged me as a father but it was your Wiccan whore who laid me low with her dark arts..."

"Stop denying the truth!" Harold snapped. "Azrael didn't have three fathers; he had *four*! Something evil crossed over with that alien device; a seed from an ancient race cast into the Void for storming the Gates of Heaven. These Fallen Angels want to destroy every sentient life-form in God's Creation out of sheer *spite*. Even though Azrael was trapped in that device, he's manipulated your Order for centuries; quietly creating the state of mind necessary to spread the Revelation Virus and kill billions – all in the name of God! Surely you appreciate the biblical irony of that?"

"Pah! I expected such quicksilver words from the lips of a Prince of Lies," Schimrian countered. "Because of your Wiccan, I recall little of what happened but Almighty God has restored me! Let us cross swords in His name so that I may have the pleasure of cutting that blasphemous tongue from your Unworthy mouth!"

"You can try!" Harold raged. "But here's the kicker: a Fallen Angel that wants to purge Creation was bad enough but by hacking that device housing him and then wiring in your brother's brain has created a monster that *enjoys* killing and inflicting pain and he wants to do it over and over again using that resurrection machine! You have to destroy it, Schimrian! If he ever becomes flesh again, he'll make Hell a reality for *all* of us!"

"Liar! God Himself recognised our devotion and sent down his Holy Angel to guide us but you destroyed him, you *Lucifer*!"

Harold was about to reply when he was startled by a tug at his sleeve. "Oh, Mouse! I'd forgotten about you! Listen, I'm sorry: I should've sent you up to Uppermost with Surl and the others but can you keep an eye on Fern and the other two for me? That weird light show just now has knocked them out."

"Saul says they're in some sort of deep slumber after fighting off Azrael, Light-Father. They're twitching but he can't rouse them - they seem to be having a really bad nightmare."

"I'm not surprised if they took on Azrael with... with whatever that shining light... thing was all about. It must've worked: I can't feel him trying to get into my head any more."

"It's called a Five Soul Fold, Father," Mouse said gravely. "It's very dangerous but something broke the link before it was too late. They all could've died."

"Answer me, Lucifer!" Schimrian taunted. "Will you meet me in single combat so you can depart this *vallis lacrimarum* with at least *some* shred of honour to your risible tally?"

"Huh! He's trying to distract you," Mouse scoffed, standing on tiptoe to peer through a gap in the barricade. "They're not attacking here so they must be up to something somewhere else."

A rumbling boom echoed and re-echoed across Muspelheim like a roll of thunder. "You're right, Mouse!" Harold said, his heart sinking. "They're trying to outflank us. Ah, I think I see torches at the Southern Stairway! Hell's teeth, they've broken through! We'll have to pull back up to Folkvangr and hold that barricade there. We have to retreat!" he ordered. "Can some of you carry the Wiccans? We can't leave them behind."

"Well, Light-Father?" Schimrian mocked. "Will you always be remembered as the eternal coward fleeing from your foe? Are you man enough to face me sword to sword? Will you grant me the satisfaction of dying upon my blade?"

"You're just a diversion," Harold yelled back. "Doesn't it bother you that Pious is a walking corpse? Nothing in the Bible about that is there? In your heart you know that he's Azrael's creature not yours and that *thing* will be the one who ends your twisted existence when your 'beloved son' gets bored with you!"

"Liar! Blasphemer!" Schimrian screeched through the loud-hailer. "Awrecai! Leored! Take your men and charge up those stairs now! Inquire of them, my sons, Inquire of them!"

The two Fathers and their Brothers, terrified by Hvretsope's death and the brutal murder of their injured brethren, ran up the Stairway with Awrecai's and Leored's machine-guns chattering away and the Brothers firing volley after volley with their rifles. As they were completely panic-stricken, few bullets actually struck the barricade. Harold took aim as Ken, Linden and Seainare arrived, breathless after racing down the Stairway, and took up positions alongside him to open up with their machine-guns.

Harold fired his rifle twice and struck Awrecai in the chest while Leored and the twelve Brothers, one of whom was carrying a begiuller, were mown down with no hope of ever reaching the barricade alive. One tried to hurl a plasma-grenade but he was hit and the blast killed the last three surviving Brothers. As the echoes of the carnage faded away, six rapid reports sounded from the Core below and then the unexpected happened: Dreorman and Schimrian appeared, slowly backing up the stairs whilst pointing their swords at eight Ferals who were glaring at them with a dreadful hunger in their eyes and clutching a variety of weapons.

Schimrian threw his empty revolver at them in disgust and almost tripped over a corpse. "Stay back, hell spawn!" he yelled. "We'll not die at the hands of mutated filth like *you*!"

Dreorman despaired to see rifles and machine-guns pointed at them, realising that only two choices remained to him at the end of a brutal, sadistic life: death by Feral or death by bullet. Schimrian was unfazed and bared his teeth at Harold, the thin veneer of civility sloughing away from him. "Ah, *there* you are, Lucifer!" he sneered, brandishing his sword. "My offer of an honourable death still stands. Will you not honour my challenge?"

"Not today," Harold said, shaking his head slowly. He drew one of his handguns and pointed it at the Great-Abbot's head. "My father always said you should put a mad dog down."

Before he could pull the trigger, he heard the sound of running feet, the clatter of a discarded machine-gun and Saul crying: "You'll not have him!" as his katana clashed with the sword of Pious a mere six inches from the back of Harold's neck.

Startled, Harold spun round to empty his gun into Pious before the others could react. Pious grinned and actually spat out the round that had impacted his face leaving a hole in his cheek which was rapidly healing to everyone's disgust and disbelief. He extracted two flares from his pocket and pulled the fuses, tossing them to one side. "Now, what did God say unto the Void?" he mused in his rasping, wheezing voice. "Oh, yes, let there be Light!"

He launched himself at Saul as the darks of Muspelheim were rent by the hellish red glare of the flares. He rained powerful strikes upon the youth, drawing sparks from both weapons. Had Saul not been genetically enhanced, those blows would have numbed his sword-arm completely but his heightened reflexes served him well and both blades were blood-red blurs in the crimson glow.

Behind Pious, all hell was breaking loose with the echoing of distant screams and gunfire and feeble lights pricking the pitch-black underbelly of Muspelheim. Ken snatched the rifle from the bemused Olias and shot Dreorman in the right leg but it jammed when he tried to shoot Schimrian. The Great-Abbot took one contemptuous look at the Ferals and immediately leapt over the barricade to swing his sword at Ken only Harold blocked him, finding it quicker to draw his katana than his second gun.

Ken rolled away gratefully and joined Beorstahl and Naeglin to guard the Wiccans whom they'd dragged to the foot of the Stairway leading up to Folkvangr. "Shoot them!" he screamed.

"We're trying!" Olias replied, grabbing another rifle from Marc. "But all the firing mechanisms keep jamming!"

"And ours!" Michael added, wrenching at his rifle bolt. "This is impossible! The mechanisms should work!"

"Club the *aglaecen* then," Ken roared in desperation as Harold desperately blocked several rapid thrusts at his abdomen.

Templein raised his rifle like a club and smashed Pious across the back of the head. The Abbot's head bobbed forward slightly but the ragged gash in his scalp healed almost instantly. Templein looked down in helpless horror to see that Pious had reversed his sword, whilst keeping eye contact with Saul, and had thrust it backwards into his abdomen just beneath the sternum.

Pious inhaled a rasping breath to speak: "I cannot be killed, *worm*." Then he twisted the blade slowly as Saul took up a defensive posture, unable to intervene as he was gasping for breath. "But know that it pleases my Master to kill you thus!"

As Templein fell to the floor, trying in vain to keep his bowels inside his body, the others did not see Dreorman succumb to a mass of vengeful Ferals and begin a death as prolonged and as savage as any inflicted by the Erdethric Hybrids.

Try as they might, neither Ken nor Beorstahl or any of the others could fire a single shot at Pious or Schimrian. They couldn't even use their knives as the strength suddenly ebbed from their limbs if they came within three yards of both men. Ibrahim battled through the numbing geis and swung his axe repeatedly at Pious but the blade constantly veered away from his target until he was howling with frustration and retreated, utterly exhausted.

"See? We're protected by God!" Schimrian gloated, feinting at Harold who was 'heeding the soul of the sword' as Saul had once described the technique of fighting with a katana.

Harold knew Schimrian was toying with him and guessed that Azrael was preventing anyone from physically interfering with the swordplay. He had a sudden vision of the winged angel seated upon a throne gazing benevolently down like Caesar watching gladiators fight to the death in Rome. Schimrian was instantly upon him with arcing overhead strokes but Harold suddenly remembered the pattern from the Great Annex and countered the reverse slash to his abdomen which was unprotected by the stab vest. "Well parried, Lucifer," Schimrian conceded grudgingly. "But as for your Harlots over there: we shall hand them bound and naked to the novices for sport. We'll make sure they take *months* to die."

Harold ignored the goading. "Ken! See to Templein! The rest of you, help Bas and the Ferals!" he ordered as blue flames rippled down his katana and that of Saul's whilst coils of black vapour caressed the blades of their enemies. "There's nothing you can do here. The Powers That Be are here with us!"

"But our weapons are useless, Light-Father," Camus protested. "We'll be at their mercy!"

"Trust me, Azrael won't protect those Brothers! He's focussed here and doesn't give a toss about them. He wants *all* sentient life to suffer and die including these two morons!"

Michael and the others warily skirted the four combatants and gladly rushed into the shadows of Muspelheim to search for enemies they could kill leaving the three exhausted and helpless Wiccans sat upon the steps to watch the swordplay. They were flanked by the terrified Naeglin and Beorstahl who heroically battled their fight or flight instincts and held their knives at the ready. Unseen, unheard, down the steps beyond the barricade, long dead families were being avenged as Dreorman was torn apart...

~~~~~

"There are fifteen beneath us, Yin-chan," Kayleigh murmured, peering through a duct vent into Auros Avenue below where most of the squat, fortified gold bullion trading houses were situated. "What foresight of ours to remove the grills."

Pomona notched an arrow to her bow and aimed at a Brother who was holding a lantern above his head. "Indeed, sweet Yang-chan," she whispered lovingly. "We had the foresight."

"Bas, there's a vertical shaft with rungs connected to the duct to your right," Kayleigh explained. "Tell your Ferals to go down to the vent at street level. When we shot Brothers years ago, they scattered everywhere and never, ever bothered to look *up*. Sheep they are so when we start killing them, you and your Ferals can hunt down those who flee into the alleys. See? They're not moving - they're lost in the dark and that map confuses them."

Bas peered down though the vent and twitched her ears. "You're right, Kayleigh," she hissed, baring her fangs. "They're cursing that monster, Pious, for running on ahead of them."

"We'll go with the Ferals," Amos volunteered. "Fria and I can see everything in the dark with these goggles. I just hope we can use our knives and hammers - we haven't practiced with these things yet," he confessed, patting his gun holsters.

"I'll come with you," Bas told them.

"They may move on at any moment but we'll count to one hundred before we start killing them," Pomona said. "So you'd better hurry. Go! Go!"

The Ferals needed no urging and swarmed silently down into the side-streets like a tide of rats. Amos had to massage his bruised fingers as he emerged from the vent as they'd been trodden on several times by Fria as she descended the shaft above him. His temper was not helped by the fact that had he lost his grip, he would've fallen some thirty yards down into the Core.

The Brothers were huddled together in pools of lantern light around the map in the middle of the broad avenue but all of a sudden, to the north, a brilliant red glow appeared casting immense shadows across the vaulted ceilings, buttresses, pillars and air ducts of Muspelheim, making the alley darks seem even deeper. Bas, Amos and Fria peered around the entrance to an alley still full of refuse bins and bales of paper waste. "What the *hell* is that accursed light?" Bas spat. "Wait! Ninety-six, ninety-seven…"

"There!" one of the Brothers cried, pointing. "Pious must be fighting the Light-Father so that *has* to be the Northern Stairway! We have to get there and help them or Schimrian will feed us to his butchers! Brother Aaron? Have you got the begiuller ready? Those Harlots of Satan are dangerous: that flare could just be one of their glamours fooling our senses."

"Aye, Brother Wyken, I'm switching it on now," Aaron grinned. "This device will protect us from the witches."

"Oh no," Bas breathed and cringed as the sound tore into her auditory nerves but it was far worse for Pomona and Kayleigh who screamed loudly. Luckily the echoes made it hard for the Brothers to pinpoint their location and as the two girls had predicted, the Brothers did not look up but formed a defensive ring around Aaron.

357

Bas did not hesitate and let fly an arrow that whistled between the heads of two Brothers, striking Aaron in the throat.

The Brothers panicked and began blindly firing their rifles and hand-guns at alley mouths and surrounding rooftops. The money exchangers and precious metal traders had emulated the merchants in Uppermost and so priceless marble statues and gargoyles on the roofs were either marred or shattered by their bullets.

Wyken dropped to his knees to try and retrieve the begiuller but Pomona and Kayleigh had quickly recovered and he received two arrows in the back of his neck. "They're above us," one of the Brothers exclaimed and fired up at the ducts that were faintly illuminated by their powerful lanterns. Bas let loose two more arrows and drew fire at her position but she'd successfully smashed one of the lanterns. "We're too exposed," she told Fria and Amos. "We must lure them into areas where they can't see us."

More arrows whistled down from yet another vent and the remaining eleven Brothers realised too late that they were horribly exposed in the middle of such a broad avenue. Bas leapt ten feet unto a window sill and swung up onto the flat roof. "Go around the back!" she called down. "Don't be afraid to use those guns if you can't get close to them in the dark."

Kayleigh and Pomona had caught on quickly and soon only one lantern was left and near-total darkness engulfed the unnerved Brothers who fired wildly until there was a succession of clicks from their empty weapons. Three of them threw plasma grenades randomly along the avenue and onto the surrounding rooftops destroying yet more priceless sculptures then an arrow from Bas put paid to the lantern and their last glimmer of hope.

Ferals tore forth from the alleys but suffered numerous cuts and wounds as the Brothers drew knives and flailed about them blindly as the distant red beacon now illuminated *nothing*. Ferals hung from limbs and necks by fang and claw as the Brothers shrieked and tried to club them off with fists and rifle butts. Bas leapt from the roof with her knives drawn while Fria and Amos targeted two Brothers who were groping their way along a wall.

Amos found no pleasure in swinging his sledgehammer down upon the head of his helpless adversary and killing him outright. Fria cut the throat of her Brother and wiped the knives on his robes as the last of the fighting ceased. By the time they reached her, Bas had accounted for the last of the Brothers but the Ferals were gathered around three of their own, mourning their loss wordlessly in high-pitched wails and mewls.

An arrow slammed into the ground making Bas leap back several feet. "Silly cat!" Kayleigh called down. "There are fifteen or sixteen Brothers coming from the east! They heard the shooting! Get the Ferals into the alleys! Hide! Hide!"

A powerful lantern rounded a corner held aloft by a Brother who had a machine-gun at the ready in his other hand. He spotted the dead Brothers and quickly guessed that they'd been ambushed. "I am Brother Brodiglede," he declared arrogantly. "We'll take our revenge for our fallen brethren upon you and this Light-Father. Are you out there, Ursaf? Or is it that traitor, Camus?"

He stepped into a nearby alley and to their surprise, he doused the lantern. Bas retrieved her bow and quiver from the roof and leapt down into the alley where Fria and Amos were hiding. "We'll outflank them using the side streets," she whispered. "I just hope the Ferals have the sense to do the same or we'll be outnumbered. I'm going back onto the rooftops to cover you."

"Please be careful, Bas," Amos said impulsively. "We don't want to lose you!" Through his night-vision goggles he could see Bas peer down at him over the edge of the roof with a peculiar, unreadable expression on her face before vanishing from view. "Come on, Fria," he urged. "Let's do what we can."

Kayleigh and Pomona had been told about begiullers and now recognised the weapon beneath them using their untrained but acute far-seeing abilities. "I don't want to feel that pain again, Yin-chan," she growled. "I *hate* these bad men!"

"As do I, Yang-chan, but there are good men."

"Oh? Like the light-Father?"

"Yes, like the Light-Father!"

The Brother with the begiuller did not even feel the arrow enter behind his clavicle to piece his heart. Again, the Brothers failed to look upwards and instead opened fire at rooftops and imagined enemies in windows cascading glass shards and gargoyle fragments down upon the pavements. Amos fired his handgun into the clustered Brothers from a narrow alley and hit one of them but had the sense to retreat with Fria around the back corner of the trading house as a plasma-grenade came tumbling after them.

Bas found it almost impossible to take aim at the Brothers as they were raking the rooftop edges with rifle-fire. Then her heart fluttered as she saw faint lights emerging from the red glow and heading quickly towards the Brothers who were now standing in a defensive ring at the cross-roads of the two avenues.

"Where's that murderous pig, Brodiglede?" one of them demanded angrily. "He's supposed to be leading us!"

"There!" another warned. "There are torches approaching us down this northern avenue but I don't think they're our brethren. Let's split into two groups and take cover either side of the avenue over there and douse the lanterns! Let them come to us; shoot at their torches and throw your plasma-grenades at them. Those accursed archers won't be able to see us either!"

The tactician didn't realise that they were still easy targets for the craft of Pomona and Kayleigh who had raced through the duct system to be above one group while Bas had leapt from roof to roof to fire down upon the other. Fria and Amos were creeping to the west to come at that group from behind but the Ferals beat them to it, rushing past them to leap upon the backs of the Brothers.

The other group of Brothers suffered death and arrow wounds from above and panicked, firing wildly upwards just as Camus, Michael and the others rounded the corner unchallenged to engage them at close quarters with rifles and knives and, as Harold had predicted, their rifles now worked flawlessly.

Fria and Amos ran down two Brothers who'd broken through the Ferals and were fleeing westwards. They halted and cowered in the pitch black, begging for mercy whilst blindly groping for their enemy. "Do you yield?" Fria said only for the Brothers to home in on her voice and fire their rifles at her. Amos had reacted instantly, dragging her down and receiving a bullet graze to his back. He lay on top of her, knowing that they were both about to die.

Instead of the gunshots and oblivion he'd expected, there was a rapid succession of grisly sounds, grunts and thuds and when they looked up, they knew Ibrahim was glaring down at them through his night-vision goggles. "You idiot, Fria!" he snapped. "These are fanatics! They're nothing like Ursaf, Ignatius and the others. You almost got yourself and Amos killed!"

He hauled them roughly to their feet. "I'm s-sorry, Ibrahim," she stuttered, shame-faced. "I don't know what ever made me say that! It won't happen again! "

"It'd better not," Ibrahim grunted sourly. "Still you did save these two devils for me. My inner demon thanks you."

"Ugh, the Ferals didn't leave much of those Brothers behind," she shuddered. "But at least they didn't get a chance to throw their plasma grenades at us."

"Uh-huh," Ibrahim muttered, scanning the alleys and rooftops anxiously. "Now where is my sister? I need to find her!"

~~~~~

Bas was about to fire an arrow when a metal inspection plate smashed the bow out of her hands. She turned to find Brother Brodiglede calmly aiming a machine-gun at her and tapping his night-vision goggles. "I *knew* I'd find an archer on the roof but by the blackened bones of Saint Casalle, I never thought I'd find such a cute cat-girl up here! I suppose I could just shoot you with this but where would be the sport in that, *freak*?"

Two arrows whistled down to knock the machine-gun from his hands, sending it skittering over the edge of the roof. "Oh, how clever of the Light-Father!" he laughed delightedly. "He's posted two guardian sprites up there to protect you! How absolutely divine! Oh, I do hope they'll let us play, *kitty*!"

He adopted an Eastern martial art posture as the fighting continued in the avenues below. "Hand to hand or shall we use knives, kitty-cat? Wait! Of course! I expect the poor little kitty thinks she's the *only* little kitty in the whole wide world, yes?"

"What do you mean, monster?" she growled, crouching and drawing her knives. "I am unique. There are no others!"

"Yes! Fire! Passion! I like that in a *feline*."

"You're going to die," Bas snarled as he drew two knives from her belt-sheaths. "So you might as well explain yourself."

He looked up at the ceilings and ducts. "What's this? No more arrows from above? It seems that your guardian sprites don't want to save a freak like you after all, kitty-cat."

"They know I would punish them for denying me my prey," she hissed, slowly circling and looking for an opening. "Before I kill you, monster, tell me what you know!"

"Yes, yes, I am a monster, I suppose. A monster blessed by God, no less. So many Inquisitions; so much *fun*! Ah, don't make that face, you're *such* a pretty kitty-cat, yes you are!" His face became serious: "Very well, I'll tell you. I was at Erdethric when Farzad and his lackeys were splicing more than just wolf genes into those children. They used dogs, pigs, deer, chimpanzees and *cats*. There!

361

You may have some sisters still alive! Am I not generous? I get to give you all this forlorn hope before I kill you!"

He leapt forward and caught Bas by surprise as she was too close to the roof edge to dodge him effectively and suffered a long scratch on her right forearm. "First blood," he crowed, licking her blood off the blade. "Let's dance, little kitty-cat."

Something snapped inside Bas and she crouched low, emitting a growl from her throat and pounced but Brodiglede was too fast. He executed a roundhouse kick just before she landed catching her in the midriff and sending her tumbling back to the roof edge. She rolled to one side to avoid the follow-through but again it was a complex move by her opponent who kicked her to the head, dazing her. "See what happens when you focus on the knives, kitty-cat?" he admonished. "Anyway, I'm bored now. Lesson's over."

As he thrust a knife down at her chest, she spun round on her back and kicked his legs from under him. She continued the movement as he was falling and drove a knife up between his ribs. He crashed down on his back and smiled at her. "Unh! Lesson two, kitty-cat," he gurgled, the blood trickling from his mouth. "You're only overconfident once in this life. Learn this well... ah!"

She struggled silently with violently conflicting emotions on that rooftop while Brodiglede breathed his last but most of all she wanted to claw his face to ragged, bloody shreds. She looked over her shoulder to find Ibrahim staring at her. "We must get back to the Light-Father, Bas," he urged decisively. "You need to spend time with him before you lose yourself!"

~~~~~

"All I can see are after-images," Nightshade complained. "It's like each sword is swinging through several dimensions before they connect. I want to help the Light-Father but I can't *focus!*"

"You have to do *something*, Wiccans!" Naeglin urged, unable to take his eyes off the spectacle. "Saul and the Light-Father are going to be killed unless you do!"

Fern grabbed Naeglin's arm and hauled herself upright and leant on her staff for support. "Azrael has drained us dry but you're right: we must help them," she said, gritting her teeth.

"That blue aura on Saul's sword and on the Light-Father's must be Ormuzd's craft at play," Nightshade concluded. "She can't cross over into Gaia so she's fighting Azrael through them!"

Harold felt like an ice-giant swinging his sword to carve out the mountains and valleys of virgin worlds. The power surging through him was so seductive yet his katana moved as if by its own will. He could sense Schimrian was drawing energy from Azrael as he was drawing his from this Ormuzd. Anger stirred within him as he fought: he was nobody's *proxy* no matter how powerful they were! He was Harold Norman Porter. He was the Light-Father and he had to save his Scatterlings! He'd known this since he'd first opened his eyes in this world and now these Powers That Be - creatures beyond his ken - were moving him, Schimrian, Pious and Saul about like pawns on some bloody celestial chessboard.

Suddenly, he had Schimrian on the defensive, driving the Great-Abbot back towards the barricade and raining blow after blow down upon him. Schimrian side-stepped a thrust causing Harold to lose his balance and, in a blur of motion, he drove a kick into Harold's lower abdomen, badly winding him.

"You're mine now, Light-Father!" he cackled then he gasped in agony because Mouse, hidden in the barricade, had hurled her spear at him and pierced his side. Harold didn't hesitate and drove his katana deep into his enemy's abdomen. "*That's* what your so-called 'son' did to me, you bastard! Enjoy the karma!"

Pious saw Schimrian drop his sword and stagger backwards clutching at his wound. He immediately seized Harold by the throat with his left hand. "*Die, Light-Father!*" Azrael hissed through the Abbot's dead throat but Saul saw the opening and severed his left arm from his body. Pious dropped his own sword to clutch at the stump, emitting a hissing scream of pain not unlike a kettle upon a stove. "Thou young upstart!" he wheezed into Saul's face. "Thou shalt not take either of us this day!"

Before Harold or Saul could move a muscle, Pious surged forward at an unbelievable speed to sweep Schimrian off his feet and leap clear over the barricade, scattering the Ferals like bowling pins. "After them" Harold cried out, tearing open a gap in the barricade. His body awash with adrenaline, he bounded down the steps closely followed by Saul, Naeglin and Beorstahl who had snatched up Schimrian's sword.

Fern drew in a deep and shuddering breath. "Oh, thank Gaia, Azrael's gone from us!" she sighed in relief, stretching out her arms. "Stay here. I'm going to go after my Light-Father!"

"Me too," Mouse declared brightly, retrieving her spear.

Nightshade stood up and assisted Ivy to her feet as Fern and Mouse weaved quickly through the gap in the barricade. "Let's not do that again for a while," she grumbled, massaging her stiff neck. "Where does she get all that energy from?"

"The Light-Father," Ivy smiled. "Even though he doesn't realise it yet... by Diana's tears, look at that *arm!*" she cried out.

In the last gutterings of the flares, they could see Pious's severed arm twitching, the fingers clenching and unclenching then the flesh suddenly dissolved into a black powder that *flowed* beneath the barricade leaving behind an empty sleeve.

"That's necromancy and no mistake," Nightshade grimaced in disgust. "This is well beyond our craft, Ivy. If Azrael ever regains physical form, we'll be snuffed out like candles."

"Diana teaches us that wherever a human heart beats, there's always hope. We must hone our craft. We must become stronger if we're going to save the Light-Father and all his children."

"Perhaps we should start with poor Templein over there."

~~~~~

Harold was the first to confront Pious on the Wealthorpe viaduct which was littered with the bodies of Brothers and Tally-men. "It's over, Pious. There's nowhere left to run. You two bastards deserve death more than any creature that's ever lived in this world!"

"Who are *you* to judge *us*, Light-Father?" Pious demanded in his bellows-wheeze of a voice. He effortlessly leapt up onto the viaduct retaining wall with the semi-conscious Schimrian slung over his shoulder. "You have no more free will in this farce than we do!" He closed his eyes and slowly toppled backwards off the wall taking Schimrian with him into the Milverbore far below.

Beorstahl peered over the wall: "They're not surfacing, Light-Father! That has to be the last of them! We're free!"

Harold slumped down onto the rail track ballast stones and rested his back against the retaining wall, glad of the sea breeze and the sight of Fern and Mouse emerging from the wreckage at the Mouth of Thor. The reaction was setting in and his muscles were trembling and cramping. He looked up at Saul then at Beorstahl and Naeglin, realising how much these three young men had suffered compared to him: he'd been here mere weeks when they'd lived in fear and pain for six *years*. "It's not over," he said grimly. "Not as long as that bastard, Azrael, is out there."

Fern came up to him so he laid aside his bloodied katana and levered himself awkwardly to his feet to take her hands. "That Five Soul light thing you did was amazing," he said gratefully, putting his forehead to hers. "I never thought I could love you as much as I do right now." He looked down at Mouse staring up at him expectantly. "And you!" he laughed, placing a hand on her head. "What you did was amazing too. Azrael didn't notice you until it was too late so I owe you my life, Mouse."

She reached up and patted his cheek affectionately and grinned. "You're welcome, Father! That sword fight was un-*geh*!"

"Listen, Light-Father," Naeglin interrupted. "I think Ursaf has at least one Angel in the air. I can hear chain-guns so he must be attacking the boats on the other of the city. Look! The rest have just realised what's happening and are fleeing towards Drytenham. Ha! The rats know those Angels aren't Aten's!"

Harold shaded his eyes and could just about make out the first of the terrified novices and Brothers clambering onto the quaysides but Fern turned her head away in horror: "Ursaf has just destroyed two boats but those already on shore will not escape; wolves and hybrids are waiting for them in the woods. Oh, Gaia, forgive us: most of them are no more than *children*!"

Harold put his right arm around her shoulder and held Mouse close to his side with his left. He felt numb inside as he watched Saul methodically clean both katanas on the robes of a dead Brother. "There's nothing we can do to save them and those hybrids will be coming after us next," he said despondently. "Even if Pious and Schimrian are dead, Azrael will draw the rest of the Order back here and then we're *really* screwed: we can't fight off thousands of Fathers and Brothers!"

"I'm just grateful we're alive right now, thanks to you two," Beorstahl said stoutly, clapping him and Saul on the back. "I suggest we find some bottles of whisky to celebrate both our victory and the first days of sunshine in six years!"

"I never thought I'd see blue sky again," Naeglin agreed. "Or feel the sun upon my face. It's magnificent!"

Harold placed his hands on Fern's shoulders and stared into her eyes. "I know you're absolutely bone-tired, Fern, but can you far-see how everyone is for me? I need to know."

She sighed heavily and closed her eyes. "Just give me a minute, dear heart. I'm so tired I'm going to sleep for days."

He reached inside his stab-vest pocket and was delighted to find a lighter and his cigar case miraculously intact. He extracted a cigar and lit it despite Mouse glaring at him. He luxuriously savoured the aromatic smoke as he stared westwards, half-expecting the Order fleet to appear upon the Milverbore at any moment.

Fern opened her eyes suddenly: "Ah! I'm sorry, dear heart, but brave Templein has just died and Ursaf lost two crewmen so only one Angel is airborne. The Sisters are safe but Peter, Marcus and Thanewell were hurt. Surl and Shield are still unconscious from the Five Soul Fold but, don't worry, Saul, they'll be fine."

"Bless the Virgin Mary for small mercies. Thank you," Saul smiled gratefully, sheathing his katana. "But what of Bas and all the others who were fighting in Muspelheim?"

"They're alive and the Brothers are all dead but we've lost another ten of our poor Ferals," she said, bowing her head in grief. "We've *got* to destroy Azrael or this misery will never end! Bas desperately needs your magic too, Light-Father. They all do. You can't hide in your Tower of Grieving any more."

Harold nodded and solemnly took his katana from Saul to sheathe it in its saya. He looked up as Ursaf's Angel clattered overhead towards Drytenham to attack the four boats yet to reach the quaysides. As he exhaled a cloud of cigar smoke, he wondered why he felt so little sympathy for those Brothers and novices about to die. He gritted his teeth: he *had* to hold on to his humanity otherwise there was no point in fighting Azrael!

Fern kissed him on the mouth having read his thoughts. "Yes, Harold," she smiled. "There would be no point. But Mouse and I will always be by your side, won't we, Mouse?"

Mouse hugged them both. "I promise, Father, but what will we do about all these dead bodies?"

Harold sighed and waved a hand at the corpses of the Brothers and Tally-men scattered about the viaduct as carrion crows began to circle above them. "It's tempting, Beorstahl, but the whisky will have to wait. We have work to do."

~~~~~

366

Lightning Source UK Ltd.
Milton Keynes UK
UKHW020120011119

352680UK00008B/551/P